PRAIS

'Joe Donne'
... N

'Exciting and highly readable' – Gua

'Donnelly's depiction of the natural world is as
interesting and carefully drawn as that of the
supernatural' – *Observer*

'Pulse-racing horror ... very satisfying'
– *Glasgow Herald*

'Donnelly scores with unusually believable
characters, well-realized settings and thoroughly
researched mythological backgrounds'
– *Daily Telegraph*

'*Havock Junction* raises Donnelly to being one of
the two best horror writers in the UK ... Probably the best horror novel of 1995' – *Fantasy
Bookshelf*

ABOUT THE AUTHOR

Joe Donnelly was born in Glasgow and is the author of the highly acclaimed novels *Havock Junction*, *Shrike*, *Still Life*, *The Shee*, *Stone* and *Bane*. His recent psychological chiller, *Twitchy Eyes*, is published by Michael Joseph. A journalist, writer and broadcaster, he has won several awards for investigative reporting, including Reporter of the Year. He is still involved with newspapers and also writes plays for television. He now lives with his family in Dumbarton, Scotland.

Incubus

JOE DONNELLY

A SIGNET BOOK

SIGNET

Published by the Penguin Group
Penguin Books Ltd, 27 Wrights Lane, London W8 5TZ, England
Penguin Books USA Inc., 375 Hudson Street, New York, New York 10014, USA
Penguin Books Australia Ltd, Ringwood, Victoria, Australia
Penguin Books Canada Ltd, 10 Alcorn Avenue, Toronto, Ontario, Canada M4V 3B2
Penguin Books (NZ) Ltd, 182–190 Wairau Road, Auckland 10, New Zealand

Penguin Books Ltd, Registered Offices: Harmondsworth, Middlesex, England

First published by Michael Joseph 1996
Published in Signet 1997
1 3 5 7 9 10 8 6 4 2

Copyright © Joe Donnelly, 1996
All rights reserved

The moral right of the author has been asserted

Printed in England by Clays Ltd, St Ives plc

To
Cissie and Helen Kinney

Author's Note

Barloan Harbour, Levenford, Lochend and the other places described herein are based on real locations. The events, however, are completely fictitious as are the characters, unfortunately. The irresistible power a baby wields is all too real.

CHAPTER ONE

The clatter of urgent footsteps slapped on the walls and came echoing back, hollow as drumbeats, with a flight rhythm all of their own.

Somebody was running.

It was a girl. She was hurrying along the alley, body held in tight, breath puffed out in plumes as she passed the cascade of waste-bins at the back of the Loo Fung Chinese restaurant. Andy Skinner, who used to be something big in double glazing but had hit the skids after he'd hit the bottle and had now come to rock-bottom, was rummaging around in the trash for chicken wings and cold leftovers. He saw the girl come flitting by, though flit wasn't how he'd have described it.

The face was ghostly, a pale oval shape in the shadows. A pale oval shape with dark ovals for eyes and a wide oval for a mouth. She was hunched over, and looked up at the same time as Andy. Her eyes opened wide, so wide they looked as if they could have popped out.

It was then that Andy saw she was carrying a bundle close to her body, but she was moving too fast and it was too dark to make it out. For a minute he thought she was carrying a baby, and that was a surprise. Down in the alley in the back of the Loo Fung, you saw plenty of winos and every now and again you'd get somebody sticking a needle in a vein in their arm by the light of the back kitchen window. You never got girls with babies in their arms.

It must have been something else, he thought, turning away, minding his own business. He paused and turned back, slowly, the way you see drunks do that shows their springs and shock absorbers are well and truly shot, along with their reflexes. He thought he'd heard a cry, high and keening, and it could have been the girl. If she was running down here, it was a fair bet somebody would be after her. She might be one of the girls from Ramage Street who hung around waiting for the bars to empty out so they could clock on for the night shift. Maybe it was the police chasing her, or her stickman, or maybe it was an angry john she'd stiffed for his twenty. Whatever it was Andy didn't need the worry. Something to eat, some chow mein would be nice. Something to eat and a warm place over by the back vent where he could sleep. That was all he wanted. No trouble. He eased himself back into the shadows while the girl stumbled on, heels cracking hard on the old cobbles. She got past the black bags and the old galvanized containers that smelled sour and fatty, breath still feathering out in front of her face. She got to the light at the near end and he heard the cry again.

This time she turned to look at him and in the yellow light he saw her mouth open in a gape that told him she was about to scream. There was fear written all over her face.

Andy knew a thing or two about fear. Whatever was scaring her, whoever was scaring her, it wasn't his problem. He started to turn away but the dark hollows of the girl's eyes held him and made him stop in mid turn. Her mouth clamped shut and the scream stayed stuck where it was, silent and pinioned inside her throat. The tendons of her neck were stuck out in vertical ridges, making her head shake. He could see that quite clearly even in the pale and watery light reflecting from a storeroom window. She was only a few feet away and he could sense the tension and the tremble in her body, like she was wound tighter than a top C string on a guitar. For that small space of time she slowed. Her feet stopped their clatter on the hardcobble and they stood, the tramp and the girl. A slick of hair had curled down on to her brow and stuck there just above her eye. There was a glisten of sweat there, as if she maybe had the flu or a fever, and at this time of the year that wasn't beyond the bounds of probability.

The eyes held him. Down in their depths there was a glint of light, a powerful glare of life. She tried to open her mouth again, as if fighting pain, but her jaws snapped together, and across the space between them, Andy heard her teeth grind, like small stones underfoot. Any harder and they're gonna break, he thought. There had been a time when all he'd have thought about was the orthodontist's bill, but on this night, looking at the stricken face and listening to that strange creaking sound

2

coming from inside her, he thought about the pain it must have been causing the poor cow.

The whimpering noise came again. It was high and somehow hoarse. For an instant he thought it was the cry of a baby, but the sound was too abrasive, too jagged. The girl's eyes opened wider. The light flashed in them and he saw pain there in the rictus of the grimace stretched across her face. She was a good-looking thing, tall enough and not wasted like some of the hookers, and her teeth were straight and even and, despite the dim light, they looked white, which you never saw on any of the junkies *except that the grinding went on and they'd crack and shatter and then she could work here anytime* who did tricks for enough to buy the next fix.

The sound bleated, this time more of a growl. Like a ferret maybe, even one of the city foxes that came prowling around to compete with Andy for the Loo Fung scraps. The sound of it made the hairs on the back of his head stand right up on their ends and quiver. He could feel them rise and tensed up as if a cold hand had grabbed the skin between his shoulder blades. Right away his belly clenched tight, another cold hand gripping hard, and he could feel the muscles of his sphincter open and close. His breath stopped and backed up, clogging his windpipe.

The fear came almost hard enough to knock him down.

It shuddered through him, a shunt of absolute, inexplicable dread. Andy was certainly no stranger to fear. He'd been mugged many a time and got scared, but that was the day-to-day fear of life on the cobbles. Worse than that, no matter what anybody said, once he'd got down and got dirty and looked at the world through the bottom of a bottle of Buckfast fortified rocket fuel, was the mad fear of the heebie-jeebies when his dead wife and dead kids would come stalking him through the shadows dripping flesh and rippling with the fire that had blackened their bones.

The fear that riddled through him was like that, except it was worse, much worse. It hit him almost hard enough to make him stumble and fall. It was every primitive fear that had ever been spawned. And it was all sparked off by that little whimpering growl. The sound of a baby crying, yet somehow not that. It was a sound that had no place. It was simply *wrong*.

3

Andy did stumble back. The girl began to turn. The dread was swelling inside him like a live thing. His eyes were still held tight by the girl's own gaze.

'Holy fu–' he started to mouth.

The girl turned and as she did, her coat opened, just an inch or two. Andy got a glimpse of something small and crumpled in the shadow. A flash of something that could have been a reflection, could have been an eye.

The terror soared. The skin of his scrotum withered and wrinkled as his whole body squirmed to get away.

The girl moved on. Her eyes swept past him, a terror as black and as poisonous as the fear inside Andy Skinner twisted her features into something hag-like and ugly. Then she was gone and the blanket of dread that smothered Andy was dragged away. He stood there, shaking with the force of it, his own eyes staring and threatening to pop out and swing on his own gaunt cheekbones. The nerves at the back of his knees twitched and jittered and almost turned traitor-toed to spill him on to the pile of trashbags. His scalp was still crawling and the slithery fingers were still gouged into the skin of his back but the fear was ebbing away.

He let out his breath. The echoes of the girl's footsteps rang out, as she moved out of sight.

The fear diminished with the distance. He stood there, listening for that sound again, but apart from her receding footsteps and the murmur of traffic along the main street there was silence. Andy stood still, waiting for the pursuit to clamour along, pressed back in the shadows just in case somebody mistook him for something more than a tramp.

Nobody came.

He waited a while, among the slimy smells and scents of the Chinese garbage, feeling the sudden craving for a drink to stop the shakes. Nobody came along and the girl's footsteps faded to whispers and then died.

Andy headed for the light down on the street. Whatever had reached and touched his nerves, whatever it was had sobered him up. His hands might have been shaking and his heart pounding, but he was more sober, more lucid than at any time in the past five years.

He reached the wine shop on the corner where he could get a

4

plastic bottle of high-octane brain rot, but he stopped before he went inside.

For the first time in a long time, he didn't want a drink. He stood there, trying not to think about the awful fear that had taken him over, unable not to think about it. He was confused and bewildered as any man can be. For those few moments, he did not know what to do.

Down the street and over the backs of the houses, the bells of St Stephen's punctuated the hour, a clear and smooth sound that cut through the cold air and reached Andy as he swithered on the wine shop doorstep. Father O'Toole would know what to do. It wasn't too late, was it? Not too late in the day, and maybe not too late in the game.

Andy Skinner went down the main street and turned at the lights, weaving through the unseen traffic, heading for the dark spire of the church. Half an hour later, despite the bitter smell of new sweat on old, Father O'Toole heard him confess to the drunken and reckless killing of his wife and family in the car accident he'd escaped nearly seven years before.

Andy Skinner did not want a drink that night. He wanted more than anything to feel the nearness of God and the touch of his grace, though he hadn't contemplated his creator in all of those years. He did now, because down in the shadow of the alley where the Loo Fung threw its garbage, he had felt the touch of something bad.

David Harper had his collar rucked up against the chill of the winter air. The breeze swirled round the blackened and crumbling corner of the old warehouse down close to the harbour. It was hardly more than a breath, but it sucked the heat from his cheek and the cold of it seared the inside of his nose. He dug his hands in his pockets and waited, trying not to stamp his feet in the time-honoured tradition of policemen in cold climates. From somewhere beyond the corner of the lane, the faint and high-pitched tunes of Christmas carols came filtering through the mist, a monotonous and somehow melancholy sound of winter city streets. The shops were only a hundred yards away, maybe even less, as the crow flies, but David Harper and Helen Lamont were not crows. A hundred yards that made the difference between the bustle of the city with its fast and frenetic hordes of gatherers doing their festive shopping after work, and here, behind the façade of the mall and the main streets, where the dark alleys and serviceways headed down towards the river. Here, the old warehouses, by-way shabby because they were not built to please the eye, huddled against the mass of railway arches and old shipping offices. In a year or so, they would all come down and make way for new works of architecture. For the moment they were solid and shadowed, roll-down doors battened against the night, windows bricked or shuttered against the intruder.

Somewhere down the river, a foghorn bellowed, far off and mournful, and the sound made David think of dinosaurs. The gaunt shipyard cranes looming out of the fog on the other side of the river, lit by the flashing beams of the steady traffic passing over the curve of the bridge, looked like swamp monsters of pre-history. The shadows on the girders made them seem to move. David wanted to move. Standing in the cold, hidden in the dark of a doorway where hookers performed *alfresco*, and where drunks pissed and vomited every Saturday night in this no mean city, was not his idea of a good time. It was work. It was a job, but it was not fun.

Further along the road, where it joined with Riverside Lane, behind the shopping mall, Helen Lamont was almost completely hidden from view. She had the vantage of the north side of the street. David could just make out the pale blur at face height. She must be keeping very still. She must even be keeping a hand in front of her mouth to prevent the tell-tale plume of breath from billowing out. There was back-up down at the corner where two uniforms were sitting in the relative comfort of a van. David's doorway and the niche of an old entrance where Helen Lamont merged with the shadows were the only cover on this part of the street. A parked car would have been spotted from two hundred yards away, and anyone approaching on wheels would have neither slowed nor stopped.

A slight cough on the radio jerked him out of his thoughts of dinosaurs and river beasts in the night. He thumbed the receive on his radio, pressing it close to his ear with the volume turned down so low the voice on the other end was almost drowned in the hiss of static.

'Company.' Helen Lamont's voice, even in the tinny overlay, was abrupt and clear.

'Check.' He keyed the radio off again, feeling his heart speed up just that little bit as he went on the alert. Five seconds later, the twin lights of a van, just the side lights, no main beam, cut through the swirl of mist, expanding as they approached. The rumble of the engine caught up, an old, tired diesel with a pinhole in the manifold that made it sound even older. The van came closer, juddering on cobbles that had been laid a century before, maintaining its speed as it approached. For a moment, David thought it might pass on by. He tried not to look at the lights, to maintain his night vision, wondering if he'd been given clean information.

The van slowed beside the metal gate on the far side. A blur up on the driver's side showed a pale face behind glass that was dirty and hoared with frost on its edges. Brakes squealed tinnily and the van stopped, an old, decrepit and nondescript pantechnicon, the kind that is always seen blocking alleyways or unloading from dingy storehouses at odd times of day. It lurched on springs until it settled. The door opened immediately. Somebody got out on this side. Two others stepped down quickly from the blind side. There was no rush, but David Harper's heartbeat moved up a notch. He glanced at the niche where Helen Lamont was still all but invisible. That was good. She hadn't moved, waiting for his signal. She was keen and she was pretty good. They'd worked together for six months and he knew he could rely on her to keep her head.

Tonight was no big deal. The Christmas rush was big business for everybody, and there were shares on all levels of the economy. Tonight, according to the wire, it was a simple pick-up of compact discs and assorted electronic hardware from a warehouse that had been turned over a week before. David had got the word from a good source. It wasn't a big job, and there were no heavy people, which was why it was a two-man hit plus back-up.

The roll door on the far side screeched upwards with a sound of tearing metal, high enough to send a shiver down the back of his neck. He waited some more while they all went in. A light came on, not bright, but enough to see by in the storehouse. He made out figures moving with deliberate speed. It took them five minutes to get the van half loaded. They'd been stupid enough for the three of them to pile into the store without leaving a lookout, which told him they were far from organized. He allowed them another two minutes, thumbed the button on the radio, gave Helen the two words and then waited. She came out of the shadow, a slight figure in a heavy flying jacket, more a waif in the dark than a policewoman. Without any delay, he crossed the road and walked straight to the doorway as two of the men were coming out, arms laden with boxes of interactive CD machines.

He held up his black flashlight, butt first. 'Put those hands up,' he barked, glad to be moving and suddenly unable to resist the joke. The first man, maybe the same height as himself and several pounds heavier, squawked in alarm. He only saw the figure with a hand stretched out, took in the black barrel, and did exactly as he was told. Three boxes went spilling to the ground in a clatter and thump of cardboard.

'What in the name of . . .?'

'You're under arrest,' David said. 'Put the boxes down and line up against the wall.'

A smaller man close by the door put his stack down. Over by the wall, a younger man, stick-thin and angular, had stopped in the act of bending. He straightened up, spun, and leapt for the space between David and the doorway. Just as he did so, the smaller man dropped his load and scuttled straight out into the street. David grabbed at the thin one, got a hand to an anorak hood. He snatched it and jerked back and down with a hard twist, trying to spin the other man, and the whole hood came ripping off with a pluck of torn buttons. The thin man did spin but, more by luck than anything else, regained his balance and came out of it facing the right way for flight. He was off and running, hard on the heels of the smaller man who had gone out first.

David cursed. For a split second he couldn't decide whether to stay and capture the third man, but the decision was made for him instantly when he heard Helen shout from outside.

'Stop right there.' She was trying to take two of them. David launched himself out of the storeroom, knowing he'd recognize the third man again no matter what, and ran after the fleeing figures. Helen was running in the opposite direction, aiming to cut the men off. The small man went straight for her. She didn't stop, but instead brought her own flashlight up. From only a few feet away she flicked it on, sending the beam right into the man's eyes. He made a guttural sound, put his hands up to his face. Helen side-stepped, bent, and at the same time put her foot out, swinging forward to sweep the man's legs from under him. He cried out again, went into a half somersault and came down with a sickening thud. Immediately Helen was on him, twisting his arm up his back, telling him in a yell that he was under arrest.

The thin man hit her hard enough to send her sprawling.

The toe of his boot caught her right under the ribs and knocked her straight back. From twenty yards away David heard the crack of the connection and the hard grunt of pain. Helen hit against the wall, slamming hard with her shoulder, letting out another incoherent yet eloquent sound.

'Fuckin' bitch,' the thin man screeched. He had stopped, possibly unaware that David was right behind him, or perhaps because the fright of the sudden surprise had put him right over the edge. Despite the violence of the kick and the slam against the wall, Helen got to one knee, grabbed his leg. He tried to kick her again. By this time the small man had rolled, groaning, and made it to his feet. The thin one aimed a punch directly at Helen's head and she warded it off with her forearm. He managed to get another kick at her, catching her in the pit of her belly, while she still hung on to his leg.

David hit him so hard the blow almost dislocated Helen's shoulder.

The skinny man went staggering off and David followed, slamming him again, right up against the wall which he hit with a surprisingly meaty thud. Without hesitation, David smacked him on the back of his head, driving his face forward into the crumbling sandstone. He heard the crack as the man's nose broke. The thin man squealed. David grabbed him by the collar where the hood had come away, dragged him back. The small man was on his feet, getting ready to hare off down the road. Helen's hand flicked out in a cat-swipe, snatched his hair and spun him round, bringing him close to where David was standing.

In the dim light of the back street she pivoted on one foot, still grasping the small man's hair while he mewled in pain and fright, snapped her leg up and drove her knee hard and fast into the thin man's groin. He jack-knifed instantly and David let him drop.

'Thanks,' she told him.

'Any time,' he said, grinning, though he would have felt happier if the collar had been easier. There should have been no trouble in making the arrest and he should not have let any of them out of the door. He bent down, took a hold of the collar again, hauling the thin man upright, and began reading him his rights. The prisoner was blubbering now, his face a mask of blood and snot, both hands sunk in against his crotch, while his body tried to stay bent double.

Right at that moment, the van's engine coughed into life. It revved hard and without hesitation, it came rumbling along the narrow road towards them.

'What the hell?' Helen snapped. The thin man tried to pull away and she clamped his wrist, driving it up his back. The van came roaring down, just a black shape, with no lights on. For an instant it looked as if there was no driver. The nearside wheel hit the kerb, mounted the pavement and the van came swerving right for Helen.

'Jesus Christ,' the small man bleated in a high-pitched, panicked voice. Helen turned, saw the black shape bearing down on them. Her mouth opened in a perfect circle.

David ran forward, dragging the thin man with him. He twisted, swinging the other man out in front of him, placing him directly between the van and Helen. Lights or no, he knew the driver could see enough.

The engine growled. Up in the cabin the pale smudge of the driver's face pulled back. For a second it looked as if the van would crump both David and the thin man against the wall. Then at the last possible moment, the wheels spun. Bright sparks fountained from the wall where the wheel arch scraped and then the van went hurtling away from them. It missed David and the thin man by inches. Unable to stop it careened across the road and slammed into the opposite wall with a deafening crash.

David dragged his captive with him as he strode towards the van. With one easy movement he brought out his cuffs, slapped them on the thin man's wrist, jamming them as tightly as he could to cause the maximum pain. He snicked the free end on to the lug at the back of the van. A smell of spilled diesel spread out from under the chassis. David sniffed. 'If this blows, you'll blow with it,' he told the thin man, whose mouth dropped wide in fright, showing a snaggle of stained teeth.

David got to the door, jerked it open, reached in and hauled the third man from the cabin. The driver was moaning in pain and panic, both hands up against his head where he had driven forward and hit the windscreen. David got him outside, turned him round and, with surprising gentleness, pulled the man's hands down from his face. 'Kenny Lang,' he said. 'I thought it was you. Are you all right?'

He leaned forward, in evident concern for the other man's well being. Kenny Lang lifted his face, spread his arms just enough to show that he thought he might live. David looked him straight in the eye and in that moment the anger flared in sudden heat. This cretin had tried to kill his partner. He had deliberately run the van straight at her to smear her against the wall. Another second and Helen Lamont would have been lying there in a crumpled heap.

David Harper drew his head back, drove it forward with all his weight and smashed his forehead on to the other man's nose. Kenny Lang dropped like a sack, making no sound but the noise of his weight hitting the ground. His face was opened like a ripe tomato.

David crossed the road. Helen had the other man cuffed and face down on the pavement. He got his hands to her elbows and raised her up. There was a dirty smudge on her cheek where she had made contact with the wall. In this light it looked like a bruise on her pale skin. The orange street lights at the far end caught her eyes and made them glitter. David got an arm around her, feeling the slightness of her body against his, and the shiver of the adrenaline rush that just about matched his own.

'You OK?'

'I'll live,' she said, breathing heavily. He could hear the anger in her own voice, along with the pain. She was bent slightly to the left, favouring her injured side. 'And thanks again. You're making a habit of this.'

'What's a boy to do?' he said, managing to get a smile from her.

The patrol arrived from the end of the lane and David relinquished his hold on her, though not before the uniforms exchanged knowing looks.

'Call for the wagon,' David told them curtly. 'Constable Lamont may need medical treatment. Book all three of these.'

'What's the charge?'

David looked at the bulky man who still lay on the street, conscious but hardly aware. 'Littering the road for a start. We'll work it up from there when I get back from casualty.'

He walked Helen the two hundred yards to the car, past Carrick Street, which led right down to the river's edge. Just at the corner, somebody passed them, heading west on the old cobbles. Neither of them looked, but both of them got the impression of a young woman walking quickly. In the distance, the choirboys in the shopping mall were still singing their non-stop dirge and here, closer to the shopping centre, the bustle of the city was louder and more urgent.

The fast footsteps clacked on the cobbles and the figure hurried away. A breeze stirred and brought up a smell from the dirty waters of the river, an acrid, rancid scent that was sharp as the winter air. David wrinkled his nose, wondering what toxins had been flushed into the water. He blinked quickly, feeling the anger inexplicably swell inside him again. He took a deep breath to force it away. By the time he eased Helen into the car, the street was empty.

She was running.

She scurried down in the dark and shadow of the alleyway, staying clear of the lights and the bustle of the main street. Her heartbeat was a pounding in her ears and the pulse a thudding in her head, hard and persistent, like a migraine without the blindness.

There was a red tinge to everything, as though she were seeing the world, dark and shade, through coloured glass or a film of blood. She wondered, dimly, what was wrong with her eyes. Something had burst. She had felt it when she was running, a sharp shock of pain on the crescendo of the thudding pulse and then a draining sensation as it faded under the grinding throb.

Panic flared high and hysterical *oh Jesus don't let this be happening to me* and was instantly swamped down to a low guttering flame. She turned the corner, holding herself tight, clutching the bundle in clawed hands, clamped against herself under her coat. She could feel it press up against her breast and the panic soared again. The mewling sound came, soft and close, but it went through her like the screech of a stone-saw in the masonry yard where her uncle worked and she felt it like a physical sear.

The alley was long and narrow, jinking in a dog-leg at the far end where the shadows crouched and huddled away from the light. She clattered down on the cobbles, feet pattering and echoing back from the high walls. Round the corner she came, slipping on something slimy and slick, regaining her balance before she slammed against the roughcast on the corner of the back-alley storehouse and came along the straight serviceway behind the main street stores. Here and there, fruit-boxes and plastic bread-boards were stacked or heaped, there was a smell of old mould that would have been strong on the cold air but for the all-pervading flat and sour scent that clogged her nose and somehow conjured up images of weasels and reptiles. The reek hung about her like a cloud and made her heart beat fast, too fast, in her chest, but she could do nothing about that now. All she could do was run down the alley, holding on, holding tight.

She went scuttering past the piled black bags beside the dumper skip at the back of the Chinese restaurant when something caught her eye, a grey motion in peripheral vision, and she turned her head.

The thing came lumbering out from the shadows, not close but not far away, and she slowed, quite reflexively, the way she would have done on any street, in any alley – though there were few alleys she'd gone tripping down in recent years – but it was only instinct, not fear. There was no room inside her for any more fear. She turned and saw the man, gaunt and grizzled, his grey hair wild and awry, almost a caricature of someone who has stuck a finger in an electrical socket. His face was grey but his eyes were wide and his mouth even wider. She did not know that unconsciously the man was parodying her own expression.

Something, some cry, some word came blurting to her lips and almost made it out into the cold air but then her jaw snapped shut – *was made to shut* – and the word was strangled to silence. She could hear her own teeth grinding there as her muscles clamped and clenched and creaking noises of hard surface against hard surface vibrated through her head.

Go on go on go on don't stop.

Not quite words. Just an urgency. A motive force. It twisted within her and willed her feet onward, making the nerves jump and the muscles twitch. The man stared at her, eyes owlish and suddenly fear-filled. She could see it there, mirroring her own terror, as if he were looking at a devil. She tried to speak again but nothing happened. Her teeth clenched and the tendons in her neck felt as if they would break with the strain of it.

Go go go go get gone. Go now.

She could feel herself turn and pull away, only to stop still. Her mind tried to fight the dreadful imperative, but a sharp pain, keen as glass, razored in behind her eyes, crystal clear and so powerful it blinded her momentarily. She shook herself, more in reaction to the hurt, to shuck it away, and when her vision came back all the dark images were tinged in a deeper red and they were doubled up, wavering apart in dizzying duplication before they jostled back into conjunction.

Oh please. Mother. Oh no. Her mind, the part of it that she could still use, was babbling in baby talk.

The man with the grizzled fright-hair and the terrified look on his face backed off. She turned and went running down the alley, leaving him in the shadows. She stuck to her own, clinging close to the wall where it was dark. The alley forked here. The left track doubled back down to the main street where the library stood blocky and solid on the corner opposite the double hump of McDonald's. Down there, people were parking their cars and eating out of polyfoam platters. Families would be huddled round tables, groups of boys would be exchanging bashful insults with groups of girls, the way she had done only a few years past.

A million years, it felt like.

Down there were people, ordinary folk going about their lives, and she wanted to call out to them but she couldn't make a sound. Her breath rasped at the back of her throat and whistled out through her teeth as she grasped her arms tight around the bundle and went staggering up the other fork in the alley to the end, at the back of the pizza place where she used to work Friday nights when she was still at school. The smell of onion and mozzarella and pepperoni came thick in the steam from the vents, billowing out in ghostly hauntings of scent, but it smelled bad here, foul and sickening, alien.

She felt her throat clench against it and the pounding came harder in her ears. For a moment she thought she might vomit in a bitter spray against the wall, but while her belly heaved, it all stayed inside her. Beyond the corner, on the far side, a corrugated shack stood adjacent to a fenced compound filled with bent and broken cars. She stumbled past and two big dogs came loping out of the shadows, startled by her passing, and launched themselves at the chain-link wire. Ordinarily the frantic and vicious snarling would have sent her away screaming in fright, but she was beyond that now, carried along on a wave of utter horror of her own that transcended any simple alarm. The dogs slavered and growled, eyes reflecting the orange of the street light, noses wrinkled, lips pulled back from gnashing teeth.

A small whining sound responded, not loud, but cutting across the snarls from inside the compound. A different, corrosive smell sprayed out.

The effect was electric. The dogs leapt back from the fence as if they'd been kicked. The larger of the two, a big German Shepherd with a shaggy coat hackled into spikes, twisted round so quickly it slipped and rolled on the wet ground. The other one yelped a whinny of protest and surprise. It spun round in a complete circle, clashed against the chain-link and then leapt for the far shadows. The second dog screamed an oddly cat-like sound and tumbled after it, tail tucked right under its belly. Far back in the compound, among the hulks of broken cars, they could be heard howling in fright, a strange and shivery, quite unearthly sound in the dark.

She continued up the alley, ignoring the canine terror, went round the corner to the accessway behind the terrace of houses on Dunlop Street. She scrambled past the hedges, careless of the scrape of sharp twigs against her good winter coat. Her breath plumed in front of her, picking up the light of the moon. Five or six houses along she came to a white barred gate, pressed against it and swung it wide with a faint creak of the hinges. Inside she scurried up the flagstone path and went round the side, up the short flight of stairs. Her fingers, still clawed and numb, managed to get a hold of the handle. With a wrench she got it open and pushed her way inside.

Her hand automatically reached for the light switch.

No . . .!

The wordless command froze her rigid, hand stretched out in the dark. The awesome fear burgeoned in a black tide and she sagged against the wall, limbs suddenly weak and shivery, as if she'd run a marathon, as if she was felled by fever.

Hot tears sprung to her eyes, wavering pink as they brimmed over and spilled down her cheeks.

She slowly lowered herself to the floor, slipping down against the wall until she was hunkered against the skirting board, breathing shallow and fast. The door snicked shut on the latch leaving her in darkness lightened only by the paler rectangle of the curtained window.

The small sound came again, cold and shuddery, quiet as a creaking hinge, rasping like gravel on a far shore, but loud in her consciousness, a demanding sound.

'What am I doing here? she thought to herself. What on earth . . .?'

The bundle in her arms whimpered its dry little rasp. The scent came wafting up from the folds of her winter coat and a hot shard of pain twisted against her breast. She turned, squirming against the sensation, letting her coat open wide. Her eyes were more accustomed to the dim light and she could clearly see the white of her blouse, coned out where her other breast pressed against the smooth fabric.

A dark, damp stain was spreading across the surface, turning the white to grey. She stared at it, puzzled. Behind her nipple, an odd, pulsing ache, not quite pain now, but a pressing sensation, swelled and waned. The stain spread and the odd scent came strong again, now tinged with a sweeter smell. It was then she realized that her breast was leaking milk.

Oh please no. Don't let this be happening to me.

The panic welled up again and the scent came thick and choking in her gullet, enveloping the dread. The fear was smothered and squashed down inside her.

The baby's head, a small smooth shape in the dim light, moved quickly. She felt the cotton of her blouse tug away from her and the edge of her bra scraped against her skin. The baby's head moved again, nuzzling down, and it clamped on her nipple, sucking hard, pulling furiously at the erect little nubbin. She could feel the liquid, her own milk, squirt out of her and even as she lost herself in the darkness, she knew that she could not possibly be nursing a baby. She couldn't be breast feeding. She had no milk to give.

Yet the baby sucked and pulled. It made small, feral, gobbling noises down there in the dark of the coat folds and Ginny's panicked breathing began to subside. The sobs that made her lungs hitch in sudden jerks faded away and an irresistible sensation of fulfilment enveloped her. It layered itself on the spark of her own self that was still aware and writhed and twisted inside her, clamouring to be away and home and safe.

Very slowly, as if all the strength had drained away from her, she leaned back against the wall where her coat made a damp smear on the flock paper.

The baby did not stop feeding.

CHAPTER TWO

The woman spun around in the centre of the mall. Her arms were spread wide and she looked like an elderly ballet dancer trying a final slow pirouette. Two girls passing close by turned to look at her, sniggered and moved on. Over by the Italian delicatessen, a couple watched the sluggish, graceless spin. The woman's handbag spun away to the left, hit the tiles and slid along the floor to the wall. Up above it the lights caught the Christmas tinsel and a choir of plastic angels swung their heads idiotically from side to side as they sang doleful carols.

The woman, tall and angular with grey frizzy hair, opened her mouth in a silent yell. Her eyes rolled upwards until only the whites were visible and then she fell with a resounding thump to the floor. She jerked as if a savage current of electricity were discharging through her body, back arching right up from the surface. A gout of spittle coughed from the back of her throat. A dry, desperate croak rasped from her yawning mouth. A pair of boys almost fell over the skinny, splayed legs and swerved to avoid the obstruction without stopping.

Two assistants came rushing out of the Body Shop and reached the stricken woman. One of them, red-haired and freckled, hung back nervously. The other, short, plump and dark-haired, crouched over the fallen shape. 'Are you all right?' she asked, the question everybody asks when it is clear that nothing is all right.

The old woman gagged again, mouth now twisted into a grimace of pain. Her hands were clamped in against herself, one on her thin chest, the other on her belly. Her legs were spread wide, bare and bloodless, shivering and thrumming uncontrollably. The woman's head rattled hard against the floor.

'Get a doctor,' the girl said, turning over her shoulder to her friend. 'Phone an ambulance. Quick.'

The red-head hesitated, wringing her hands together, somehow dismayed and revolted at the same time.

'Come on Jeanette, *run*. She's really sick.'

From another shop doorway, another woman came hurrying across from the Rolling Stock car-accessory shop front. 'What's the matter?'

'She just fell down.'

The sprawled woman's eyes rolled downwards and for an instant they locked on the kneeling girl. Her mouth opened and closed several times. Three small moles, equally spaced in a line, marked her face like ink blots.

'She's had a heart attack,' the second woman said. Her name was Jenny McGill. 'That or a stroke. Try to get her on to her side.'

'*Baby.*' The word came hissing out, almost a snarl. A spray of spittle came out along with it, making the word incomprehensible.

Jenny McGill from Rolling Stock pushed at the prostrate form. 'Christ, she's stinking,' she said, not unkindly. It was true, the woman smelled pretty awful. She looked as if she hadn't eaten in days, or washed in longer than that. Despite the smell, old sweat and damp clothes and something else besides, Jenny pushed and hauled until she got the victim on her side. She tilted her chin back to clear the airway and recoiled again. The breath came panting from between teeth that were grey and rotten. It stank of decay. Ignoring this reek, she pulled open the thin cardigan and thinner blouse, careless of the few buttons. A surprisingly swollen breast pushed out of a grey bra and she shoved it to the side.

'Is she going to die?' the plump girl asked. A crowd was gathering around them. People's voices held the hushed tones of the curious, ready to be shocked at the nearness of tragedy, the proximity of death. Up on the higher level, beyond the busy escalator, a gallery of folk, boys, girls and adults, were hanging over, spectating greedily.

'Don't know, dear, let me have a listen. I've done first aid.' Jenny bent right down, turning her head to the side, and got an ear to the heaving chest. The skin was clammy and hot, too hot. She clamped the heel of her hand against her exposed ear, cutting off the tumult of sound, though the plastic angels still managed to get through with 'We Three Kings'. She pressed harder until the festive music faded out and closed her eyes to concentrate.

The woman's heartbeat was faint but fast, tripping like a woodpecker burr against the ribs.

'Fibrillation,' Jenny said. 'She's going.' She heaved the woman until she faced upwards.

'What?' the plump assistant asked.

'It's her heart. Is your friend phoning for help?'

The other girl twisted her head, found a space in the gathering crowd. In the Body Shop, the red-head was putting the phone down. 'Yeah. I said to call an ambulance.'

Jenny McGill nodded. Down there against the flesh, the smell was worse. It sent a shiver through her and for an instant her own vision wavered. It was powerful and rancid, and Jenny almost turned away. The sweat stood out in strings of beads on the pallid skin. The breasts pressed upwards against the fabric, rounded and bloated, laced with dark veins. They did not look natural on the oddly wizened frame.

She leaned down again, listening to the dreadful rippling sound of a heart beating out of control. There were other sounds in there, an odd *whoosh* of turbulence, the sound of water leaking from a pipe, and a louder gurgle from further down, in the abdomen somewhere, as if the woman had been eating cucumbers or beans and was getting ready to blow.

Jenny knew it was more than that. Fibrillation meant that the heart, despite its frantic beat, couldn't get the blood pumped up hard enough. It was pooling down there in the arteries and veins in the belly, a mass of liquid pressing against the bowels and bladder. Unless the woman was stabilized, she would blow all right. She'd blow herself right out of this world.

'Stand back,' Jenny said. 'Give her some room.'

'Flipping hell, what's that smell?' a boy asked. 'Has she shit herself?'

The crowd pushed back a little. Jenny pushed herself up to her knees. The woman's eyes rolled wildly in their sockets. She mouthed silent words, only managing a hoarse gurgle.

'What's that?'

'Baby.' Finally the word blurted out in a coughing hiss. 'Got to get my baby . . .'

Must be hallucinating, Jenny thought. The woman had to be in her sixties. She put her hands together, one on top of the other, the heel of the left one pressing just under the ridged sternum. She pushed down hard. The woman's head came off the ground an inch, maybe two and slammed down again with a sickening crack. It sounded like a coconut falling on to stone. Jenny pushed again.

'What's she doing?' the boy asked.

'Giving her heart massage,' his pal told him. 'I saw it on *Casualty*. It never works. You need that electric thing. The jump leads.'

Another push. Hard and definite. The dying woman coughed once and her eyes bulged. Her mouth was working all the time.

'Why doesn't she give her the kiss of life?'

'You try it. Have you smelled her? It's worse than dog farts.'

Jenny McGill didn't stop her efforts. Her eyes were fixed on the woman. She pressed down again hard, stopped, bent to listen, heard the fluttering purr under the surface and went back to heeling her hands down on the breastbone. 'Haven't you boys got better things to do?' she snapped. 'Go out and tell the ambulance men where to come.'

The expert on smells gave her a blank look.

'Get moving,' Jenny rasped at him. He saw something in the look in her eye and pushed out of the crowd towards the door.

'Can you help her?' the plump girl asked. Her name was Carol Padden. She was normally rosy-cheeked and cheerful, but the woman's plight had drained the blood from her face. Carol was fifteen and worked only part time. She had never seen anyone take a fit or a heart attack before. All she could hear was the savage, stuttered breathing and the rolling madness in the sprawled woman's eyes and it scared her.

'Doing my best, honey,' Jenny said. 'Doing my bloody best.'

Her breath was coming almost as fast as the old woman's, a panting sound of effort. It wasn't working, she knew. The woman still writhed and twitched under her hands. There was no change in the fibrillation. Finally Jenny pushed herself up and leaned back, a trickle of sweat running down her own forehead. The woman's breath was a dry rattle and the smell, sickly sweet and powerful as rotten meat, came rising up with it. Jenny slicked a hand across her bow and as she did so, the woman's eyes swung round and fixed upon her.

For an instant they were pale and unfocused and then they suddenly cleared. In that moment they were bright with life. 'Baby,' she repeated. This time there was no mistaking it. 'Where's my baby? I need to get . . .'

'What baby?' Jenny asked.

The woman's hand came up and snatched at Jenny's wrist. The fingers closed over her forearm and gripped with desperate force. It was so tight that Jenny winced as her bones ground together.

'Wha–?'

'Get it,' the woman grated. 'Get the baby. Bring him.'

'What baby?' Jenny asked, twisting her arm, trying to free herself from the grip, but the woman's fingers felt as if they were made of iron. The knuckles stuck out white as bone. Despite the pain, Jenny thought it was impossible for the woman to be so strong. She was dying. Her heart was giving out right there on the floor. Nothing but a massive electrical shock would stabilize that fluttering uncontrollable beat.

'Find him,' the woman said again, though this time it was less clear. It was as if the very act of grabbing Jenny's wrist and speaking at all had drained the last of her strength. She raised her head up, eyes still bulging, lips drawn back over dirty, stained teeth. The smell came wafting up, thick enough to choke on. She fixed Jenny with desperate eyes.

Jenny McGill nodded, prepared to agree to anything. She pulled back and the woman's grip slackened. Her head went slowly back down to the floor. For another second, maybe two, the pale eyes hooked on to hers, sharp as needles.

Then the life went out of them.

It was just as if somebody had pulled a switch. The life went out and Jenny knew the woman was dead. Her whole body slumped, a puppet with its strings cut. The mouth gaped and a trickle of thick saliva slid out. It was pink.

Absently rubbing her wrist, where the bruise would later show the four blue finger marks and a deeper smudge where the thumb had pressed, the woman's final imprint, her last mark on the world, Jenny leaned away from the slack face and the eyes which had unfocused and were now fixed on something a million miles away, or something beyond the white light that people spoke of. It hadn't, Jenny knew, been a slow death. At the end of the day, sometimes that was all that mattered, that death was not slow.

Slowly she got to her feet, dimly aware of the ululating sirens coming closer down Meadow Street towards the mall.

'Make way, come on, give us room.' The clatter of trolley wheels thrummed over the metal strip where the security door was closed at night. The crowd, already thinning, moved back further. The drama was almost over. A woman had fallen and died, unusual, but not the end of the world. 'Ambulance,' the man's voice barked. 'Coming through.'

Jenny saw the green medics' overalls and was glad. They would take over now, relieving her of any responsibility. She raised a hand to flick away a stray slick of hair that had fallen over her eyes and she got a blast of the woman's smell. Suddenly she felt unclean.

'Right, where's the problem?' one of the paramedics said. The crowd parted wide and they came striding forward, expert eyes taking in the scene. 'Anybody know what's happened?'

'She collapsed. I saw it,' Carol Padden told him. The colour was coming back into her pretty face. 'She just put a hand to her chest and spun round and fell down. This lady said she was filigreed.'

'Fibrillating,' Jenny corrected. 'At least I think so. Her heart was too fast. I tried heart massage, but it made no difference.'

'Done the course, eh?'

Jenny nodded as the man did exactly what she had done, bending down as if in penitent prayer, and put an ear against the woman's chest.

'Not any more,' he said, wrinkling his nose. 'What the hell has she been rolling in?' He turned to his partner. 'She's stopped, Phil. Let's get her to the paddles. We might make resus.' The first man turned to Jenny. 'How long has she stopped?'

'A minute or so. Not long.'

'You don't get long,' the man said, but he grinned, showing a friendly mouthful of good teeth. He was a technician, unfazed and unshocked. He and Phil quickly lifted the body on to the trolley. The crowd melted away. The first man winked at Jenny.

23

'You did your best, love, That's all anybody can ask.' He smiled again and then they were off, heading for the doors. Jenny turned away and began to walk back to Rolling Stock where the cashier at the door had turned in her swivel seat to gawp while two small boys took advantage of her inattention to stuff their pockets with flashlight batteries. She had only walked ten paces when a dreadful scream tore the air and instantly the shopping mall hubbub was silenced. Jenny spun round. A few yards away Carol Padden turned almost as quickly.

The paramedics had almost reached the big glass doors at the west end of the mall, where the smart leather shop showed mannequins that could have auditioned for a bondage movie. The lead man had his arm held out at shoulder height to straight-arm the door wide open, though that wouldn't have been necessary because they were automatic anyway. A few yards away, tethered to a litter bin, a small Yorkshire terrier went into a frenzy of high-pitched yapping.

The shriek sliced the warm air, loud and high enough to shiver the glass on the leather shop window. Phil, pushing the trolley, head bent, stopped. Beside him a child, held in its mother's arms, went into hysterics.

'What on earth . . .?' Jenny muttered. Her heart suddenly jumped so high it was hard to swallow the saliva at the back of her mouth.

The dead woman sat upright. The lead man was in the act of turning. The woman's mouth was open in an impossible gape, ferally wide, just like an animal.

'She was dead,' Jenny finished her sentence.

The scream went on, high and glassy and completely unnerving.

The paramedic stopped. Phil's head was coming up. The door had started its slide open and the woman rolled off the trolley. She tumbled to the hard floor and hit it with a thump loud enough to be heard thirty yards away. Her coat flew open and a bloated breast spilled out, grotesque and rubbery, filigreed with veins. The grizzled hair sprung out in all directions. There was a cracking sound as if a bone had broken, but the woman turned, almost in slow motion. Her hand reached out, fingers hooked into claws. Her scream abruptly cut off.

'Christ on a bike,' Phil said. 'What's going on, James?' He turned towards the woman who was rolling away from him, raising herself on to her knees. She crawled away from the trolley. 'I thought you said she was stopped.'

'She was. Honest to God. There was nothing there. Absolutely nothing.'

The woman ignored them. The second hallway of the mall angled away from the front door. Up on a ledge, the plastic choirboys still swung their heads in pathetic unison while the Christmas dirges implacably continued, oblivious to the drama. From here, it was clear that the sound and motion did not coincide.

The woman almost scurried across the neatly patterned tiling. A well-dressed girl came walking out of a shop, arms laden with parcels. She was oblivious to the commotion until she almost stumbled over the woman. Whatever she thought it was, it was clear that it was entirely unexpected. She screeched. All the parcels went up in the air. They came down and hit the ground with a series of thumps. The old woman scuttled past, a ragged, spidery shape with that ballooning breast dangling like a growth.

She made it halfway along the walkway. Phil and his partner went chasing after her, but they needn't have rushed. Whatever burst of strength the woman had managed to summon left her just then, when she was halfway to the far wall where baby buggies and walkers and prams were parked in a line.

One moment she was scuttling on hands and knees, a grotesque, fluttering shape on the floor. The next her hands slid from in front of her and she tumbled headlong. Her forehead hit the tiles with a sickening crack. She rolled over, twitched twice, and was still.

The medics reached her, one of them dragging the trolley behind him. Without any hesitation they heaved the woman back on again.

'Make sure she's strapped in this time,' James said.

'Make sure she's dead next time,' Phil snapped back. Over by the bookshop, an old and elegant woman's mouth fell open into a shocked oval.

'Sorry, ma'am,' James said. He tried to smile but couldn't.

He had never seen anything quite like this before. The dead did not get up and walk, or crawl. Not in any of the manuals. And she had been dead all right. He'd heard nothing inside her except for the gurgle of settling fluids. She'd been dead and gone.

But she had screamed loud enough to wake the dead and she'd gone crawling like a ragged spider.

He shook his head. His partner strapped the form on to the flat and they ran for the doors. They opened in time and the medics got to the ambulance.

Inside the mall, Jenny McGill watched in stunned silence. Her heart was beating fast and she felt suddenly faint. The sight of the hunched and grotesque shape scuttering across the floor had scared her so badly her hands were shaking. She put them up to her face and again she smelled the woman's scent. It smelled of death.

'Step on it, James,' Phil urged. 'Get this thing moving.' The siren was screaming as loud as the woman had done and the ambulance rocked from side to side as the driver hauled it round a tight bend.

Phil had slit the faded blouse down the centre and got the black pads of the portable resuscitator on to the ribs under the rubbery breasts. He thumbed the node and, despite the insulation, he felt the hairs on his arms stand up when the current discharged. The woman's muscles contracted violently, back arching off the trolley despite the restraining straps. Her arm, which had rolled off the surface and had hung limply, fingers pointing at the floor, spasmed in a sudden snap. It came up, fingers now clenched into a fist and punched Phil's left testicle with enough force to make him cry out in pain.

'You OK?' James called back.

'Bitch hit me,' Phil managed to reply.

'What?'

The fingers unclenched and the hand fell back down again. Phil bent, trying to ignore the pulsing ache, secured the arm under a strap and tried again. The body flailed once more, but the monitor line stayed horizontal.

'Trying adrenaline now,' Phil said. 'Fifty. Straight in.'

He aimed the thick needle at an angle under the breastbone, pointing it upwards and slightly to the right. Without hesitation he started to depress the plunger and the hormone went straight into the heart muscle.

'Nearly there,' James said. 'Got anything?'

'Nothing yet.'

The ambulance sped through the gateway, siren still yelling urgently, and ran straight for the covered bay in front of the accident unit. While Phil had been delivering the cardiac shock, James had been on the radio calling in. A crash team were waiting to take over. The brakes squealed and Phil was thrown forward. Just at that moment the woman's body gave an enormous shudder. Her eyes flicked open, pale and blue and faded. They looked around. Phil turned. Her hand jerked against the restraint.

'Baby,' she whispered. 'Got to get my baby. He needs me.'

Phil stared at her, stunned into silence. The adrenaline hadn't worked. The shocks hadn't had any effect. Yet now she was alive again.

'There's something funny going on here,' Phil said. The hairs on the back of his neck were crawling. The woman's eyes swivelled towards him.

'My baby,' she whispered again. 'Bring him.'

Phil opened his mouth to speak when another enormous convulsion arched the woman off the trolley. It happened so quickly that he had no time to react, and with such force that one of the restraining straps broke and sent the fastener flying to smack against the roof.

The door opened. Hands reached in. The woman flopped back down and the life went out of her eyes again.

Somebody unsnapped the brake and the trolley was hauled outside. Phil followed behind.

'I gave her fifty of adrenaline,' he told Brendan Quayle, the young emergency doctor who was already pressing his stethoscope down against the woman's ribs. 'She came round. But it didn't look right.'

The team trundled their package inside. James came round and the two medics followed them into the unit.

'Can't feel a thing,' the doctor said. 'Did you shock her?'

'Twice. Up to four hundred. Not a thing. The line was flat.'

'But she came round after adrenaline?'

'Not right away. It was maybe a minute, a bit longer.'

'Can't have been. Wouldn't take that long,' the doctor said, though not unkindly.

Phil shook his head. The sudden lurch inside the ambulance and the croaking whisper from the woman had badly unnerved him. He had seen many things on the road. Dying children, mutilated crash victims, frozen bodies in the snow. They were all part of the job. You bit down on the shock and went on and eventually you treated them like numbers because it was easier that way.

But this had been different. She had been dead twice and she had come alive and there had been a mad look in those rheumy eyes. Whatever had happened to the woman, it had not been natural. Phil didn't quite articulate that thought, but something inside him knew. He shivered again.

It took the crash team less than five minutes to pronounce the woman well and truly dead. Phil looked through the port-holes of the doors, half expecting her to come lunging up from the table. A nurse drew the sheet over her head. Nothing happened. The woman's nose and her oddly full breasts poked at the surface of the fabric, but she remained still.

'You've gone all white,' James said.

'Nearly shit myself,' Phil said. 'And she nearly neutered me.'

'You can't win them all. Come on, I'll get you a cup of tea and we'll write the report up later.'

A tall nurse came and wheeled the gurney away down to the mortuary. Phil followed its progress until it went through the swing doors and disappeared from sight.

CHAPTER THREE

'She just fell down,' Carol Padden said. 'I was right at the front of the shop. It sounded dreadful, just a terrible thud and all her breath came out.'

David Harper nodded. He was sipping a cup of tea in the back shop, his fourth of the morning, and he knew he should refuse any other offers or he'd start to choke. Either that or he'd be jangling by nightfall.

'And that's when you and your friend, what's her name, Jeanette, went out to help?'

'Yes. But there was nothing we could do.'

'Did you see anybody with the woman?'

The girl shook her head. 'No. She was on her own. I'm sure of that.'

It was going to be a slog, David knew. The uniforms had already been round asking the questions and had got nowhere. Normally the beat teams who patrolled the Waterside Mall and the whole of the shopping centre of the town would be enough, but he'd been sent along to lend his weight and that was odd enough. It was just a sudden death. No suspicious circumstances. A middle-aged woman who had upped and died in public. A Jane Doe. Ordinarily, she was of no great account in the scheme of things. People died when they got to their time and the world still turned and it wasn't a job for a detective sergeant to be wasting his time on.

The nameless woman had spun round, fallen and died of natural causes.

Except that the natural causes were a puzzle.

There had been something wrong with her that the experts at St Enoch's hospital couldn't figure out and that's why he'd been sent out to root around. David didn't know what it was that they'd discovered. Nobody knew, or at least nobody was saying – not yet. He'd find out in time, that was for certain.

'We need a name and an address,' Donal Bulloch had said. He was the CID head for the city-centre division and everybody said he'd be the Chief before long. 'Don't ask me why, for I don't know. Professor Hartley tells me there are some anomalies they're having a problem with.'

'Is she infectious? Contagious?'

'Your guess is as good as mine, David. They don't know yet. No, only kidding. They don't believe she's infectious but they think she might have picked something up from somewhere, and they want to find out what. Hartley says there's something in her blood they haven't come across before. Anyway, if they're puzzled, then I'm puzzled and we'd better get a handle on this. The beat boys have come up with nothing at all, so you can do me a favour and get a name and address and a background I can give the sawbones. If you need help, just shout and you'll get it, OK?'

David shrugged. It was a beat job, door knocking and asking questions, and he had better things to do. The previous night's grab had in itself been an interruption to something more important, but he'd worked it because it had come down his own line from a good source. He'd been spending most of the week with the team on the Tollcross post office raid, sifting through all the statements, and the scene-of-crime evidence, piecing together the clues, building them up bit by bit, and he'd felt the pattern emerging. It was a talent he had and his bosses knew it. Now they'd taken him off the team when he was getting that little tickle of certainty and they'd asked him to check out a sudden death in the mall.

Bulloch looked at him. 'Good collar the other night.'

David nodded appreciation.

'Is that a bruise there?' the boss asked, pointing to a mark just under David's hairline. Bulloch smirked. Kenny Lang had been charged with police assault and they could have jacked that up to attempted murder, but there was no point. He was just a small-timer who panicked. He would not try to run a policeman down again, not ever. Bulloch grinned. The bruise was familiar. Anybody on the force recognized the imprint of a Glasgow kiss.

'How is Lamont?'

'She's got bruised ribs. A bit sore. She's getting checked out later so she'll be back tomorrow probably.'

'Good. Take her out with you if she's free. She's got promise.'

The dead woman had to be important. David had figured that out already. They wanted to find out who the woman was, where she came from, and from the sound of it, what had killed her. Down in the mall, David sipped his tea.

'Had you ever seen her before? Maybe she's bought something before?'

Carol Padden shook her head. 'I don't think so. She didn't look like she used Body Shop stuff. Didn't smell like it either.'

'Smell?'

'Horrible. Really disgusting. Like she hadn't washed for ages. It was really weird. Would make you sick. But it was worse than that. It was, like, sick. No, *wrong*. It just smelled all wrong. It made me think of nightmares. I don't know why. When I smelled her everything went dark for a minute and I thought I was going to faint, but I was dead scared as well, like I was in some kind of danger. For a minute everything looked really different, all the people crowding in. But I think it was just because I got such a fright seeing the woman fall like that. I never saw anybody dying before. She was making a terrible noise in her throat as if she couldn't breathe and she was trying to say something, but I couldn't hear it.' Carol's eyes were focused on the distance, in her memory. 'The woman from Rolling Stock. I've seen her before. She tried to give her restitution.'

'Resuscitation?'

'Yes. That. Pressing down on her chest. And the woman grabbed her hand and said something about a baby. That's what it sounded like. But she never had a baby. I think it must have been something else.'

Jenny McGill was more positive.

'Definitely she said "baby". Clear as daylight. She grabbed a hold of my arm – look, there's the bruises to show you. I thought the bones were going to crack and it gave me a right scare, I can tell you.' Jenny rubbed at her wrist where the bruises were purpling up well. ' "Get the baby, was what she said. Get *my* baby." But she was so far gone I think she was delirious, or hallucinating or something. I tried my best to give

31

her heart massage, but it was no good. She was dying. I could hear her heart running riot in there. The only thing that will stop that are the electrical pads.'

'You seem well up on it.'

'I did two years' night school in first aid. I've got certificates.'

'Somebody mentioned she didn't smell very clean,' David said.

Jenny's eyes widened. 'You can say that again. Worse than unclean. When I got home I soaked myself for hours. It was awful. If I hadn't been all worked up with her dying right there in front of everybody, I'd have been sick. But it was more than just somebody who's not been washing herself. Some of these buskers could do with a scrub with carbolic, but this was a lot worse than that. It was rotten. I don't know, like the way you'd imagine gangrene smelled. Or something gone off. It just didn't smell natural. When I got close to her it was really bad. Made me feel all shivery inside and I could feel myself get all hot and clammy. I nearly threw up. For a minute I nearly passed out. She's not diseased or anything, is she? I haven't caught anything off her, have I?'

'No, I think it's all right. We just have to find out who she is.' He took her address and phone number. He still didn't know what was puzzling the medical men at St Enoch's, but if there was some sort of disease, then they'd want to find everybody who'd been in contact.

'Had you ever seen her before?'

Jenny shrugged. 'Maybe. There was something familiar about her, but when you work in here, right on the main walk in the mall, you see hundreds of faces, thousands of them every day. I probably saw her passing, but I don't think she was a customer. Somebody in the other shops might know.' She leaned forward. 'Do you want a cup of tea?'

David's bladder told him he didn't.

It was late that afternoon before paramedic Phil Coulter and his partner got off duty. David went through it again with them. Phil was reluctant to talk at first, but James Bradley started describing what happened and that got Phil going.

'Swear to God, she scared the living daylights out of me. Twice I knew she was dead and then she came back to life. I told Brendan Quayle on casualty and he looked at me as if I was daft. But it's true. She had no heartbeat at all, but she fell off the trolley and started crawling away. Ten, maybe twenty seconds before she dropped. Like a puppet with its strings cut. When we got her back on again, there was no sign of life.'

'That's true,' James agreed. 'I checked the pulse in her neck and there was nothing.'

'But it was in the ambulance that she really scared the life out of me,' Phil continued. 'Jim was driving and I was in the back. I gave her two hits with the pads, juiced right up to four hundred, and I got nothing but a flat line and a punch right in the balls.'

David raised his eyebrows. 'She attacked you?'

'Galvanic jerk, that was all, but I won't be having any fun for a day or two.'

'Only way he'll get a woman to feel him up,' James mocked. 'I prefer to get them drunk, myself. Nothing better than a Carlsberg leg-opener. Works every time.'

Phil ignored him, though his mouth twitched in a half-smile. David could tell that they were pretty close as partners. They'd seen a lot together, and probably saved many a life in the process.

'I gave her adrenaline, injected straight into the heart muscle. Sometimes that kicks everything up again, but nothing happened. Not for a minute, maybe two. Then she comes round, opens her eyes and stares right at me. I can tell you now it gave me a real fright. It wasn't right. I've seen corpses come back to life before, but this was different. It was as if she was dead, but there was something making her keep going.'

'I've told him that's a lot of crap,' James butted in. 'We probably missed the heartbeat.'

Phil shook his head. 'There was nothing. The ECG was dead. But there was something trying to keep her alive. Like willpower, or some sort of after-death thing, maybe even afterlife. Whatever it was, she opened her eyes and looked right at me and started babbling on about a baby.'

'A baby?' David asked, for the third time that day.

'That's what she said, and her voice sounded awful. Like it was coming from down a well. Honest, she was dead, but she was still talking. She was dead, but she crawled off that trolley and along the floor in the mall. I know what I'm talking about, sergeant.'

'And what do the doctors say?'

'They say there must have been something we missed. There's no trouble or anything. Prof. Hartley, the consultant, he's given the OK to everything we did. Can't fault us on procedure, but I know there's something wrong. And now you're round asking questions and that makes me even more convinced.'

David shrugged. 'Just trying to find out who she was.'

'Something else, though.' Phil stopped and looked at James who seemed to think for a second, then gave a small nod.

'When we got back later, they'd taken her out of crash and down to the mortuary and after that they got her out of there. One of the nurses says she was up in microbiology, and that doesn't normally happen. The crash cubicle was sealed off for a while, though nobody knew why. So now I know there was something funny going on.'

'If there was anything dangerous, they'd have let us know,' James said. 'We'd have been the first to be called in for checks. If they haven't done that, then it can't be infectious.'

'I don't know what it was,' Phil replied. 'All I know is that she was trying to talk to me, and she was bloody dead. I'll never forget that, swear to God.'

David found a bathroom and got rid of the tea before deciding to go back to the mall. The ambulance drivers were a long shot, and there was an even longer shot back in the central concourse, but he thought it might be worth a try. What Jenny McGill and Phil Coulter had told him was odd enough to make him think.

It wasn't just the scare the paramedic had got that niggled at him. Maybe he had seen plenty of things, but there was always one more surprise round the corner. David himself had been in on the Toby Cannel capture after the Waterside bank raid that had happened only a block away from the mall in October. Toby had not come quietly. He'd fired three rounds and then he'd taken six shots, two of them through the heart, but he'd kept on running, a hundred yards or more down the alley with exit holes the size of fists in his back. A seventh shot had shattered the thigh bone and Toby had crashed and rolled and yet he'd still tried to get up. When David and big Jock Lewis had reached him he was trying to get to his feet, spraying blood like a pig on a shambles-hook and swearing to Christ that he'd kill them all. It had taken three of them to get him down and take the gun from him and Toby had fought like a madman. He had collapsed ten minutes later and a post-mortem showed that the shots had shattered his spine and completely destroyed the left ventricle of his heart and that he couldn't have walked a yard, never mind run a hundred, and he couldn't have fought three big policemen. That's what the pathologist had said, but it had happened. David was sure something similar had taken place here. Some people just didn't die so easily. Some had a hold on life that you had to pry off with a crowbar.

David knew it wasn't just the scare they'd had that niggled and itched at him. It was not just the scare, nor the unexplained resurrection. It was the baby.

Both Jenny and Phil had mentioned the baby. The dying woman had been trying to tell them something. Even young Carol Padden had thought she heard the word, though she couldn't be sure.

A *baby*.

That didn't seem to make much sense, but it could mean anything. The unknown woman could have been remembering something from her past; that, David knew was not an uncommon event in close proximity to death. She could have been minding a baby for someone, and had possibly come out to the shops for a quick errand, though that too seemed unlikely. The only houses within a quarter of a mile were in the Merchant City where the old offices had been converted into flats for young lawyers and media folk. The dead woman was not among their ranks, that was certain.

Back at the mall, the choristers were still twisting their heads mechanically as they sang 'Jingle Bells' and David wondered how the shop assistants could stand the constant barrage of fake merriment. The incessant noise only reminded him of how close Christmas was and that he'd better find a spare half-hour to get his shopping done. June would already have his gifts wrapped and ribboned: a sweater, same as last year and the year before. Two shirts. Aftershave and talc. He needed a new zoom lens for his camera to take shots of the snow geese flighting in up on the hill lochs, but he knew he'd have to buy that for himself. June faintly disapproved of his weekend trips. Down in the mall, the shoppers browsed and the choirboys urged them on. David wished he'd done his festive buying in the summer and got it over with. Christmas was not his favourite time of the year.

John Barclay – known to his former colleagues as Jab, thanks to his middle name of Anthony and the fact that he had been a fair boxer in his day – had an office on the first floor, built on to a corner with windows on either side which gave him a vantage down the entire main section of the mall. He welcomed David with a brusque but friendly handshake and offered him a seasonal whisky, which made a change from the tea. David sipped the malt slowly, savouring the peaty backtaste.

'So there is life after the D-Division,' David said.

Jab grinned and raised his glass. 'Could be worse,' he said. 'Full pension and criminal injuries and I walked straight in to this. There is a God and he smiles warmly down on me, for which I am eternally in his debt.'

'How's the hip?' Barclay had taken a crowbar blow that had shattered the bone when he'd tried to arrest a hit-and-run driver who turned out to be a thief on his way home from a job on a jeweller's safe. David and he had worked together on a couple of cases.

'Still gives me gyp, but I'm not on my feet all day long, like some folk.' He smiled over the lip of his glass and gave David a wink. 'Surprised they sent CID out on this. Looks like a natural-causes job.'

'That's most likely. They just want a name.'

'Can't help you here,' Jab said, 'but I've got the tape from yesterday. I've been over it a couple of times and I've record-protected it so it won't wipe. '

'Can I see it now?'

'Sure. I thought you'd want to.' The office had a bank of monitors, all of them flickering that blue-grey colour that security screens emit. They covered every angle, showing all the store fronts. Some of the larger departments had their own

36

security cameras which fed here too. Barclay used a remote to fire up a set in the corner. It clicked twice and the screen came alive. At the top, the day, date and time showed in white numerals and letters. The seconds scrolled up mesmerically. The ex-policeman leaned forward and pointed. 'There she is. Coming out on the left.'

David watched. On screen the woman came angling across the concourse, past the escalators and the bench seats where throngs of teenagers gathered in a crowd. She moved slowly along, tired and shabby-looking, shoulders hunched. Past the glassy observation elevator she stopped and leaned against one of the columns that supported the high roof. Off to the left, the little plastic choirboys swung their heads from side to side.

'She's carrying something,' David said. He moved closer. The woman had a white carrier bag in one hand. When she turned slightly, it was clear that she held a smaller handbag which had been hidden by the other one.

'Mothercare,' Barclay said.

A baby . . .

On screen, the woman, tall and angular, spare and skinny-shanked but strangely buxom, paused and bent down as if she was out of breath. 'Watch this now,' Jab told David.

The woman convulsed. There was no other way to describe it. Her head and shoulders had lowered, as if she was crumpling to the floor. Her face must have been only feet from the tiles and then suddenly she snapped straight back up again. David had seen the motion before, a couple of times, but only in brawls. It looked exactly as if she'd been punched in the belly, making her swing down, and then kicked in the face, throwing her back up again.

'Heart attack,' Barclay said. 'Seen it happen before. I'd stake my ex-career on it.'

'Big gambler,' David murmured, but his attention was on the motion on the screen. 'Can we get sound?'

'What do you think this is? Universal Studios?'

The woman's hands jerked up. The carrier bag flopped against the pillar. The handbag went spinning away to the left and out of sight. She stumbled forward, tottering from side to side into the clear space between Rolling Stock and the Body

37

Shop. Her arms rose right up to the side in a crucifixion pose and she spun slowly. For an instant, she stopped, one hand came clamping in against her chest and the other went down to grab at her belly. Her head went back until she seemed to be staring right up at the roof and she fell like a sack, hitting the floor with obvious force. The picture fuzzed out right at that moment, as if a sudden discharge of electricity had jammed the reception, then it came back on again. The shape on the floor jerked violently, the back arching right up from the tiles. Despite the poor resolution of the distance, they could see her mouth wide open in a silent scream.

People passing by just looked at her, in that curious but uninvolved way. A pair of boys almost fell over the skinny, splayed legs and swerved to avoid the obstruction.

'Heartless little bastards,' Jab muttered.

Jeanette and Carol came hurrying over from the Body Shop. The taller girl held back, but the other one went right down, obviously trying to help. A small crowd began to form. The red-head – her hair looked fair in monochrome – pushed her way back to the shop. Jenny McGill came from the other direction. The two men watched as she opened the blouse and bent to listen, then saw her shoulders heave as she tried the heart massage procedure.

A movement at the edge of the screen caught David's eye. A small woman in a grey coat bent forward at the side of the pillar, slowly and casually picked up the Mothercare bag and stuffed it inside a shopping bag of her own. She turned and disappeared. David asked Barclay to rewind the scene and when it came back on, with Jenny McGill desperately thumping at the woman's chest, he pointed out the slick snatch.

'Bloody ghoul,' Barclay said.

'Do you know her?'

The ex-cop shook his head. 'One of millions. Just an opportunist.'

'But we know the woman was in Mothercare. I can check there. Maybe find out what she bought.'

He turned, thinking. Something was nagging at him. The Mothercare bag wouldn't necessarily give any clue about the woman's identity. But there had been another bag. David looked back at the screen. He reached forward and pointed to the left of the screen where the walkway took a dog-leg turn towards the west entrance.

'Her handbag went flying over there. Can we find out where it went?'

'I never saw that,' Barclay conceded. 'I only thought the main action was important. The tape might have been wiped already. I can have a look. It could take some time.'

'If you don't mind,' David said. He knew he could instruct the other man to give him everything, but it was better to play it nice and soft.

'Sure, ' Jab said agreeably. He poured out two more scotch whiskies in the heavy-handed way that Scots men do, despite the fact that David had hardly touched the first one. He crossed to a tall cabinet, opened the door and showed David the stack of tapes. There were dozens of them.

'Got them colour-marked,' Barclay said, 'so it might be quicker.' He checked with a small chart taped to the back of the cabinet door, and brought out about a dozen video cassettes each bearing a red sticker. He put the first one in the machine, let it run for a few moments, then ejected it. It took five more tries before he sat back.

'I think we could be in luck.' He thumbed the fast forward, let the tape whirr for several minutes, pressed 'play'. It took him several tries, running the cassette back and forth until they got close.

'There,' David said. There were a number of people in the picture, two coming out of a confectioner's shop and the others standing in front of the chemist's. As one, they turned to face the right of the picture. Over by the wall, there was a line of supermarket trolleys. Two women started to move closer to the camera, foreshortening as they approached, then walked out of sight.

'They were in the crowd,' David said. 'The one with the hat was there. '

They watched the scene. Right at the far edge of the picture, the small woman in the grey coat moved towards the pillar.

A sudden blur flashed across the screen.

'That's it,' David said. Barclay stopped the picture and the screen jittered to a blur. He rewound for several seconds and replayed the scene. It wasn't pin-sharp, but it was the handbag. It came flying in from the right, hit the ground and skidded on the smooth tiles. They watched it slide right to the far wall and hit against the wheels of the trolley. It lay there, black and shapeless but still clearly a bulky handbag. For more than a minute nothing happened.

Then a girl walked into the picture. She was thin and dark-haired, wearing jeans and a long flapping coat. She looked over her shoulder, turned to watch down the length of the con-course, then very quickly she stooped and lifted the bag from the floor. Cleverly she kept walking, not opening the bag to check the contents. She put the strap across her shoulder, held her head up and walked casually towards the exit. She just looked like a girl out shopping.

'Carrie McFall,' both men said at almost exactly the same time.

'Theft by finding,' Barclay said. 'She won't be handing it in to the station.'

'I'd better find her. If she's still got the bag, it'll be a mir-acle, but I've worked longer odds than that.' David turned to the mall's security chief. 'If I don't get anything, I'll have to come back and go through all of these tapes.' His own sen-tence surprised him because it just sprung to his mind and was spoken before he'd even thought about it, but it was out and it was right. Sometimes he was lucky enough to get a hunch and he'd worked them long enough to go with the flow.

'Jeez, David, that could take a while. And I need them, to keep these cameras running.'

David shrugged. The sudden intuition was buzzing at the back of his head. 'You know how it is. I'll make it as short as possible, but don't wipe any of them.'

'Come on, man. The firm'll go crazy if I lay out on new ones. You know what the guards get paid an hour here? The company doesn't exactly throw money around.'

'Have to insist, Jab, and I'm really sorry, but Donal Bulloch put me on this one, and neither of us wants to give that big Highlandman a bad time or he'll do our arms *and* our legs.'

The importance of saving all the tapes was somehow sharp and clear. 'So let's not fiddle with big Donal's evidence, eh?'

He didn't like doing it to Barclay, especially when he was ex-job, but it had to be done. It was just a little lean, nothing heavy. Jab looked him in the eye, realized the score, and gave in gracefully.

'I suppose you're right. Donal's done me a good turn in the past. Couldn't let him down.' He grinned to let David know there were no hard feelings, turned and locked the cabinet door. 'Want another?' he asked, indicating the bottle. David shook his head. He hadn't touched the second one. Barclay saw him to the door, limping hard on his left side where the hip had been smashed, as if he was still in some pain.

'I'll be back quick as I can. Thanks for the hospitality, and the help. Once I find young Carrie I'll give you a call and we can all stand down. '

'Make it fast then,' Jab urged. 'This is a nice little number. I'd hate to lose it.'

CHAPTER FOUR

It was on her.

It had her in an embrace so foul that the very contact was enough to drain the life from her. It was eating her, sucking her dry, filling her with its poison and she could feel herself rot from within, bones and flesh melting and dissolving as her blood mingled with whatever foul stuff was running through its veins. It held her tight and she held it tight, both of them locked together in a deadly, dreadful enfolding.

A dream, only a dream, she tried to tell herself, even in sleep. *Wake up wake up, wake up*.

It tightened against her, clammy and amphibious, cold as ice and hideous to the touch. It was feeding on her, gobbling her up, sucking and slurping, and she could sense her own self diminish and shrink as it gathered energy and waxed strong.

It was a dream. A part of her mind, the internal sentry that kept watch in the dark, listening for danger, told her it was a dream, a nightmare, but she could not free herself from it. She could not waken.

It had changed, in the way that dreams do when they alter from the acceptable and familiar into the surreal, when they crest on the brow of night and go swooping down the black backslope into the chaos of tormented vision.

She had been coming home. An early finish, stepping light despite the drizzle and the early darkness of midwinter. A few days before Christmas with most of her presents bought, and all of her cards written up and posted for a change. She was heading past the shopping centre, listening to the little choir-boys singing her favourite carols. There was a sparkle of tinsel and a twinkle of lights on the Christmas tree and she was looking forward to the holiday, her mother's good cooking and Dad snoring in his chair by the fire, still wearing his paper hat and giving off the faint aroma of his annual cigar. She walked briskly, planning to pick up a couple of small gifts in the shops, just stocking-fillers, before going round to Celia's to feed the cat.

They'd asked her to go with them, and she'd been tempted. Two weeks in the sun of a Greek island, away from the cold and clammy winter, would have been wonderful. She'd almost agreed, but at the last moment she'd thought of her father's angina and the way her mother would look if she told her she wouldn't be home for Christmas. And there was Tony too. They hadn't been going out so very long but already they were close and she wanted to spend part of this time of the year with him.

There would be other Christmastimes, other winters when the lure of the sun might drag her away, but she'd plenty of time. The weathermen said there was a possibility of snow as a high-pressure area brought cold down from Greenland and there was a chance the pond would freeze over and they could go skating.

All of this, the recollection of thoughts and fragments of emotions, whirred past in her dream as she saw herself come into the mall. The doors whisked open silently and a warm blast of air from the overhead draughtbusters came billowing down in a welcome breath. The choirboys sang out louder now she was inside, clear recorded voices piercing through the hubbub of the crowd and the clack and clatter of heels on the tiles. She stopped at the leather shop and picked up a pair of chunky earrings, moved on to the Tie Rack for a pair of neat leather gloves for her grandmother. She was just putting them in her handbag as she was leaving the shop when she became aware of the commotion on the central walkway.

Somebody had been screaming. She wasn't sure whether she had heard it or whether one of the shop alarms had gone off further along the mall. She turned towards where the crowd was gathering. A woman was hurrying from another shop, her overall flapping. The woman was running, but of a sudden she was moving in slow motion. Everything started to lose speed. The world took on a viscid, syrupy texture.

The sound of the choirboys faltered, as if drained of power. The low hum of the escalator became a deeper, growling sound, hollow and mechanical and strangely animal. Over at the middle, the crowd were bending down to the flapping thing

43

on the floor and she could hear their hushed, startled sounds, like distant, muted echoes.

She was moving away. Someone was hurt and she didn't want to see it. Of a sudden she was scared. She turned involuntarily, almost reflexively, and moved to the right, feet silent now on the hard tiles, as if she were gliding along, not quite making contact with the ground. She could have been a feather drifting in the wind, so little control did she have over the direction she took.

A woman was coming round the side of the pillar. A small black shape was crumpled up against the wheels of a trolley.

She glided on past the line-up of buggies and prams, suddenly aware that something was wrong. Everything was wrong. The choirboys were tolling out a slow, tuneless dirge. Their clean little plastic faces seemed to run and melt. The escalator wheels were shifting and grinding. The tinsel sparked and spangled with a strange, electrical illumination. It writhed in the curved bows suspended above her.

She stopped.

The smell engulfed her. In an instant her stomach clenched in a spasm so tight it sent a bolt of pain through her, worse than cramp. She grunted and the sound came out long and slow, thrumming in a way her voice never did.

Take me!

The command bloomed inside her.

The smell billowed into her nostrils, rank and somehow musky, thick and cloying in the back of her throat. It scraped against the receptors of her membranes and for an instant she almost fainted. She was standing stock-still, a hand clamped against her belly. The pain faded just a little, but it spread upwards, forked left and right, flowed into her breasts in twin warm and tingling streams. Without warning, the pain flared there too.

Oh . . . *oh!*

Her voice seemed to have the cracked tones of an old bell.

Take me take me. LOVE ME!

A dreadful imperative shuddered into her mind, more painful than the twist in her breasts or the augur in her belly. It was a mental blast. A wave of heat ran through her veins, fast and

44

jittery. Beads of sweat sprung out on her forehead and made it clammy. Her breath came short and shallow. All the twinkling colours reflected from the window faded out for a moment.

Take me NOW!

She felt herself turning. An old grey pram, one of the coach-built ones, maybe an old Silver Cross that had seen better days, stood alone at the end of the rank, just beside her. The courtesy chain that would have secured it to the bar on the wall dangled free. The folding hood was up, shading the inside, and the weather guard was firmly clipped in place. From where she stood, she could see nothing.

But she could smell something strong and volatile that made her emotions spin. She tried to walk on but her feet refused to obey her. She moved towards the pram, shoes dragging on the tiles. Something inside it moved, just enough to make it shudder and rock on its old-fashioned curved springs.

A small sound, something like a grunt, something like a cry, came out from the shadow. It riveted right into her.

The noise of the commotion faded away and the choirboys' bass atonal singing rumbled to silence. In that instant there was just her and the battered pram, enveloped in a musky, invisible cloud. Her heart was tripping erratically and her skin seemed to crawl with a life of its own. She reached out and unclipped the snapper on the weather shield. She lowered it slowly. Down in the shadow, something moved.

Without any volition, she unsnapped the second catch and leaned forward.

For a fraction of a second, eyes fixed on her, pinning her with a sharp and hot connection of will. She saw a face that at first had no real shape, just a rippling blur of flesh. A scream started to wind up down inside the hot clenching in her belly. She stumbled back, but the mental imperative stopped her. In that brief space of time she was held, shuddering with fear and alarm while another, stranger, and much more powerful emotion was building up inside her.

It drew her back again and she looked under the hood. Her eyes blurred, focused again and the impossible rippling sensation faded and stopped. She saw the baby.

The big eyes looked up at her, glistening with baby tears. Its round face and little smooth red cheeks were streaked with them. Its soft lips were trembling, as if it was about to burst into a spasm of sobs.

Her heart swelled. The urgent thumping faded instantly. The pain down in her core shrank away. The pulsing pressure in her breasts did not diminish, but swelled fiercer, but now it was no longer real pain. It was the pressure of need.

She leaned towards the child. 'Poor little thing,' she heard herself say, her voice automatically talking in the sing-song cadence of an adult comforting a baby. Inside her, a part of her consciousness screamed at her to run away, to flee. It smiled up at her suddenly. Its eyes were huge with appeal. The wide brow showed a twist of dark curls poking down from under a knitted hat. The baby smell infused her.

Take me take me take me . . .

The demand was urgent now, irresistible, inescapable. The fear was strangled back to whimper deep in her consciousness.

Mother me!

'Yes, ' she said aloud, letting the word trail away in a long sigh. She bent right into the pram, pushing the hood back a little. The baby blinked its eyes tight against the light but she wrapped it in the old shawl and gently lifted it out. She opened the top buttons of her coat, overwhelmed by a sudden protective instinct, and clutched the baby in against herself. She turned around, looking up to the end of the concourse and down again to the near door where she had entered. For a moment of indecision she swithered, taking one step to the left, another to the right.

Over in the centre, the woman kneeling beside the dark, prostrate body was slamming her weight down hard on the chest, using the heels of her hands on the breastbone, trying to restart a still and lifeless heart, trying to resurrect the dead.

The need to get away came sweeping through her. She turned, keeping her head low, and pushed her way through the passing crowd of shoppers towards the nearest exit. As she passed, some of them, the women, turned suddenly, following her with their eyes. She could feel them on her but she tried to ignore them. She hurried forward. Down the centre, past the escalators she turned and her coat flapped open. Immediately the baby squirmed hard, and she felt a bolt of pain lance into the back of her head. Without thought she clasped her collar up to cover the small bundle. Moving fast now, as fast as she dared without breaking into a run, she got to the far doors which opened with a slow gush of sound like a harsh intake of breath.

Out in the air it was winter-dark and a *smirr* of rain was misting the air, though it was cold enough to be sure to turn to ice in the night. She swung to the left again, keeping her head low, and hurried up the pedestrian walkway, swerving to avoid passers by.

The urgency was inside her. She had to keep moving, just get away. She had no direction yet, only the imperative to move, to flee. She walked up and over Hanover Street, down Wellington Street, past Victoria Square, all of them hung with fairy lights and each shop competing in the choral cacophony, but she heard none of it.

Her entire being was focused on the internal voice which urged her on and on into the night, and the need that surged within her in a powerful tide of emotion.

At her breast, the baby shifted position, nuzzled further in against her warmth, and the mother-love burgeoned like a flower. The scent of the baby was all through her now, a warm narcotic that nurtured her as she would nurture the baby.

But first she had to find shelter. She hurried out of the shopping precinct, heading parallel to the river. She reached the junction that was the unofficial boundary of the city centre and turned right on Levenford Road beyond the Chinese restaurant.

The alley yawned and she was scurrying up it in the darkness. She was almost running now, heels slapping on the cobbles. A shape moved out of the shadows and she saw the grizzled old tramp. She looked at him and he stared back and the fear in her welled up in the depth where her own sense of self lived. It made her want to scream out loud and beg for help because over and above the powerful urge there was something wrong that she couldn't fathom but deep inside herself she was dreadfully afraid. She tried to stop and ask the man for help, not knowing why, only realizing that something was happening to her, but the enormous gravity of the force inside her dragged her away and on and on and on. The dogs came and snarled but she hardly noticed them as she scurried along the path, pushed the gate open, found the door handle and let herself inside a house she had never seen before.

The fear was rising faster now, a black tide of it, threatening to swamp the other emotion, the awful need. She went into the lounge, still in the dark, and leaned against the wall, feeling the strength drain from her as her knees gave way. She slid down against the wall leaving a damp stain on the wallpaper.

Another damp stain was spreading across the surface of her blouse. In the dim light she watched it expand, grey against the white. A different scent came now, one that made her think of weasels and scaly things. It came strong now, tinged with that other musky smell that seeped into her pores and into her blood and into her mind.

Her breast was leaking milk.

What's happening to me?

The panic welled up again and the scent came thick and choking to mask it, smother it, clamp it down. She felt the baby nuzzle down.

She woke with a start, hauling for breath, shaking with the force of the dream. The room was dark, the curtains drawn, and she did not know where she was. She was cold and stiff and the images of the nightmare hovered at the front of her mind, dreadful pictures spangling and expanding in the dark, changing with the flicker-flick speed of film sequences.

A huge sigh escaped her. She was stiff and sore, as if she'd got cramp or flu. That was surely why she'd had the appalling dream.

She closed her eyes and her head thumped against the wall as the tide of the nightmare washed over and through her. What a dream, she thought, hearing the words coherent in the tumult of the aftermath. *I stole a baby.* It was an appalling notion, and that showed she must be coming down with something. She was lacquered with sweat, but cold. Her hair smelled damp.

She had dreamed she'd looked in a pram and seen a beautiful baby and she had taken it and gone on a nightmare run through the rain and the dark to a strange house in an unfamiliar part of the city. It had been awful, but now she was awake, shivering in the aftermath. Any moment her mother would come in with a cup of tea. Any minute now . . .

'Must be getting broody,' she told herself, her mind still vague and numb.

A griping pain twisted down in the basin of her pelvis, sharp and cramp-like. The pain looped up like heartburn and spread across her ribs to pool in her breasts. She thought the flu was worse than she'd supposed and maybe it was something worse than that. She closed her eyes, twisting them shut against the sensation.

And something moved on her skin.

She woke completely then, every pore of her body tensed and galvanized, every downy hair on her neck and arms standing to attention.

'Oh . . . *aah!*' Whatever she tried to say, it only came out in a little double gasp. She twisted away from the motion. It was small and slender. She could feel roughness scrape against her smoothness.

'Oh please . . .' she bleated.

The dream came back, swooping into her mind with powerful mental force, overlaying the conscious sensations.

She pulled back, turning as she did so. She was slumped on the floor, not on the bed. Her arms were clamped around the thing inside her coat. She tried to unlock them but they were stiff from the force of her grip and they refused to move. In their embrace, the motion came stronger. She tried to look away, sudden appalling terror welling up inside her in a gush of abhorrence. The thick smell came billowing up, rank and foetid and overlaid with that sickly sweetness. It suffused her again, this time not in a dream, this time all too real as the dream had been a recollection of something all too terrible.

She felt her head turn of its own volition and she looked down into the shade in the folds of her coat. The small smooth head moved against her. It turned slowly. An eye opened, gazed into hers, held her for an instant, connecting with her, before it slowly closed again.

'Oh mother oh Jesus oh.' The words tumbled and tripped over each other in an incoherent gush. Tears sparked and filled her eyes.

The small shape turned again, eyes closed against whatever light was coming through the curtain but the pervasive scent came stronger. Ginny's tears blinked away and the baby was in her arms. Away from the light, its eyes opened and its innocent gaze fixed upon her as if she encompassed its whole world.

The rank odour faded to a sweet baby scent and she felt the sudden love and the fierce need swell inside her. The deep, primitive part of her consciousness protested and fought, yelling hysterically and incoherently, a blare of pure fear, but the need within her grappled it and she was paralysed, unable to move.

There was blood on her blouse now, a faded patch where it had mingled with the milk.

She knew she had no milk. She couldn't have milk to feed a baby. Her breasts could not be bleeding.

But there was a bloodstain on her blouse and her breasts were swollen and aching, pressing painfully against the cotton. The fear rose and the need clamped it down and her emotions wrestled and rolled while the baby fixed her with its wide, mesmeric eyes before it turned and burrowed down where the buttons had come free. She felt the scrape of skin as it sought her nipple. Her skin puckered, as if it was trying to crawl away from the contact. A shudder ran through her yet her body responded to the need and she twisted to assist. The mouth found her nipple and clamped upon it. It started to suckle, tugging hard, hard enough to cause the burning pain to return, but she was paralysed, locked within the fear and the mother-love, thoughts turning and tumbling and whirling within her, utterly terrified, completely smothered in maternal instinct, clutching the small thing that she'd stolen from the mall.

After a while, she began to sob softly in the dark.

CHAPTER FIVE

Helen Lamont looked up from her desk in the squad room when David Harper came in, running his fingers through his short hair to shake off the mist droplets that had condensed and settled in a dew as he walked back to the station.

'I heard you were looking for me.'

'Nothing too important,' he said. 'I'll need help to go through some videos.'

'Picking up porn now, David?' She gave him a wide-eyed innocent look and he went along with it, trading her an easy grin.

'Don't you wish, sleazy cow.'

Her eyes opened wider and her mouth formed a small circle of surprise, even shock. 'That's sexist. I could have your legs done for that, chauvinist pig.'

'Whenever you can tell me who Chauvin was, I'll hold my hands up and take the rap.' He knew she was kidding, and so did she.

She returned his smile. A bruise swelled purple just under her eye and two scrapes went down the side of her cheek where the skin was still risen slightly. Apart from that, she looked undamaged, though he knew there was a handspan black-and-blue mark across her ribs where the doctors at casualty had taped them tight, and another deep purple blossom on her belly where she'd taken the full force of the boot. She still looked almost frail, but he also knew she was as tough as anybody on the shift, as the knee in the thin man's groin testified. Back in the station he had claimed she'd assaulted him. His lawyer advised him against proceeding further. He was an accessory to a potential charge worse than receiving stolen goods. He had backed off, very gingerly, for his testicles were still paining him the following day.

David gave her an exaggerated up-and-down once-over, still kidding, though while he appreciated the fact that she was a good cop, a really good cop, he was also male enough to think she was a good-*looking* cop, and there was nothing wrong with having good-looking policewomen around. She barely came up to his shoulders and she had a dark-eyed, almost soft appearance, but her looks were deceiving. On the first day they'd worked together he'd seen her square up to Walter Gourlay down on Pollock Road when he'd come at her with a baseball bat. She'd ducked and there had been only two hits. She'd hit him on the throat and he'd hit the ground. He'd hardly been able to talk when faced with his oppressor in the Monday morning court, and the judge had taken a look at the differences in their size and sex and laughed big Walter down to a year in Drumbain jail.

'Before I forget. ' Helen turned round, making a face as David shook the droplets from his coat. 'May called.'

'June, ' David corrected automatically. He was getting used to Helen Lamont's quirky sense of humour.

'May, June, whatever,' Helen said, trying to keep the smile off her face. 'Anyway, she called half an hour ago while you were out doing your Christmas shopping. She wants you to pick something up.'

He rolled his eyes to the ceiling. 'Does she ever want anything else? What is it this time?'

'Something from a delicatessen. For a fondue or whatnot. You're apparently having people around tonight. I put a note on your desk. She wants you to call.'

David slumped down on his seat and ran his fingers through his hair again. It was short and dark, almost severe. It gave him a clean-cut capable aspect, almost tough. He was tough enough.

'Tonight?' he asked, letting his breath draw out in a sigh. 'She actually said it was tonight?'

Helen nodded. 'Sounds like you're in trouble, boss, and now you're heading into more. It's the same old story. She's got you on a pretty short leash.'

He lifted the phone and turned away while he dialled, putting his feet up on top of the old radiator which clanked loudly as it joggled on its loose wall bracket. She turned back to her notes and tried to ignore the stage-whispered conversation. It went on for three or four minutes and then he put the telephone down. There had been no goodbye. No tailing off in the conversation.

'Where were we?' he said. She could see the glitter of annoyance in his eyes. 'Matter of fact, where were you today?'

'I hope I'm not going to suffer over the fondue, sarge?'

He looked at her, eyes still fiery. Then he blinked and was normal again. 'No, course not, Helen. Anyway, the fondue is off. I'm too busy. She's known my rota schedule for weeks.'

'Big trouble?'

'Jurassic.'

'I'd rather hear about the porny videos. I'm up to here with relationships.' She indicated a distance somewhere above her head. 'My sister's engagement is off. My cousin's getting a divorce. And my mother's met some car salesman down at the ballroom and she's doing some pretty fancy footwork for a woman her age. Her hormones have gone haywire. All that and Christmas just round the corner. Let's not talk about relationships.'

'Suits me,' David said, shrugging off his annoyance. June was becoming more demanding by the month, both of his time and his attention, and the more insecure she seemed, the more he found himself resenting her. That just made him feel guilty, for they'd had a good couple of years.

He backed away from thinking of her, realizing that was something he had been doing for some time. Turning to Helen, he told her about the video and how Carrie McFall had snatched the handbag. 'Red-handed, as they say in the movies. It was pretty smooth, no hesitation, right on to the shoulder and away. Cool as ever was our Carrie.'

'And a heartless little bitch,' Helen said. 'The shoplifting's bad enough, she's been doing that since she was ten. But stealing from somebody who's dying on the floor, that's really a bit off.'

'Don't worry. She'll have a great time at the preview première. We've got to get the bag back, if we can. I have to find out who the victim was.'

'What's so important about her?'

'Who knows? She's caused a bit of a stir at St Enoch's. Something wrong with her blood. I'll tell you the details later. Donal

Bulloch asked me to give it a look, and that's good enough for me.'

Carrie McFall was easy to find, despite the fact that she'd changed address twice since David had booked her last. She still lived on the north side, in Blackhale, where the planners had opted for a supermarket housing policy. They stacked them high as they could, then forgot about them. Up in this part of the town, business was drink or drugs or moneylending. The local economy boomed and everybody was in the same gutter along with the shell-suits and pit bulls who ran the smack. Carrie McFall was just a product of a succession of slumps. Her record was pretty much up to date, and a little longer than the last time David had seen it.

Her boyfriend, a skinny runt with a bowl cut and a ring though one nostril, opened the door, stuck a foot under it when he saw it was the police, but removed it pretty quickly when David leaned inside and snagged the ring between thumb and forefinger – all the while finding it hard to believe how stupid anyone would be to leave himself so vulnerable. David twisted just a little and the boyfriend grunted, more in fright than in pain. The door opened and the boy pressed himself against the wall of the narrow hallway as David and Helen went past.

Carrie was watching television, sitting with her feet drawn up under her on a low sofa that had seen better days, lazily smoking a cigarette and chewing gum at the same time. She had dark hair almost to her shoulders and a silk scarf tied casually round her neck. Helen recognized the quality and she knew Carrie didn't have that kind of money. The girl turned round slowly. Her eyes widened just a fraction, hardly at all. She was cool. She was used to this. She eyed them up and down with hardly a flicker of emotion, then stubbed her cigarette out. In the bedroom, a baby squalled.

'Got a warrant?' Carrie McFall demanded.

'Got a conscience?'

'You're not giving this place a spin without a piece of paper. I got turned over only last week.' Carrie blew a pink bubble for emphasis. It burst in a small puff of smoke.

David leaned to the left, eased open the narrow cupboard. Black plastic bags bulged down at floor level. 'Well, you should be a little bit more careful. What's in the bags?'

'Christmas presents. Open one of them and it'll be inadmissible, you know that.'

'You've been watching too much television,' Helen said. She pulled the cupboard door, giving it a quick jerk. One of the bulging bags toppled as the pressure on it was released. At least a dozen perfume bottles, still in their cartons, all of them expensive, slid on to the floor.

'Oh dear. Your presents seem to have all fallen out. Lovely stuff. Paris. Givenchy. Not cheap. Got receipts for them all?'

Carrie shot her a deadly look.

David sat himself down on the couch. It was cleaner than most in Blackhale on the north side of the city. Some people called the scheme The Sump, and not without reason. It was where the dregs finally settled when their jobs had vanished, when their self-respect had gone. They had fallen well clear of any social safety net. In some of the high concrete towers, you'd be lucky to find a seat and if you did, you'd never sit in it for fear of getting a needlestick puncture in the backside.

'But today's your lucky day. A very merry Christmas, I shouldn't wonder. Because I could forget all about the sweet smell of success in the binbags.'

Carrie moved away from him. Her eyes flicked from David to Helen, suspicious as ever. She'd never had any reason to trust a policeman. Both of her brothers were up in Drumbain jail and neither of them was coming out again for some time.

'I could forget all about it,' David repeated, 'but I do want to know all about your new handbag.'

For an instant, Carrie looked genuinely puzzled. David kept his eyes on hers.

'What new hand–?' David caught the spark of understanding, swiftly masked.

'Yes, that one,' he struck. 'Good performance. You should be in the movies.' He gave her a wide smile. 'Oh, come to think of it, you *are* in the movies. We've got a lovely shot of you in the Waterside Mall. Very photogenic. What a mover.'

Helen sat on the other arm of the settee, diverting the girl's attention. 'And we want the bag.'

'I never took it. It was empty, so I just dropped it.'

'Nice try,' Helen said. Her voice went brittle and cold. 'The second camera picked you up going through the exit. Bang to rights, I can tell you. But remember, Carrie, this is not a smack-on-the-wrist job like lifting a few bottles of fake perfume. You see, you took a handbag that belonged to somebody who collapsed in there. That wasn't very nice.'

David butted in, forcing Carrie to swing round to face him.

'Trouble is, her medicine's in the bag. She suffers from a very rare condition. They've got her hooked on a life-support and they need her medicine. If they don't get it and she dies, then what are we looking at? Culpable homicide? For sure. Could maybe even crank it up to murder, if you insist. If you persist.'

'I never saw any pills,' Carrie said, eyes shifting from one to the other, sensing real danger now. 'There was hardly anything in it, honest. Just a purse with some money. I threw them away. But I can show you where.'

David smiled again. It had been far too easy. The story he had spun had more holes than a garden riddle, but Carrie was in no position to be objective.

Half an hour later, a shivering Carrie, who had been so convinced she was facing a long stretch that she'd come with them immediately and forgotten to take her coat, showed them where she'd thrown the bag. She directed them down the narrow streets near the river, not far from where David and Helen had arrested the three men with the stash of hardware. They passed under the motorway bridge, a black arch that rumbled with the passage of overhead traffic, making the ground shiver. The streets narrowed further the closer they got to the river. An early evening mist curled up from the water, softening the outlines of the buildings. It was cold and dank, and there were few people here at this or at any other time. There had been a day when these streets close to the old quayside had teemed with life and bustled with commerce, but no more; like Blackhale, this too was a derelict part of town. Close to the river, where the railway paralleled the bank, there was a stretch of waste ground bounded by a tall barricade made of old railway sleepers. At one time it had been a shunting branch for the main line, serving the long-gone yards and wharves, but now it was overgrown with the scrub alder and exhaust-blackened birch that colonize gap sites in all cities. The place was less than five hundred yards from the glitter and sparkle of the shopping mall, but it could have been a hundred miles away and a century distant. Here the buildings bounding the old sidings were tall and crumbling, and the alleys between them narrow and lightless. Here the junkie hookers did a little business, hiking their skirts up in the dark behind the barricade. An occasional drunk would turn up stiff as a board, red eyes frosted open on a winter's cold morning.

David made Carrie show him exactly what she'd done. She pointed to a gap at the corner where some time in the past some vandals had set the old sleepers alight. He shone his small flashlight through. She had only slipped the bag in between the stanchions and jammed it down among the jagged twigs of the undergrowth. He reached through, groped blindly, snagging his fingers on the sharp ends of broken branches and getting a thin splinter jammed up under a nail. He cursed, found the bag's shoulder strap and hauled it out. It was old and tattered and, inside, the lining was shredded and torn from long use. The purse was cheap and plastic, gaping empty except for a small black folder tucked into the outside pocket. Beside the purse a tattered account book was losing one of its covers.

'Can I go now?' Carrie asked. She was hugging herself tight against the cold that had come down hard, turning the thin mist into a sparkle of frost.

David motioned to her to stay. Helen stood close. He shone the beam over the front page of the book. It was a rent-receipt account.

THELMA QUIGLEY, the name read, written in block capitals on a light patch reserved for it. He flicked the cover open. Her name and a scrawled signature were repeated inside. There was an address. The small wallet showed a couple of photographs done in black and white. They looked old and faded. There was some faint writing on the back, not easily legible, but also old-fashioned script, maybe from the fifties.

'See,' Carrie said vehemently, hopefully. 'There was no medicine. If she dies, it's not my fault.'

'Oh, I should have told you,' David said, giving her his best smile. 'She's already dead. They couldn't save her. And how do we know there was nothing else in here?'

Carrie's mouth opened so wide her chin was almost on her breastbone.

'So it's murder then?' Helen asked.

'Looks pretty much like it.'

Carrie started to babble. Her shiver became a shudder that had nothing to do with the cold. She was protesting her innocence, the words guttural and frightened, almost incoherent. Finally David held a hand up. He had what he wanted.

'OK. Enough. We'll think about it. You can go for now. We'll be in touch.'

The girl looked at him, disbelief slack on her face. He nodded to confirm what he'd said. She stood frozen for almost half a minute and then turned on her heel and ran away from them, her expensive running shoes thudding down on the hard surface, echoing back from the gaunt walls.

'I reckon that gave her the message. Scared the daylights out of her.'

'But she shouldn't have taken the woman's bag in the first place,' Helen said, her voice colder than the sparkling frost. 'Not when she was lying there dying.'

She went into her own bag, drew out her radio and thumbed the switch. When the control room came on line, she stood there, eyes fixed on David Harper, and told them she had reason to believe there was stolen property at an address in Blackhale. When she had finished, she clicked the switch with a hard jab of her thumb. 'I don't mind the shoplifting,' she said. 'But she shouldn't steal from the sick. Or the dying. She's a damned parasite, and the world's too full of them.'

David looked down at her. In the dark of the badly lit street, her dark hair was tumbled over her eyes, framing the heart shape of her face. She looked soft and mild-mannered, almost innocent, despite the shadow of anger in her eyes. He remembered how she'd tackled the two men who had run out of the storeroom, how she had hung on despite the brutal kick in the ribs.

'Remind me not to get on your bad side,' he said.

'Oh, you'll never do that,' she told him. 'You stopped me getting the rest of my ribs stove in, and that makes you one of the good guys.' She gave him a big smile and it lit up her whole face. 'Even if you are a chauvinist pig.'

It was more than a mile from the riverbank sidings to the address in the tattered rent book. David was driving his own car, a mud-spattered four-wheel drive which had seen better days and worse roads. The frost was condensing out of the still air, forming orange haloes around the lights on the far side of the water where gaunt cranes loomed dark and angular over the black turbulence of the river's downflow, stretching up to the dark sky, catching the occasional sweep of lights from a car on the bridge. In the mist they seemed almost to move.

'Like dinosaurs,' David said, driving slowly. 'Brontosaurs.'

'Brachiosaurs,' Helen told him.

He looked round at her. 'I stand corrected. You're right.'

'In this light, you can imagine them moving, all charging through the fog. They'd make the ground shake.'

'Make *me* shake,' he admitted. 'And fill my pants.'

She laughed out loud. The anger had gone from her voice. They moved on, past the tall bridge which spanned the river, its lights like a string of bright pearls on the suspension cables. Just as they came out from under the first span, an immense flock of starlings came whirring across the water, all screeching in unison, the sound of their wings loud enough to be heard over the sound of the engine and the low fog horn from five miles downstream.

Helen looked up at the birds as they came wheeling in, turning as one entity to sweep under the shadow of the bridge to their roosting place. 'Why do they swarm like that?'

'Apparently they're just checking the talent,' he said. 'I read somewhere they flock like that to get an estimate of their numbers. If the swarm is too big, they lay fewer eggs the following spring, so there's enough to go round. One of nature's control mechanisms.'

'I didn't know you were a bird man,' she said. A hint of a laugh made her voice warm in the shadows of the passenger seat.

'Ah, there's more to me than meets the eye. I take photographs of birds.'

'More porn?'

'No, real ones. Whenever I get the chance. Birds, animals, any kind of wildlife. Been a hobby since I was small. I've had a couple featured in magazines.'

'So you've not been a hard-bitten detective all your life, then. I thought you were a born cop.'

He laughed this time. 'There's no such thing. I used to believe there were. There's only some good ones and some bad ones. Nobody's born for this.'

'And you?'

'You already said. I'm one of the good guys.'

The starlings screamed like banshees in the winter dusk while the cold frost came dusting down from the darkness overhead. David drove along the river road, past the warehouses and the grain stores that had stood empty since the ships had abandoned the dying ports and the shipbuilding yards had left the giant cranes as reminders of their own extinction.

They reached the house they sought. It was a ground-floor apartment in a small terrace off the main street in an old, rundown part of the city, but it was as nondescript as anywhere could be. The garden had been covered in concrete which was now cracked and eroded. Bare tendrils of some creeper, an ivy that had withered and shrivelled, clung to the crumbling wall. The paint on the door and the window frames was peeling and behind the glass the curtains were shut. There was no name on the door, no plate to carry a name. It was completely anonymous.

David turned to Helen, asked her to check round the back of the house. She disappeared into the shadows and came back a minute or so later.

'No sign of life.'

He reached to the door handle, gave it a twist. It made a low, creaking sound of protest, but it turned all the same. The latch clicked hollowly and the door opened a crack.

He pushed it, listening to the whine of the hinge until it was wide open. The hallway was just a mass of shadows.

'Hello?' David called out. His voice boomed hollowly in the darkness. There was no reply.

★

It nuzzled into the warmth, eyes tightly closed, reaching out with its senses.

It, *he*, was safe for now. Safe in the hot dark and the smoothness of the new one. He turned his head just a little and found the nipple, let his lips stretch and flow over it, pull together and begin to suckle.

The milk came slow, not yet the full flow, but that would come in time. He was hungry, as always, but instinctively did not suck his fill. The milk was rank and weak, too sweet and dilute. It did not have the nourishment he needed. He would get hungrier still, and desperate until she changed, this new mother. That would take time. He could sense her battle for control, could feel the internal jitterings and writhings as she fought for her own self. But he would win this one.

She was difficult, but it had happened all so suddenly and he'd been forced to take her very quickly. The old one had been dying. She had been drying out, shrinking into herself. He had sensed her slow decay, but it had still been too sudden when it came. His need had finally drained her, despite the flow of milk that had still been thick and strong. He had stolen her strength at last, sucked her essence dry.

But she had gone with dreadful suddenness, leaving him alone and helpless.

He had sensed the change in the old mother as he sensed the pull of the moon and the tides of the sea and the coming of the dark. He reached out his awareness, stretched it out around him, pinpointing the hot warmths that moved with sudden swiftness and uttered their thoughts aloud in jarring cacophonies of sound. Although he had been aware of that alteration in the old mother, he had been distracted by the new growth in his own body. That was something different after all this time of suckling and feeding and it had taken him unawares, and changed his perceptions. He would have prepared, as he always had done, when the old mother began to falter. He would have chosen a new one first if he could, letting the old mother slowly fade out, dying from his hunger and discarded because of his need, while he reached his thoughts inside another one to prepare her to feed him. He had been diverted and the life in her had blinked out.

61

The loss had been intense.

It was as if a physical umbilical cord linking them had been severed. She hadn't faded away, she had broken. She had burst inside, so violently it had stopped her in her tracks. The pain had come lancing across the distance, magnified by its purity, and had slammed into him as he lay in the dark. He had called to her, suddenly – for the first time in memory – afraid of losing her and being left alone in this place.

He had no recollection of fear, because he had never lost a mother before.

She had responded because she carried the essence of him in her blood and the blood sang out in terror. She had tried to get to him. Her mind had sparked and crackled, fading then swelling strong as the lack of oxygen competed with the urgent demands of the other thing in her blood. She had tried to get to him but she had fallen and she couldn't force her broken body across the distance.

All around her he could sense the heat of the others, milling around, touching her. He could feel the stroke of the other one's hands and the punch-pound weight on the mother's chest transmitted from her mind directly to his and all the time her panic and fear had soared. He was losing her and she was losing him and her mother-love screamed out from her in desperation. The life had started to fade. He could sense the sparks of it, little flares of incoherent thought and need, and his blood was sizzling inside her veins as it still battled to return, to reach him.

Then he screamed for help.

He had screamed the way a baby does, the way an infant will snatch at a human's emotions.

But he had screamed with his mind and all of his instinct. The glands had opened up and pulsed and the scent had gone hissing from him.

Far off, he felt the responses. He sensed a shudder here. He heard a groan there. Mental pictures danced within his own cold consciousness, picked up by the reflexive scanning that had powered up in this moment of intense danger. Bright columns of warmth hovered close, passed on by. Way in the distance, hundreds of them milled together, each one a potential source of food and warmth. He screeched again.

Close by, one response was stronger and he instinctively homed in on it. He focused his demand and speared it outwards. Way beyond him, he could sense the old mother's disintegration as her mind faded, leaving only the essence of himself in her blood which spasmed and kicked reflexively. He called out again, a powerful cry, but fined down so that it was aimed at the one target. The urgency was clamouring in him and the fear rising: there were minds out there that would not tolerate his, would not love him. There were minds out there that were cold as stone, that he could not appeal to, could never influence.

The moving warmth stopped. He felt its indecision, the sudden mélange of repugnance and fear coupled with the new stirring deep within it.

He demanded.

She wavered.

He strained, focused tight and *commanded*. She turned towards where he lay and as he felt her approach a surge of satisfaction rolled through him. The old mother was fading away, the broken and empty chrysalis, discarded and useless. The new mother bent down and pulled the covering away. Bright light seared his eyes; he hissed like a snake and his glands had opened under the intense pressure. She had looked down at him and recoiled and then the scent, coming reflexively in that first sight, had infused her.

Take me take me take me. His demand was a mere twist of thought pulsing out from him, irresistible, inescapable. The sudden fear inside her was strangled back to whimper deep in her consciousness.

Love me!

She had reached and taken him and pulled him into her warmth. He had felt the smoothness of her skin and his desperate fear had instantly begun to recede. He had made her move, chivvied her along his own familiar paths, brought her back to a place he knew.

Now in the dark, he suckled slowly, tasting the thin, weak milk, but he could also taste the trickle of blood oozing from where he had abraded the skin. Already, his own essence would be mingling with the blood, flowing inside her, making the changes he needed. It would take some time, but he had time.

63

She was young and she was strong and she would last, this one would, for as long as he needed her.

In the dark of the room, pressed against the warm smoothness, he could feel the ripples of her body as the slow sobs hiccuped through her. He picked up her confusion and the desperate schizophrenic battle between her panic and her need. It would take time, but he had her now and she had him and he would bond her to him with an unbreakable imprinting that would last until beyond the span of her life. That was how it had always been.

CHAPTER SIX

'Hello?' David called out. His voice boomed hollowly in the dark hallway. Somewhere in the dark, a small thing moved or rustled. There had been a noise. He'd been almost sure. For an instant he thought he heard a kitten whimper. There was a scrape, like a chair being moved, but just then a car turned at the far end of Latta Street, its diesel engine rumbling loud through a hole in its manifold, and momentarily drowned out all sound. When the car had gone, there was a silence. David called out again, louder this time. The words echoed back from the narrow walls and he was not sure that he had heard anything.

He pulled the flashlight from his pocket and swung the beam ahead of him. 'Looks like there's no one home.'

'That's no surprise. Nobody's reported her missing. Even though it's only been a day, if she had family here I reckon somebody would have called us.'

He motioned ahead of him, put a foot over the doorstep and slowly walked inside, following the cone of light. There was no window in the hallway, just the walls, papered in an old-fashioned print. There was a small telephone table bearing a bunch of dried flowers that looked as if they'd been there since the sixties. There was no telephone.

'Why don't I just put on the light?' Helen asked. He turned to face her, seeing only her silhouette against the faint glow of a street lamp somewhere out there in the frosted night. 'After all, it's not an armed robber we're looking for.'

'Go on then,' he conceded.

She fumbled for the switch, found the brass plate at shoulder level close to the door, flicked it down. Nothing happened.

'Maybe she never paid her bill,' David said. He moved forward. The hallway was dry and dusty and even in the dark it gave the impression of being festooned with cobwebs layered with dust. Off in the shadows, the darkness seemed to twist with motion. David pulled back.

'What is it?'

'I thought something moved,' he whispered. The dark had seemed to roll forward, billowing towards him. He knew it was just imagination, but it was a strange thing to have imagined. He blinked and, as he did so, sparks of colour flashed in front of his eyes, like the kind of after-images he got when the sunlight reflected off the water on the estuary while he was taking pictures of the wading birds. But here, he had not been looking into the light.

He moved further down. Something rustled. Helen gave a start.

'Police,' David called out. 'Don't be alarmed.'

Nothing moved. He swung the beam up. There was a narrow door, slightly ajar, just a crack. The noise hadn't come from there.

'Maybe not,' David answered his silent question. 'There's nobody here.' For some reason he was tense and suddenly strained. It was an odd sensation of hyper-alertness. His heart gave a thud and raised its beat to a higher speed. Daft bugger, he told himself. Settle down.

Yet strangely, in the narrow confines of the hallway, right at that moment, he sensed danger. It was a completely inexplicable sensation, and a peculiar one, because it was not a physical danger. For that brief instant, it was a shudder at the unknown, at the oddly moving dark in the tiny dilapidated house.

He got halfway down the hallway, taking each step slow, trying to avoid making the floorboards creak. Then he walked into the smell. It came thick in the air, musty and musky, powerful enough to taste.

'Bloody hell,' he coughed.

'God, that's awful,' Helen said, gulping as if about to retch. 'What on earth is it? Smells like something's died in here.'

For a moment, David considered calling in to get a team round to turn over the shabby little apartment. The smell of decay really was like the reek of a shallow grave, and both of them had experienced that before. This, though, was somehow different. David pulled a roll of tissues from his pocket and handed half to Helen. She clamped it over her face and they moved on, reached the door. He fully expected to find a mouldering corpse lying in a greasy heap. David pushed the door open, his nerves twisting with that strange anticipation, and they moved in.

This time the smell took them hard. David took a breath and his vision blurred as if chemical had been squirted into his eyes. Helen gave a little cough and then a soft groan that told him she really was holding back on vomit.

He turned. 'Keep quiet, for God's sake.'

As soon as the words were out, he wondered why he had spoken them. They had just blurted out, an angry slash at Helen. He faced her, swinging the beam of the torch low. The shunt of anger flared and his shoulders and forearms tensed to trembling tautness as a surge of adrenaline hit into his veins. In that instant he could have lashed out at anything.

'What the fu–?' he started. He didn't even know what he intended to say, whether it was a question directed at Helen Lamont or at himself. His belly muscles spasmed hard, as if a hand had twisted his intestines. The flashlight beam swung and caught Helen in its periphery. Her eyes were wide, not to compensate for the dark, but with the same bewilderment that mirrored his own.

'Oh Jesus,' she muttered, sagging back out of the light. 'Oh my . . .' she started again, but faltered once more.

Her own belly was suddenly roiling, but not in anger. She was reeling within the scent that filled the dark of the room. Her eyes swam with blurting tears. A wave of longing rippled through and within her. Right on its heels came an appalling sense of loss and an utter, unnameable need. A flush of heat like a fever's bloom crawled under her skin, infusing her temples, burning her ears. Her stomach clenched and her breasts instantly throbbed, nipples suddenly taut and tender against the cups of her bra. Deep in the basin between her hips the muscles cramped again and she felt the unmistakable draining sensation down there.

The smell clogged the musty airlessness of the room. 'Gas,' David coughed. His throat was trying to close in involuntary twitches. The hairs on the back of his neck felt as if they were marching in unison. The strange, unbidden rage flared to a bubbling heat and he felt as if his head was beginning to inflate.

67

In the dark of the room, pictures flashed and flickered in the front of his consciousness, and his body was pumped up ready for fight or flight, every nerve sizzling in readiness. The need to hit out lurched through him and he knew this was not his own emotion, not a genuine feeling. He had to be reacting to some chemical agent. His heart thumped a quick drumroll and he could hear the pulse in his veins.

'Gas.' He spat the word out again and, without hesitation, he reached for Helen. In that split second, he could easily have grabbed her and slammed her against the dark wall. The violence swelled huge within him. But as soon as his fingers snagged the corduroy of her jerkin he dragged her towards him. He forced the fury away from him, mentally punching it out of his head while his thoughts were still reeling in the dark. It had to be contamination, some sort of pollution. Rational thought was almost impossible but he made it to the window, swept the thick curtain back and got a hand to the catch. Helen came dragging along with him, gagging all the while. Pictures flickered in front of his eyes, wavering images in splashes of flat and somehow poisonous colours. Helen's knees were giving way and threatened to spill her to the floor but he gripped her collar tight, lifting her almost off the ground. She was blinded by the tears and the bleak sense of abandonment that emptied her heart.

'I can't,' she started to say in a voice that was hardly more than a whimper.

He opened the window wide with one push of his arm and thrust her in front of him, right into the cold air. The breeze from the open door at the other end of the room swept through in a cold draught that made the ragged curtain billow outwards. Immediately the smell began to dissipate rapidly. He scooped in a lungful of air. Little sparks orbited and wheeled in his vision and the breath was cold and frosted, sharp in his throat. Helen gagged and sagged again. He could feel her choking, her sides heaving. A black tide of rage surged up inside him, faded just as quickly and was then swamped by a secondary wave of dreadful guilt coupled with the explosive decompression of relief. He could have hit her. He could have slammed her up against a wall. *He could have done something much worse than that*. For a moment, for a dreadful dizzying few seconds, he had been pure and savage animal. He could have ripped her clothes off and thrown her down on the ground and spread her wide to slam himself into her again and again.

'What the fuck's going on?' he rasped.

'Oh David,' Helen blurted. 'I'm really sick.' She heaved in a huge breath. The wind whistling round the chimneys and rustling in the dead ivy that crept over the little brick porch came blasting in the door and blew the stench away. A cat swaggering tail-high by the scrubby hedge caught the scent and screeched. Its fur stood on end, like a caricature of a startled tomcat. Its back arched and then it snapped into motion. One instant it was a shuddering ball of fur and the next it was a streak of black. It crossed the concrete patch in a second and hit the crumbling wall with such force that it bounced back in a complete somersault. Without a pause, and with no cessation of its caterwauling, it ran at the barrier again, went straight up like a rocket, its momentum taking it two feet higher than the top of the wall, then down the other side. It went screaming away out of sight.

The pinwheeling lights faded out and the adrenaline surge emptied out of David's blood, leaving him trembling and weak. Helen started to raise herself up, breathing hard, but not sick now. He swung the beam round. A small table light with a dark shade was close by on an old-fashioned chest of drawers. He reached and tried it, surprised when it came on, letting a feeble light swell in the small room.

'God, I thought I was going to be sick,' Helen said. The bleak and empty sense of loss had drained away. It was as if it had never been. With the window open, the smell had faded to barely a background scent. 'What the hell was it?'

'I thought it was gas, but it's not. Maybe some chemical. Cleaning fluid or something?'

'Did it make you sick?'

'I nearly puked all over you,' he lied. He couldn't tell her how in that split second he could have clubbed her to the ground. He could hardly believe it himself. The image of her lying naked, legs splayed, hovered on the edge of conscious thought and he tried to close his mind to that for, once planted, the thought had triggered an excitement he did not want to feel at all. The anger, however, had burst like a balloon, leaving him deflated, and even the recollection of it was difficult to conjure up again. He flicked the flashlight off and they stood there, embarrassed by their reactions and shaken by the strange, surreal experience.

The room was small and narrow. There was an old bed at one end and a door halfway along the wall that led into a small kitchen. There were two seats, unmatched overstuffed armchairs. In the corner a mound of children's soft toys was piled in a pyramid. There were teething rings and rattles. Beside the bed a white plastic baby bath sat in a frame and a selection of oils and lotions were lined up surprisingly neatly.

A Moses basket that might have been made before the war stood over in the corner, but it was piled with folded sheets in laundry bags. The bed, low and narrow, was covered by a pile of blankets that were tumbled and twisted into a circular shape, as if whoever had slept there had eased out so as not to disturb them. It reminded David of a vole's nest down by the riverbank.

'She said she had a baby,' David said.

'Who would let somebody bring a baby back here?' Helen sniffed, got an aftertaste of the rancid scent on the still air and the strange sense of longing throbbed again, just a tickle at the back of her consciousness. She squashed it flat for she recognized the sensation of need within herself. It had taken her by surprise; she had never experienced it before and did not welcome it now. Nor did she welcome the other need she'd felt when he'd grabbed her and hauled her towards the window. As soon as she'd breathed the fresh air and the nausea had subsided, she had been suddenly aware of the grip of his hand on her neck. His touch had tingled through her skin and flared in a burst of heat and another kind of longing that had flowed over and through the other.

'A baby,' David repeated, and she shook her head emphatically, telling herself not to be such a bloody idiot. His hand was reaching towards the mantelpiece. For a shuddering instant, she wanted to feel it on her again. She drew her eyes away, looked up at him.

'That was what the paramedics said,' David continued, 'and

the assistant from Rolling Stock. She told me the dead woman had a baby with her and nobody believed it.' He was trying to recall exactly what he'd been told. 'Phil Coulter said she had tried to get away from them because she had to get to her baby. He thought she was delirious.'

'I thought she was alone,' Helen said. 'And nobody came to report her missing, did they?'

He shook his head, eyes narrowed, thinking. 'She told them to find it. It wasn't on the video, but we didn't look at them all.' He tried to think back to what he had seen; Jenny McGill pounding the chest; the expert lift on to the paramedics' trolley; the woman reaching to snatch the Mothercare bag. Then he recalled Carrie McFall bending quickly to pick up the handbag beside the line of trolleys. Something was itching in his memory, but not yet hard enough.

'There's been a baby here,' he said, letting his eyes wander around the cramped little room. It was not damp, but stale and unclean. The odd smell that he'd taken for contamination had blown away now, leaving only the odour of dirt and sweat and lack of hygiene. The nest of blankets looked as if they'd be crawling with lice. A strip of wallpaper had peeled away from the wall at the ceiling and in other places there were signs of dusty mould. 'She's been looking after a baby here,' David said. 'So she's got relatives, or she's a childminder.'

'If she was a childminder, then whoever gave her a licence should be shot,' Helen said. 'It would be a crime to let a child in here.'

'We were concerned at first,' Simpson Hardingwell said. 'But then, when you get a case as unusual as this, it's always best to take a step back and be systematic.'

Hardingwell was the consultant microbiologist at St Enoch's. He was tall and gaunt and had an enormous axehead of a nose which made him look pompous and aristocratic, but he was pretty straightforward as far as David could make out, and not at all patronizing.

'There are still one or two things that puzzle us greatly. Professor Hartley, he's the pathologist as you'll know, called me in almost immediately and we both made a further examination of the woman.'

'This was after the post-mortem?'

'No, this *was* the post-mortem. Young Quayle at casualty got Gordon Hartley in right away. The paramedics had told him she'd revived *en route* and then, on arrival, she had shown some signs of life in the crash unit though there was no heartbeat and no sign of brain activity whatsoever. Occasionally you observe reflexes for some time after death, but Quayle said she had spasmed quite violently and had been foaming at the mouth, gushing saliva. His first thought was rabies, because these symptoms are quite characteristic of the virus, though we haven't had a case here in years.'

He leaned back and ran his fingers through thick white hair. 'When Hartley looked at her down in the mortuary, there were still slight tremors in the muscles, though the spasming had stopped. He was concerned about her physical condition. In many respects she was emaciated: an elderly woman who seemed to be half starved. Her body fat was almost non-existent and her skin colour indicated she was anaemic. She appeared to be in her sixties, early sixties I would have said. Now that gave Hartley a problem and he'd already asked me in for an assessment of bacteriological or viral risk. To tell you the truth, I've never actually seen a case of rabies, in the flesh, so to speak, and I was quite interested, though I was sure this would be something else.

'Anyway, to get back to the initial picture, she was in her sixties, but there were anomalies.'

'That's what my boss said.'

'Quite. The first difference was in the condition of her breasts. Quite a contrast with the rest of her appearance really. They were neither flaccid nor lumped with cellulite or fatty deposits as you might expect in someone of her age. They were swollen, very full indeed. That could have indicated a number of pathological causes. Beriberi, for instance, but that's hardly common here. Hartley thought there was an inflammation, perhaps caused by a blood disorder. There were marks around the nipples and the aureole area, abrasions and bruising, some of them quite severe. Much of the tissue was swollen and it was clear that blood had seeped from the abrasions. My first reaction was Kaposi's sarcoma, which is one symptom of the final stages of HIV.'

'You mean she had Aids?'

'No. The haematoma were different in shape and colour for a start, and later tests showed she was not HIV positive.'

He leaned forward again and put both hands on a pristine blotter pad. 'That was just the initial observation, you understand. Once Gordon went in, we found things were very odd indeed. I took swabs of all the mucous tissue, samples of blood and both muscle and integument. I waited until Hartley was further in before I got the fluids from stomach and bowel and nothing at all from the brain until close to the end.

'What we have is a puzzle. From the pathology point of view, Gordon's as baffled as I am. Contrary to expectation, the breasts were fully functional and still lactating. In fact there was still a slight leakage of milk and that's extremely rare in a woman that age, almost unheard of. There have been two cases recorded and third in a woman in her sixties on hormone replacement therapy. Not full lactation, you understand, but merely a slight resurgence of glandular activity.

'Our woman – what's her name? Quigley? Her mammary glands were fully functional. Comparable to a woman in her twenties within two weeks of birth. The bruises, it transpired, were not the haematoma common to bruising from a blow, but suck-punctures. The Americans would call them hickeys. You would say love bites. They had been worked with some force, enough to rupture minor capillaries and draw blood through the pores. There were odd abrasions too, shallow scrape marks with lined striations which were deep enough to break into deeper capillary vessels.'

'And what would that mean?' David asked. So far he was just curious, and he was aware that Hardingwell was indulging him. The consultant seemed to be enjoying it too.

'Something had sucked on her. Adult or child, it's hard to say. I'm not in forensics.'

'And there was more?'

'Oh yes. Her ovaries were still fully functioning, though greatly enlarged, which might explain the excess of progesterone in her blood. She had unusual abrasions on the vaginal wall

73

and, another surprise, she was still menstruating, which might account for the anaemia. Hartley ascertained that she'd suffered a massive rupture of the left ventricle.'

David had watched enough hospital scenes on television to get the picture. 'A heart attack?'

'Catastrophic. The wall had ruptured almost completely. It was paper-thin and must have been giving her pain for some time. It was a wonder she was able to walk. Further examination showed aneurisms in a number of blood vessels in the brain, bubbles in the walls which could have burst at any time. It was a race between a cardiac arrest or a stroke. It was clear that she had high blood pressure, despite the anaemia, but the damage to the heart wall was quite significant. It was as if the muscle had been leeched away, causing severe reduction in tissue mass and strength. It was a third of its normal weight.

'My tissue samples were equally perplexing. That's why we called Mr Bulloch. Blood showed severe depletion of red cells and a corresponding increase in white. Pre-leukaemic, I would normally say, but that's academic of course. She had raised levels of progesterone, well above normal levels one would expect even in a woman of pre-menopausal age. And then there were the antibodies.'

'She had an infectious disease?'

'Not quite. Antibodies are the body's defence against disease. They are triggered by contact with viruses or bacteria, any invasion at all. Current theory is that we have dormant antibodies for every disease that has ever existed, a sort of biological overkill. The scanning electron microscope also showed a rather large compound of proteins and amino acids, long polypeptide chains, like new genetic material. It is unlike anything I've ever seen, and my colleagues are equally baffled. All I can surmise is that the antibodies are a reaction to some infection, possibly to those complex molecules, though it will take some time to isolate what the vector is. If it's viral, it could take months. I don't believe it's serious, but I would prefer to take no chances. I have to consider the possibility of a mutation – which happens from time to time – in the formation of an antibody, or even a new strain of virus, neither of which might be serious. But we would prefer to be sure. That's our job.'

'So you do think she's had some sort of disease?'

'Oh she had disease all right. Heart disease, embolisms, distension of the ovaries, over-production of hormones. She was a sick woman. I'm trying to find out if she had a disease she could pass on to anyone else and I also want to find out whether the bug she may be carrying is what caused the other conditions. As I say, it could be a new strain. I'd like to find out if our Thelma Quigley had been abroad recently, or if she's been in close contact with someone who has come from the tropics.'

Hardingwell looked across at David and gave a twist of a smile. 'At least we know it's not rabies, and that's a blessing. But we want to find the source of this new cellular material if we can. It could be a mutation, which is unlikely, but it could be something as simple as a parasitic infection, one that is new to us. Apart from the other questions, it's fairly miraculous that the woman was walking and talking instead of being hospitalized weeks ago.'

'What about the paramedics? They said she was dead, but she came back to life. Could that be something to do with it?'

'More to do with the heat of the moment. Despite what they tell you, medicine isn't an exact science. It's most likely that her pulse had dropped to an extremely low level because of the rupture, but there was still some brain activity. The heart might still have been operating on the other side, which wouldn't have made a great deal of difference, but there is a remote possibility she could still have been alive then and in crash. The signs would be very easy to miss.'

David drew out his notebook and flipped over the pages. He found the notes he had made and read them quickly. 'The witnesses said that she spoke about a baby. In her home, we also found evidence that there might have been a baby at some time. Is it possible she did have one?'

'She could have looked after one,' Hardingwell conceded.

'But the milk thing, and the ovaries. Is it possible that she had actually given birth?'

Hardingwell laughed, not unkindly, but in real mirth. 'If she had, somebody would be rushing to get a paper out on it even as we speak. I'd even be tempted to write to the *Lancet* myself. But no. She could not have given birth.'

'She was too old?'

'Oh, there was that, although those damned Italians are pushing back the age frontiers faster than you would imagine. It won't be too long before a woman of that age will actually give birth. She'd have to be healthier though.'

'Maybe looking after a grandchild?'

'Not that either, I'm afraid. She could never have given birth at all.'

'Why?'

'Because she was a virgin. Hartley found her still intact.' The consultant smiled. 'She really was an old maid.'

The search of the flat had not taken long. The drawers of the dresser had been filled with baby clothes, all of them laid out and folded neatly and most of them showing no signs of wear at all. There were tiny cardigans, and larger pullovers, as if someone had been buying for a baby's growth. In the kitchen, there were sterilizers and plastic bottles, unopened tins of baby food and rusk teething biscuits on which the cellophane wrapping was still shiny and tight.

'None of this has been used,' Helen said. 'Not the bottles and the clothes. They're all brand new, but some of them are *old*.'

'Don't baffle me with logic,' David told her. 'I didn't understand a word of that.'

'They're new in the sense that they have never been used, but they are old in the sense that some of them came out of the Ark. Look at that romper suit. That went out with button boots. I used to wear something like that.'

'Not yesterday then?'

'Very funny. No, not yesterday. It looks as if she's just been collecting baby gear and storing it away.'

'A weirdo?'

Helen looked over at him. She was crouched down, careful not to kneel on the threadbare carpet. In her hands she held a jumper in knitted pink, with two tiny ribbons as ties. 'Depends on your point of view. Maybe she just *wanted* a baby. Like an obsessive. Some women can't have them and it drives them over the edge, according to the psychology course. They can even fantasize that they actually have a child. Sometimes it gets worse than that and they steal one.'

She got up from the floor and held up the small garment. 'I think she was a very disturbed old lady. None of this stuff matches, either in fashion or sex.' She half smiled, thinking of how disturbed she herself had been only half an hour before. David was rubbing his jaw with his free hand, making the hairs on his chin rasp. The sound, completely masculine, tingled on her nerves. She ignored it.

'I wouldn't know,' David told her, and she laughed out loud, hoping it wouldn't sound forced.

'Of course you wouldn't. No offence, but you're a man and I've never yet met a man who knew that only baby girls wear pink. Some of these are blue and the rest are pink. It's as if she didn't have a clue what she was buying. Some are for a child more than a year old and others are for newborns.'

'You know a lot about it,' David observed.

'I'm the youngest of a big family. My sisters breed like rabbits.'

'And you?'

The image came back to him, the mental picture of her lying spread. *Breeding like rabbits.*

'Give me a break. I buy the kids sweets and Christmas presents and that's where my maternal instincts end. I think there's something wrong with my hormones.' She gave him a lop-sided grin and tried to shuck away the reverberation of the twin aches that had rippled deep within her. The first powerful compulsion had drained away almost as quickly as it had swamped her but the memory still hovered scarily close. The second remained with her, strangely strong.

David returned the smile, but he too was trying to focus his mind on the maternal drive. June had been pushing him to get engaged. She wanted to settle down and start a family. He wasn't ready for that, he knew. He'd resisted moving in with her and he was coming to realize that his reluctance was nothing to do with settling down and having kids. It was to do with him and it was to do with her. He'd have to do something about that. He looked at Helen Lamont and wished he'd never brought her here. He could do without any complications.

The wardrobe at the far end of the small room had more bags of baby clothes and an old-fashioned hatbox that was filled with newspaper clippings and some tattered exercise books. At the bottom, there were two old diaries filled with neatly looped handwriting that at first sight looked similar to the woman's name on the rent book. He took them with him when they left the house and went back to the station. David dropped Helen off on South Street, only half a mile from his own place and then drove home.

Of the three messages on his answering machine, two were from June, the second more irate than the first, demanding to know where he was and telling him he had spoiled her evening. She asked him to call immediately. The other was from John Barclay at the Waterside Mall.

'I've had a look at some of the early tapes,' John said. 'There's something you maybe want to have a look at.'

David called back, but there was no reply and he made a mental note to call the ex-policeman the following day. He made himself a cup of strong, sweet coffee, which went a long way to taking the winter chill from his bones. While he sipped he opened up the box and began to sift through the old cuttings and pieces of paper. He hefted one of the diaries, opened it and began to read.

He never returned June's call that night.

CHAPTER SEVEN

It was bitterly cold. Hoar-frost made filigree jewels of the
spiders' webs stretched on the hedge along the back of the
lane, but she did not see them. The air was chill in her throat and
she huddled down against it, her movements fast and jerky. It
was still dark, midwinter-dark, in the dregs of the morning and
she was stiff and sore from the night slumped against the wall in
the corner of the room.

She had tried to call out when she heard the movement outside the strange house where she'd hidden in the dark, but it
had touched something inside and stifled her. It had made her
move, urgently, digging at her with mental spurs, and she had
run, quickly, out of the back, as soon as she had heard the
knock on the door. It had told her to find sanctuary. It had
reached into her mind and found a place she could take them.
Ginny had scuttled out and along the track, past the fence
where the dogs immediately went frantic and launched themselves, not at the fence close to her, but on the far side, as if they
were trying to escape in the other direction. Their howling tore
at the air. She had floundered past the ragged bags of refuse
behind the Chinese restaurant, down the far alley and taken a
side street that followed the line of the waterway parkland
where the canal meandered through the green belt of trees and
narrow, fallow fields.

Move move move MOVE! The urgent commands pushed and
jolted. Her lungs ached after a while because she could not
pause. Every turn she took, with the baby huddled in against
her, was down a darkened street, past a shady wall, in the lee of
a hedge. She was instinctively avoiding light. It took three-
quarters of an hour and she was almost fainting from exhaustion when she got to Celia's house. She scrambled up the
narrow path, got the key free and, after several futile attempts,
stabbed it into the lock, turned hard to the left, pushed the door
and was inside.

It was cold, but not freezing. She sagged down on the carpet, panting like a beaten animal, listening to the rasp of breath in her own throat. The only illumination was the pallid touch of the moon out in the evening sky and the green pulsing light on the coffee table in the corner. It held her eyes while she sat there feeling the weight against her breasts.

Some time later, the phone trilled and she started back, hard enough to bang her shoulder against the wall. She turned, heart hammering yet again and almost reached for the receiver, but once more the mental injunction froze her to stillness.

The telephone rang, four, five times, insistent and urgent in the darkness, but she could do nothing. It clicked. There was a hollow purring sound then a double crackle of electronic interference.

'Hi, this is Celia Barker.' The voice was bright and lively. A voice free of cares. 'I can't come to the phone at the moment, so leave a message and I'll call you back.' The purr returned, then a rapid series of blips and a long whine of noise.

'Hi again, Ginny, I called earlier.' The lively voice was different, fresher then before. 'Just to say I've arrived and this place looks marvellous. Blue skies and a warm breeze coming in from the sea. And the boys. Mmmm. They're all Greek gods. Wide shoulders, tiny backsides, rippling torsos. We're going to have the time of our lives. Don't worry, we'll be careful, because we can't possibly be good. Just a pity you couldn't come along. You'd have a ball. Several probably. Anyway, thanks for looking after Mork and Mindy for me. There's plenty of tins in the cupboard. Just make sure Mork stays out of Mindy's bowl. Don't have any wild parties and if you do, make sure you tidy up after you. Love and hugs . . .'

The voice was gone, a brief bubbling stream of words and laughter. The machine clicked, whined again, then shut itself off. The green eye winked steadily and the silence stretched out.

She stayed still, hunkered down against the wall, eyes fixed on the green light, through her mind was a whirl. She was trying to hold on to the familiarity of the voice on the phone, her friend's abundant normality. But it was difficult to think clearly. It was almost impossible to think at all.

The night had been crazy. It had been filled with strange dreams and awful visions, and when she awoke she recalled what had happened and the baby was down on her, sucking hard, draining her. She had tried to resist, tried to haul it off her breast. The instant wash of repugnance had made her want to grab it and rip its mouth from her skin and throw it to the ground. She had suddenly wanted to hurl it to the floor and stamp on it until its sucking pout stopped.

She had tried and the pain had come.

The pain had come in a corkscrew of hurt right at the back of her head. It felt as if the inside of her skull was being split down the bone sutures and the pain had been so immense that for a moment she had blacked out. The room had swum in wavering double vision and she had been swimming in a sea of suffering so fine she could hear it resonating on the inside of her teeth. It was such an agony, so devastating and overwhelming that she could not even cry out.

No! A wordless command sliced inside the pain.

The motion of her hand froze in mid strike, hovering paralysed inches from the back of the baby's neck. Everything seemed to happen in slow motion, the way it had been in the dream, but this was no dream, she knew now. This was a nightmare maybe, but no dream. The pain subsided fast and left her gasping with sudden relief.

Her hand was stayed. She blinked twice and great tears rolled down from eyes that were raw from the dreamlike sobbing of before. The baby's head was still pressed against her skin. Its silky hair was black and shining and there was a line of matte down trailing on the slender neck and between the pink shoulders. The cold puckered the skin into shivering gooseflesh. Her hand was freed from its stasis and she looped the edges of her coat around the tiny frame.

The baby turned, mouth still fixed on her nipple but no longer sucking. It opened an eye which again seemed to be red and protuberant at first and then changed, wavering to blue. It fixed on hers and the scent came rolling up like a mist to infuse her senses.

GET OFF ME! Her panicked thought came in blaring capitals and the pain flared instantly. The revulsion and loathing was squashed underneath the sudden weight and the scent filled her head and the repugnance fragmented, then coalesced as some other emotion.

Mother me . . . the command shunted into her senses. *Love me.*

The pain faded again and was replaced by a sudden warm infusion of unexpected pleasure. She tried to fight it, tried to keep her mind clear, but it was impossible. She felt as if she was being torn apart while her emotions wrestled and heaved and her thoughts jittered and sparked and the fear and the alien sense of need looped and writhed around each other in a confusing maelstrom.

She drew her hand down and cradled the baby's head against her, dizzy with the conflicting sensations. Its skin was warm and dry *yet underneath that perception she sensed something cold* to the touch as it nuzzled gently, tugging the way Tony had done only a few nights before behind the steamed windows of his car.

After a while she was able to move. She rose from the corner, still hugging the little thing against her. She knew she needed to wash, but there were other needs clamouring at her. All of a sudden she understood she had to move, to get out of the flat. The urgency swelled in her mind and, without hesitation, she went into Celia's bedroom. The bed was neatly made up, very feminine, with embroidered pillowcases to match the eiderdown. She drew it back one-handed while the other hand clamped the baby to her breast. All the time, her mind was reeling, though underneath the mental storm, everything was icy cold and clear.

She drew the cover down and then the sheet, folding it corner to corner then doubling that until it formed a square. Finally she was able to take the baby away from her. It twisted, letting the nipple slide out of its mouth with a rubbery little pop. It turned and its eyes swung up to her. They were wide and clear, big baby eyes that stared into hers with mute appeal.

My baby.

The thought came strong. The infant hand moved away, small and pink, minute fingers clenched into a fist. For a brief instant, a mere fraction of a second, she imagined its skin began to ripple and tendons writhe under the surface. A shimmering iridescence, as if the dim glow of the street lamp were being reflected back from minute facets, broke the light into fragments. A tickle of pressure nudged in her brain and the iridescence vanished. The tiny fingers opened, closed and then slackened again, clean and rosy, each little nail perfectly formed.

The baby gazed liquidly, needfully at her, and she felt her heart flip over. She was borne high on the surge-tide of mother need. It was impossible to resist.

Ginny bent quickly, her hair sweeping down on either side of her face with the sudden motion. She laid the child on the blanket and wrapped it up, tucking the hands in tight. She swaddled the baby into a bundle then turned round. Beside the telephone, the twin green eyes of the machine's answering lights blinked mutely.

She found her own bag on the carpet where she had spent the night, rifled it quickly, taking her credit card out along with the rest of money she'd taken to buy Christmas presents. It wasn't much and she needed more. She went back into the bedroom and checked in the drawers on either side of the bed, but found nothing except bottles of pills and a substantial package of condoms. Under any other circumstances she'd have made a comment, probably one of surprise, but they hardly registered on her mind. The dresser on the far side yielded two twenties, tucked inside a make-up case. Back in the living room there was a sideboard where Celia had stashed her work-a-day handbag. She dragged it out, experiencing a warm, almost savage glow of triumph. She had known it would be here somewhere, and inside, she knew she'd find Celia's bank card.

'I'd better leave them here just in case,' her friend had said, practical as ever. 'If I lost it abroad with the rest of them, I'd have no money when I came back.' The card was in a small blue plastic case. She knew the number was simply the day and month of Celia's birthday.

The door closed with a dull thud, muffled by the swirling mist that was more frost than fog in the early silence of the morning. The orange lamps were haloed and somehow eerie. Some distance away, a truck engine coughed into life, sounding like a large animal. Further away, miles down the river, a ship's foghorn came wavering on the still air, a distressed bellow in the far distance.

The cold was intense and she wrapped her coat around the bundle, cinching the belt tight. The little face was snug against the warmth of her blouse and the huge eyes were closed. It made no sound, but she could sense its warm thoughts inside her own. It was protected, safe in her arms. Her heart flipped over in the powerful wash of mother love.

And beneath that, struggling desperately, her own sense of self was thrashing frantically like a drowning creature in a pit of black tar.

The path behind the houses took her back down towards the alley. The dogs were either sleeping or they recognized her. They made no sound from behind the chain-link fence. There was no sign of the tramp. She made it out from behind the Chinese restaurant and on to the road.

There was no one about at this time in the morning. Her heels clacked on the concrete and the sound came reverberating back at her, deadened by the ground mist. She passed the church and reached the high street before she saw anyone else. It was a police patrol car nosing along, two bored officers close to the end of their shift, looking forward more than anything else to a cup of hot tea and a warm bed. Both of them looked round to follow her progress as she hurried past the shop windows, head down and shoulders up against the chill. She was no threat, no burglar. The car moved on. It turned the corner and she stopped, retracing the forty steps to the bank she'd just passed. Without any hesitation she slid the card in the slot, punched in the number and hit the key for a balance inquiry.

There was less than a thousand in the account. Celia, normally a good saver, must have taken plenty out for her holiday. It would have to do. She keyed for the maximum, waited until it coughed out two hundred in clean twenties, folded and wadded the money into her purse and hurried on.

She experienced no guilt, not on the surface. The baby needed the money. And still, underneath the numbness and the strange overwhelming mother-love, she was screaming in terror and revulsion.

In the dark of the early morning, she made her way back to Celia's place, taking great care to avoid being seen on the main streets.

It was after two by the time David Harper looked at the clock, realized how long he'd been sitting and dragged himself away from the small pile of papers. He had a long, hot shower and toyed with the idea of another malt whisky before deciding against it. He went to bed. It had been a long day and a longer night, but despite the physical tiredness, his mind was still wide awake, trying to make sense of what he'd been reading.

Thelma Quigley.

That had been the name on the rent book, but he was convinced that it was not the name of the woman who had died screaming in the Waterside shopping mall. He had spent most of the night reading the diaries and going over the notes and the cuttings from old newspapers, yellowing pages, brittle and fragile with age, worn at the folds.

There had been two diaries, both from the mid sixties, tattered and loose in their covers. With them had been a number of school exercise books, all of them different colours, and a pair of spiral-bound notebooks – the kind reporters use.

She had been a note-taker, Thelma Quigley, or the woman who carried her rent book and used her name had been, a compulsive recorder of events; though apart from the diaries, there was no way he would know, unless he passed them along to forensics for paper typing and dating, to which period the other papers belonged. Oh, there were clues, and he supposed if he sat with them a while longer he might spot a chronological give-away, but for the moment, all he had to go on were the battered diaries.

March 17, 1967.
Thelma wants to go to France this summer. She's so adventurous. I asked what's wrong with Brighton and she laughed. She says the French men are much more romantic than the English, and they don't have all those Mods and Rockers causing fights and trouble. She'd got a part in *The Sound of Music* at the Citizen's Theatre and she wants me to audition for the chorus, but I can't sing as well as she can.

More along these lines: a woman in her thirties, a little shy, a few years older than her best friend who had theatrical ambitions and who had further horizons than a holiday in Brighton. The diary of a woman who had been cloistered by nature and by circumstance and who experienced the world vicariously

85

through Thelma Quigley's eyes. The name, repeated often enough, began to nudge a distant memory.

May 22, 1967.
I haven't been able to write for all this time [this after more than a week of empty pages and the ink is smudged where tears have softened the page long ago]. I went up to her grave, but there isn't a headstone there yet. I can't believe she is gone. Dead. Just like that. All the life and all the smiling. The police came round to ask me more questions, but there was nothing I could tell them. Thelma had lots of boyfriends, but nobody serious. I wanted to see her before the funeral but they said best not to. It was a closed coffin because they said she was marked and I can't believe that somebody would do it to her. Oh, what a terrible thing. If I could catch him I would stab him myself until he was dead. I miss her. I wish I'd told her I would go to France.

July 26, 1967.
The headstone is in a polished stone with her name on it. My flower holder with the white heart in marble is still there and I put some carnations in it. Her name looks so lonely there on the stone and I can't still believe that she is down there and not up and dancing around the way she always did, laughing and joking with the boys. They haven't caught him yet, the b*****d (God forgive me but I can't forgive him). Tomorrow, I'll go up to the bridge where we went with Tom and Geoffrey last year when Thelma fixed up that double date without telling me and then we laughed all the way home because she said Geoffrey looked like Adam Faith except smaller and everybody knew Adam's only five foot nothing. That was the last real laugh I remember and since then it's all been grey. Nothing matters any more. I have nobody to talk to. My mother says just to snap out of it and Dad doesn't know what to say. Nothing matters and I don't have any other friends and I'm so very lonely. I'm going to go up to the bridge tomorrow, because wherever Thelma is, she'll be laughing and she'll make me laugh again.

There was a space in the diary for the next fifty pages. Nothing had been written from July until some time in September. David could have been forgiven for assuming that whoever had written the lines in July, a woman clearly grieving and suffering a deep sense of loss, had done as she said she would do and gone up to the bridge, wherever that was, and joined her dead friend.

But no.

September 22, 1967.
He wants fed, poor little thing. He needs to be fed all the time and when he turns those big eyes on me I almost melt. I go all squishy inside and I know Thelma would have just adored him. She always said I'd be a great mother, and she was right. I take care of Baby Grumpling better than anyone could and I love him to death. Really I do. I just can't wait for him to learn to speak and I know just what his first words will be.

The writing was clear and rounded, exactly the same as in the earlier pages before the blank stretch. They had been written by the same woman.

I'll have to get another pram for him because the wheel on the other one is buckled and he doesn't like to be jiggled about. I always know when he's not happy. He soon lets me know. That's just the way babies are. He sucked me really hard today, and I got a big bruise, but he can't help it. He must be really hungry all the time and I don't mind because he needs his food and he won't take anything else.

December 20, 1967.
I got him a big teddy and a furry hedgehog that looks really cuddly. He'll start playing with toys soon but he's too young yet, just a tiny little thing and so helpless. He needs me so much and I know he loves me. All I want to do is hold him in my arms. I have to go out to the shops for more liver. I never liked it before, but I need more all the time. Funny, isn't it. They say you get notions and cravings *before* you have a baby. I'm getting them all the time. Liver and eggs and eggshells. Funny that. I'm so looking forward to Christmas. Just me and the baby. It'll be like the first ever Christmas and he's so sweet, just like the baby Jesus. Maybe I'll sing him a carol.

The next diary had been more of the same. Not every day had been filled in, sometimes there were gaps of weeks, but every entry consisted of nothing else but the rituals of feeding and clothing 'Baby Grumpling'. As he read on, David sensed the strange alteration, the obsession the woman had with the baby, but it was not that realization which made the hairs on his arms begin to crawl.

There was something odd, something unnatural about the whole thing. Some time during the reading, he'd got up and poured himself a decent measure of Islay Malt and he'd sipped at it, savouring the smoky ancient taste of peat damping down the fire of the liquor. Still, the whisky couldn't take away the strange taste that the diaries imparted.

There had been something wrong here. He couldn't put his finger on it although there were glaring omissions. They weren't what gave him the creepy fingers up and down his spine. It was beyond those omissions – that he would have to check out in any case – way beyond them. He sensed something that was just wrong. Not criminal, though that was a distinct possibility, but simply wrong.

The diaries gave him a puzzle that he would have to solve. Some of that would be easy: just a matter of record. Thelma Quigley had been murdered. It was clear from the pages of the diary that she'd been stabbed to death and her body buried in a shallow grave and that it hadn't been found for some time. This knowledge was already making the faint memory stronger. Thelma Quigley. He *had* heard the name before. Once he ascertained who Thelma Quigley had been, he would find out the dead woman's identity.

He closed his eyes and tried to get to sleep. Outside the wind picked up, driving shards of hoar-frost against the pane in a winter whisper. Out in the dark, a cat screeched and David recalled the blurred motion when he and Helen Lamont had leaned out of the window in the dead woman's house.

There had been something wrong with that place, more than just a foul and musty smell and the collection of children's clothes and toys that had never been used. His thoughts jumped from the dingy flat to the black-and-white video unreeling on the screen in John Barclay's office. He recalled the woman's shivering body, then the jerk as she tried to raise herself up. He hadn't heard the words, but Jenny McGill from Rolling Stock had reported she had said something about a baby, which was also confirmed by the paramedics. The dead woman had been carrying a Mothercare bag, long gone now, but the shop specialized in infant care.

Also snagging at his mind was Hardingwell's laugh when he'd said she'd been a virgin, but then his puzzled observation about the woman's condition. She'd been well into her sixties and leaking milk like a newly delivered mother.

Finally David drifted off to sleep. In a jumbled series of dreams he saw the black-and-white video of the woman's collapse unreel, though this time it had sound and the camera zoomed in on her stricken face and she was screaming for her baby, mouth wide to show stained, discoloured teeth and amazing breasts ballooning out as grotesque swellings, each of them dribbling a viscid mess that could have been anything at all. In the blink of an eye he was back in the unkempt little apartment, surrounded by a dead silence. He was alone this time, turning from the window, his vision sweeping past the narrow little door and towards the rumple of bedclothes that were knotted and twisted into the shape of a nest. He turned again, listening for a sound he thought he'd heard, aware that he was no longer alone. A slight, scraping sound came from under the bed and he tensed, expecting something to come leaping out at him. In the dream he crouched, still jittery with tension, and the sound changed. It came the way things do in dreams, without reason, without warning. It changed from the scraping sound of a mouse to the shivery cry of a newborn baby. David got to his knees and scanned the darkness under the bed and the sound changed again into a gurgle of laughter. He turned away from it, suddenly drenched in fear, and as he did so the pile of cuddly toys, now a pyramid in the corner where two walls met, collapsed on top of him and he found himself under an avalanche of soft toys which rained down until he was completely smothered and his breath was backed up in his throat.

He woke up gasping for breath and slick with sweat. The shivery aftermath of the dream stayed with him until he got up and made himself a coffee, drinking it down hot and sweet. Outside it was still dark and a light snow was blowing in against the window. No creature stirred out there.

CHAPTER EIGHT

David drove through the winter fog to the office, thinking about the woman and trying to shake off the strange feeling of apprehension that had hung around him since he'd awoken from the dream. Donal Bulloch was down in London for a conference so he reported to Scott Cruden, the inspector who worked directly to the boss.

'I'll have to check with the landlord this morning and maybe have a word with the neighbours,' he said. 'We still don't know who she is, but we should get a positive line on it today.'

Cruden thought it was time wasted on a natural-causes death, but if it had been sanctioned from higher up than his altitude, then he declined to argue, at least for today. 'Quick as you can, but you can't have Lamont, not for this morning and probably the next day or so,' the Inspector said, without rancour. 'She's checking out a missing person up in Whitevale. Girl's done a runner, so it seems.'

David shrugged nonchalantly, but he knew he was disappointed. He told himself it was because Helen Lamont was a good partner, someone he could rely on. An image flitted across his mind, though not the brutal one he'd imagined in the dead woman's house. He just got a picture of her smiling up at him as he stood with his hand on the mantelpiece. Had he read something in her look? He shook the thought away. He needed no further complications in his life.

A word with the Rachman who rented out the crumbling property, and a knock on a few doors, wouldn't take much time. He went to his desk and wrote out an information request which he passed through to the records office. It was a simple file check on Thelma Quigley, the dead woman who, it seemed, had died twice. The run-down of the neighbouring tenants might make that request redundant, he knew, but it would save time if he drew a blank.

Helen passed him in the corridor along with two uniformed policemen. 'Going back out?'

He nodded and she shrugged apologetically. 'I should be back in an hour or so. I got a missing girl in her twenties, but it's very early days yet and it's ten to one she'll turn up, so give me a call if you need a hand.'

He gave her a silent OK sign with his middle finger and thumb and went out into the cold. He did not see her watch him from behind the glass as he walked down the steps towards the car park.

The landlord was an estate agent in Miller Street beside the canal which skirted the north side of the city and wended its way towards the river much further down, towards the firth, near Barloan Harbour or Levenford. He was out, but his son was in the office, a young man somewhere in his mid twenties in a fairly well-cut suit, but with an accent rough enough to grind glass.

'Old Thelma? Been there for years,' he said, after David flashed his warrant card. 'Rent paid by benefit. Never bothers a soul.'

'Have you had a look inside the place?'

'My old man maybe looked in once in a while, I believe. She's quiet enough. No loud parties, no pets. No trouble. That's all you want in this line of business.'

The young man had the cocky kind of arrogance of those raised to money-grub but couldn't say anything much more. He checked the records and confirmed that Thelma Quigley had been a tenant for five years. That was it. She was a name on a register and social security money in the bank and as long as she didn't party down until the small hours, then the landlord couldn't give a damn. David felt the swell of anger again then forced it down. There was no point. There were a million Thelma Quigleys in a million houses in a thousand towns. Nobody gave a damn about anybody these days. Money talked louder than ever.

Old Mrs Whalen who lived three doors down was stout and motherly and had a face that was laced by a filigree of wrinkles. Her husband Bob was huddled by a coal fire, still wearing a flat cap and an ancient army overcoat draped across his shoulders. He coughed gratingly from deep down inside himself and hawked a gob of something putrid into the fire where it hissed and sizzled for a few moments. Mrs Whalen gave him a nonchalant slap on the shoulder and told him to mind his manners while the police were in the house.

'Asbestosis,' she said. 'Been bringing that stuff up for years, poor old soul. I tell him he should get out in the fresh air, but he can't walk the length of the room now.'

Despite the gloom in the little house and the flat smell of plaster that was never going to dry out, the place was clean. The furniture was old and scarred from long use, but polished, and there was a line of photographs on the mantel that showed the up-and-coming generation of Whalen grandchildren. The old couple had lived a full life.

'Twenty-one wee 'uns and four great-grandchildren. I need to rob a bank every Christmas,' she said, bending over arthritically to pour a cup of tea. David felt a roll of weary sadness for them, old Bob with his asbestosis filling up his lungs to drown him in his own mucus and the little lady with the job of looking after him and the line-up of grandchildren on the mantel. He forced himself to stop once more. It was not his fight and she was not complaining.

'Thelma? Oh, she kept herself to herself, you know. I only ever saw her down at the shops and she'd say hello. Sometimes she'd hang out the sheets. She was forever hanging them out on the line when it was warm. That was the only time you ever saw her without the babies.'

'Babies?' he asked.

'Oh, she always had babies. Don't know whose they were, but she looked after them the whole time she lived here. Real shame about what happened to her. I heard it from Mrs Corrigan who got it down at the post office. Amazing how word always gets around, eh?'

David conceded that it was. He was interested in the babies. A bad feeling was trying to insinuate itself into his mind and he clamped it away. He'd read all the papers on the Dennis Nilsen case, the bodies buried under floorboards and cut up and dumped down the drain-pipes. He'd studied the Frederick West case with the corpses in the garden and mummified in concrete.

There had been a smell in the flat. He tried to recall it, but couldn't quite. If it had been the smell of a decomposing corpse, a rotting human, he'd have known it from experience. He shook his head absently, shaking the thought away. He wouldn't have missed it, surely. The thought nagged at the edge of his mind.

'Were they her grandchildren?'

'Don't think so. She never had a wedding ring, though that stands for nothing these days. Maybe she was childminding or something. One thing was for certain, she was always talking baby-stuff, leaning over the pram and goo-ing and gaa-ing, the way people talk if they want the kids to grow up doolally, but if you ever went near to have a look, she'd put the cover up quick as a flash. I always thought that was funny. Funny peculiar, that is. Most people can't wait to show a baby off, even if it isn't theirs. And everybody puts a coin in for the baby's luck. You would never have thought Thelma was rich enough to turn her nose up at some extra money. She never looked as if she had two pennies to rub together.'

Old Mrs Whalen insisted David had a biscuit and said it was all right if he dunked them in his tea. She acted as if he was one of her grandchildren and when he thought about it, he probably was young enough. Old Bob hawked again and stared at the flames, his seamed face bracketed by long lines in leathery skin. He'd worked a hard life, that was for sure. His hands were big and gnarled and looked as if they'd once been strong enough to swing a pickaxe or build ships, but his eyes were old and tired and burned out.

'How many babies?' David finally asked.

'Oh, couldn't say. I never really got a look at one, but there must have been different ones. Maybe four, perhaps five over the years? Sometimes you wouldn't see her for a month or so, mostly in the summertime when it was hot. I think she must have gone away on holiday. But then she'd be back with another one in a different pram. That's how we could tell. Maybe that's how she paid the rent, but she didn't act like a childminder. They've always got five or six to look after and that's too many in my book. That's just being greedy.'

'Nonsense, woman,' Bob finally spoke up. His voice sounded like boots on gravel. 'You had eight yourself.'

'That's because he was a dirty-minded old besom,' Mrs Whalen told David with a crinkly smile of genuine mirth. 'And anyway, they were *my* babies. All steps and stairs, one after the other with hardly a break to get my breath back, and every one of them loved to death.'

David snapped back, almost spilling his tea. *I take care of Baby Grumpling better than anyone could and I love him to death. Really I do.*

'It was a happy home,' Mrs Whalen said, unaware that David's attention had wandered. 'That's the pleasure babies bring, and once you have one, you want another, like chocolates. Mind you, there was no room at all to swing a cat in here and never a spare penny either, but we got by, we did, and that's because they were all loved. There was always the sound of kids in this house until they grew up, and whenever they come to visit, it's like being young again.'

'Och, don't talk rubbish, woman,' the old man growled in a dry wheeze. 'You'll put the young fella off his tea.'

'Never pay no heed to him,' the old lady said. 'He was never home, always out earning, and he loved them just the same. You only had to see his face the first time he held one of them in his big rough hands to know he'd have fought the world for them.'

David got the picture. The old man turned back to the fire and went back into his memories, chest heaving like bellows, breath hissing like a punctured tyre.

'But you don't know where Thelma got the babies?'

'No. Nobody knew where she came from herself. Around here everybody knows something about everybody else's business, but Thelma was different. A real mystery. Oh, she was polite enough. Always said hello, but she'd never stop and pass the time of day. Only ever spoke to the babies, really. I suppose she always had somebody to listen to her.' She gave her husband another hearty slap on the shoulder. 'Not like around here, you ould bugger,' she cajoled, but the laugh was in her voice and the old man ritually ignored her.

The other neighbours told the same story. The woman had bothered no one and had wanted to be left alone. Nobody had intruded. They all mentioned the babies in the prams, how the

94

woman was hardly ever seen without a child. Apart from that, they knew nothing more.

Thelma Quigley was a mystery.

David did not tell them that she was not Thelma Quigley. Of that he was almost certain, from what she had written in her diaries, unless she was schizophrenic and had twin personalities. He didn't think so.

But she was indeed a mystery. Almost everything about her was a puzzle: where she had come from; the babies she looked after. Something else was nagging at the edge of David's thoughts and he couldn't quite put his finger on it.

It was only on the way back to the station that it struck him quite forcibly. She hadn't been with a baby when she died. Yet she'd spoken of a baby with her last dying breaths while the blood drained away from her burst heart and pooled in the pit of her belly.

Records had left a sheaf of papers on his desk. Among them was a photocopy of a woman's face. Thelma Quigley smiled out from the page and despite the grainy quality David could see the life sparkle in the woman's eyes. She had dark hair caught up casually on top of her head, some of it tumbling down to the left, finely arched eyebrows and a dazzling smile that showed perfect teeth. Her skin was clear and unblemished.

She looked nothing at all like the elderly woman who had collapsed in the Waterside mall.

And it came as no surprise to David to read that Thelma Quigley had been stabbed to death in a frenzied attack way back in the free-love days of the sixties. The knife had gone through the jugular vein and her windpipe, severing her carotid artery. The attacker had plunged it so many times into her chest and belly that there was hardly a piece of skin left uncut. The file showed a set of copies of pictures from the shallow grave, taken in the harsh light of the camera flashgun. The puncture wounds were twisted and shredded at the edges, the flesh macerated and grey. She had not been found for almost two weeks.

The diaries had not lied. The woman who had been living as Thelma Quigley, who had brought babies home to the dingy little apartment, had been somebody else entirely. David's mind was whirling with possibilities. Finally he shook the jumbled thoughts away and sat down to read the report.

Thelma Margot Quigley. B. June 22 1942. Parents: John and Louise Quigley.

The first few lines were statistics, the whens and the wheres of a girl's life printed out on the lines of an official form. School, national insurance number. Date of birth, date of death, estimated to the nearest two days. A bright girl who worked as a secretary in a whisky brokerage in Edinburgh and dreamed of becoming an actress. The words conveyed little except the cold flesh round bare bones. The report went into detail, as police reports do, still stark on the odd tinted sheets rolling from the fax machine, sheets first printed from the old microfiche files in the dead store. The detectives had interviewed more than a thousand people, many of them friends or boyfriends of the outgoing girl who had been brutally and inexplicably murdered, but the killer had never been caught, David noticed, again mentally tallying this with the handwritten words in the old diary.

'Anything good on the go?'

David turned in his seat. Helen Lamont was passing by, dressed for the cold weather in a padded coat and a beret which made her look less than ever like a policewoman.

'Still on our flake-out in the mall,' he conceded.

'Don't tell me you've got to go through old records. Maybe you should knock on a few doors, lazy bugger.' She winked and gave him a wide smile.

'Done that all morning,' David said, trying not to read anything into the smile. 'This whole thing just got a whole lot weirder.' One of the other detectives looked up from his desk and David changed the subject. 'How about you? Scott said you were chasing a runner.'

'If she really is a runner,' Helen said. 'I'm hoping she might just be an overnighter with a bad case of embarrassment. She's been missing thirty-six hours, so it's a bit early to say. The Inspector wants a bulletin printed out for all the cars.'

Helen held up a picture of a fair-haired, intelligent-looking girl in her early twenties, not quite smiling, but close enough to it to give the impression that she might be about to burst into laughter. There was intelligence in the blue eyes, and the photograph conveyed the impression of someone who was capable and fit.

'Ginny Marsden. She never came home from work night before last. Hasn't been seen since. Usual story.' The curious detective got up and strolled out of the room with a bundle of files under his arm. Helen turned the subject back. 'So what's happening with the creepy lady?'

'As our brothers across the water would say, there's some weird shit happening. Firstly, Thelma Quigley's not her real name. The real Thelma died thirty years ago, near enough. That's what's in here.' He indicated the sprawl of papers spread across the desk.

'So who the hell is she?'

'That's what I'm trying to find out. Fancy a trip to Edinburgh?'

'Love to, but I'm tied up.' Helen said, pulling her lips down in an expression of disappointment. 'I have to start moving on our runner before the trail gets cold, just in case she hasn't done a flit. Ask me in a couple of days and make sure you've got tickets for anything not written by Lloyd Webber. Then you've got a date for definite.' She gave him another wide smile and was gone before he realized what she'd said.

David turned back to the old files on Thelma Quigley. He had just bent his head and focused on the first page when the phone rang. He thought it might be Helen, but it was June and she was far from happy. He pulled the receiver away from his ear and listened to the tinny squeak, unable to comprehend a syllable of the unbroken stream. After a while she stopped and he could make out the staccato 'Hello? Hello?' He thought about simply cutting her off and he realized that he really had to do something about this.

Finally the sound began to falter and he brought the receiver back to his ear. 'Hi, June,' he said. 'I'm fine. How was your day?'

CHAPTER NINE

'She just never came home. Her dinner was in the oven because she'd phoned to say she'd be an hour late getting home. She had a couple of things to do. Buying Christmas presents and wrapping paper. Just to make sure she had something for everybody.' All the short sentences came out in brief bursts.

The woman's hands were shaking and her eyes were wide with the glazed and certain look of a mother who has lost a child.

'She's dead, I know she is. Something awful's happened to her. I can feel it.' The voice started to break up into a gabble of choking sobs. Helen Lamont waited until they had subsided. Winifred Marsden's husband put his arms tentatively around his wife's shoulders and patted her gently before drawing her close. She turned his head into his shoulder, like a child seeking comfort. He did what he could, but there was no comfort for Winnie Marsden and there was no warmth in her husband's eyes. He was looking into the far distance, seeing his daughter run through the flower beds as a tiny child and overlaid on that picture, in awful stark colours of red and black, he saw her sprawled in some alley or under a hedge, ravaged and ravished and stone-cold.

'She always came home, or if she was staying out she'd always call,' Winnie said. She was a tall woman with silvering hair that had once been blonde. She wore no make-up, or it had been washed away by tears and dabbed off by wet handkerchiefs. Her nose was red and her eyes puffy, but Helen could see the underlying elegance of the woman. Her hands, though shaking, were slender and smooth and her nails long and varnished. Two days ago she'd have turned heads in the mall. Now, though she was only forty-six years old, she looked sixty.

'And she did call to say she'd be late?'

'Yes, she did.' John Marsden replied. 'It was me who answered the phone and Virginia was surprised that I was home. I was early that day.' He was a handsome man with wavy brown hair and strong, capable hands, one of which enveloped both his wife's hands when she finished dabbing her eyes. 'She said she was going down to the shopping centre for some last-minute bits and pieces. She always had a thing about Christmas. Made sure everybody got something, you know.'

Helen nodded. 'And she never came home.'

'That's what we told the police yesterday. Night before yesterday in fact. They should have done something about it then.' Helen could see the pressure of anger build up in the man's eyes. He was keeping himself under tight control for his wife's sake, and for his own sake too. 'I mean, we knew she was missing. We checked with all her friends, and with Tony.'

'Tony?'

'Her boyfriend. They're thinking about getting engaged. We checked with them all, but nobody saw her after she left the office. That's when we called the police, but they said there was nothing they could do.'

'Yes, that's right. We have to give it twenty-four hours at least unless it's a small child.'

'But we knew she was missing, didn't we? We told the police that. She always comes home.'

'Yes, I understand.'

'Do you?' John Marsden demanded, glaring at her, suddenly vehement.

'I hope so. But I know I do want to help,' Helen said. She did not react under the focus of the man's brimming emotion. His voice was tight and hissed through clenched teeth and a vein had risen on his temple. It was better for him to vent the pressure now, before something burst.

'It's not her fault, John,' Winnie Marsden said placatingly. She turned her eyes on Helen, trying to apologize over the distance between them. 'She wasn't there.'

'Most young people do turn up, if it's any help,' Helen said. 'Ninety-nine per cent of the time they've spent the night with friends or boyfriends or at a party. Honestly, it's true.' Helen tried her best but it did not help these people. It was odd, but their certainty that their daughter would have come home no matter what, unless she had been physically prevented, was strong enough to convince her that something really had happened to Ginny Marsden. She had sat with many parents before, listened to them telling her how their boy would never run away from home, how their daughter could not possibly consider leaving, and seen them proved wrong. But for some inexplicable reason, this was different.

Virginia Marsden was twenty-two years old and worked in a lawyer's office near the Riverside precinct of the city. She liked to play badminton and had joined an aerobics class. She sang in the choir on high days and holy days and she never forgot a birthday or an anniversary. She was studying business administration at night school and was determined to carve out a real career for herself. She had everything to live for. She loved her parents. She always came home.

Helen knew that when she turned up, *if* she turned up, then the parents would be stunned and happy and would accept any explanation, no matter what. On the other hand, if she didn't, then the real questions would start and John Marsden would be put through the wringer. Every statement would be calibrated and measured, every family photograph would be assessed and evaluated. They would turn him inside out to see if his love for his daughter was just what he said it was, or if it was something more than that, something darker and deeper. He would jump from one hell to another and his wife would see him peeled like an onion, layer by layer.

And the boyfriend would be opened up just the same way, so that he would not know himself and for the rest of his life would always wonder if maybe he *had* done something terrible.

That was if she did not turn up. Police investigations are dreadful diggings into dirt and motive, a necessary function of the protection of life and property. Helen Lamont hoped the girl would walk through the door. If not, the hell for the Marsdens and those close to them was just beginning to get stoked up.

'So she called just before she left to say she had errands to run?'

'Yes,' John Marsden told her. 'Christmas shopping. I'm sure that was it. I was watching the news at the time and Winnie was in the kitchen. She said she was going with Celia, I think. The television was on and I missed some of it, but Ginny was in a

bit of a hurry, so I just told her we'd put the dinner in the oven.
It was lasagne.'

'Couldn't have been Celia,' Winnie said. Her slack brow tightened into a frown of concentration. It took some effort. 'Really
it couldn't.'

'Why's that, Mrs Marsden?'

'Because Celia's gone on holiday. They wanted Ginny to go
along, but she didn't want to. Said she'd never been away from
home for Christmas. I told her, John and I told her that it was
fine and she should just go and enjoy herself, because she'd
worked so hard this year, but she said she always looked forward to Christmas dinner. That's just how she was. She would
never leave without telling us.'

Helen filed this for future reference. She'd have to check
every friend and acquaintance.

She stayed with the Marsdens for two hours and when she
left she had a clear picture of their daughter, plus a good
colour print taken only a month or so before. It showed a slim
girl, quite tall and with blond, wavy hair tumbling down to
her shoulders. She had a long dark coat that came almost to
her ankles, the very coat she had been wearing two days ago
when she left for work. She had her mother's elegant looks, the
same high-cheek-boned structure. The difference was in the
eyes. Ginny's expression was bright and alert, and Helen was
sure that three days ago, Winifred Marsden would have looked
similar, just a bit older. Now she sagged emptily, her mother-
love twisted and shredded under the appalling pain of fear and
loss.

David stayed up with his copy of the file on Thelma Quigley.
Scott Cruden would soon be pressing him for something on the
case, anything at all just to get a tab on the dead woman and
clear her away neatly. It wasn't as if she'd committed a crime or
was wanted by Serious Crime or Special Branch or SO 13. She
was just somebody who died, someone they would call a Jane
Doe on the other side of the Atlantic. Already David had heard
the expression a couple of times in relation to this case and
thought it was better than simply 'dead person'. It gave a
corpse a name, even if only a temporary one, but it turned a

corpse into a human, somebody who'd had life. The two simple syllables were also easier to type on to the report form.

If he'd been asked he'd have said he wanted to clear up this case and get back to real police work, but that wouldn't have been the whole truth. The mystery snagged him and he wouldn't let it go until he knew all the answers. He'd brought the files home to go over one more time before driving through to Edinburgh to find a connection. Inspector Cruden hadn't been overjoyed at the news, but since his own boss had sanctioned the effort, he went along with it.

When David left the office, still thinking about Helen Lamont and her offer of a date – and that had taken him by surprise too, and he didn't know if she was kidding or not – he'd dumped the file in the back seat and gone up to June's place on the Westland Hill near the university. She lived in a narrow avenue close to the old canal which meandered round the parkland where the trees stood bare and gaunt. The welcome he got on her doorstep was just as bleak as the winter view.

'So what happened to you?' The interrogation began as soon as she opened the door to his knock. She'd obviously watched for his car and was ready for him. He had hardly touched the knocker when the door swung wide. June was a pretty girl, small and neat, with short fair hair and even teeth. She'd have been prettier if she'd been smiling. She wasn't. She stood there, legs braced apart, eyes flashing. She had one hand on the door and the other on the wall, unconsciously barring entry. On her feet she was wearing outsized slippers that looked exactly like pink bunny rabbits with huge eyes. For a strange, unreal moment he saw the scene from two different perspectives. Part of his mind took in the incongruous stance and the anger in her eyes, coupled with the contradictory, ridiculous appearance of the novelty slippers. Another, deeper part of his mind took in only the fact that they were furry animals, just like the ones in the boxes in the Jane Doe's apartment, the ones he had seen in his dream come tumbling down from their pyramid heap, somehow alive and threatening, to smother him under their warm weight.

He took a step backwards, momentarily wrong-footed.

'I . . .' he started.

'Yes?'

'I could stand out here if you like and let all the neighbours hear.' He refound his balance and said the right thing. She lived in one of the old tenements that had been renovated and sand-blasted and gentrified. The empty stairway outside her door would carry every whisper up to the top landing.

'You'd better come in then,' she conceded, dropping her arm. He could see the tension in her and right at that moment his annoyance drained away. It was not her fault and it was not his fault. He passed her by, stooping to give her a kiss on the cheek. She let him, though he sensed her stiffness and wished it could all be easier. In the kitchen the coffee smelled good and there was something tasty cooking in the oven. He slung his coat over the back of a chair. She picked it up and hung it in a hall cupboard, the way she always did. He sat down, inadvertently scuffing the chair on the floor tiles, wincing reflectively and uncomfortably at her own irritated wince.

'You could at least have made an effort,' she started, carrying on the phone conversation as if she'd never stopped.

'I could and I did,' he said, not entirely truthfully. 'I was busy, you know that. Donal Bulloch put me on to something and when he does that, you don't hang around. Anyway, you know what the job's like.'

'But we had Peter and Jean round. I told you about it on Tuesday, remember?'

David went through the motions, feeling dreadfully uncom-fortable. They had been seeing each other for two years and in the past year he'd begun to run out of excuses for not getting a flat together. She'd been prepared to give this place up, albeit reluctantly, but she would have done so and moved in with him. He'd countered that it wouldn't be a good idea, because of his irregular hours and the late-night call-outs, but the pressure was on and he recognized it.

Most of June's friends were married and those that weren't were engaged. Her biological imperative was beginning to crank up to a crescendo. She wanted to get married. She wanted to settle down and be able to go out on foursomes and sixsomes. All she wanted to do was get married and have chil-dren and live happily ever after.

He was fond of her. For a while, he'd been sure he was in love with her, but now he wondered about that. He'd kept his own place where he had his books and his darkroom and his rock music and blues tapes from way back. One of these days he'd make a good father. One of these days, one of these years he'd make a damned fine father. Very possibly. Some time.

But not yet.

There were things to do and hills to climb and rivers to cross, physically and figuratively. He wanted to take his camera equipment to the wilds of Burma and Borneo, following in the trails of David Attenborough and Peter Scott and Flora Spiers while he still had the chance. He wanted to climb in the Alps and the Himalayas while his muscles were good and firm.

After that, he'd maybe get the urge to settle down. Maybe.

For now, he was running out of reasons. She was a good girl and he realized, despite the fact that he couldn't quite understand the drive within her body and her mind, the great hormonal shunt of reproductive need, that he was not being entirely fair. He didn't understand it, but he recognized it, and he knew he could not, or would not, be able to give her what she needed.

She'd made a casserole and dished it out, talking all the while about the couple who'd been over the previous night, how disappointed they were that he'd not been there and how Jean had given her meaningful looks which she'd taken to be condescending. David tried to tell her that if her friend was like that she wasn't much of a friend. She had just got engaged to Peter who was something in hospital management and David, who'd grown up in Kirkland with three brothers sharing a room, was working class enough to take a dislike to him just for that reason. Peter was a suit who smelled of expensive aftershave and spent a lot of time talking about how the personnel didn't understand the problems of the unit and it had taken David half an hour to realize that he was talking about nurses and hospitals. Units and personnel. After three years on the beat before his transfer to CID, David had seen enough hard-working nurses push themselves to the far edge to widen that dividing line between life and death on a rough Friday night in this no-mean-city on Clydeside.

As he ate the casserole, which was, as usual, another of June's triumphs, he mentally noted that he'd been right in the first place and he was glad he'd had other things to do. Shaking down Carrie McFall and dumping her on the sidings down by the river might not have been anybody's idea of fun, and wading through the reek in the dead woman's apartment had been no Sunday picnic, but, in retrospect, it had been better than a night with Peter the suit and Jean with the sparkly engagement ring flashing in front of June's mesmerized eyes.

He did his best to placate her, not willing to get involved in an argument, but halfway through the meal he realized his thoughts kept drifting back to the mystery that had landed in his lap. When he thought of the trail of the dead woman, he thought of Helen Lamont and saw her dark eyes flashing up at him. Later, in his own living room, he felt another pang of guilt at how he'd declined June's invitation to stay over. He could have made the effort, he told himself. He just wasn't sure that he wanted to.

He switched on the television, made himself a coffee which he knew he would regret in the dark hours as he tried to get to sleep, and watched the news which was full of doom and despondency and nothing of particular interest to anyone. There was a game show or sport on every other channel, so he automatically reached for the remote for the video and began to play something he'd taped. It was one of the natural history series he'd missed the previous year and was now collecting as it re-ran, adding to his library of nature films. The familiar narrator's voice came out in a whisper as the screen showed a naked and shivering hatchling in a nest of grass and moss. As David opened up the file on the real Thelma Quigley, the motion caught his eye.

The tiny bird, shivering with cold and effort, its huge eyes still shut blind and its skin bare and pink and vulnerable, was squirming in the nest, bracing its skinny legs on the edges, twisting and turning against the nearest egg. It took several tortuous minutes and at every stage the hatchling stopped, exhausted, panting with exertion. Finally it got the egg on to its back and carefully raised itself up until it was in danger of toppling out of the safety of the nest. It was the egg which dropped.

'And the baby cuckoo will continue until the other pipit eggs are disposed of,' the famous voice intoned, 'thus ensuring it has a monopoly on all the food its foster parents will bring, and ultimately, its own survival.'

David watched the whole operation, fascinated at the effort and the evolutionary imperative that made the cuckoo a successful brood parasite, even to the extent of mimicking the colour of the eggs in the victim's nest. As a ten-year-old, using his uncle's camera, he'd managed, more by luck than design, to get a picture of a cuckoo sitting on a robin's nest in his own back garden, and had been overwhelmed with pride when the photograph had been used in a nature magazine.

For a while he sat at the table, the papers forgotten, as he watched the cuckoo grow and grow, demanding more and more food from its exhausted foster parents who could do nothing but respond to its yellow gape and shrill cries.

Finally he switched the television off and turned to the file and the pile of papers he'd found in the woman's apartment. He went through the Quigley file again, skimming the words for anything he may have missed, and then reached for the 1967 diary. As he did so, his hand nudged his half-empty coffee cup and in trying to prevent it from spilling its contents on to the papers, he dropped the diary. It tumbled to the floor and landed with the pages fanning the air. A piece of paper fluttered out and landed on the carpet nearby. David bent and picked it up.

It was another newspaper cutting.

HOPE FADES IN HUNT FOR MISSING WOMAN

The headline was grey against the yellow of the paper which was so thin and dry it looked as if it would crumble to dust. The name of the newspaper was not evident but a part of the date, just the six and the seven, told David it had to be from the same year. The paper had been stuck in against the back cover. He unfolded it carefully, moving slowly in case it shredded, and managed to get it spread out on the table.

Police hunting for missing secretary Heather McDougall fear she may have been abducted and killed.

And they believe she could be the victim of the brutal killer of Thelma Quigley whose mutilated body was found in a shallow grave near Duncryne Bridge in May.

Miss McDougall, who vanished two weeks ago, worked in the same whisky brokerage as the murdered girl and they were the close friends. The disappearance, months after the murderous attack on Thelma Quigley, who was set for a glittering stage career and had just landed a major part in a musical show, has led to speculation that Heather McDougall is the latest victim.

And if this is the case, although no body has been discovered, then it is almost certain that the two women knew the killer.

While police have claimed that such speculation is not relevant to the case, local people have been quick to spot the link between the killing and Miss McDougall's disappearance. The two worked together for several years. They often went out together and even travelled abroad. They were in the local Treadboards Theatre Group where Thelma Quigley starred in *Calamity Jane* only months before the murder.

It is also clear that the police have made the connection, because a massive search has been in operation for the past week in the heavily wooded area around the bridge and the stream. Teams of tracker dogs have spread the hunt up over the north side where the public paths lead to a well-known lovers' lane.

Miss McDougall's mother Catriona was unable to comment, but her aunt, Mrs Janet Ferguson, said: 'There doesn't seem much hope now, after what happened to Thelma. Heather is a very quiet girl and she would never have gone off without saying anything. My sister fears the worst.'

Superintendent Philip Cutcheon, leading the investigation, said: 'At the moment this is a missing person operation. Anything more is pure speculation.'

Mr Cutcheon's men have already spent several days in the Duncryne Bridge vicinity after the recent horrific accident in which woman was injured and a baby killed when it was thrown from its pram into the river below. The tragedy happened two weeks ago when spinster Greta Simon was struck by a lorry. The baby in her care is believed to have fallen into the gorge. Its body has not been recovered. Police are also trying to trace the parents. The search continues . . .

The story ran on, regurgitating all the malevolent facts of the body-in-the-woods murder, as it was described back then, and more details of the horrific accident on the bridge. It carried a photograph of Thelma Quigley which was instantly recognizable, but of much better quality than the one on file, and another of a shy-looking chubby woman with thick, dark hair. Heather McDougall was not looking at the camera. She was not pretty, but she was attractive in a moon-faced way. Three small moles lined her cheek.

David put his hands on the paper, flattening it down to the surface of the table, and sat thinking for a while. He'd just been handed another mystery.

He was changing. It was deep inside, the growing thing, the sense of alteration. The panic had flared again when his out-reach senses told him of their approach in the old nesting place. He would have felt the vibration, but his questing sentry, his mental radar had touched them as they came nearer and the fear of exposure had shocked him awake.

He had reached out, eyes wide in the dark, while the mother slept fitfully, dreaming her jumbled visions. He had made contact, just a light stroke at first, on the warmth of another female. He pulled back instinctively, then stretched out again with his mind and touched once more. There had been two of them: a female, a potential mother – he tasted her automatically, like a dog sniffing the air – and a male. Males were different, un-pliable, deadly; he knew from the depths of his instinct. He felt the danger as he scraped on the male's surface and he had woken the mother then, roused her with a jittery mind-squeal and she had slammed awake. There had been no time. He simply stabbed her with his need and she picked him up and moved to the back of the house. He always ensured he had a nest with an escape route. That was as natural as breathing, as instinctive as the suckling reflex. He made her move on and she pushed out into the cold air. He huddled from it, burying himself close to her heat. Trying to pick a direction to travel, he took pictures from her mind and urged her on. The approach, the warm one – *could she be a mother? There was something in that brief slither of contact that had jolted him* – and the deadly male, receded, but still he had to hurry fast, to find another nesting place.

After all this time of suckling and feeding, he was changing at last. The sense of transition was burgeoning through him, quickening all the while. He could feel it spurt and stretch and he was carried helpless on its bow-wave.

It was a huge thing after all this time and instinctively he knew it was right. Tiny tremors rippled through flesh that was beginning to toughen, bones that were starting to lengthen. Sinews pulled and hauled, testing themselves. Where there had been gristle and cartilage, new bone was forming and as it happened his hunger grew. He needed more now, more than just the milk and the leechings of blood.

He would need a place to shelter and stay quiet until the change was complete. Inside the new mother he could hear the steady pound of her heart as the hot blood raced, carrying his essence along with it. It would change her as he was changing, but for now it was not easy. Too much of him, too much of his mind and his energy was invested in the new thing, the metamorphosis, so that she was not completely subdued, not completely transformed to be his mother. That would take time. He could feel her mental bayings and resistance, her rational terror as she kicked and heaved against his goad. It would take time and he did not know if he had the time to take. This one was different, he realized now. He had blundered, caught unawares and vulnerable. When the old one had fallen he had sensed only his own need and the new one's potential, smelled her scent as she had smelled his and he had reached and grabbed in panic and fear.

That had been the mistake, because this one was different. She had fought him, squirming and twisting to wrench out of his control. Whatever thing he touched inside the other mothers, it was somehow different in this one. He had snatched her because she had been close at his moment of greatest need, instead of choosing her because he could reach inside and alter her to suit his needs.

It was too late now to do anything but wait. He had invested too much in her to reject her and find another. He needed her to last through his new phase, whatever this was. Instinctively once again, he knew it was momentous and powerful and that he would be strong.

Maybe he would not need a mother.

That was a new thought.

Maybe he would be able to feed for himself.

The concept was so colossal that it sent a shiver of excitement through him, causing him to rasp against the skin. Immediately, without any conscious thought, he clamped his mouth on the feeder and sucked. Automatically, he shot out his tongue on to the smooth swelling of the skin to let the tiny denticles on the surface abrade a layer so he could suck the blood up through the straining capillaries, but his tongue was changing. It was smoother now than before, unable to scrape at the skin.

A small tumult of panic lurched within him but he forced it away. In his gums, there was a gnawing pain, throbbing under flesh hardened from a lifetime of suckling. Already the skin was swollen, tender and beginning to break. He could feel the tiny slivers pushing through, sharp and close-set. Reflexively he turned his head and pressed down with strengthening neck muscles.

She groaned in her sleep and tried to turn.

The craving came on him fierce now, more savage than before. His skin was tight and dry and pained him when he moved. The new joints had grown quickly and they tensed, needing to try their strength, needing to move. His leg kicked involuntarily, striking the mother on the thigh. She grunted in half-sleep. The room was dark, but there was light outside, not the harsh light of day that seared his eyes, or the lights in the street that caused him to flinch, but the white moonlight catching the frost on the window and limning the room with an eerie blue. He could feel the pull of the moon on the tides within and knew his time was near.

He had struggled to get his mouth to the teat again and snagged it with his dry lips. The skin was peeling on the top edge and he could feel the swell of new flesh underneath. The milk and his own essence came welling up into him, filling his mouth, and he suckled noisily, grunting his new, deeper sound of satisfaction. He sucked harder and the mother shivered in the sudden pain. The fabric surrounding them pulled on his skin and rustled like dry leaves. He opened his eyes wider to savour the blue light of the moon. His legs twitched again, flexed and bent. His toes spread wide and there was a pulse under his armpits where new pressure squeezed at him.

The excitement of it made him twist his head as he nuzzled. He sensed the lines of heat under the mother's skin, and followed them, letting the nipple slide out of his mouth. It made a faint popping sound which he ignored, tracing instead the deep stream of heat, clambering over the mound of swollen breast to the vein which throbbed temptingly. He got his mouth over the spot and nuzzled in again, driving his head down. It took a while. There was some resistance and then a faint *tick* of release.

An instant gush of taste flooded his mouth.

The mother whimpered in her torpor, twisted as if trying to wriggle away, but he held on, held her with his concentration while the flavour of her filled his mouth and his throat with spurts of intense ecstasy. The heat and energy suffused him, sending trails of fire deep down inside him and then radiating it outwards to tingle on his skin. His eyes widened as he let the sensations surge inside him, the taste, the pull of the moon, its wan and perfect luminescence, the surge of new blood and the inescapable change in his own body.

It would be soon.

He nuzzled closer and another strange sensation impinged itself on his mind.

Down below, between his new limbs, the caudal appendage had begun to shrink and shrivel while the buds formed themselves into jointed legs, the way a tadpole's tail shrinks as it develops its limbs. Between them, the boneless flesh was narrowing down, resorbed and altered, but still a part of him. He felt it twitch and turn, almost as if it had a mind of its own. A new centre of heat developed within him, a new sensation of awareness.

The appendage uncoiled like a soft, prehensile tail, like the tongue of a butterfly. It unravelled from its tight twist of flesh, probed slowly and found the warmth. Without hesitation, but so softly it seemed simply to flow, it moved inside.

Taste exploded all through him, the taste of his own essence and the taste of the changes he had wrought. Here was another source, but an infinitely richer one. The other part of him pulsed and flexed in a strange peristalsis that brought the new sustenance into him. For a second he was completely suffused with it, his cold mind suddenly hot with new excitement.

Instantly his body responded. All his muscles quivered uncontrollably in a spasm of ecstasy and in that surge he could feel the change speeding up.

This was what he needed. He had been feeding on honey, but now he had royal jelly to advance the transformation. His entire being seemed to surge with new-found energy.

Ginny Marsden felt the sudden pain and woke from one nightmare to another.

In that moment, she knew who she was and her mind reeled in the immensity of her fear. It was feeding on her, draining her away. It had turned its mind away from her, removed the tight focus of its attention and she knew who she was.

Yet she was paralysed. It was all over her, its mouth was on her shoulder, close to her neck and she could feel the rasping burn where her skin had broken. It was like a series of pinpricks, not much more than a scrape, but she could feel the drain of her own blood.

She moved, just a shiver as her body reacted to the dreadful knowledge, and the thing tensed. In the dark she could see nothing but a faint outline in the dimness of the room, but she could feel everything.

Oh Jesus it's in me.

Her mind shrieked. It was on and over and inside of her. The dryness of its skin rustled and dragged over her own smoothness. Its mouth moved on her skin and she felt the rasp of its lips and the lap of a cold tongue.

And down between her legs she felt the awful peristaltic pulse of that other part which probed deep inside and drained her from within.

Holy mother please save me.

She knew she was in hell. She was in hell and a devil was feeding on her.

Ginny Marsden was locked in the horror. Her body tried to react but couldn't and her mind was split and split again in the enormous terror of it. A part of her, an icy bubble of her own self, tried to think, tried to remember what had happened. Had there been an accident? Had she been hit by a bus on the way to the mall?

Yet another part of her recalled the dreadful dream where she saw the woman collapse to the tiles and she remembered the beckoning pull inside her head, the slow approach towards the old black coach-pram. She saw herself bend and look inside at those big baby eyes drowning her with their irresistible appeal.

No . . . no . . .

She tried to shake off the memory of the huddled scurry along the precinct. She remembered it as if it were a distant dream, as if it had happened to someone else, yet she recalled the sensation of the frosted air rasping in her throat and the sudden and all-encompassing need, and deeper still, the twisting alteration inside her even as she scurried, not knowing where she was going, where she was being led, to the shelter they needed.

And now it was on her and in her and she was powerless. She shuddered again and it tensed once more. Its fingers were splayed on her skin and they closed slowly, nipping at her flesh. For an instant the nuzzling stopped. The pulsing inside her slowed. There was no sensation in the pin-prick punctures, none at all, but she could still feel the leakage, and from her breasts the milk oozed under her own strange internal pressure. It smelled sweet and warm, but in it there was another smell and she knew it was the smell of the thing that suckled at her. She felt diseased.

It moved slowly and she could not turn her head as it turned its own towards her. The eyes were huge and glassy, wide open and bulging. The head swivelled and the eyes reflected the pale light of the frosted moon, just enough to cover the red-black with a silver ice. It blinked once, making an audible snick of sound, then fixed her with its stare. It squeezed down on her, using arms and legs, and she felt the probe of its mind, like the touch of a dead but still crawling hand, impinge on her own brain. She tried to writhe and twist away from it, but it flexed again and the cold air was suddenly saturated with the musky scent. Ginny Marsden reared back from it, trying to hold on to her own thoughts, knowing she had to get away, free herself from this nightmare, and realizing under it all that it was no dream. The scent filled her and she felt her own self fading away. It made a grating sound, like pebbles crunched underfoot, like the rending of metal, but she only heard the bleating, the defenceless baby whimper of need and she responded to it. It vibrated within her, mirroring her own resonance and she was lost to it.

But in the deepest corner of her mind she was still screaming in utter terror.

CHAPTER TEN

'She always came home, or if she was staying out she'd always call. But she never came home again and her dinner got burned in the oven.'

Neither of them knew it, but the old woman was repeating almost word for word what Virginia Marsden's mother had told Helen Lamont. Her name was Catriona McDougall. She had just been told that her daughter had died in a shopping mall in a city the old woman had never visited. The voice was tremulous and quavery, and every now and again it would break off into a sudden silence as if the air had been cut off. The pain was thirty years old but it had not diminished in any way. There was not a whit of difference between the old woman's grief and what Winnie Marsden was suffering.

David had driven across rolling country to get to this village, an old place where the buildings had crow-stepped gables and the streets were narrow and rutted from past decades of trundling cartwheels and iron-shod hooves. The village was a huddle of houses in the lee of a hill that might have been the spoil heap of an old mine. The people were squat and broad-shouldered, like mining folk, and their accents flat and dour. A small church had a graveyard in its lee, sheltered from the wind, where old headstones canted and slumped, and David knew that if he scraped the moss from them he would read names that would be the same as the ones on the doors of the low houses. The town was clean, scoured by cold blasts from the sea a few miles distant, but country-clean, as if it had some pride left, unlike the rest of the mining villages that had been left forlorn and dying in the past years.

The old couple lived in a small cottage tacked on to a row of houses off what could have been the main street. The house backed on to sloping fields where the grass was weighed down by hard frost. There was no sign of life in the fields, and few passers-by in the streets. David got the impression that this was a self-contained place, where people huddled together, like the houses they lived in, and kept their own counsel. An outsider would stick out in a village like this.

Despite that, the old woman, Catriona McDougall, had invited him in, pressing herself against the wall to let his bulk pass her in the narrow hallway, and had made him a cup of tea and offered thick scones. Her mantelpiece bore a picture of a shy-looking girl with three tiny moles in a line on her cheek. David knew he would have to tell an old woman that her daughter was dead.

'Never came home,' the old man, said, parroting his wife. He was sitting hunched in his seat, a rickle of big bones in a hollow skin, pale blue rheumy eyes fixed on his massive, faltering hands lying like dead roots on his knees. 'Not never.' His face was quivering very slightly, as if there was an awesome tension within, but David knew it was the palsied tremble of senility.

'It was in all the papers,' the old woman said, 'and we had the police here day in, day out, always coming to ask another question, or show us a picture of this man or that one to see if we could spot somebody that might have done it, but it never made a bit of difference. She never came home again. She just vanished. It was about the same time as the baby was killed up there at Duncryne Bridge.'

'Not never,' the gaunt man repeated, though his expression didn't change.

'It broke him in half,' Catriona McDougall went on, nodding in her husband's direction. Her shaky voice still held the trace of the Highland accent she'd grown up with, the soft lilt of the west coast. 'Broke us all in two and that's the truth. She was our only one, you see. It was a great shame that we could never have another one, but Callum said it was fine, as long as she was healthy and whole. He said no matter what we'd love her just like a whole tribe of them. She was our only one and she never came home.'

The old woman was about ninety. She was tiny in comparison with the huge scarecrow of a man who sat motionless but quivering on the seat by the small coal fire. Outside, a smatter of hailstones rapped against the window, driven in the east wind that came straight over from Siberia and down across the North Sea to chill the whole of the shoreline of the Firth of Forth.

The wind moaned down the chimney and the old woman reached over to pull the heavy blanket around her helpless husband's shoulders, gently smoothing down the old woollen fabric with a stroke of her hand which conveyed, in one soft movement, the enormous love and loyalty they'd shared during the good times and the barren days and still burned strong in her heart. The capacity for human love, David thought right then, must be unfathomable.

He was reminded of old Mrs Whalen, a few doors down from where the dead woman, this woman's daughter, had lived. There was the same compassion and concern, the same old, warm love that bound two people together. David Harper could only marvel at the strange and powerful drives that kept a man and a woman linked so unbreakably long after the flush and the heat were gone. He wondered if such a thing could happen to him. There was a difference, though, between the two old women who looked after their ruined old men. Mrs Whalen had brought eight children into the world and raised them through the better and worse times and seen them off into their own lives, reaping the harvest of grandchildren.

Old Catriona McDougall had given birth to the one, a difficult and harrowing birth that had almost killed her and the baby both, and she'd never been able to have any more.

And then that one, whom she'd cared for beyond the normal span of years of motherly care, had been taken from her, though her mother-love still burned within her, a torch of sadness and hope and prayer and need that would never be extinguished.

'After Thelma went, Heather was never the same again. They were so close. It was Thelma who got her out of herself. You know what I mean. Heather was always the shy one.' Catriona McDougall pointed to the picture of her daughter on the mantelpiece, right in the centre, in contrast to Mrs Whalen's array of descendants. The three little birthmarks, set in a slant like the stars in Orion's belt, were exactly like the ones in the other photograph which he'd seen of the dead woman, eyes half open and blind in death on the slab. The moles provided the only visual similarity, though there had been other identifying marks. Like the picture in the old newspaper cutting, the young woman in the picture looked nothing like the raddled, oddly proportioned corpse in the mortuary.

'Oh, don't get us wrong. Thelma was wild in her way and sometimes we'd worry that she'd lead our girl astray, but Heather told us she was old enough to make up her own mind, and it was true. We just never wanted to see her getting hurt, or into trouble, you know?'

David agreed that he understood.

'Never came back,' the old man chimed in a voice that was as hollow as his skin.

'But after what happened, she just seemed to crumble. It was like the light went out of her life, and that's what happened to Callum here. The light went out of his, so I lost the both of them really, more or less. They never ever found her, so they could never say for certain what happened. Oh, sure, everybody said it was the same beast that killed Thelma must have done away with her.'

The old woman's eyes filled suddenly with tears and she broke off, turning to dab a small embroidered handkerchief there.

'I couldn't bear to think about it. We knew what had happened to the poor girl. Stabbed and mutilated she was, it was dreadful, just animal, and if they'd caught the man who did it, he'd have been torn limb from limb by the folk around here. But they never found him and they never found Heather. The police asked if maybe she would have run off with the man and I remember I got angry and nearly threw them out of the house for ever suggesting such a terrible thing. Thelma was younger than our Heather, but she was good for her, we realized later, because we'd brought her up close, you know. Sheltered. Because she was the only one we had and we were always scared of her getting hurt. But Thelma really was good for her and she'd never have had anything to do with anybody who'd hurt her friend.

'It was after that the police, yon big man that Callum knew from the bowling club, Superintendent Cutcheon, told us that it was likely she'd been killed and we shouldn't expect to see her again.'

The old woman looked over at David who sat patiently,

holding a saucer in one hand and a half-empty cup in the other. 'But I never gave up hope, for there was something inside of me that could still feel her. Oh, I could never explain it to anybody and I can't explain it to you either. You don't know what a mother has inside of her. I knew from the moment . . .' She stopped and looked over at the ruin of her husband, slack-mouthed and empty-eyed, and an expression of wonderful tenderness came over her face. The love conveyed in that one look was so powerful that in that instant David could see the young woman behind the wrinkles of the ancient face.

'. . . I knew from the moment she was conceived. That's hard to believe, but I knew then that I was carrying her. She was a part of me from that night, a living part of me. I felt her grow. What does the Bible say? I felt her *quicken* in me and I said a prayer of thanks. Callum, he just laughed the next day, the big lump, and he was off to the war two days later before the sickness started and he'd have laughed on the other side of his face if I'd have got a hold of him then. But I'm telling you, Mr Harper, you know when a part of you has died, and I never felt that until now.'

David raised his head as if startled. 'Pardon?'

'I was making the dinner, just a piece of boiled fish, for that's about all he can manage these days, and I was bending down to take it off the stove when I fell down. I was there on the floor and I thought this was it, that my Maker was calling on me while I was making the dinner and I thought it was not a good time and then I got scared thinking of what Callum would do because he'd just be sitting there and never know what happened.'

Mrs McDougall dabbed her eyes again and sniffed. 'But then, right at that moment, I saw Heather standing in front of me, just the way she was. She was waving to me like she did in the mornings when she went off to work and then she was gone and she really *was* gone. I couldn't feel her inside of me and I cried and cried, just like I'm doing now, silly old woman. I don't know what happened, but since that moment, not even a week ago, I've known she was gone. Maybe I just couldn't admit it to myself all those years, but I don't think so. The light just went out and the torch inside of me that would have lit her steps back home went out along with it.'

She stopped sniffing and turned her eyes on David. They still glistened, but they were bright with intelligence. 'And then you turn up on my door asking questions.'

'The bridge,' he said. 'That's what I wanted to ask about. It's in the old files.'

'Not so old, Mr Harper. It's as clear as yesterday to me. And probably to him an' all,' she said, nodding in her husband's direction. 'For he isn't in the here and the now. That's where they found Thelma. Hardly buried at all, just covered with leaves and all cut up by that madman. He could still be living, but I'd sooner he was burning in hell, may God forgive me. It was up by the bridge at Duncryne. It's not far away, just a half a mile along the road and then a sharp turn to the right that takes you up the valley. It was Lord Duncryne built it in the old days, before my time even, and that's a *wheen* of years ago, I can tell you.'

I'm going to go up to the bridge tomorrow, because wherever Thelma is, she'll be laughing and she'll make me laugh again.

The lonely, rending words in the diary came back to him. Heather McDougall had decided to go up to the bridge and it was clear from the diary that she'd intended to throw herself off and drown herself. He hadn't been up there yet, though his curiosity would drag him in that direction, nothing surer, but he knew beyond a shadow of a doubt that there was deep water under that bridge and if she had jumped off she would have drowned.

His thoughts flicked back to the rest of the story in the newspaper, the tag-on filling around the tale of the missing girl. There had been another death at the bridge, and something more besides. Somebody had gone over the parapet and had almost drowned in the pool there way back in the sixties, at the same time as Heather McDougall had disappeared.

Now he knew that she had not been abducted. Not murdered. Neither had she thrown herself from the bridge in a despairing reaction to the brutal death of her friend.

She had simply disappeared and she had been gone for thirty years, using her dead friend's name, living for some of the time in a damp and cramped little apartment in a city on the other side of the country.

And this mystery planted its daughter mysteries, more conundrums and riddles. Old Catriona McDougall, a Highland woman who had the lilt of Gaelic in her voice, had obviously inherited a touch of the second sight. She had never truly believed her daughter was dead. Not until only a few nights past, the very night when the woman travelling under Thelma Quigley's name had fallen to the floor of the mall.

The thoughts were tumbling and whirling now, too many questions and no answers at all. A part of him considered it would be better if he dropped the whole thing, went back to Donal Bulloch and Professor Hardingwell with the information he had gathered and at least allow the police on this side of the country to close an old case that was still technically open.

Perhaps old Catriona was not the only one who had an extra sense. David didn't call it second sight, he called it intuition. Whatever it was, it was sounding an alarm bell inside his head and prickling the hairs of his forearms. He had always had faith in his hunches and he decided he had to trust the feeling now.

Helen Lamont knocked on the door and waited in the cold for a reply. She could have sent a uniformed patrol round to check up on the address, but it was on her way back to the station and after seeing the despair in Winnie Marsden's eyes, she had decided to make a special effort. David had gone through to Edinburgh that morning while she was getting the photograph copied for inclusion in the bulletin for the beat men and the patrol squads to show at the doors.

There would be a lot of footslogging on this one, she realized, because Ginny Marsden had been popular and she'd been busy. Everybody she knew, from colleagues to friends to the girls at the aerobics class and the night school, would have to be interviewed. The girls at Kellacher and Frick, the solicitor's office down on the Riverside, had been little help – until the very end, but that hadn't been their fault. They were just teenagers with their minds on Christmas and boys and nail varnish and little else. None of them were at night school for a business diploma.

'Oh, what about Celia?' one of them asked.

'Celia Barker?' Helen had taken a note of the name at the Marsden house. 'Isn't she on holiday?'

'Yes, she is. Greece I think. I'm sure it's Greece. Or maybe Ibiza. Oh, it doesn't matter. But Ginny was thinking about going with them and then she changed her mind.'

'And?' Helen asked encouragingly, hurrying the girl along.

'And I think she asked Ginny to feed her pets. I'm sure she did. They were good pals, and Celia always got somebody to look after the animals. She's got a cat and a goldfish with funny names. Minky and Dinky. No, Mork and Mindy, but I don't know which is which.'

Helen took a note of the address. She'd planned to ask about the Barker girl, simply because she was Ginny Marsden's closest friend and there had been a possibility, a long shot maybe, that she had changed her mind at the last moment and was now too scared to phone her parents to tell them she was on an island in the Mediterranean. It was a long shot that had bottomed out anyway. The girls confirmed that Celia had flown off the day before the Marsdens had put their daughter's dinner in the oven to keep it warm. Ginny had been at work all day and the other girls in the office reckoned she had gone down to the mall for some last-minute shopping. The one who remembered the pets' names recalled walking down to the corner with her.

Helen jotted the date and time down in her book. She looked at the figures, drew her eyes away, looked again. Something tried to snag her mind. She reached for the vague connection, failed to grasp it. It would come back later, she told herself.

The line of low houses on Dunlop Street was shaded by pollarded lime trees which protected them just a little from the swirling frost. It was getting late by the time Helen got there and while she would have killed for a hot cup of tea she was conscientious enough to get out of the car and push open the wooden gate of the garden of the house at the end of the row. There were no lights on in this house, or the one next to it, and Helen knew it was unlikely there would be anything here worth bothering about, but she had already called in her intended movements and it was best to do this step by step. Ginny had apparently intended to go to her friend's house some time to feed the cat, so it was logical to check it out. The possibility that she had a secret boyfriend her parents and Tony didn't know about had occurred to her. This place might have been the ideal place for a clandestine meeting.

'Rather catch you getting a leg-under than find you lying in the bushes,' Helen said, almost aloud, speaking to the image of the missing girl she had got from the photograph. She chuckled to herself. Better that, better all round than putting Tony through the hours of questions he'd face if Ginny didn't turn up very soon. He was next on her agenda, right at the top of the list. The poor sod didn't know what was about to hit him.

She knocked on the door and waited in the cold for a reply, feeling the rasp of the winter chill in her throat.

Something scuffled inside the house. It was just a small scrape of noise, but it was unexpected and made Helen jump. She knocked again.

'Hello?' She bent down to peer through the letterbox. Inside there was darkness and shadows.

A floorboard creaked.

Helen's heart rate edged up.

There had been a movement. She had heard it twice. She stood up, wondering what to do. She started to bend to look through the letterbox then changed her mind. The noise had been tiny, so it was probably the cat. But there was a chance that there was someone behind the door. She straightened up, thinking, then turned and went back to the car for a flashlight.

Call in, she told herself, but another voice said that would be stupid and could make her look foolish. The torch was big and heavy in her hand. The gate creaked when it opened again, the hinges contracted with the cold. Instead of going to the door, she walked along the flagstones towards the window. The curtains were mostly drawn, but there was a space she could peer through. The beam reflected from the glass, but she shaded her eyes with a hand bridged from her brow to the pane. Inside a long couch and a small coffee-table were just visible. Back at the door she knocked again and, standing back, she pushed the letter-flap open with her fingers, keeping at arm's length just in case something sharp and blinding came lunging through the gap. It had happened before, everybody knew that, a stab through a letterbox that had punctured eye and brain. Only nobody knew *whom* it had happened to.

'Ginny Marsden?' she asked. The words were swallowed up in the darkness inside. She waited a moment or two, then repeated the girl's name. There was no reply. The flashlight beam angled through the slot and found only a shadowed hallway with a tall coat stand on which a coat and hat made an eerie representation of a hanged man.

Then the sound came again. A little creak as if a slow foot had gone down on a board, putting just enough weight for the old wood to protest.

A shiver went up Helen's back.

Call in!

She thought about it again. It could be a burglar, somebody who'd seen the curtains drawn for a day or two, somebody local who knew the girl was off on holiday. Possibly it could be Ginny Marsden herself.

Call in. It was always safer. If necessary she could have a squad around here. She could even get a warrant to have the place searched. But she could see the look on the patrolmen's faces when they turned up, the big boys, the macho cavalry, who weren't afraid of noises in the dark. She cramped down on the mental insistence. She could do this. It was only a house.

Slowly she let her fingers draw back from the hinged flap and stood up. Diamonds of frost were dancing in the torchlight and her breath plumed out into the cold night air. She swung the beam to the left to shine on the path around the side of the house, and then she followed the beam, keeping it low and covering most of it with her hand to make it less obtrusive. A wicker gate at the side opened without any problem and hardly a rustle from the scraggly honeysuckle festooned around it. She reached the back of the small house. Overhead, an overflow pipe grew a long and deadly spike of ice, which was suspended over her like a sword. She moved out from under just in case, past a small window which was shuttered by venetian blinds. Here at the back of the house, the ice crystallizing in the air became a thicker mist curling around the eaves and the down-pipe, softening all the outlines, moving in thick translucent tendrils and slowly billowing rolls of fog.

Get a hold of yourself, Lamont, she ordered herself. It was only a small terrace house on the end of a row. There were no suspicious circumstances other than the fact that a girl had gone missing. A cat-flap was a pale white against the dark of the door and she remembered now. Mork or Mindy. The other was a goldfish, according to the girl in the lawyer's office. Helen tried the handle, turning it very slowly, pleased and somehow relieved that it made no sound at all. She knew she should knock, identify herself, but she tried the handle anyway, assuming the faint scrape of noise had probably been made by the cat.

The door opened with a brushing rasp. She froze, taken by surprise. Her breath plumed out again and she realized it had backed up unconsciously. Helen thumbed the torch, keeping the beam down on the ground, and swung it slowly forwards, through the two-inch gasp. The floor was tiled. She waited for another five breaths, ignoring the insistent mental command to get a uniformed patrol round to the house.

She swung the door open until she stood in the frame. The kitchen was cold and empty. Beside the sink there was a bowl with a name printed on the side. A collection of pots hung from hooks on the wall. A dishtowel had slipped to the floor beside the sink, black and white on the red tiles, just out of the direct beam of the light. Helen took a step forward, two. She was inside.

The mist followed her in, twisting creepily in the light, like an uninvited, insinuating ghost.

A small noise came from beyond the door, which was not quite closed. Just a slither of sound, fabric on fabric, and it was followed by the faintest mewling sound, hardly more than a squeak.

Damned cat, she breathed. It was the cat. Of course it was the cat. A strange relief oozed inside her, draining away the tension. She turned, moving towards the door.

'Here, puss,' she called softly, in the tone that every human being uses. 'Puss, puss, puss.' She pursed her lips and made little kissing sounds. She reached a hand forward to push the door open, expecting the cat to come squeezing through the gap. Just at that moment, something registered in her brain. She froze again.

It was the dishtowel on the floor beside the sink, a black-and-white shape crumpled on the floor. She was in the act of turning towards it when a sudden rap of noise came from down in the darkness of the hallway beyond the door. In that instant the skin puckered down the length of her back as if a cold finger had trailed between her shoulderblades. The flashlight beam jerked. She was still in the act of turning when the light caught the scrap of cloth on the floor.

It was no dishcloth. The cat was lying sprawled against the little hatch under the sink. A puddle of blood had pooled out around its head, black against the light colour of the tiles, glistening in the beam. It was lying on its side, half turned so that one paw jutted up, tensed in the final spasm of death, every sharp claw unretracted, forced out in vicious little curves. Its lips were drawn back in a death-snarl, pulled so tightly that the sharp teeth were clearly visible top and bottom as if the animal was frozen in a screech of hate. It made the little cat fierce and feral in death.

But there was more to it than that. Despite the somehow menacing little knock in the still darkness beyond the door, part of her mind was clearly and completely focused on the dead animal.

It was not the yawning scream fixed in rigor mortis or the hooked claw that made it look as if it had been caught in the act of a final vicious swipe. It was the dark and ragged pits where the pet's eyes had been. The head was twisted right round on the neck so that it stared up towards the ceiling, but its stare was blind and cavernous. There was nothing but deep holes on either side of what once had been a cute button nose. The eyes were gone, and in the gaping recesses there was nothing but the glint of congealed blood or some other glutinous fluid that caught the light of the torch and threw it back. A flap of skin had been peeled away from the cheek, skin, fur and muscle, leaving a hole where the bone showed through.

'Oh my . . .' she muttered, trying to draw her eyes away from the mutilated little animal.

Down in the hallway another board creaked and the sense of danger simply exploded inside her. She turned away from the door, heart suddenly pounding, one part of her mind fixed on the cat with its eyes torn out and another focused on the noises and yet another, deeper part of her mind suddenly awash with the fear of the unknown and the supernatural. The child-fear of creatures in the dark swelled within her, threatening to blot out everything but the need to turn and run.

'Get a grip,' she hissed, trying to quiet her suddenly pounding heart. The rush of blood soughed in her ears and her throat clicked dryly. It couldn't be the cat. It could be a burglar, someone caught in the wrong place at the wrong time, surprised in the act of ransacking the empty house.

And if it's only a burglar why are you so damned scared? she demanded to know. A burglar she could handle. She snicked the torch off, though it still shook in her hand, and gripped the handle tight, raising it protectively to shoulder height.

Not a burglar. Housebreakers didn't pluck the eyes from pet cats. Then what? For some reason she could not have explained, she did not think of who.

Her heart wouldn't slow down despite her best efforts. The powerful occult sense inflated and she tried to flatten it down, but it was uncanny and unexpected and so primitive that her conscious mind could not squash it. Her legs were quivering with the tension of it. It was completely incomprehensible, but it was real.

'This is the police,' she called out, forcing the words through her teeth. They sounded very quaky there in the dark of the kitchen. 'Do not move, do *not* try to run.' Helen went into professional mode and that made her voice a bit stronger. She held the flashlight tight and put one finger on the button ready to make it shine. She took a step forward, through the door and into the hall.

Something mewled. It was a faint sound from down in the dark. There was a rough edge to it, like the cry of a small animal. It repeated, a little louder. Helen's heart thudded again, making itself flop inside her chest. She took a second step forward, and another.

The smell came then, a powerful wave of scent billowing in the dark, thick as the mist that had followed her inside. She recognized it instantly. It was the smell of the house where the dead woman had lived in the clutter of ripped blankets and the mounds of toy animals with their beady little eyes all reflecting the light.

Her eyes stung and her nose smarted and her throat tried to close itself against the stench. She blinked hard, trying to clear the sudden spark of tears that made the dark shadows waver. Something scraped roughly down among them and the sound registered in a series of dwindling vibrations, as if every element of the noise had been slowed down and separated into a rasping chain of sound.

Helen pulled back. The smell was everywhere, so thick it could almost be felt, much stronger than it had been in Thelma Quigley's house. She turned, trying not to breathe it in, but sensing the musky particles settling on her skin and entering her pores. She was in the act of turning when colours erupted in her wavering vision. They simply exploded in a series of shimmering pulses, as if all of the rods and cones in the receptors at the back of her eyes had fired up simultaneously. The colours danced in her vision, sparkling and luminous.

Poison! The recognition hit her the way it had come to David Harper in the other house. It had to be some sort of nerve gas.

The colours expanded in putrid shades of orange and yellow, lava-reds and pulsing purples. Shapes swelled and fragmented. A green face went whirling past her eyes, dripping sparks of watery silver. A child screamed far off in the distance, a high and piercing sound that went on and on and on, ululating madly before tailing off in a series of heartrending sobs. Off to the right, the sound of a blocked sink, the sound she had hated as a child, came gurgling up through the floor, rekindling an old fear of swamps and wet darkness. Her foot kicked against the door and the thud chimed in her ears in a loop of sound that echoed from wall to wall. Her heart was kicking madly against her ribs, her fingers paralysed on the flashlight, unable to make it switch on. The sink by the window twisted and warped out of shape and the taps turned to powder and crumpled into the maw of the drain. The cat on the floor rolled over and stood up on its hind legs and reached out that one paw, each of the nails hooked to rend and slash, while in the blank sockets of its eyes she could see a phosphorescent light glaring balefully.

Helen tried to call out again but there were no words. Her

throat managed a dry croak before it closed over in a strangled clench. In the dark she saw her grandmother turn towards her, face cobwebbed and crawling with spiders from some long forgotten but somehow living nightmare. She heard her name called over and over again in the far distance by a boy she had seen killed by a truck on South Street next to the river. The cat was dancing to fiddle music and insects were crawling all over her skin. Maggots came humping from the spikes swelling to ripeness on the shimmering door while down in the dark of the hallway, where the colours faded to deep black, something dreadful was coming.

Her stretched senses reached and touched something alien and scabrous.

She was still turning, trying to flee from the dark, when her reeling mind brushed against another and she felt the cold and repellent touch of another mind.

She tried to scream and nothing happened. Inside her chest her lungs were filled with fire and her teeth ground together causing sparks to leap from one surface to another. Her hair whipped like tentacles and she began to fall in the dark.

Then a dreadful jittering thing came rushing at her.

CHAPTER ELEVEN

She was coming closer. He reached out with his senses and touched her.

Here in the dark he had became very still. The mother moved and he made her stop. She made a low noise and then was silent. There were glass sounds of ice forming in the air. A small thing rustled in the dead flower beds out there and that caused a reflexive pang of hunger which he pushed away. The footsteps were loud, picked up by his new and heightened ability, crunching harsh on the frost on the flagstones.

They paused and there was another silence broken only by the whirr of starlings' wings in the sky and the chittering cheep as the flock wheeled towards the church tower to roost. The gate shrieked, a scream of protest that sent his own hackles rising. It sounded like a challenge and he responded to the high rasp with an involuntary twitch. Inside of him excitement surged for an incandescent moment and then slowly deflated.

The footsteps came closer and he forced his senses out further, until he trailed them over her warmth. The new hunger swelled again. She was hot and pulsing, tense with readiness. Something familiar came to him. He concentrated, focusing tight.

And he recognized her.

He had no words, not yet, but his senses picked out the differences in texture and shape and heat and a thousand other subtle differences that enabled him to tell one from the other. This one had come before, to the other place where the old mother had nested. She had come with the other one and he had been afraid, vulnerable in the disorientation that followed hard on the loss and the change to a new mother and the imminence of the change.

Was she hunting him? Was she a danger?

He snuffled with his mind, questing and probing, but he was not strong enough yet for anything more than a brush of contact. It was difficult, impossible to tell, but still he felt the uneasy sense of approaching threat. His instinct was to avoid it, to stay still until it had gone. He could wait in the darkness, safe in the mother's warmth until it passed.

The gate shut with a clatter of the hasp, cold metal on metal. The vibration racketed against the glass of the window and sent it shivering in sympathetic resonance. He concentrated his thoughts as the footsteps stopped by the window where the curtains almost met, allowing in a sliver of moonlight to send a bright line running down the side of the wall. A shadow moved, cutting off the light, turned away to let it spear back inside again, then blocked it off once more.

Tension rippled inside him and his excited perception narrowed to target the approach.

A different light came swinging up through the slit between the edges of the drapes and he recoiled as a searing pain drilled into his eyes. If the light had caught him directly, they would have smoked and sizzled with the unexpected heat of it. A small sound blurted out from him and the mother went into a sudden spasm of shivering in response.

Outside the new one shivered too, suddenly tensed, responding unconsciously to the sub-sonic hiss.

The shadow moved away and the cold moonlight was back again, wavering in his stinging vision. Something thumped at the door and the mother twisted at the sound. He sensed her protesting, felt her sudden lurch of hope and he clamped down on it hard. She grunted softly as the conflict within her mind and body pulled on her like warring tides.

The door rattled and a metallic click came. He had heard letter-flaps open before and dismissed the noise as insignificant. A human sound came echoing down the hall, garbled words that made no real sense. Just then the mother moved, her weight shifting off balance. She put a hand out to stop herself falling from the couch beside the door. A floorboard creaked.

The stranger shivered hard, not physically, but mentally. The vibration came singing through the dark, a pure and clear note, the primitive beginnings of fear. He felt a swell of satisfaction and another hunger followed instantly. He swivelled his head, waiting for the next move. Almost absently, he urged the mother to pull back to the corner beyond the scope of the light should it come again. She responded sluggishly, a deep and untouchable part of her fighting him all the way, but he plucked on the inside of her nerves and she moved slowly. Her knee came down on the sprung board and made it creak again.

The reaction from outside was instantaneous. He could feel the cold shiver in the new arrival transmit to him. Through the wall, through brick and mortar, he saw the warm colour doppler down to a cool nameless shade as the tension altered the very vibrations of the other life. The alteration in sensation faded off quickly and the woman moved away from the door. He sat there in the dark, beside the lounge door, clasped tight in the mother's arms while she trembled almost imperceptibly. The new one moved, almost out of range, beyond the side of the wall and then came back again at the back. He strained to pick her up, almost ready to move, when there was a noise from the kitchen,

She was inside.

It was completely unexpected. Over by the far wall, the green eyes of Celia Barker's answering machine blinked at him. The colour represented a small animal but he had learned to ignore the reactions the eyes sparked off within him. It had no *sense* of life. He ignored them now because of the noise in the kitchen. She was in now.

The sensation of approaching danger inflated wildly.

In the kitchen the woman called out in a low, unintelligible series of clicks and booms that sounded raw in his ears. She came closer, bright in his night sense, and he reacted to the nearness.

The mother moved. She tried to call out and he reacted. His glands were primed, pumped up as never before as he prepared for flight or fight, though his instinct told him it was not yet the fight time. The mother tried to pull back and he wrapped his tail around her, looping it round her neck, hauling it tight to strangle the sounds that were about to blurt out and reveal them both. It held her taut and she gurgled mutely.

He was ready.

The presence came towards the door. The mother drew back and he forced her forward, one step, two steps. Beyond the door, the noise came again, a short mutter stretched by his altered timescale of sudden alertness. The mother's foot rapped against the skirting board.

On the other side of the door the heartbeat thudded in sudden fast pulses of colour. Feral anger and hollow need rippled through him as the apprehension came to him in waves. His glands swelled yet further, lumping up beneath the skin, pressing tight under the surface.

The woman called out, a stuttering rumble of noise that bounced and echoed from the walls of the narrow hallway. She came out of the kitchen and into the hall. He mewled. The sound came from low down in his chest, a smothered whimper of fury and his own kind of fear. He made the mother press herself in against the wall. Muscles inside him clenched tight, pressing like a pain, suddenly urgent. Spiracles down the length of his abdomen, little parallel rows of holes that trailed from under each limb opened. There was no volition, no choosing of the mix he would need, the way he did with the mother or the others who had to be manipulated. This time it all came out, every gland sphincter opening like a mouth, every muscle squeezing in an instant of relief. He could hear the pheromones spray from him in a hiss of mist.

The mother went rigid. It was instantaneous. She jerked as if she'd been hit with a hammer right on the forehead and he gripped her tight. Her head rapped against the wall, her whole body vibrating so fast and so hard that the back of her skull rapped on the surface in a rapid series of dull thuds. Her mouth opened and a drool of saliva spilled out in a sticky rope. Inside her head, frantic fear screamed in a mental blast and he absorbed it with his own mind, soaking it instantly to damp its force.

Out there the spray caught the other one and she stopped dead, just out of the kitchen, one foot still raised from the ground. He felt it slam into her like a physical blow. His concentration was wound up so tight that all his receptors were wide open. She reeled back with the enormous force of her physical reaction to the responses triggered by the pheromones. Adrenaline spurted into her veins. Complex dopamines and melatonins flooded receptors in her brain. Even more complex sugars urged in a powerful hit of energy that could not be expended. Her ovaries squeezed progesterone and oestrogen into her system and she fell back, almost doubled up with the overwhelming chemical overload.

He felt it sizzle through her, perceived her galvanic reaction. Inside her head the neural connections sparked and forked uncontrollably. She staggered, her mind emitting sharp and crazy pulses of thought-static that he picked up in the dark. It was like watching an explosion of light and colour, like tasting the concentrated essence of his own self in a mother's blood. It was like draining the pure distillation from deep in a mother's depths.

For a moment he too was in sensory overload, experiencing everything that erupted within the new one. He was almost paralysed on the crest of the momentous reaction.

In his grasp the mother vibrated, her own receptors shuddering under the impact but already, even in so short a time, inured to its full blast. He loosened his hold just a fraction and she gagged, choking for breath. The fear was swirling inside her in a hot stir while the mother-need clashed with it, sending counter-pulses through her. Her mind was ripping apart. He swivelled his head to peer through the crack between the door and the wall. In the hallway the new shape stumbled back.

He moved then. He turned back and focused on the mother. She moved too. There was no hesitation. He pressed hard and swamped her fear and the panic with the urge to protect.

Even in the dark, Ginny Marsden saw her baby's wide eyes and she sensed the danger.

She came out of the chemical assault, eyes staring. The dreadful fear was crushed down to a hot coal, while the mother-love simply ballooned. She felt her legs move, muscles still trembling hard enough to spill her to the ground. Something was coming for the baby. Something wanted to hurt it. She did not think, just reacted. She lurched out through the doorway, now holding the baby tight in her arms, and banged against the wall. It whimpered. She groaned an unintelligible sound of panic and anger and threw herself forward.

A shape was moving just inside the kitchen door, its outlines blurred in the dark. This thing was threatening the baby. She ran forward, clutching the mite against her, feeling its soft skin, her mind flickering with the irresistible need to protect.

She hit the floundering shadow, reaching out with her hand to push it away. The back door was wide open. The silhouette whirled away from her, careered against the sink and bounced back. She saw a hand reach up and knew it was reaching for the baby. She tried to turn and then something happened.

Ginny did not see it, but suddenly the shape was reeling back once more. There was a clatter of noise and a sharp unmusical crack as something made of glass broke and then shattered. A metal utensil fell into the sink with a ringing sound that seemed to go on and on. Something screamed loud and deafening in the enclosed space.

Helen saw a lurching shape come through the doorway. She was still turning, trying to flee from the dark and the nightmare images that wavered and exploded in her mind. Enormous jolts of distilled terror sent shocks through her. Then her mind brushed against something scabrous and completely alien. In that moment, despite the fragmented horrors rolling and tumbling inside her head, a part of her knew this was different. The cold and loathsome touch slithered across the surface of her brain and she reeled from it.

A scream tried to blurt, but no sound came out from her strangled throat. Her hair whipped like thick tentacles, slapping against her cheeks as she shoved herself away from that appalling touch.

A dreadful jittering thing came rushing towards her. She had no time to react. The sensory overload was so devastating that she could not stop herself in the act of turning, could not raise a hand up. The shape came slamming out through the other doorway. A hand reached out, pale against the dark, expanding in her vision. It looked like a white and writhing spider. Her own hand, stretched out as it was, almost touched the fingers. They pulled back unaccountably. The shape lunged towards her.

Oh my God it's got two heads.

The sudden clear thought blazed. The thing had two heads. It was a monster coming at her from the dark of the hall. Some rational part of her mind told her it was another hallucination caused by a gas or a drug that she'd breathed in. Another part of her, completely primitive, completely fundamental, told her it was a gorgon. It was a nightmare come alive and coming for her. Her mouth opened and this time a gurgle of fear escaped her. Her head twisted to the side. A pale face turned away from her, moving, it seemed, in slow motion. She saw fair hair whip around, bouncing almost elegantly in the air. The first hand whirled away, flying of its own volition.

And another face loomed up.

Her heart punched into her throat and kicked so hard she was sure it would choke her to death.

The face leaned forward, its features twisted and gnarled, eyes huge in the dark, large as golf balls, protruding from a face that she could never have dreamed. The eyes were staring, emitting a light of their own. The mouth was small and puckered, forming an almost perfect black circle inside which needle teeth looked like splinters of glass. The lids pulled back so far that the amphibious eyes looked as if they would pop out and burst on the sunken cheeks. A papery, shiny substance fluttered on the skin.

It screeched at her, so loud and so high she felt the bones inside her ears and the very shell of her skull vibrate so rapidly it caused a drill-bite of pain to cross her brow from one temple to another.

Her eyes were locked on to the protuberant eyes of the two-headed thing. It opened its mouth and its scream turned into a hiss. The smell came again, more diffuse than before. The shape blurred and changed. The colour, even in the dark, wavered from shades of grey to pale pink. The eyes shrank, swelled, shrank again. For an instant she thought she saw a baby. Some other wrenching sensation kicked in her belly, a twist of need in the midst of the appalling fear.

Then something came whipping out and caught her just above the eyes. Needle-sharp points poked at her skin. She felt a rip. The face blurred and ran like wax, leaning in close to her. She sensed a dreadful hunger and recoiled, aghast. On her forehead a pain erupted in a slender point of fire and she fell back. The last thing she saw was the two-headed thing dance back along the line of the sink. Helen's head hit against something hard and colours spangled in front of her eyes, but they were real colours, not sick and alien. The darkness closed in on her and she realized with fading horror that she would be left alone in the dark with the monster. The shadows of the kitchen spun away from her as a deeper black came in and she felt as if she were falling down a long well.

'The door's unlocked,' David Harper told the two uniforms. Another patrol was just coming up the alley. There was hardly any daylight left, but he hadn't wanted to waste time, not since the talk with Heather McDougall's old mother. John Barclay had left two messages for him at the station, both asking him to call urgently. David knew the ex-cop would be wanting his video-tapes back, or at least to get the go-ahead to re-use the ones he already had. David promised himself he'd call in the morning, once the search of the dead woman's house was finished. Inspector Cruden had not been easy to convince, but the neighbours' statements that the woman they knew as Thelma Quigley had always been seen pushing a pram and had always had a baby were definite enough to make it worth the check. If there had been a baby, they had to find it.

'It could be another West case,' somebody had said in the squad room and Cruden had lifted his eyebrows just enough to think about it some more. 'She's always been seen with a baby in a pram, but it's definitely not a neighbour's kid and she had no relatives to speak of. The house was full of toys and baby clothes. She could have been a weirdo, or just some sad old lady with a complex, but if she wasn't . . .'

'You're sure she's Heather McDougall?'

'Certain of it. We're getting dental records checks right now, but it's a formality. The three birthmarks on her cheek match exactly. No point of trying for prints. She was pure as the driven snow. Prof. Hardingwell confirms that too.'

'But you've already been to the house?'

'We didn't know about the babies then.'

'Sounds a bit of a long shot to me,' Cruden said, but he was policeman enough to consider the possibility, however remote. David Harper was a good cop, and not given to flights of fancy.

Finally the Inspector gave the go-ahead for the search and they got the warrant signed within the hour. There were one or two things David hadn't mentioned, not to anyone, because the information he'd got from Edinburgh was old and purely coincidental. It kept nudging in on his conscious thoughts quite insistently and he had to shove it away.

'Is Lamont back?' he asked as he was pulling on his coat. He wanted her back on the case with him, telling himself it was only because of her professionalism. Another internal voice told him he was a damned liar, but he ignored it.

'No, she's still out,' Cruden told him. 'She's still working on the runner. Gone over to Gilmourhill to knock on a door or two.'

David shrugged, buttoning the coat up to the neck for the short walk across the car park. 'If she gets in, tell her to call me.'

It was bitterly cold now in the still air with darkness falling swiftly and a pale moon rising over the rooftops. The two patrolmen stamped their feet hard on the flagstones, making the ground quake. Their batons and cuffs clunked and jangled. David pushed the door open and flashed his light into the hall.

'Bulb's gone here,' he said. 'Take one from inside and set it up.'

'What are we looking for?' one of the officers asked. He took several steps up the hallway, then stopped. 'God, what a stench. Has something died in here?' he turned, still holding his torch up. The beam caught David in the eye and he flinched back from the glare.

'Turn that off,' he snapped. The smell was different now. He recalled the surge of anger and the undertow of violence that last time he'd been in the dingy room. He remembered the other sensation, and the image of Helen Lamont pale and spread-eagled. He forced it away yet again. Now the smell was thinned, but it still had the musky reek that conjured up images of stoats and ferrets and movement in the dark. David realized he should have pulled a search team together the first time. If there had been a baby, and if the baby was in the room, he'd not only be turned over for missing something quite literally under his nose, but he'd find it hard to forgive himself.

If there had been a baby and it had still been alive . . .

He turned away from that kind of thought. It would get him nowhere.

'Left is the living room. Beyond there's a bathroom and on the other side a kitchen.' He gave them directions and the five of them began a systematic search. The nest of blankets and sheets was still in a swirl where he'd last seen them. The team carefully unravelled the tangle, screwing up their noses at the smell that still lingered on the fabrics.

'What did she keep then? This is worse than cat's piss.'

'Dog farts. Worse than that.' His partner went one better. 'This would make you puke your guts.'

David was on the far side of the room checking among the piles of toys. Opposite him, a young policeman was going through the small cupboards on the dresser, neatly placing everything on the floor beside him. He drew out a cardboard shoebox, opened it slowly. The top slid to the side, and David turned just in time to see the recruit stumble back so quickly he fell on his backside with a thump. The box flew out of his hand, twisted in the air and a white ghostly shape came floating out.

'Holy fuck . . . ' the patrolman at the bed barked. The youngster on the floor scrabbled back as if he was being attacked. The shape spun slowly in the air, a translucent face staring blindly and hollowly, and then sank to the floor. It landed with a rustle and crumpled where it fell. The cop on the floor was still scrambling backwards and his movements were enough to cause an eddy in the cloying air of the room. The papery thing rolled over, scraped against the edge of the dresser and immediately began to disintegrate.

David crossed the room in three strides and tried to get a hold of it. He reached a hand out and stopped.

The face moved. Small shoulders shrugged as it rolled, thin and narrow, oddly slender. The face was in profile, flat and somehow wizened. The eyes were huge and blind and the ears, set high on the sides, were hardly more than pointed flaps. There was no real nose. As David reached lift it, the whole thing crumbled.

'What the hell is it?' one of the men asked.

David did not reply. He was hunkered down, watching the papery shape fragment into flakes. It was like a skin and it reminded him of something he'd seen before. Even as he watched, it came back to him. It was like the covering of a dragonfly larva after it had split to free the jewelled adult.

It made a tiny sighing sound as the breath of air stirred by his very reach shifted it again. The small face collapsed in on itself. The translucent arms folded and bent. There were no legs, just a tapering body that ended in what looked like an umbilical cord. There was nothing he could do but watch as the little shape fell apart into tissue scraps The face broke into a hundred pieces, more fragile than butterfly wings.

'Jesus, sarge, I thought it was a friggin' ghost,' the young policeman said. 'Scared the shite out of me.'

'It's a caul,' David said, almost, but not completely sure. 'There must have been a baby here at some time.' The thing was unrecognizable as anything now.

'I'm sorry, sarge. I just opened the box and it came out. I didn't mean to let it drop.'

David let it go. He stooped and collected some of the flakes and put them back in the box. His mind was working fast and he could have kicked himself for not searching the place more thoroughly the first time.

'What's a caul?' the young man's partner asked.

'Something babies can be born with,' David explained. 'It's like a fine skin, mostly covering the face like a membrane. It peels away after birth.'

The officer made a face. 'Why would somebody keep it?'

'For good luck,' David said, but he didn't feel there was any luck in this. A caul would have to come from a newborn baby, which meant there must have been an infant here at one time, maybe even born in this room. If that was the case, what had happened to the mother? None of the neighbours had ever seen her. They had only seen the old woman with a baby.

The image of the fluttering, decaying shape crumbling on to the old floorboards stayed in his mind. It had been a queer, wraith-fine shape, with bulging eyes and a flattened face. No legs, but long arms. It hadn't looked like any baby David had ever seen, but then again, he'd never seen a caul before. But this one, if it really was a birth-mask, could be another clue to add the rest that surrounded the woman who had taken the identity of a girl murdered thirty years before.

'Never came home,' old Mrs McDougall had said. 'She just vanished. It was about the same time as the baby was killed up there at Duncryne Bridge.'

The words kept coming back to him, demanding attention. What old Mrs McDougall had said had been repeated in the tag-on to the murder story and the tale of the missing girl. There had been another death at the bridge on the day Heather McDougall had disappeared.

She had gone up to Duncryne Bridge to throw herself off, to join her murdered friend, but she had not killed herself. She had simply vanished for thirty years. There had been a baby on that day and there had been a baby now.

That nagged at David's mind. Was it a coincidence? Or was there something deeper, something more sinister?

Down on the floor the flaky remains of the membrane formed an oddly sprawled light patch on the old wood. David had already taken some samples for tests, to make sure it was what he thought it was. He scraped some more into the shoe-box and again he thought of the bulging eyes of the dragonfly as it peeled off its skin to emerge a fast and dazzling predator from a black and scaly thing that lived in the dark. The eyes on the caul had bulged.

The search turned up nothing new. There were stains on the sheets at the centre of the jumble, which could have been blood-stains. David had the men fold them for forensics. Apart from that there was little to be found. There were no trapdoors to get under the floor and no evidence that any of the boards had been lifted in recent times. A hatch led up to a small loft above the kitchen, a tight and dusty space where the rank scent lingered. It had a narrow skylight that gave on to a low, sloping roof at the back of the property. In the beam of the flashlight, David could see scrape-marks on the moss where something had slid towards the guttering that abutted the adjacent flat, and he tried to recall the sounds he'd heard the first time he and Helen Lamont had come to this house.

There had been a noise. He'd been almost sure. A whimper-ing sound that he'd taken for a kitten, the slight scrape of a piece of furniture being moved. He had not been sure then, and he was not sure now, but now he wondered.

Had there been someone in the house all along?

Helen Lamont staggered to her feet, gasping for breath, gagging with a sudden roll of nausea that swelled up in a sickening rush.

Every beat of her heart sent a wave of pain through her head and she felt a trickle of blood slide down her forehead and between her eyebrows. Her flashlight had spun away and landed somewhere and she was in total darkness. Even the light of the moon had gone. For an instant she was completely disoriented, struggling to comprehend what had happened.

Monster . . .!

No, not a monster. The sudden jolt of apprehension had brought back an image of something that had lurched out of the shadows. She'd thought it was a creature with two heads, but that had been a hallucination. Either that or she was going completely crazy. Hot on that thought came the realization that she had to get out of there. There was a smell in the air, still rank and sickening, though diminished now from what it had been. That's what had caused the hallucination, she told herself, some chemical, some poison in the close atmosphere of the room. She stumbled to the door and yanked it open, vaguely aware that she had not closed it when she came in.

Out in the dark of the winter the air was cold and clean and she haled it into her heaving lungs, feeling the rasp of its icy touch at the back of her throat, yet welcoming it. She leaned against the wall at the back of the house and retched violently, bent double with the force of it, though nothing came up except a trickle of saliva. Heartburn flared under her breastbone and acid burned her gullet, but she kept everything inside.

. 'Stupid bloody bitch,' she told herself 'Should have called in.' Now she had to get on the radio and that would mean a red face at best. She was still trying to work out what had happened, now completely unsure of the train of events. Something had come lunging at her.

Hadn't it?

She could not even be sure of that now. There had been the smell, like the foul reek in Thelma Quigley's house. It had come billowing up, thick and greasy, and then suddenly she'd gone completely crazy. There was no other way to describe it.

She'd fallen and banged her head. That was true enough, for there was a lump rising on the back of her skull, still pulsing urgently, and another pain on her forehead where the trickle of blood welled from a cut. Something had come lunging out of the dark, a dreadful shape that wavered and twisted and looked as if it had two heads.

Hadn't it?

'Damned silly bitch,' Helen scolded herself again. She got to the car and on to the radio. The control-room girl patched her through; a squad car arrived in four minutes. David Harper was the first to get out. He saw her in her own car and came walking quickly across. The two uniforms followed behind.

'We were just passing,' he said. 'What happened?' He leaned right over her, almost protectively, put a hand on her shoulder. She felt herself sag against him, felt the warmth of his solid weight. For a moment she wanted to hold on to him, hold on tight, and let loose the tears that were close to the surface. He steadied her, eyes full of concern.

'Got a bang on the head, that's all,' Helen said. She was still unsure, still confused. She didn't want to say the wrong thing. 'Could have been a burglar, but it was dark and hard to tell. I think I was dazed for a minute.'

'Did you get a look at him?'

She shook her head. 'No. Couldn't say if it was a man or a woman. Just a shape in the dark. Slammed into me.'

'So why were you checking a place out on your own?' he asked. 'You should have called in.'

Helen shot a look at the two policemen who had just reached the pavement. She quickly drew her eyes back to David, giving him a sign to leave it alone. He picked up the message, but his eyes had that confusing mix of concern and anger.

'I thought I saw something and slipped when I turned round. It was nothing. I was just on a routine check, a long shot. I'm still looking for the girl and there was a possibility she might have come here to feed the cat.' She kept her eyes on him, knowing he was right, but unwilling to take it in front of uniforms. 'I'll put it in my report.'

One of the patrolmen walked up to the gate. 'Want us to take a look around?'

Helen swivelled round. 'No. I've done that. The place is empty.' David saw the tension in her look. For some reason she didn't want them going into the house. He went along with that for now.

'That's OK with us,' the man said. 'We're off shift ten minutes ago, sarge.'

'Fine. You might as well knock off. I'll check the place out and then I can take DC Lamont back.'

Once they were gone he turned to Helen. 'I should get you back to St Enoch's.' He reached towards her and felt the back of her head. She stayed still while he palpated the lump, but winced slightly under the pressure of his fingers. 'You got a right crack there.' He brought his hand round, cupped it under her chin and tilted her face so that she was looking directly at him. 'And a cut here too. How many of me can you see?'

'Just the one, and that's enough,' Helen said. 'I didn't need a rip in front of the boys. It was just a routine check. I never expected anything.'

'OK. I wasn't ripping you. I was worried, that's all. But then you didn't want them to go inside. So what's up?'

'I don't know,' Helen said, glad of his concern. She could still feel the pressure of his fingers on the back of her head where the lump throbbed in time to her heartbeat. 'It's really weird. I didn't want to make a fool of myself, but there's something funny going on. You remember Thelma Quigley's place? The smell?'

He hadn't got round to telling her he had identified the Jane Doe.

'Well, it smells like that in there, but worse. I couldn't be sure what happened. It made me dizzy and I might have fainted. I'm not even a hundred per cent certain that I was knocked down, but I think I was.' She explained what had happened, or what she thought had happened, and then he made her stay in the car while he checked out Celia Barker's small house himself There was nothing much to find except for a swirl of blankets on the floor and the dead and stiffened cat. If there had been any smell inside the house it had not lingered long. A faint, acrid scent was barely discernible and could have been anything, but he knew Helen Lamont. If she said it was the same as in the dead woman's house, then he'd believe her. There was no sign of anything that could have caused it, no canisters of chemicals, nothing. The dead cat was a puzzle, but it was close enough to the door to have crawled in through the cat-flap. It looked as if it had been mauled, maybe by a dog, and the missing eyes told him it had been dead a while. Even in winter, they were always the first to go. He dumped it without ceremony in the waste-bin outside the back door rather than leave it to rot any more. A dead cat was not important.

CHAPTER TWELVE

'Curiouser and mysteriouser,' David said. 'I'll get a team out to the Jane Doe's place to lift the floorboards if I have to. She definitely had a baby there at some time, and maybe more than one. Almost definitely more than one. Christ alone knows what she was up to.'

Helen sat curled up in an old armchair close to the imitation coals of the fire which sent a flickering glow dancing on the walls. She was wearing an outsize sweater which swamped her and cradled a brandy in a fine-cut glass. She had a small pink dressing on her forehead. The nurse in casualty had looked at the narrow, deep cut, swabbed it with stinging alcohol and sent her home again. She wasn't even bruised.

'It was the same smell, or very similar. I really thought I'd been poisoned. It was like having a trip, and a real bad one too.'

'I suppose you're talking from experience?'

'Give me credit, David,' Helen shot back until she saw the look on his face. She tendered a smile that faded quickly as she thought back. 'It was like walking into a nightmare. Everything in the room changed shape and the colours went through the spectrum, except they were all sick colours. It felt as if I was on a rollercoaster, but a mental one, as though all my senses had been wired up the wrong way. I was scared and angry and depressed and completely confused all at the same time. It's hard to explain exactly what was happening. I remember thinking I was having some sort of breakdown, a psychotic episode or something.'

'I get that kind of feeling just watching Rangers in extra time,' David said. She hit him with another look and he gave her an apologetic shrug that told her he was trying to keep it light. 'Maybe there's something new on the market. Ecstasy? Jellies? Something like that? A new brand of PCP?'

She leaned back and sipped her drink. 'Whatever it is, it's not pleasant, I can guarantee that. I can't imagine anybody paying money to feel like that.'

David had to agree with her. He remembered the odd, unnerving twist of emotions that had rocked him when he'd stepped inside the dingy room in the dead woman's house. The sudden violence had been the most disturbing part of it all, the instant, vicious anger that had swept through him; that and the sudden surge of raw need.

'I got something like that in Quigley's place,' he said slowly, battening down the image in his mind that tried to transpose itself on the real Helen Lamont. 'I mean McDougall's house. I thought it was gas at first, or some fumes, like lead paint or ammonia, but it was none of those. Remember I got you to the window?'

She nodded, recalling the sense of loss and the other, weird need inside her. She recalled the grab of his hand on her neck and the shunt of sudden want.

'It was then I thought of nerve gas. I saw a programme on Porton Down. Sarin gas, the kind they used on the Tokyo underground, that was what they were testing, that and a few others. They can give people real hallucinations. As soon as I breathed it in, I wanted to hit somebody. If I hadn't got to the window, it could have been you.'

Helen gave him another smile. 'I saw what you did to Kenny Lang. You dropped him like a sack, so I'm very glad you decided against it. You should have told me this before.'

'Well, it passed pretty quickly, and of course it couldn't have been anything lethal, I suppose,' David said. 'I'm allergic to a couple of antibiotics. They give me anxiety attacks. I just assumed there was some sort of cleaning fluid that had evaporated and left some traces that affected me the same way.'

'Was there anything inside Celia Barker's place?' Helen asked.

David shook his head. 'Nothing out of the ordinary. The bed was still unmade and might have been slept in. A couple of blankets and sheets were on the floor by the wall. It reminded me of the bedding in the other house. I've taken some of that for sampling, plus the caul.'

He'd already told her about the macabre find in the shoebox. Helen herself had heard of the phenomenon, so he didn't have to explain in great detail. It was just a mystery that sparked more questions. 'I'm more interested in who hit you. Cruden's sure to give you a bad time for going in on your own.'

'I told you, it's just a missing girl who's got no history at all. The address is a workmate's house, and she's clean too. They're normal folk, from quiet, law-abiding families. Both girls have good jobs, good careers. There was no reason to expect anything, none at all. I was surprised to find the door open, and there was always a possibility that the girl could have been lying there hurt. It was a judgement thing. Anyway, that's in the past. I'm not sure what happened. Remember, I was seeing things, and I didn't want to let the uniforms know that. I don't want that kind of thing on my record.' She turned to David again and gave him a half-smile that conveyed a number of different messages. 'I can tell you, though. Perhaps there was something there, but I couldn't swear to it: I might just have fallen. I did think I saw something, but it was some kind of monster, some creepy thing out of a Hammer movie. It had two heads and one had a face like a gargoyle, but then again, there were spikes growing out of the door and blood running down the walls. There was definitely a chemical in the air, but it cleared when I opened the door.'

'So what made the mark on your head?'

'Your guess is as good as mine. I wish I knew. If it had been a burglar, I could have taken him down, or at least made him fight his way past me. Under any normal circumstances I could have done that, but believe me, the situation wasn't normal. I'd like to find out what it was I breathed in, because it's powerful stuff.'

Helen said she'd prefer to accept she'd slipped and fallen on the frosted tiles, at least on the official record, than to have let an intruder escape, assuming there had been one, after going in without back-up. David didn't think it was such a good idea, but he went along with it.

'And how was your day?' she asked, draining her glass, drawing him back to the present. She reached for the bottle, caught his look which silently asked if it was wise to take another drink on top of the painkillers, but she poured anyway and took a sip.

'As weird as yours. Christ knows what I'll be able to tell the boss. Thelma Quigley turns out to be Heather McDougall, her best friend who's been living under an assumed name for at least five years, possibly more, maybe even as many as thirty. I'll have to do some real backtracking to find out. Quigley was murdered back in the sixties and Heather disappeared a couple of months later, on July 27, 1967. I spoke to her old mother who's still pretty sparky, though her dad's lost it a little. Things got a little complex from then on. I can't make head nor tail of it.'

'Tell me then.'

He leaned back and reached for the small folder into which he'd slotted some of the documents. He took out a folded sheet of paper and handed it to her.

'See for yourself,' he said.

July 28, 1967

BABY DIES IN BRIDGE PLUNGE

A baby is believed to have drowned in a river plunge after its pram was hit by a lorry. The tragedy happened at Duncryne Bridge in the village of Blane just north of the city when a woman thought to be the baby's grandmother was crossing a road. The child's pram was thrown against the parapet of the bridge which crosses the Balcryne Stream. Police believe the infant was hurled out and down to the deep pool below.

The woman is critically ill in Blane Hospital where surgeons last night operated on horrific headwounds suffered in the accident. A hospital spokesman said the woman, who has yet to be identified, was still in intensive care suffering from multiple fractures and internal injuries.

The tragedy happened yesterday afternoon on the north side of the Duncryne Bridge opposite the public walkway well known in the area as a lovers' lane. The crushed pram was found only yards from the spot where, in May this year, the mutilated body of amateur actress Thelma Quigley was discovered. Police are still hunting for the killer who buried his victim in a shallow grave after stabbing her to death in a frenzied attack.

Teams of police, using tracker dogs which are already familiar with the steep-sided valley, were out in force combing the area around the banks, and a team of divers were being flown in from the Navy Base on Finloch to search the deep pools in the river known locally as the Witches' Pots. So far no trace of the infant has been found.

Last night lorry driver Brian Devanney, who is employed by J. C. Carnwath Hauliers, was charged with reckless driving. He is expected to appear in court this morning. It is the third fatal incident this year involving the transport firm and already pressure is mounting for a full Ministry of Transport inquiry.

Devanney was initially taken to hospital for shock and head injuries suffered when his cab veered off the road, narrowly avoiding a plunge into the chasm, and demolished a row of ash saplings planted by Councillor Agnes White early this year.

Hospital sources say that the driver claimed the woman had run in front of his vehicle. This allegation was not completely discounted by Mr and Mrs George Crombie who arrived soon after the tragedy and helped Mr Devanney from his cab.

'He was in a dreadful state,' Mrs Crombie said. 'He said he'd just killed a woman who had ran out in front of his lorry.'

The story went on, brown ink on grey paper, still smelling of chemicals from the microfiche printer. It was just one of a handful of sheets of old newspaper David had got printed out from the library's storage system when he came back from his visit to the old couple. The report carried a picture of the bridge, which had not changed in thirty years – David knew that from the walk he had taken up the track, spurred by curiosity. The spot where Thelma Quigley, the real one, had been butchered, and where the baby had been catapulted over the parapet and drowned in the river, was quite spectacular, even in winter. In summer it must be beautiful.

'I took a walk up there, just for a look-see. Heather McDougall said she was going up to the bridge and that's where she was headed, apparently, on the day she went missing. Her idea, as far as I can see, was to top herself. I'm convinced she planned to jump from the bridge and join her dead friend in the hereafter. Something stopped her, and that's the real puzzle.'

He took the piece of paper from Helen's fingers and folded it once more. 'She never went home again. Her parents expected her back that day but she didn't turn up. And thirty years on, she turns up dead on the floor of Waterside Mall. That's really weird. Her notes really point to a suicide attempt, and it was the same day as this baby was sent flying.' David put the printout into the folder.

'That's an awful story.'

'True. When I heard it, it rang a bell in my mind. It was one of the biggest cases at the time. Devanney, the driver, was sent to jail for manslaughter.'

'The woman died?'

'No. It wasn't her. It was the baby, though oddly enough they never did find the body. That's what made it stick out in my mind. Devanney was initially done for dangerous driving and they boosted the charge up to manslaughter. He took the corner too fast and was on the wrong side of the road at the time – or so the court was told, anyway, though he denied it. His defence couldn't have been trying too hard, for the case would never stand up nowadays. Anyway, he was charged with the culpable homicide of the baby, even though they never found it.'

'I'm not with you.'

'You must have heard of it. This is the Bridge Baby case.'

Helen shook her head. 'Before my time.'

'And mine, but I do read, you know.' He indicated the sheaf of papers jutting from the folder he still held in his hand. 'It's all here in the printout. What happened was that this woman, Greta Simon her name was, had a baby with her. It was knocked out of the pram and over the parapet into the water. There was a spate at the time, a heavy rainfall or something, and the baby was washed away. Nobody even knew who the kid was, because Greta Simon couldn't tell them. She was brain-damaged and hardly able to speak, but her neighbours knew she'd been looking after a baby. Just like Heather McDougall, in fact. They thought it was her granddaughter. She was too ill to appear in court, but there were enough witnesses to say she'd been walking along the path to the bridge with the baby in the pram.'

'And they convicted a man for that?'

'He did nine months. The baby never did turn up and, according to the experts, it was probably washed down into the River Forth and out to sea. It could have been anywhere. The search took the whole length of the stream and they dragged every pool and culvert. The dogs found nothing either, though some people said maybe a fox or a badger, or even a domestic dog might have found it and eaten it.'

Helen shuddered. 'That doesn't bear thinking about.'

'No. But it's a coincidence. Really odd. I wish I'd never started on this.'

'Why?'

'Because I'm getting nowhere and it's got to me. I've a million other things to do and Scott Cruden's expecting me to get this one tied up as soon as possible. It was supposed to be a simple job of backtracking on a dead woman with something odd in her blood. The more I look into it the further away any answer seems to be.'

'But you won't be able to let it go?'

He shook his head. 'My old mum always said my curiosity would get me into trouble. She's probably right. But you have to admit, there is something weird in all of this. We get a Jane Doe in the mall . . .'

'You're beginning to sound like an American dick,' Helen said. She looked up at him and narrowed her eyes mischievously. 'Or maybe just a dick.'

'Very funny. We find Thelma Quigley who turns out to be Heather McDougall who did a runner thirty years ago on the same day that a baby is killed. She turns up in another town halfway across the country with a baby that's now gone missing and we know it can't be hers, but the medical reports say she was lactating and possibly able to feed a baby.'

'You never told me that. I thought she was about sixty. Was she on some kind of hormone treatment?'

'That's why I was put on this in the first place. To find out if she'd been away and picked up a strange tropical disease. Anyway, in her flat we find baby toys, clothes, and then there's a caul. I've taken some pieces for analysis and the rest of it crumpled to dust. It should tell us something.' David paused, trying to recollect where he had digressed. 'Yes. So McDougall went missing – just like your girl, what's her name?'

'Ginny Marsden.'

'Her. She – McDougall – just never turned up. They thought she'd been murdered, but she hadn't. All this time she's been living very quietly as Thelma Quigley, her friend who *was* murdered and buried in a shallow grave up near the bridge. Lovely spot, by the way. Really spectacular. You'll have to come and see it. I saw a little bird there, a dipper, poor little thing, trying to find a hole in the ice.'

Helen sat back. 'You've sidetracked yourself again. I thought it was me who had the bump on the head.'

David came back on line. 'So then *you* turn up at the Marsden girl's place, or at least her friend's place, and it's got the same smell, the same kind of chemical as we found down at Latta Street. That's too many coincidences for me.'

'Maybe it really is some kind of cleaning fluid,' Helen suggested. 'I get reactions to some of them. Maybe that's it.'

'It's an easier explanation than nerve gas,' David allowed, though his expression said he was far from convinced. 'Maybe I'm allergic to it as well, and possibly we should call in the health department just in case there's been a spillage. Aside from that, there's something in this whole story that doesn't add up. It's going to niggle at me all night.'

He flicked through the papers, letting the other chemical smell of the microfiche printer drift up. 'Look at this,' he said, leaning towards her. The picture was grainy and smeared, but unmistakable. An old-fashioned black pram lay crushed against the stone wall just at the side of the bridge. A patterned baby blanket lay on the road. 'Nobody knew who the baby belonged to. Nobody knew its name.'

'I thought you said it was that woman's. Greta.'

'She *had* the baby all right. But it wasn't hers. She was too old. There was plenty of evidence that she was caring for one, but nobody knows whose it was. There isn't even a name, although the neighbours said she called it Tim. Tiny Tim. There were no records of adoption, and no relatives came forward at the time. Greta Simon herself was a bit of a mystery. Nobody was sure of where she came from, although most folk thought she was English. That was it. She was crossing the bridge and a truck smacked her into a plantation of shrubs and knocked her baby over the wall and into the river below. End of story.'

'But you don't think so?'

'No. There's something odd here. It's too much like the Heather McDougall case.'

'But separated by thirty years.'

'Separated yes, but connected. She went up to the bridge on the same day. That's in her diary, and her mother confirms it. Thirty years on she turns up dead and allegedly, *possibly*, a baby has gone missing.'

'Sounds like history repeating itself. What do you think? This Heather McDougall, do you think she was a baby snatcher? Some kind of crazy?'

This time David shrugged. 'Could be. I don't know. I did a check this morning on recent snatch cases. There's damn few of them, and as far as I can see, there's never been a case where a baby's been stolen and gone unreported. Not unless . . .' he paused.

'What?'

'Not unless she's been bumping the mothers off first. Maybe poisoning them? Perhaps that's what the smell was. Some sort of poison that she gassed them with.'

'You don't really believe that,' Helen said.

'No. I don't believe it at all. The McDougall woman was sick and she was old. She couldn't have overpowered a mouse. She was probably looking after someone's kid. We just haven't turned that person up. As I said: if I have to, I'll dig up the floor. It could be a Fred West case all over again, but I doubt it. I just think there's something weird in all of it. I look through all these clippings and I think for a second I'm getting to the bottom of it, and then it's gone.'

He stood up and put his glass down. 'And now I'm gone. I'd better shoot.'

She made a disappointed face. 'Just when I was beginning to enjoy this.' She eased herself off the chair and snaked her arm around his. 'Thanks for coming to get me today. And thanks for keeping it between us. I won't forget it.'

He gave her a wink that told her it was no big deal. She leaned her weight against him again and he could feel the warmth through his shirt. It was a friendly gesture, the kind a partner would make, but in that instant he sensed something more. He almost wrapped an arm round her to draw her close and stopped himself just in time.

'I'll give you a hand with your runner,' he said quickly. 'Because I want you to stick with me on this Jane Doe. Come and pick me up in the morning.'

'You don't have to do a runner too,' she said. She smiled up at him, let the smile fade. Her dark eyes looked straight at him and her skin felt hot on his. Helen saw his hesitation, mistook it for incomprehension. She shrugged quickly to disguise what could have been an awkward moment.

'Not so soon anyway.'

It was cold and dark. Outside the mist oozed and crept, almost alive, seeking the dark corners to fill with thick and clammy damp.

Ginny Marsden shivered, half asleep, slumped against the potato-sack matting in the corner of the garden shed. How she had got here she could barely remember. The flight was a series of jumbled images, shapes and shadows flicking past in peripheral vision. She recollected the shape that had loomed in the kitchen, she had struck out and then she'd been running, protecting the baby. The threat had gone. It had reeled back and fallen and Ginny had got the impression, no more than that, that it had been a woman.

She had been dreadfully afraid that the intruder would hurt the baby. The fear had swelled in a hot gush that had blanked out every other thought. She had gone blundering out into the cold, breath pluming in the frigid air, running as if devils snarled at her heels. She hadn't stopped when she reached the end of the lane at the back of the houses. She'd taken the right turn up the next road and then carried on for almost half a mile, unsure of where she was going, but guided somehow by instinct, until she reached the pathway that led up the side of the allotments where rickety shacks and huts and old greenhouses that had seen better days huddled together in the little patches of cultivated ground.

She knew this place. Her grandfather still worked here in the summer, tending his chrysanthemums and dahlias and weeding his little plots of prize onions and leeks. She had played here as a child, tasting the mint and the thyme that grew beside the greenhouse. She had played with the big fat toad that lived under a terracotta pot and ate the slugs that ate the cabbages. It seemed like a million miles away in time.

The gate was locked, barricaded against vandals and crowned with a piece of barbed wire. She ignored it, ignored the pain as she clambered over the wooden slats, ripping her palm twice in the attempt while still holding the baby close to her. It urged her on, its fear driving her. It needed warmth and shelter. She got to the other side, letting herself down heavily, then scampered up the aisle between the frosted leeks and Brussels sprouts to the hut at the far end. The padlock was closed but she knew where the key would be. The pot shard sheltered another toad, this one stiff in its winter hibernation, looking more like a rock than an animal. Beside it, the silver key glinted. She opened the hasp. The door creaked as she let herself inside and she closed it firmly before allowing herself to stop. In the dark, guided by the powerful emotive force, she crept to the corner where the potato sacks were piled in a heap. She arranged them around herself, pulling them over and tucking them, until she and the baby were almost completely covered. The baby nuzzled in at her, forcing its head in against her warmth, searching for a nipple. It found it, plugged in, and she felt the intense merging sensation as it drank of her.

Some time in the night, she woke briefly, shuddering at a dreaming image, her breasts sore and throbbing and her blouse smelling of sour milk. Her back ached and her palms throbbed where the barbs had punctured the skin. Her eyes were heavy and gritty under the lids, as if dust had got under there to rasp at the tender flesh. For a moment she tried to recollect what had happened but her mind was sluggish and turbid. For an instant the image of the hibernating toad came back to her. That was an accurate reflection of how she felt: her muscles were drained of power, as if she'd been sucked hollow, and the cold had stolen into her bones, making her weak and strengthless. The sacks smelled musty, of loam and old potatoes, and overlaid with that other smell that was becoming familiar now, the bitter sweetness that it secreted.

It.

Ginny Marsden gave a little start in the dark.

It. The baby. It had snuggled into her and fed and she had given of herself, feeling the urgent pressure in her swollen breast lessen in a pleasurable seepage.

It wasn't there. She turned, just a little, feeling her numbed muscles respond so slowly it was like being cocooned in treacle. The baby was gone. Her mind began to come alive again, suddenly thrown out of the torpor by that knowledge of release.

The baby was gone. The thing that held her had left her. Her heart gave a little double beat. She moved, and heard the joints creak painfully. The darkness inside Grandfather's garden shed was almost complete, save for a pale rectangle high on the wall where a piece of perspex had been screwed to the wall as a windowpane. It was still night then, for the moonlight came glimmering through the scratched plastic, barely strong enough to outline the shapes of the garden tools hanging from the nails on the beam nearby.

It was gone. She could escape. The images of her dreams came back then: the scaly sensation of something inhuman crawling all over her; its cold, puckered skin making her own cringe and buckle into gooseflesh. She felt again its probe between her legs, slender and cold, hugely repulsive, appalling in its invasion, draining the goodness from her blood, from her marrow.

Just at that moment, she heard a slithering motion close to the door. There was a movement, a scuffle that ended in a tiny, almost inaudible squeak. Something small died in that instant. Her heightened senses picked up its sudden snuffing out, just as they perceived the other presence.

It had not gone at all. It was still there, in the dark. It had crawled away from her and caught something. It was there by the door, a scuttling shadow – *Oh my god oh my god, I have to get* – that would come back and snare her again.

Ginny attempted to gauge distance in the dark. She flexed her arm, trying to warm it quickly, knowing any delay would give it a chance. Of a sudden a desperate need to be free almost paralysed her, coming as it did on the waves of fear and horror.

There by the door, something crunched gently, the sound of a bird's eggshell crushed. A faint warm smell of blood came on the cold air, mingling with the other smells and the similar metal scent that she knew would later come from the oozing drag deep inside her. The shadowy thing made a scuttling noise again, two, maybe three yards away, hardly more than that. Beside her the garden fork dangled next to the old spade that Grandfather used to make the even rows for potatoes. The four tines were close to her head height. An instant solution came to her and with hardly a pause she got to one knee, reaching a hand to unsnag the fork.

Her muscles groaned. The bones in her knees and the joints at her thighs ground together like rough stones. The thing in the shadows by the door moved quickly. She sensed it turning. Desperately she reached and got a hand round the shaft of the fork.

CHAPTER THIRTEEN

'What a lovely bunch of flowers.' The voice on the phone bubbled with laughter. 'And completely unexpected.'

'Come on, Ma,' David protested. 'You always get flowers. I even used to pick them for you up in the glen. Remember the bluebells?'

'And they wilted in ten minutes,' his mother's voice came chuckling down the line. 'I remember. I also remember you were covered from head to toe in mud where you fell into the marsh. Anyway, I just wanted to say thanks for remembering. I called you earlier, but there was no reply.'

'I must have been in the shower. You can't hear the phone from there,' David said. Helen Lamont raised her coffee cup to him. She was wearing her sheepskin-lined flying jacket against the cold of the day. It looked too warm for indoors. 'Anyway, I always remember and it's always flowers. The only thing I forget is your age.' He held his hand up as if his mother was standing right in front of him. 'No, don't tell me. That's *your* secret. You look just the same anyway. Always do. Not like me, I've a face that's worn out two bodies. A face only a mother could love, eh?' He laughed, bullshitting fondly. 'So how is he? Tell him I'll go fishing when the weather's better. And tell him to stay out of the cold, you know how it gets to him.'

Helen sat at the table listening to him on the telephone. His shirt was unbuttoned and only partially tucked into his trousers. His hair was still wet from the shower and it gave him a fresh, boyish look. He absently rubbed it with the towel, unaware of her inspection. The muscles of his forearms bunched then released, and she remembered the sudden protective strength when he'd hit the thin man down on Waterside Street and slammed him against the wall.

One of the good guys. She had called him that, and she meant it, now more than ever. In the past week, in the past few days, her perspective had strangely altered. She remembered the strength of his body outside Celia Barker's nightmare house, solid as a rock when she leaned against him. She could still feel the touch of his fingers on the back of her head. Helen could have told herself she was imagining a reaction, but she did not. For a reason she did not quite comprehend, she was able to perceive at a deeper level. She could sense something in him that he himself was probably unaware of. She considered calling over to him to tell him his coffee was getting cold, wondering what his reaction would be to the inevitable question on the telephone, but she changed her mind. The son's affection for his mother was evident in his tone and posture and she let him banter with her for a while before she brought the coffee over. He gave her a wink, just like the one he'd thrown her the night before, just before she'd told him he could stay a while longer. He smiled and took a slurp.

'Yes, Ma. I'll make sure I get something to eat. No. I'm fine. Yes. A sweater would be great. But not a Pringle. You know I never wear anything with a name on it.' He laughed out loud at something she said. 'Yes. I know you've seen my birthmark. No. Nobody else. Honest. Think I'm a pervert?'

Finally, with more laughter, he hung up.

'I must remember to look for the birthmark,' Helen said, and he laughed again, his face glowing from the heat of the shower and from the warm enjoyment of the teasing with his mother.

'Her birthday?'

'Yeah. She'd kill me stone-dead if I didn't send flowers. I didn't manage two years ago when I was undercover on the Toby Cannel job. I was out of touch for a week, down on Riverside close to where we were the other day, and I completely forgot about it. We'd been out of touch so long I didn't even know what day of the week it was. That was when big Toby got shot. Took six shots and had holes the size of dinner plates out the other side. That scared the hell out of me, watching him keep on running, like he was a machine. Like the Terminator.'

'You've done it again, sidetracked yourself,' Helen stalled him. 'Can't you stick to a subject?'

'Right. Anyway, she'd left a million messages for me and when I didn't come back she called Donal Bulloch. She had to go though five offices until she got him, for he was the only one who knew where I was, except for Jock Lewis who was with me

160

the whole time and did nothing but eat beans, which I swear was pure murder after the first day.' He caught Helen's look again. 'The boss told her I was out on a very important job and that I was fine and what was more, he even sent her a bunch of flowers himself. But when the papers carried the pictures of Toby Cannel lying on the cobbles, my mother knew what the big important job was. She's not stupid. She wanted me to quit then and there.'

'You ever hear that old Dean Martin song? "A man who loves his mother"?'

'In the film? *Robin and the Seven Hoods?*'

'That's the one,' Helen confirmed. ' "A man who loves his mother is man enough for me." It's nothing to be embarrassed about. It's natural.'

There were two other messages on the answering machine. David hit the play-back button. June was first. The sound was muted and from that distance Helen couldn't hear any more than a murmur, but she could get the gist from the way he turned away. She stayed where she was. David didn't say very much and a pang of pity stole through her. It passed very quickly. June was going to lose him. She knew that for certain. And she knew why.

Without looking round, David changed his posture and she knew he had passed to a different message. He listened, head cocked to the side, and clicked the button again before beginning to redial. As he was hitting the keys, he turned round again, and asked Helen to bring over the folder with the photocopies. She slid it across the coffee table and he stretched to get it. He selected the picture of the crushed pram.

'It's John Barclay down at the mall. He's been trying to get me for a couple of days.' He held up a hand, indicating someone else was on the line. He spoke for a moment, said he'd be down within the hour and hung up.

He picked up the print which showed the tangle of buckled wheels and crumpled metal. 'John's found a pram down at the Waterside Mall. One of his boys stored it away after locking up on the night Heather McDougall died. That's just an aside. I thought he was desperate to get his videotapes back into the machines, but he says he's had a look at them and he's found something else.'

'What is it?'

'We'd best both have a look. Something strange.' He seemed glad to have a practical matter to think about. She felt a smile start inside.

He had woken hungry.

It was a different hunger now. The mother had moved in her sleep, automatically and instinctively protecting him from her weight, huddling him close. She trembled deep within herself and he withdrew slowly, unwilling to break the contact, fully awake now. He would have to wait until she was ready before he drank again. Already his limbs were strong enough, the bones quickly grown and articulated. He could move now.

He had felt the surge of fear when the nest had been invaded in the night, for he had recognized the human, a female one. A potential *mother*. He had read her scent and her movement and had recognized her from the other time. He had sensed danger and invasion and the need to flee because he was not strong enough, not yet. There was something about the other one too. As she had reeled back he had touched her, put his mark on her. He had felt her deep strength. Something inside of him had stirred there and then, even in the height of the emergency. Now her scent and her vibration were imprinted inside him.

Out there in the dark something was quietly creeping. His appetite flared reflexively. He remembered the other one that had come close in the warm place, how he had struck, moving faster than he had ever done in his long and placid life. He had not planned it. The thing had come close, mewling in some alarm, entrapped by the scent. There had been no thought, just action. He had reacted in an explosion of speed, and it had died. The blaze of its mind had flicked out almost in an instant after he had hit. The blow had shuddered up from the end of his arm to the strangely articulated socket, but there had been no pain. The pain of touch was foreign to him. Until now there had been only two pains that he could comprehend, the hurt of bright light and the bite of hunger.

The new hunger pangs twisted inside him. They had jolted

him from sleep. He had felt the movement outside. His eyes blinked open and his other sense reached.

Over there, a point of warmth moved, blazing fiercely against the rolling grey of the background sparked by the tiny, unfocused lights that showed the ants and other insects in their thousands under the protective lining of the wood.

He moved then, again instinctively, ferret-smooth, cat-slow, yet with the steadiness of a spider. All of his senses were focused forward. For that moment he forgot the mother. She was lying curled up in the nest. He turned his mind away from her and concentrated on the warmth ahead. The hunger gnawed within him. Unused muscles in new limbs flexed. He shivered in tension, as if all of his energy was singing along the length of his slender spine.

He struck in a blur and the warm thing squeaked as it felt his rush. It ran for the door, doubled back, almost as fast as he was. It turned, faced him defiantly, its weasel mouth opening to show deadly little spikes of teeth. Without hesitation he snatched it. It twisted in his grasp, tried to bite him, a hunting weasel now caught. He leaned forward, impaled it with his eyes and it died with a feeble screech.

He bent his head, licked at the morsel, savouring the heat and the musteline scent it had sprayed in defiance and defence, so like his own spray. His mouth stretched over the head and his juice ran into its eyes, making them steam and run. He sucked then and swallowed quickly, pressing his own tiny teeth to pierce the thin skull and let his own poison drain inside, dissolving the brain and the nervous tissue. He squeezed and emptied the thing into himself, savouring the taste as it slipped down inside him. Instantly his whole body glowed with the heat of new nourishment. He bent again to the tiny, shrivelling husk. He froze.

Sudden alarm shivered through him. The mother was awake and he had let her go. He turned, eyes wide in the darkness. He could feel her fear and pain the way he could sense the other things in the night. Underneath it, even stronger, her desperate bubbling anger came to him. He saw her pale hand reach slowly for the fork. His own senses were wound up to a jittery speed that made everything seem sluggish. He saw the four curved points. It came swinging down. He moved to the left, new limbs thrusting against the ragged floorboards in a powerful shove. A clanging noise rolled out, deepened now in his hot speed, sounding like an old gong. The vibration shivered the air.

He flicked forward. She never had a chance to move again. He launched himself at her, scuttling up her dark shape, glands swelling again.

She made a sound, a whimpering noise that sounded like a low grunt to him. He fastened to her. His tail went around her neck, coiling and tightening. She grunted this time and the fork dropped away to land with a quivering thud on an old grow-bag of compost, impaling it to the floor. He sprayed instinctively and she fell back as if her ligaments and nerves had been severed. He waited in the dark until he knew she was subdued, then loosened the coil from her neck very slowly, listening to the slow pulse of her heartbeat, feeling it through his own skin.

His new hunger was sated, but he had other needs. He sat in the dark, his night-vision eyes fixed on her, slowly loosening his grip and nuzzling down in against her heat. There was no fight in her now, but he would have to be wary. This was the only one who had ever fought, the first who had tried to break away, who even *could* break away. There was a danger in that.

He waited for a while until he sensed the impending arrival of dawn, and then he woke her, urging her to move. He heard the creak in her bones as she made the effort, but he did not know what caused that. He had no words and no real knowledge outside his own self and the mothers. But he was learning quickly.

Down in the security office in Waterside Mall John Barclay offered them coffee but David and Helen were more interested in what he had to show them. All of the screens in his office were on, a bank of flickering grey-and-white squares showing all the views. It was still before nine, but already the place was filling up with early-morning shoppers, hurried people, not casual browsers, picking up what they wanted on the way to work. As David and Helen watched the screen, Carrie McFall came walking quickly past on the main floor close to the escalators.

'This is it,' John said. 'I've been through them all and I thought you'd want to see this.' He thumbed the cassette into the slot, hit replay and they watched the blurred figures race backwards, their steps odd and jerky and vaguely silly. Finally he slowed it and the whine ground to a whisper. 'Here. This is from camera four on the side foyer. Watch.'

'What are we looking for?'

'Your woman, the collapser. We've got her coming in.' John raised a hand and pointed. 'There she is. The one behind the fat man. That's her.'

'Are you sure?'

'Couldn't be surer. I spent a whole afternoon going through the tapes after you left, mostly because I wanted them back, but after I saw this, I thought you should have a look too. Didn't you get my messages?'

David shook his head. John gave him a disbelieving look. They turned back to the screen where a portly man in a heavy coat and a hat too small for his round head came bulling through the door. Behind him, a tall, spare woman came walking forward, head bowed.

She was pushing a dark-coloured pram.

'That's the same one our boys found round the back. One of the men stuck it there after the place was closed. He thought somebody had just dumped it, for it's pretty old and one wheel's got a squeak that sends shivers down your backbone.' John stopped the video. Heather McDougall, if it really was the woman, flickered unsteadily on screen, her head half turned into the shadow. 'It was only after I saw this that I asked and somebody remembered finding the thing. What we've got here's a real puzzle.'

He thumbed the switch again. The spare woman came in through the automatic doors, into the light. She raised her head, moving slowly, almost painfully, to the left. Even in the wavering image on the television screen, she appeared gaunt and dishevelled. The pram looked black and its hood was raised. They watched in silence as she moved further to the left and then began to head out of the picture.

'That's it?' David said, though his brain was already trying to work things out. There had indeed been a baby, assuming there had been one in the pram. Either that, or she'd been a bag-lady, just using the old pram as a trolley. He was about to say something else when the woman, right at the far edge of the screen, leaned forward over the push-handle to stoop over the pram. The definition was not clear enough to see her lips move, but her head did sway from left to right. It was clear she was talking to something inside the pram. She was talking to a baby the way mothers do. It was clear in the sway, in the timing. Seconds later, she moved beyond the scope of the camera. John Barclay stopped the machine.

'You can have that one. Now look at the tape from Number Three, next to the escalator.' He slid it in, switched on, and the picture came to life. 'I should have made a compilation to save time,' the security man told them, 'but I don't have editing facilities here.'

Heather McDougall came towards the camera, still pushing the pram. Two girls crossed her path, passed her by, then both stopped. They looked at each other and one of them shook her head violently. Her friend put a hand up to cover her nose and mouth. They hurried away. The woman walked to the wall where two other buggies were parked. She stooped forward again, reached into the pram and made some small movements, as if she was tucking a baby in tight. When she leaned back she raised the cover and snapped it firmly in place. Slowly, painfully, she turned and walked off towards the Mothercare shop, slowing momentarily as if catching her breath. The motion of the camera, timed to swing left to right and back again in the space of a minute, followed her progress as if directed by human hand. Helen recognized the handbag as the one they had found in the bushes where Carrie McFall had thrown it. David recognized the creaking falter of a woman with only minutes left to live.

'You've seen the next bit,' John Barclay said. 'You've still got the tape. I thought you should see what happened.'

'I appreciate it, Jab,' David told him. 'The medics were right. And the woman from Rolling Stock, she told them she'd a baby.'

'But whose?' Helen asked. 'And what happened to it?'

John's face creased into a wide smile. 'I wondered when

you'd ask that. That's exactly what I asked when I saw her walk off towards Mothercare. We saw her coming back again and throw a wobbly in the middle of the mezzanine, so after I found her coming in, pushing the pram, I had to look through the rest of them. Lucky they're all timed. It's a fiddly job, but you can work out a sequence.'

On screen, Heather McDougall, walking as if she was struggling uphill at the end of a long day, merged with the early evening crowd at the door of the shop and then disappeared from view.

John lifted the next tape from the pile and exchanged it. David and Helen stood facing the screen expectantly. 'I hope I can get to use the rest of the tapes after this,' John said. 'And I reckon the force could stand me a few drinks.'

'May the force always be with you, John. We appreciate this.'

The ex-policeman hit the button again. Once more, the figures danced and jiggled backwards. The camera panned from right to left, taking in the crowd of people comically staggering up the escalator in fast reverse. The lens swung beyond them. Right at the edge of the picture, they could see a part of the crowd that had gathered round the fallen shape slumped on the tiles.

A small woman in a grey coat bent forward at the side of the pillar, just inside the frame, turned and merged back into the crowd with the dropped shopping bag. Just within view, Carrie McFall came walking quickly, heading for the spot where the handbag had fallen. Both of them disappeared from the shot. For a second, the only people visible were the two girls who had passed by Heather McDougall and reacted strangely. They were turned towards each other, obviously comparing purchases.

A figure walked past them, moving quickly, with an almost jaunty step. She was slim and fair, her hair pleated and pinned up, as far as they could tell, under a neat beret. Her long coat was open and flapped in time to her step. The picture was not pin-sharp, but even so the girl looked as if she might be smiling.

'Good heavens,' Helen whispered. John Barclay held up a forestalling hand.

'Watch this,' he said. It was only then that the camera

reached the end of its travel and began to swing to the right again. The girl was coming more into the field of view. The camera swung just enough to pick up where the second one had left off. The small row of prams and two baby buggies stood against the wall.

The girl came sauntering past. Her head turned slightly to the right, and although they couldn't see anything else in the frame, they knew she must have been glancing at the commotion in the centre of the walkway. She slowed, peered, obviously curious, then started walking again. From her gait, it seemed she couldn't make out what the disturbance was and quickly lost interest. A hand went into her pocket, and a small movement brought that side of the coat flapping round in a wrapping curl. David could see the health and confidence in that simple movement. The camera tracked her as it had followed Heather McDougall. The girl came abreast of the small queue of baby carriages. Very briskly, obviously intent on getting where she was going, she strode past them.

'Here,' John Barclay said, quite unnecessarily.

The girl walked three steps, slowed at a fourth, almost stopped on the fifth. Her head went up, showing her full face for the first time. She was pretty and regular-featured.

'Bloody hell,' Helen said. 'That's her.'

'Hold on,' Barclay forestalled again. 'This is the bit.'

The old black pram was right in view. The new arrival was standing just beyond it, maybe three paces past the upraised hood. Her head came up and turned just a fraction to the right. On the grainy screen, it looked as if she was sniffing the air.

Something cold trickled down David Harper's back. A strange and curdling sense of prescience rippled along with it. He knew what was going to happen.

The girl stopped dead. She sniffed again, though they could see nothing but little twitches of her head, blurred on screen. She half turned away from the pram, as if determined to walk away. One foot took a step; the other seemed to be stuck to the floor. Her handbag swung with the momentum and came back to strike against her hip, dangling from the strap. A hand came out of the pocket and reached forward, away from the direction of the pram, as if the girl were trying to push through an invisible barrier, maybe even trying to haul herself away.

She stopped again. Her mouth opened. The three of them could see the black circle. No teeth showed. The girl could have been punched in the belly from the suddenness of the expression, like all the air was whooshing out of her. The mouth opened further, in a strange and tortured gape.

'She's going to be sick,' Helen said.

'No.' John Barclay didn't elaborate. He didn't have to. They were gripped, unable to draw their eyes away. David could feel the prescience building. For some reason he could not explain, completely unnatural, or preternatural, he wanted the girl to keep walking. A sense of chilling menace reached from the black maw of the pram where the hood showed a square of inky darkness. It travelled through time, through the four days since Heather McDougall had died. Travelled through the air fast as light into the camera, through the wires, on to the tape and back into the screen and he could still feel it. Helen was sitting close enough to feel him shiver and wondered what the hell was happening to him.

Move, he heard his inner voice urge. *Walk on, love.*

The girl turned, moving very slowly, for all the world as if the camera had slowed down. John Barclay's hand was nowhere near the controls. There was no sound of course, but David had the impression that if there was, it would be dopplered down to deep clunks and groans like a tape that had slowed almost to a stop. He did not know why that thought came to him, but it came with an inexplicable sense of foreboding.

She swivelled towards the pram though even then they could see the pull of her body trying to move away. Her feet were almost hen-toed in the obvious internal struggle. She leaned forwards, pulled back. Her foot moved again, took a step in its direction. She turned again, her face twisting back towards the light. Her shoulders twitched and the long, elegant coat twitched with it. Off to the left of the screen Carrie McFall, the shoplifter, came briefly into view and disappeared, unaware of the drama happening not twenty yards away, interested only in her new find.

The girl in the coat walked forward, legs moving awkwardly,

like a zombie in a B-movie. It would have been comical under any other circumstances, but none of them felt the humour. Her steps were ungainly, forced, somehow obscene.

'Oh, Jesus,' Helen said, feelingly. It was a strange cliffhanger of a moment for them. Even John Barclay, who had seen the sequence before, seemed to be holding his breath.

On screen the girl reached the pram, body still twisting, all the elegance gone. She seemed to have no control at all now, no volition. It was all in the posture and the motion. A mime artist couldn't have conveyed it better.

She stood stock-still, trembling, both hands visibly fluttering. Then she stooped low over the pram. The black square under the hood darkened further with her shadow. She reached inside. They could see her shoulders working as she manipulated something with her hands. She stood up clutching a baby tight against her, huddled inside her coat.

'Good God,' Helen breathed. 'It *is* her.'

'I could hardly believe it myself,' John Barclay said. He stopped the video, leaving the girl standing there, half turned towards the camera, with the little bundle wrapped in a shawl clutched in against her chest. Her eyes were wide and her face completely devoid of expression, as if all the muscles had sagged. The smile was gone.

'That's Ginny Marsden,' Helen told David. 'I'm sure of it. Her parents said she was coming here anyway. I should have thought of going through these tapes, but it never struck me. Honestly, David, it really is her.'

He was standing, eyes glued to the screen, seemingly unaware that she had spoken. He turned to Barclay. 'Turn it back on, John. Let's see what happens next.'

The camera was moving once again, tracking the motion as if some conscious power were guiding the lenses. The girl turned away from them, heading for the far door beyond the mêlée where the paramedics were just in the picture now, racing for the door.

'You'll have to watch this closely. I can rewind it if you want, but look at the top of the screen.'

David found it hard to take his eyes from the girl. There was something unnatural and dreadfully fearful about her posture.

She had changed utterly from the confident young woman who had come swinging down the main walkway of the mall for last-minute Christmas presents. She had crumpled and altered, in the space of a few seconds, into a flaccid, somehow pathetic figure. David had seen the attitude before; on the shell-shocked victims of Dresden as they stumbled through their smoking streets, shadowy and indistinct in the old newsreels. He'd seen it in the posture and expression of the people in the cattle-trucks on their way to Auschwitz and Birkenau. It was the knowledge of certain, unavoidable catastrophe. A trickle of sweat ran down the side of his ribs.

John pointed a finger. The trolley was moving towards the door. A number of people were coming through and, despite the silence, they reacted to the obvious shout from Phil Coulter. One woman stopped in her tracks. Her husband pulled her to the side by her arm. The trolley stopped rolling. One of the medics had a hand out towards the door.

'Here,' Barclay said.

The dying woman on the gurney sat up, face contorted as badly, as painfully, as the girl's had been. Her mouth opened and closed as though she were gasping for air. Phil Coulter reached a hand out towards her. She twisted, rolled off the trolley and hit the ground. Without any hesitation she was crawling, like a flapping black insect, towards the woman with the baby. On the silent screen, she was a strange and grotesque apparition, moving jerkily on the patterned floor. A small dog tethered nearby strained against its leash, mouth scissoring angrily, even fearfully. The woman scuttled past it, a round, pale breast dragging close to the floor like a monstrous tumour. A girl came walking out of a shop, laden with parcels, unaware of the scene right in front of her. She almost fell over the crawling woman and the parcels went up into the air. The old woman scrabbled past, made it halfway along the walkway. Just on the very edge of the screen, the flapping coat of the girl could be seen. She stopped, turned quickly and came back towards the camera. The old woman stopped, flopped forward with the momentum so that her forehead smacked the floor. Even in the silence it looked like a heavy blow. She rolled over, twitched, and then was still.

'What do you think?' John asked. 'Is this weird or what?'

David stood open-mouthed next to Helen whose expression mirrored his exactly. The girl walked quickly, but still jerkily as if her muscles were responding to mixed-up commands. She clutched the baby in against her coat. The closer she came, the more her face expanded on the screen.

'That's Ginny Marsden,' Helen said. 'I'm sure of it.'

'Who's she?' John Barclay asked.

'She's a girl I've been trying to find. She went missing a couple of days ago.'

'Well, now you know why. She's a bloody baby-snatcher.'

'Look at her face,' David said.

Ginny Marsden's face was contorted in a dreadful grimace. She now looked as if she was struggling with all her strength against an invisible barrier. Her mouth was drawn back into a rictus that showed almost all of her lower teeth. The tendons on her neck stuck out like wires.

'She looks as if she's throwing a fit,' John observed.

The girl walked quickly past, heading out of the camera's range. She got to the corner, turned, and as she did so, the baby's face was just visible, turned in against her coat, clamped to her shoulder and half hidden by the wide lapel. It was just a blur, but David felt something turn over in the pit of his belly.

'Is that a baby or a stuffed toy?' John wanted to know. 'It's an ugly little bugger.'

It was just a glimpse, an indistinct shape on the screen, fuzzed by the distance and motion. But even then, the small and flickering television image was peculiar enough to make them look twice. David asked John to replay it again. They watched it three times, but the image was still blurred, though the details of Ginny Marsden's features were clear, etched with panic and shock. David knew he'd have to take it to the lab for scanning to see if they could get some enhancement that would sharpen the picture.

'I couldn't figure any of this out,' John Barclay said. 'The paramedics were right when they said she'd gone crawling off. I heard the same thing happened when they got her to the hospital. But I can't figure out how come she turns up here with a baby and then it gets picked up by somebody else. I was wondering if maybe they were working as a team? Maybe even using the pram for shoplifting?' He looked at David and Helen. 'That was the first thing I thought of, but then I had another look. I don't think they even knew each other. The way that girl came in through the door, she looked as if she didn't have a care in the world. By the time she went away with the baby, she'd put on ten years. I tell you, that's the weirdest thing I ever saw.'

CHAPTER FOURTEEN

'This should make it easier,' Donal Bulloch said. The CID Chief leaned back in his seat, tall and grey-haired and with the kind of suntan he could only have got from the solarium at his four-day conference. Beside him Scott Cruden looked cadaverishly pale.

'If she's toting a baby around, she'll be easier to find. At least it looks as if foul play is ruled out.' Cruden observed.

'Unless kidnapping's been decriminalized,' Bulloch corrected. Then he gave a smile. 'No, you're right, Scott, we don't know if this is really a snatch. They could have known each other, very likely did. But from what we know so far, this is a very odd case. Two odd cases. I think we'll have to get to the bottom of them.'

He turned to David. 'Mr Hardingwell tells me you went round to see him.' It was both question and a statement. David was perfectly straight in his reply.

'I thought I'd best be informed rather than go into any situation blind.'

'Not like Lamont, then, forgetting to call in for assistance. That could have been dangerous. I expect better of you. Next time, shout for back-up.'

Helen blushed to her roots. 'Sorry, sir, won't happen again.'

The Chief Superintendent nodded, closing the matter. David had shown him all the tapes, in the same sequence as he'd seen them that morning in John Barclay's office, though this time he included the collapse of the woman they'd thought was Thelma Quigley.

'I don't think they were acting together,' David told the senior officers. 'From what Helen got from colleagues and the girl's parents, she had only gone for some Christmas presents. We'll get back to them to try to find a connection, but it doesn't seem likely. It does give us another mystery, and of course we must find the baby, even if it hasn't been reported missing.'

'We've got a start on the girl anyway,' Helen put in. 'When we find the one, we'll turn up the other.'

'What about this other thing?' the Chief butted in. He moved forward and put both hands on his desk. 'You said the McDougall woman's diaries say she had a child before? Some years back?'

'I'm checking that out too. There was evidence of an infant in the house and I've sent a sample to forensics. They should come back later today or tomorrow morning. What I'm concerned about is the history. We know McDougall disappeared. Soon after that, she starts talking about a baby in her diary. Pretty sketchy stuff, and leaving a lot of gaps, but it's pretty definite. Then she brings a baby to the mall and dies. Now this one gets taken.'

He thought before continuing, gauging whether the moment was right, then ploughed ahead. 'But I'm also concerned about the first case. The entries in the diary start just after a baby went missing in Edinburgh. I discovered that when I spoke to McDougall's mother. Her daughter disappeared on the same day as a child was killed, or at least presumed dead, after an accident.'

'I remember that,' Bulloch interrupted. 'In the sixties, wasn't it? Duncryne Bridge, it was. I used to take a stroll up there myself in my younger days. A friend of mine, old Phil Cutcheon, was involved in that. He's retired now. Strange case. The lorry driver did time for it, even though they never found a body. He'd have gone down for the accident anyway, but it was a celebrated case of the day.'

'I was wondering,' David said, 'and I know it's a long shot, whether McDougall developed a habit. I mean, there's a lot of coincidences. She went missing on that day, at the same place, as far as I can make out. Her diaries begin to mention the child. She's been seen by the neighbours pushing a pram, carrying a baby, going back five years or so. Maybe more. There's something not right here.'

'I agree,' Bulloch said. 'Find the girl, and find the child. The pair of you work on this together, but try to hurry it up, all right? Give a bulletin to the patrols for the moment and if you need more manpower, we'll see what we can do.'

In the squad room, David made coffee for each of them. Helen opened her folder and brought out the picture of Ginny Marsden. It was clearly the girl they'd seen come into the mall and lift the baby from the pram. The photograph showed her the way she'd been when she came striding along, coat flapping, past the shop windows: fair haired, on the cusp of a smile and bright intelligence sparkling in her eyes.

'So why would she lift a baby?' David asked. Helen raised her eyebrows and cocked her head to the side in a facial shrug. 'There's something creepy about the whole thing,' he added and Helen could only agree.

'I could see that. She had no such intention when she came in. Then she passed the pram and everything changed. She looked as if she'd taken ill. I thought she was about to collapse.'

'Maybe she heard the baby crying?'

'Possibly, but nobody lifts a baby from a pram just because it's crying. You take your life in your hands doing that. I'm getting some of the shots enhanced. Surveillance have some scanner programme that can improve the definition.'

They got the results of the dried skin back from forensics in the early afternoon while David was reading through the rest of the notes that he'd found in the dead woman's house. Every now and again he'd pause and write something down.

It was no caul. It was skin, but not human. Bill Caldwell in the lab sent down a note to say that it was an integument of some kind, like a sloughed skin, but it was neither human nor any mammal they'd heard of and that meant any mammal at all. He suggested there might be a reptilian connection but could not be sure, and because of that he could give no clue as to the age.

David cast his mind back to the previous day when the thing had tumbled from the shoebox, drifting feather-light and translucent, only to crumple as it hit the floor, as delicate as rice-paper. He had definitely seen a head, and two arms, and a skinny chest. The rent was down the back. It had been no lizard.

But had it really been human? He did not know the answer to that.

Helen called him up to the photographic lab within the hour.

Derek Horner, a small man with thick-lensed glasses, sat at a keyboard in front of a screen. His fingers moved a trackball and he typed in commands every second or so. On the screen, Ginny Marsden turned round in slow, regular jerks as the scanner reeled the tape on. A square zeroed in on her face and shoulders, like the targeting system of a computer game. Almost instantly the picture expanded. It was fuzzed slightly, but Derek said he could clean that up, no problem. He did. The girl's face jumped into clarity, almost face-on to the camera. It was the same as the girl in the photograph, without any shadow of doubt. They could see the curve of the baby's head snuggled in to her chest. It was turned in against the fabric, almost side-on to the lens.

'Can you enhance the kid?' David asked.

'That is it enhanced. I doubt we could do much better. It's a good system here, but it won't do miracles. Forget anything you've seen in *Blade Runner*. That technology's fifty years from now at the very least. I can tickle up some definition, but it's not going to improve much.'

'Why is it out of focus?' David was used to cameras. He'd been using them since he was nine years old, taking pictures of the birds which nested in his garden. At that distance, even allowing for movement, both faces should have been clearly defined.

'Beats me,' Derek told him bluntly. 'Maybe an aberration in the lens. Maybe an odd shadow from somewhere. I can lighten it up a little.' He hit a few more keys and the area around the baby's face visibly brightened in comparison to the rest of the picture. Even then it was still grainy, just a blur, but oddly shaped.

'You sure that's a baby?' Derek wanted to know. On screen the small head looked slightly elongated and the front of the face flattened. The eyes might have been closed but they seemed large, dark shadows on the squashed face. 'It's got a face only a mother could love,' he added.

Helen laughed. 'Takes one to know one.'

Derek printed out a copy of the enhanced image, skilfully adding what approximated to skin tone. Ginny Marsden's face was exceptionally clear, but the baby was still indistinct.

'Looks as if it's melted,' Helen said jokingly. 'We can't use that on a poster.' She held the picture up again when they got back to the office. 'There's something wrong with this,' she finally said. 'It doesn't look right. I know we couldn't see it on screen, but I got a weird feeling when I saw it. I'm getting the same feeling from the picture. It's really creepy.'

David said nothing. His thoughts were occupied with other problems. He'd been back to the notes again, collating his own markings. While the exercise books, mostly tattered and brittle with age, were sketchy and undated, he could work out a sequence. Since the first mention of the baby, the sickly-sweet cooings of a new mother, there had been other entries, sometimes months apart, sometimes a whole raft of them that would continue for a month without missing a day.

They all mentioned the baby. *Baby Grumpling* was the term most often used. Never a first name. She would write down the details of the day, how he needed fed, how he needed changed. And only once, in a book that looked newer than the rest, had Heather McDougall spoken of the poor baby's skin rash, how it needed to be swabbed constantly with baby oil and then how it had peeled off like a sunburn, leaving him all pink and healthy again.

Could that have been the caul? David thought. Not according to Caldwell in the lab. That hadn't been human.

Yet on the same page where she'd marked a note, the woman had written:

I kept it to show him when he grows up. How sick he was. And now he's all better again and hungrier than ever. I think he'll drain me like a prune, God love him.

Ginny Marsden's feet led her west, taking her close to St Enoch's hospital where Heather McDougall had twitched and writhed as she died. It was a long walk, past the museum and the art galleries and across the park where the stream tumbled through the ornamental gardens. Up on the bare branches, a crowd of crows sat hunched and sleepy, silhouetted against the pale sky overhead, winter vultures waiting for the sun. They fluttered uneasily when she was directly beneath, but she never noticed. At this time in the morning traffic was light on the overpass where the bridge soared over the river, mostly trucks and double-trailed rigs hitting the road before the rush. Underneath the span she could feel the ground vibrate with their passing.

Her feet hurried her on, out towards the bus station, and when she reached it she found the waiting room empty but for a slumped drunk in a far corner. She sat patiently, huddled inside her coat, holding her bundle tight, watching the single-deckers come roaring in to collect their early-morning passengers. She had no clear idea in her head until a bus came in and sat shuddering close to the door of the long waiting room. Almost reluctantly she got up, forced the door open and stood beside the bus until the driver noticed her. He gave her a cheery grin, hit the handle and the doors wheezed open on hydraulic hinges. She stumbled on the steps, righted herself, paid with a ten-pound note which caused a delay while the driver rifled his own pockets for change and then went up to the back. The bus moved out ten minutes later, heading west out of the city towards Kirkland which was miles out into the country. There were four other passengers, two of them workmen in dirty donkey jackets, hats pulled down over their eyes as they caught some extra sleep. Nobody bothered to look at her. It was still too early.

Half an hour later, the bus pulled into a town she had passed through before but had never visited. She looked out of the window, aware of the dim reflection of her own face in the dirty glass, and saw the sign boasting Levenford Castle and the double-humped elephant's-back logo of the rock on which the ancient monument stood.

She had no real plan, but somehow, instinctively, she knew she should get off here. The sky was still dark, but there was a small café close to the bus stop where early travellers were queuing for plastic cups of coffee. She got in line, still clutching the baby tight. She found a corner seat. A bulky man in a heavy leather jacket sat opposite her and lit up a cigarette. She did not look at him, even when he tried to strike up a conversation with her.

Ginny felt the baby stir against her and turned away. The coffee was bitter but warm and she sipped it slowly while the infant twisted, trying to get closer to her body heat. She waited in the café until the sky lightened and the day began to brighten. The two women behind the counter who had worked nonstop since she'd arrived kept looking over at her curiously. Finally one of them came over with two cups.

'You look as if you could use another, love,' she said kindly, her wrinkled face in stark contrast to her jet-black hair. She pulled a chair and sat down opposite Ginny. 'New baby, is it?'

Ginny nodded. The infant stirred again. It turned, squirming hard, moving fast. The older woman reached out, pulled the lapel of the coat back, the way women do when taking a peek at a baby.

For a split second, her expression simply sagged as if all the muscles had been cut.

The musky scent came rising up, invisible but thick on the stale, smoky air. The woman blinked twice, as if her eyes were burning and itching. She shook her head just a little, as if she'd been startled, and then the motherly expression came right back into her lived-in face. 'Oh, isn't he gorgeous,' she said.

Her friend behind the counter called over. 'Don't you go giving that baby your cold now, Margaret.'

Margaret coughed, covered her mouth quickly, and gave the girl a big, even smile, showing a wide array of false teeth. 'Had this since October. It'll be the death of me,' she said, reaching into her own purse to bring out a packet of cigarettes and a cheap plastic lighter. 'So will these. Mind if I smoke?'

The girl shook her head absently. Margaret paused, dipped into her purse again and took out a silver coin. She handed it over to the girl, pressing it into her palm. 'Just for the baby's luck, love. Can't let a baby be without a bit of silver.'

'I need somewhere to stay,' the girl said. Her voice was hollow and had a slight but definite tremble. There was something about her eyes that spoke of trouble, but she didn't look to Margaret as if she *was* trouble.

'Got a bit of bother, honey?' she asked, her seamed face crinkling into a mask of concern. Dozens of people passed through the café on winter mornings: office workers heading up to the city; boys with shaven heads coming down for the early sitting of the court, some of them in ill-fitting suits borrowed to make an impression, others beyond caring; farmers down on the Highland train; and road-diggers getting a hot drink inside them before going out in all weathers to earn their bread and early arthritis. But it was unusual to see a young girl with a baby at this time of the day. She had sat for two hours, waiting for the light, avoiding everybody. Of course she was in bother, Margaret could see that, and so close to Christmas too.

The girl said nothing. She was slender and pretty with fair hair that looked as if it could use a brush. Her coat, though, looked well cut and expensive, good and heavy for the weather. Her face was pretty, but her eyes had bags under them, as if she was short on sleep, or maybe in the middle of a heavy period. Her pinched expression spoke eloquently of some sort of distress.

'Is there a place to stay?'

'Sure there is. There's a hostel up the top end of College Street. You just take the first on the left and keep going until you get to the Ship Institute. You can't miss it because there's a big boat up on the wall. The hostel's just across the road from that, and they'll let you stay there until you get fixed up, and they'll help you find a place.'

Margaret pushed the other cup towards the girl, indicating that she should drink. The top of the baby's head was just visible under the lapel and the woman thought it was a damned shame the wee thing didn't have a hat for this weather. Once again she thought the girl must be in some serious bother. She smoked her cigarette while the girl sipped and was about to light up a second when the door swung open, trailing in a billow of cold air, and half a dozen men came in, bricklayers and plasterers from the Castlebank Church renovation, ruddy-faced and stamping their feet as they tried to shed the cold. Margaret went back behind the formica counter to help with the order and soon had the eggs and bacon sizzling on the hot plate. When she'd finished serving the workmen, she looked over to the corner. The girl was gone, leaving her coffee-cup sitting on the table. She hadn't even seen her move. She hoped the hostel had a coal fire going.

Nina Galt, the assistant manager at the hostel, showed her

the small room with its own stove. It had a bed and a square of carpet and a surprisingly pleasant view out of the window across a well-laid little public park where the shrubs were iced with a thin layer of snow. There was no television and no phone. The big armchair sagged in the middle and the stuffing in the arms looked lumpy and old. Nina gave the girl the booklet which listed the social services, the benefits office and anything else a homeless youngster might need. She asked few questions, except for a name and a previous address. As she left the room to go back downstairs to the common area – where indeed there was a big coal fire roaring in the grate – she stopped, about to turn back and tell the girl there were spare bottles and teats for baby feeding, but something stopped her. She continued on her way, wondering how many more youngsters would turn up in the next few days. For some reason there were always more of them at this time of the year: it made her think of Victorian fathers throwing their errant daughters on to the street and telling them never to darken the doorstep again. It was a damned shame, but there was nothing she could do about it. All she could do was get them settled in and give them a roof for as long as they needed.

The next day the girl was gone.

But at night, unknown to anybody, she had gone through the agony again.

Chapter Fifteen

'I found him,' the ancient woman said. 'And he was *mine*.'

Her name was Greta Simon and she sat in the wheelchair in the corner of the room, out of the light. Her hair was grey and thin and she had a shallow indentation, as wide as a tennis ball and maybe half an inch deep, on the side of her temple. It gave her face an asymmetric, somehow slumped appearance. Her left eye, on the same side as the dent, was turned inwards in a violent strabismic squint which made her look both cunning and imbecilic all at the same time.

She grinned widely, showing three teeth on the left side. The gaps gave her an odd, slavering hiss of speech as if she wore ill-fitting dentures. Her hands hugged herself constantly as if making sure she was truly there. 'I loved him and I looked after him all the time,' she said. David had to bend forward to hear. 'Little Tim. *Little Tiny Tim*. He was mine, you know. I had him and I fed him. All the time. He never stopped eating. Brought me out in bruises, he did, but I never minded that.'

She looked up at David Harper, though with her improbable squint, he couldn't be sure exactly what she was looking at. He kept a fix on her right eye to be certain. It looked the most likely.

This was the Greta Simon who had almost been killed by the lorry that day on Duncryne Bridge, the day Heather McDougall had decided to go up the valley to join her dead friend. She was old and frail and wandered, yet there was a strange life in her good eye, a peculiar, almost mischievous and somehow sly intelligence inside that deformed head.

'You can go and see her,' Phil Cutcheon had told him. 'I spoke to her once or twice after the case and she's wandered all right, but there's more to her than you'd think.'

The former detective had poured neat cups of strong coffee in a heated conservatory that let in the weak winter sunshine which, together with the greenery and the winter-flowering blooms, made it feel like a warm day in spring.

'Still miss the job,' he said. 'Miss the cut and thrust. You get used to it, and when you stop, it's as if you've had the feet cut from under you. Mark my words, you've a long way to go, but make sure you've got things to do by the time you're ready to take the pension. I've got my garden and the bowling club, but I miss the thinking, the real concentration.'

He sat back and looked straight at David, much as Greta Simon would do later, though Cutcheon had the direct look that all policemen seem to develop. The power look.

'You've got yourself a mystery, same as I had. And there was an old sergeant back in the forties who had the same thing. It's got me beat and it'll have you beat too, but there's no harm in you ploughing the same furrow. If you turned up something, I'd be glad of it. I always thought that driver should never have gone to jail. Not in a million years. But he had a cretin for a lawyer and there was nothing I could do but report the facts. From the looks of things, he was going too fast, from the skid marks anyway, but I would have said it was a borderline case. As far as the baby was concerned, we spent a lot of man hours looking for it and never turned up anything at all. What got me was that he would have been wrapped in a shawl when he went over the bridge and that never showed up either. You'd have thought it would have got snagged in the bushes or the brambles down on the side of the valley. Take a walk up there and have a look. It hasn't changed in all those years.'

'I already did,' David said. The coffee was strong and thick and he could feel his pulse speed up almost instantly. 'It's pretty steep.'

'Yes. Right down to the Witches' Pots. I used to play there as a boy, you know. Good place to swim, but damned cold, even in the summer. If the baby had fallen in there, it would have drowned or died of cold pretty quickly. But I always had my doubts, because even as a boy I knew that anything that landed in the pool tended to stay there, even when the river was in spate. Devanney, the driver, he was no use. He said the woman came running out into the middle of the road. There might have been somebody else there at the time, but he couldn't be sure and anyway he was in such a state of shock that we couldn't get a word out of him for hours. He worked for Carnwath Hauliers and there was a lot of bad feeling at the time. They were a cowboy outfit and they pushed their drivers too hard. There had been a couple of accidents before this, which was why it was easy to get a conviction, but as I said, it was a borderline case and to tell you the truth, the road up there's quiet enough for anybody to hear a truck coming a mile off. It was as much her fault, in my opinion, as his.'

'So what do you think happened?'

'Christ alone knows. I was never completely sure there was a baby on the bridge, though Greta Simon did have a kid at some stage, at least to look after. There were enough witnesses testifying to that, but nobody knew *whose* baby it was. She was in a coma for weeks and once she came out of it she was as mad as a hatter. She'll still tell you she had a baby boy and half of the time she still thinks she's got one. But it's a mystery all right. Devanney should never have gone to jail on the basis of the evidence. There was no clear proof that the baby was there, despite the wreck of the pram on the road at the bridge. Greta was a bit crazy before the accident anyway. The court decided there must have been a baby and it must have died and that was that. We searched her place from top to bottom and found plenty of new kiddies' clothes and toys, and a cot that had never been used. To me that wasn't conclusive, but I had to go ahead and make my report.'

'That's what we found at Heather McDougall's place.'

'And it stank to high heaven too, as if she'd been keeping cats or some kind of animal. There was a smell that would have burned your eyes out.'

'Snap.'

'We didn't hear about McDougall until the following day, if my memory serves me. To tell you the truth, I never linked the two cases, for there was never any pointers to show she'd gone up to Duncryne. I think maybe it's a coincidence.'

'There's plenty of them, that's for sure. That's why I came to have a chat. Mr Bulloch sends his regards, by the way. He says you and he worked together.'

'More years ago than I care to remember. He's done well for himself, young Bulloch. Got some distance to go too, I believe.'

The big ex-policeman sat back with his coffee, looking over

185

the cup at David, his grey and grizzled eyebrows drawn down. He was tall, but broad enough to disguise his height. He must have been a formidable policeman in his day, David thought. The blue eyes were still clear and bright. They measured everything.

'Anyway, what you've said has got me interested again, though I promised Maisie, that's my wife, that I wouldn't open any more cases. After I left, there were still one or two loose ends to tie up, but after a while you just sit back and let other people get on with it. That's what they're paid for, and the last thing they want is an old has-been breathing down their necks.' He grinned widely. 'But you do need something to keep the brain cells alive, so any help you need, I'm your man.'

'It's the coincidences that puzzle me,' David said. 'From what I understand, we've got two missing babies, yet nobody knows where they came from. If the McDougall woman's diaries are accurate, there's probably more than two. Maybe as many as four, because the diaries span a long time. I can't tell you if these kids were begged, borrowed or stolen, but I do know that Heather McDougall never gave birth.'

'And neither did Greta Simon. When you go down to Blairdyke Hospital they'll tell you that. She'd never had a child of her own, so she was looking after one for somebody else or she'd done some sort of fostering deal that nobody knew about. That used to happen now and again. I went through all the records at the time to find out if maybe a child had been reported missing, but even then that would have been big news. You have to remember, the pressure was on me at the time to clear up the Quigley murder. Back then, a murder took precedence over an accident, no matter how serious, and I was pretty thinly stretched at the time and so were my team. The Quigley case was a mess from start to finish. No matter, though, we did our best to find the baby, but nothing turned up.'

'And you think there was no baby?'

'Oh, there was a baby at some stage. Nobody knew whether it was a boy or a girl. Later on Greta said it was a boy, but by that time she was howling at the moon. There *was* a baby, but I am not convinced it went over the parapet and down the ravine. We would have found something. People said they saw somebody else on the bridge. We never got an identity, but there could have been somebody with Greta Simon. Who knows?'

'Somebody said maybe a fox had taken it. That or a dog.'

'We had tracker dogs all over there. If there was anything to pick up, they'd have found it. All we could do was make a report and the prosecution decided to take it all the way. It was a railroad job, but I'm a policeman, or I used to be. I don't make the rules. There was nothing I could do.' He sat back and steepled his thick fingers together. 'I spent a lot of time thinking about this later, and I can see you'll be doing the same. What I came up with was something I couldn't fathom. It's always been at the back of my mind, but I never really took it further. I think maybe I made a mistake, from what you've told me. I might owe somebody a posthumous apology. Later on, if you want, I can get you more information, but I have to tell you, it's a case of history repeating itself, and that's something I don't like to see.'

'I'm not with you,' David admitted.

'From what you've told me, you've an almost identical case and it's come too close to this old one. Heather McDougall came from here and she disappeared at the same time as the baby. Now there may be a gap of thirty years or so, but it's too weird. You didn't know that Greta Simon herself disappeared as well, way back in the forties, did you?'

David shook his head.

'Well, it's true. She came from somewhere across the other side of the country. Kirkland, Levenford, around that neck of the woods. Back then, during the war, there was a lot of movement, and there was plenty of bombing down there on Clydeside, so people went missing all the time. It wasn't until we really looked into the case that we found her name on the files and in her bag she still had her old wartime identity card. Until then, nobody really knew who she was or where she was from. Now you've got the same thing. Greta Simon, Heather McDougall, and now your Marsden girl. It's a hell of a set of coincidences, isn't it?'

'What do you mean?'

'I'm not the first to come up with the notion that it was all too pat. I heard something like this before, a long time ago, before your time. Before Donal Bulloch's time, in fact, but I never gave it any credence before. Now I wonder if I was wrong. Maybe there's some sort of virus that makes women steal children.'

'I'm still not with you.'

'No. I didn't think you would be,' Phil Cutcheon said, sitting back in his seat and running a hand through his grizzled hair. 'Tell you what. You go down to Blairdyke Hospital. Mike Fitzgibbon, he's the senior man there, I'll give him a call and he'll let you talk to Greta Simon. You can see for yourself what she's like. Once you've done that, come back to me and I'll see what I can do. You've whetted my appetite and there's bugger-all to be done in the greenhouse at this time of the year.'

Dr Fitzgibbon was tall and spare, with receding ginger-coloured hair cut very short and octagonal glasses which gave him a hard and heartless look, but he had a wide and friendly smile which transformed the initial impression. He had narrow shoulders from which a white coat drooped. It flapped behind him as he walked down the straight corridor painted in that shade of green they save for public institutions, as if it's a legal requirement to be as dismal and depressing as possible.

'Old Phil Cutcheon called me,' he said. 'It's a shame he's not still on the force. He knows more psychology than some of the dough-heads and wide boys here. He can spot a faker a mile off. Don't ever tell him a lie or he'll have your guts.'

David promised he wouldn't. Mike Fitzgibbon insisted on using first names and led David to a small, neat office with views over a regimented garden.

'Greta Simon. One of our enduring mysteries is old Greta. I've been here for fifteen years and I still haven't a clue, but you're welcome to talk to her. She can be friendly when she chooses, and then again, she sometimes doesn't say a word for weeks. It depends on the moon or whether it's raining, or if she heard a blackbird after dinner. I know her case bugged the hell out of Superintendent Cutcheon and I can quite understand that.' He crossed to the wall, opened the second drawer of a grey filing cabinet and brought out a thick folder. 'These are just the basics. There's a bundle of case notes going way back, but there's no harm in giving you the brief history.'

188

Mike opened the file and took out a sheaf of official-looking papers. To David they looked very much like police report forms.

'Greta Simon. Presented July 27, 1967 at Blane Hospital, aged approximately sixty. Suffering multiple fractures and a massive depressed fracture of the skull following a road accident. That much you know already.'

'Badly injured?'

'Appalling. She's got twenty pins in her legs. Pelvis was compacted and both knee-joints shattered. The surgeons considered amputation, but because of the head injury they thought she might not survive. It was a miracle that she did.' The doctor went down the list. 'The coma lasted approximately five weeks after which she needed intensive therapy. The damage was to the left side of the head, affecting the temporal lobe. She suffered paralysis of the right side, facial distortion and speech dysfunction, which is quite common in injuries of this nature as well as in stroke and haemorrhage victims.'

Mike looked up. 'Those were the injuries. She didn't talk for six months, maybe seven. But there were other interesting aspects to the case. We had her aged approximately sixty. To all outward appearances, from bone structure and composition, she was that age. It turned out she was nearer fifty, but that's by the way. What did surprise the team at Blane was the fact that she was still lactating.'

'Lactating?' David asked. The word made him sit up straight in his seat.

'Yes. Producing milk.'

'Yeah, I know. I was just surprised.' In fact he could hardly believe what the doctor had said. It was another coincidence. A *huge* coincidence.

Another one was about to fall his way. 'And menstruating,' Mike Fitzgibbon said, reading from the notes. 'Very unusual. Dr Tvedt made particular reference to both. He'd have loved to have done a post-mortem, I can tell from his notes. Just a shame she didn't die.' Mike gave a grin, wide and natural. 'He was an old bugger. Horrible swine of a man. Somebody did a post-mortem on him last year. Liver failure. Too much arm bending. He liked his brandy.'

The young doctor went back to the notes. 'Anyway, she wasn't expected to live, not with her injuries. The worst of all was the skull damage, and naturally there was collateral brain injury. She had three clots under the surface of the cerebrum, one of them quite massive. That's what caused the speech dysfunction, of course, and the lateral paralysis. The neuro team managed to partially raise the depressed fracture to remove some of the pressure on the meninges – that's the membrane covering the brain.'

David nodded. He'd read enough post-mortem reports, or listened to them in murder trials, to have a fair working knowledge of the terminology.

'And on the brain itself. What was remarkable was that the clots dissipated very quickly, without the use of anticoagulant. Normally we'd try to break up a major blockage and hope it dissolves before further damage is caused to the blood supply. Nobody was sure of what caused that spontaneous dissolution, but Tvedt was convinced it had something to do with the presence of unusual antibodies in her blood.'

David raised his head. 'What was unusual about them?'

Mike quickly scanned through the notes, though it was obvious he'd read them a dozen times or more. 'There was quite a range. They couldn't make out whether they were defences against bacteria or viruses, and remember this was back in the sixties. Things have moved on since then. It seemed that she'd been exposed to some infection, some invasion before the accident and her body had either produced antibodies, or these large protein structures had been introduced from the outside.'

'So what were they?'

Mike shrugged. 'Nobody knows.'

'Haven't they been checked recently? You said things have moved on since then.'

'Sure they have. We're mapping the human genome and we've techniques to identify specific antibodies, even down to their protein coats. But that was then and this is now. About six months after she arrived in Blane, there was no sign of them at all. Tvedt had thought there would be a never-ending supply in Greta's bloodstream, but he was wrong. Oh, he should have kept samples, but he didn't, and there was no way his people could induce her to produce the antibodies.'

'What made them disappear?'

'Who knows? Some believe that we've got every antibody to every disease since life crawled out of the swamp, a sort of biological array of defences that are triggered into production to counter every threat. What really kills us is the emergence of new varieties and there's new ones coming along all the time. More and more since man in his wisdom is getting down to serious genetics. Anyway, Greta, it would seem, had produced these complex molecules as a defence, or as an inhibitor. When the threat was gone, her body simply turned off the supply. It's unusual for the human immune system to leave no trace once the defences are switched off, but not impossible. Tvedt just couldn't recreate the conditions because he didn't know what had switched them on in the first place.'

Mike closed the file. 'After about five weeks, she woke, which came as a surprise to everybody, and her injuries started to mend. They did a radio-opaque scan of her brain and found the clotting gone, though there was still scarring at the source of impact. Her speech aphasia was apparent for a year or more, though she hardly talked at all. She had motor dysfunction and severe pedal handicap because of the muscle and bone injury to the pelvic area. Apart from that there was nothing much wrong with her except . . .'

David nodded him on.

'Except the brain damage was not merely confined to motor and speech functions. It left her permanently disabled, and that's why she's here at Blairdyke. She's been variously diagnosed, but in a nutshell, she's got the mental age of a girl of seven. That's just one aspect of the brain injury. From time to time she exhibits varying symptoms of catalepsy, grand and petit mal.'

'She throws fits?'

'As you say. She throws fits.' Mike smiled, but not condescendingly. 'While there is no clinical evidence, either chemical or hormonal, she displays evidence of schizophrenia, which could be attributed to new synapse pathways forming but not connecting properly. She talks to herself. She believes she is possessed. She occasionally believes she has a baby.'

David sat back. Coincidence was piling upon coincidence. 'Does anybody know whether she ever *had* a baby?'

'I'm no pathologist. I'm a psychologist. But no, she never did. Her clinical notes show that she presented with adhesions on both fallopian tubes. One of these turned out to be a tumour which was removed in the early seventies. Initially her ovaries were grossly distended and fully functional. In fact they were unnaturally active, even for a woman half her age. They were producing vast amounts of hormone when she was first admitted and there was some suspicion that this had been caused by damage to the pituitary gland, though there was never any proof. What I'm saying is that she was hormonally fertile, but physically sterile.'

'Was she a virgin?'

'No. But she never had a baby, not one of her own. Shortly after admission, at least within the first six months, the overproduction of progesterone and oestrogen slowed and then failed completely. She entered menopause almost overnight. That possibly didn't help her mental condition, but again, that was before my time. I was still in school.'

'Me too,' David said.

'So what's your interest in our Greta?'

'I don't know,' David said honestly. 'I'm following a list of coincidences that have me beat. There was a similar case to hers in my neck of the woods, somebody who would have interested you, but she died.'

'Phil Cutcheon said you might want to speak to her?'

'Yes. I would,' David said. 'I don't know what I'm looking for, I have to admit, but I'd like to check everything out.'

'You'd make a good doctor,' Mike Fitzgibbon said. He stood up and opened the door. They went back down the dismal green corridor, which echoed like a cave, amplifying their footsteps and making them reverberate in a shadowy back-beat. At the far end, a narrow stairway led down to a lower level where, oddly, the corridor was brighter and the windows let on to a small, neatly tended garden where winter roses sparkled under a sugaring of frost.

Halfway along, Mike opened a white door. He went in first, and beckoned to David to come through. Inside, the spartan room was clean and shaded. A pull-down blind came almost to the sill. For a moment David's eyes were unaccustomed to the shade but there was enough light coming in through the open door for him to see a tiny, emaciated woman sitting in a wheelchair, hugging herself tight. She shivered in a palsied tremor, the kind of motion he'd seen in Heather McDougall's old and ruined father. The eyes at first were just as vacant, focused on the far distance or on the far past.

This woman had lost her mind on the same day that Callum McDougall had lost a daughter. There was a strange symmetry in that.

'Hello, Greta,' Mike said brightly, walking towards the window. He raised the blind, not fully, but enough to let light in so they could both see without straining. A shaft of brightness caught the old woman's eye and David saw a gleam that could have been anger or mischief or complete insanity. She turned her head, still shivering slightly, away from the glare. Her hair was faded and sparse, showing a pale, mottled scalp. She lifted her head. In the silence of that moment, David heard the creak of bone against ligament.

'Shhh,' the woman said, fixing her one good eye on the doctor while the other one glared madly at the wall on the other side. 'You'll wake him.'

'Wake who, Greta?' Mike Fitzgibbon asked, turning towards David, one eyebrow raised.

'You'll wake the baby, doctor. You know he needs all his sleep, poor wee thing. You'll waken him up again and then we'll never get any sleep.'

'What's your baby called, Greta?'

'Tim. You know that. He's Tiny Tim.' She leaned forward and then pushed back, rocking slowly. Her wizened, slumped head seemed to waver and twist in the half-light. It gave her a gnome-like cast, as if her face was trying to change into something else. Despite her frailty, it gave David an eerie shiver.

'I found him, you know.' She leaned back and the chair quivered. 'Before. I found him. He wanted me, you know. He cried to me and I saved him. He needed me and I needed him.'

The old woman jerked in a sudden start, blinking quickly, three times in succession. She turned round, her good eye wide, bewildered, scanning the room. Mike looked at David again. 'This is what to expect. The alterations between her states are inexplicable and very rapid.'

'Where is this place?'

'You're in the hospital, Greta. You know that. And this is David who's come to see you.'

The old fluttery hands rubbed up and down against skinny arms, sliding scratchily over shoulders that were fleshless and bony.

'David,' she said, voice tremulous and weak. 'David. Can you find him? I lost him and I can't find him.' Greta Simon's mouth was twisted to the side and the words were floppy and unfinished. 'She took him. She took my baby and I can't find him any more and he needs me.'

'Who was that?' Mike asked.

'She did. She came and took him. I saw her.' She stiffened and twisted her head, making a circling motion that made her look even more imbecilic. For a moment there was a silence in the room and then the old woman began to hum softly. It was almost inaudible at first, like a vocal shudder, low and quavering. Then it came louder, not quite in time, but not far out. Hmm-hmm. Hum hum. Dee da. *Dee da* . . .

'I left my baby lying here . . .' The words were wet and almost drooling, but comprehensible enough. 'I left my baby lying here and went to gather blueberries.' David recognized the song. His own grandmother had sung it to him when he was a child. The melody had stayed in his head, buried under the games and the growing for twenty years or more. As soon as he heard it, an image of his own mother's face came back to him somehow, not as she was now, robust and motherly, but young and red-haired, the way she must have been when he was too young to notice her own youth.

The plaintive unmelodic tune shivered out between those few stumps of teeth. 'I left my baby lying here.' David recalled the words of the old song. The baby was taken by fairies. They stole babies in the old Gaelic myth. The woman stopped rocking. She stopped singing.

'I left him for a moment. Just a moment, on the bridge. I left him and she came and took him.'

'Who was that?' David asked. Mike Fitzgibbon put his elbows on the table, his chin cupped in his hands.

'*She* did. It made her. I turned round to look at the water and she came and took him out of the pram. I tried to stop her. I knew what she was doing and I had to get him back.'

'And what happened then?'

The old woman's good eye went still, and seemed to fog over. Her brow lifted in an expression of bafflement. Her head twisted to the side, as if listening for something, but the bewildered gaze remained.

'She's got no recollection of the accident,' the doctor said. 'That's normal, of course. Most of her short-term memory is gone anyway. Ten minutes from now, she won't remember who you are. Or me.'

Greta Simon's palsied, slumped face turned down again very slowly and the eye fixed on David again. The fog seemed to clear, as if intelligence of a sort had fled and then returned.

'Where did the baby come from?' David tried a different thrust.

'He's mine,' she hissed. The life came back into her, eerie mischief in the glint of the eye. The twisted pupil caught a shard of light and glittered grotesquely. 'He's mine, Tiny Tim, Little *Tiny* Tim. That's his name, you know. He's so small and perfect and he loves me.'

'Your baby?'

'He loves me and I feed him.' The hands were fluttering back on her thin, fleshless shoulders again, hugging herself tight, as if she held something close to her body. David could imagine a mother clutching a child. 'I found him,' she said. 'He called to me and I took him. Long ago it was.' The glitter shone in her eye and her mouth widened to a grin. 'He called to me and I took him, for he needed me. It was in the trees, beside the water. I saw her fall down and he called to me. You couldn't refuse a baby, could you? No. Not at all.'

'Saw who?' David asked, but she was somewhere else.

She hugged herself tighter. 'You don't know, do you?

Nobody knew. But I could look after him and Tim wanted me. He said, *Take me*. So I took him and he's mine.'

'Who did you take him from?'

'The lady died. She fell down and she died. She made a noise when she hit. It was by the water, where we were picking the flowers for the wine. I couldn't help her, though I tried, you know.' The voice became tremulous here. 'She fell down and the baby called to me and he needed a mother. I look after him and I feed him. He's so hungry all the time. He could suck you to death, but he needs me.'

'And when did this happen, when you found the baby?'

The old woman squinted at David. 'You can't have him. He's my baby. She can't have him neither. Bitch. Wants to steal my Timmy. Wants to take him away and mother him. That's what she wants. But she can't.' Her voice started to rise.

'Nobody wants to take him away,' David said soothingly. What he was hearing was bizarre. He'd hoped for something more from the old woman since Phil Cutcheon had told him she was still alive. He'd only been following his instincts, or at least his curiosity. But Greta Simon was simply wandering. The dent in her skull showed up in the slanted light like a crater on the moon.

Again on instinct, David asked one last question. 'How old are you, Greta?'

'I'm twenty-six.'

David looked at Mike Fitzgibbon. The doctor gave an almost imperceptible nod. 'And what year is it?'

'It's 'forty-one. Middle of May. Don't you know there's a war on, silly?'

She grinned again and for an instant her face took on a sly expression. The twisted eye gleamed. She bent her head and began to hum a tune again, very faintly. She curled her hands and shifted her arms, as if once again she really was cradling a baby.

'Oh, not so hard, Timmy. You'll empty me right out, so you will.'

CHAPTER SIXTEEN

The baby was sucking hard, making small, quite feral grunting sounds. Its fingers were clenched into her skin, gripping hard, causing pain. There was more pain on her breast where it rasped the already abraded skin and she squirmed against it.

Ginny Marsden had gone out into the cold in the early afternoon and spent a few pounds in a charity shop which had baby clothes of all sizes. The assistant watched as she chose a hat and a tiny jumper and an all-in-one little jump suit, each of them in different colours, as if she didn't care how the baby looked. There was an old-fashioned crocheted shawl which she bought. Up at the back of the shop there was a selection of used baby-walkers and buggies. Ginny hesitated for only a moment and chose an old blue pram with high sides and a hood with a plastic weather shield which could be raised and clipped to it. She paid the money and while the assistant was putting it in the till, she turned, put the baby in the pram, jammed the new clothes under the storm-cover and was on her way out. One of the pram's left wheels squeaked.

Back at the small room, she wrapped the baby in the shawl, tucking its thin arms tight, almost unaware of what she was doing. She moved slowly, hesitantly, as if she was recovering from flu, or just drained of energy. She was desperately tired and her vision kept blurring at the edges, as if she was travelling backwards down a tunnel. When she had bundled the small form snugly into the shawl she went to lie on the bed. Her blouse was open to the waist, to allow its small, snub face to press against the heat of her skin. Her skirt was rucked up at the back. All she had taken off were her coat and shoes. She lay down on the cold sheets, holding the baby tight against her while the bed warmed up. Within a few moments, the utter exhaustion overwhelmed her. Her last, vaguely conscious thought was that she must have had a pair of tights on. She couldn't remember where they were.

The darkness enveloped her as soon as her eyes were closed

against the silver line of moonlight that came through the gap in the curtains and in a matter of moments she was sound asleep. As soon as she slept, she tumbled into the black well of a nightmare.

She woke up cold and hungry, stiff and sore, with the baby tugging at her nipple, draining her. The dreams had been so malignant, so terrifying that it was a wonder that she had slept at all.

All through the dark hours, visions and images had beset her. She had dreamed she was being eaten alive by maggots which writhed and pulsed under her skin. She had been unable to move, powerless to act. She could feel her flesh tear and fragment, she could hear the grinding, sucking noises they made when they fed upon her and she realized, in the depths of the nightmare, that she would die.

Ginny awoke with this thought right in the forefront of her mind and she almost screamed aloud.

The baby snuffled again and a shudder rippled through her, an initial quiver of fear and loathing and repugnance every bit as powerful as the dream terror of the night. Then it grunted and the air filled with its scent.

She had been in the act of turning and the grey dome of the thing's head had just been visible in the edge of her peripheral vision, blurred and out of focus down below her chin. In the blink of an eye, it resolved. The lines wavered and rippled, then positively defined themselves into the pink fuzzy curve of the baby's forehead. It turned, still suckling on her, and fixed her with a wide blue eye.

The panic was squashed flat and the surge of the deep imperative to care for this baby swamped her. Yet something, a sense of contact, brushed across her mind with the texture of slub silk, of cold, foetid damp. Once again, deep inside her own mind, that part of her that was unaffected by the monstrous compulsion was bawling insanely in fear and anguish and absolute terror at the imprisonment of her very self and her subjection to the will of this loathsome parasite.

Ginny Marsden tried to move and for a moment found that impossible. Her limbs merely twitched, stiff from the cold of the night and somehow drained of energy. She tried again, succeeded in lifting one hand, one arm, though it felt as if it were made of lead, pulled down by a monstrous gravity. Her skin was numb and underneath it her flesh tingled in pins and needles which instantly recalled the appalling images of the maggots. She shuddered again, swallowing down on thick and hot bile that threatened to surge up from the back of her throat. Her shoulder creaked, sending a seismic jerk through her, while a hot and grinding pain flared there in her joint. She stopped moving instantly, waiting until the pain died away. It took a moment for it to fade down to a hot glow.

Down on her breast the baby was feeding greedily. She felt her skin drawn down into its mouth and sucked and hauled painfully. Her right breast was still rounded and engorged, tender with internal pressure. Soon the baby *the monster* would move and fasten on to the other one and drink its fill. It was getting stronger all the time. Its fingers shifted their grip on the soft skin covering her ribs, pin-points of pressure and hurt. She was powerless to resist.

Down in her belly, the cramps had started, pangs of hunger that told her she had to eat. Using her left arm to lever herself up from the swirl of blankets on the hard little bed, she gained a sitting position, with great difficulty. She felt as if she'd suffered a bad bout of flu and needed weeks to recover her strength. When she swung her legs off the bed, her knees and hips groaned almost aloud. She could feel the edges of bone snarl and grind against each other as if the contacts were all pitted and ragged.

I'm dying.

The thought came unbidden, but it landed with a deadly thud.

She understood the finality of it. Five days ago she had been strong and as carefree as a girl can be at the age of twenty-two. She'd been fit and healthy and she'd been happy. Now she felt used and rotting from the inside. Her whole body ached and her mind reeled. Down on her chest, the baby suckled lustily while she felt as if all the life was being drawn out of her. The hunger pangs twisted again and she made it to the other side of the room, walking slowly, like an old, sick woman. Over in the corner, there was a kind of work surface beside the old cooker where she'd put the purchases of the previous afternoon. She sat slowly down on the hard chair, listening to the creak of muscle and bone, and opened the package of meat she'd bought with Celia's money. She twisted slightly to enable her to use both hands on the plastic wrapping, and freed the raw slices of dark liver.

Without any hesitation she bent forward and bit into it. The meat was soft and spongy, though the surface membrane felt like rubber before her teeth broke through. An instant taste of cold metal flooded her mouth and her gorge reacted instinctively, bucking against the slithery texture and the appalling taste. The strength of the repugnance against eating raw liver was intense enough to make her quiver.

Yet more intense was the compulsion to swallow it quickly. Her hands forced the meat between her teeth and she gobbled quickly. It had the texture of wet and rotting mushrooms in a cold October, and her mouth was clogged with the iron taste of cold blood. It trickled at the back of her throat and slid down. She gagged, swallowed, gagged less, swallowed more. She guzzled the stuff, lobe by lobe, chewing as quickly as she was able, snorting and grunting in the overwhelming need to get the rich meat inside herself. Her hands were sticky and red, but she hardly noticed that. The pound of meat disappeared in minutes and the empty feeling in the pit of her stomach reversed itself to a sudden straining pressure as the heavy liver sat there, so close to her own. A wave of dizziness rippled through her as her body tried to compensate for the sudden distress of distension, but already she was reaching a bloodied hand to the box of eggs on the surface next to the empty liver pack.

She flipped the top, ignoring the sticky mess on her hands. The six eggs nestled in the papier-mâché hollows. Without hesitation she lifted one. It slipped from her fingers, almost toppling from the box, but she grabbed it again and once more, in a completely natural motion, she brought it to her mouth.

Revulsion lurched and her whole being shied away from the thought of what she was doing. Yet she still opened her mouth and thrust the egg inside. Her teeth came down on the shell and bit through. The yolk burst, raw and slick, and slid over her tongue and down her throat along with the ropy trail of albumen. The glutinous, flowery taste filled her, but she continued biting down on the shell. It crackled then crunched like grit. She chomped hard, grinding the eggshell into smaller pieces. They mixed with the remains of the egg yolk and she swallowed them all. The shards of shell scraped against her throat, but she ignored the rasp of their passage. Already she was reaching for the next one.

A few minutes later, gasping for breath and her belly distended so tightly it caused a pain to rival the ache in her joints, she finished the six eggs. She waited for a while before she opened the carton of full-cream milk and drank it as greedily as the baby drank her own. The sharp edges of the shells had cut her gums and the warm taste of her own blood mingled with the milk.

Ginny Marsden was no longer hungry. She stood up slowly, feeling the pressure of the added weight of the meal she had consumed, and ran some water from the tap. She held both hands under the cold flow, watching the water turn pink from the residue of the liver on her fingers. Small pieces of the meat, red as jelly and with a similar texture, dropped into the metal sink and swirled down the drainhole. She dried her hands on a dishtowel that bore a mitre-shaped burn from a careless iron, alternately freeing one hand from its grip on the baby's back. As soon as she was dry, it drew away from her nipple. Ginny looked down and saw the teat, raw and abraded, still standing proud of her breast. The baby snuggled closer against her skin and closed its eyes. She heard the contented breathing of a well-fed child. Her breast seemed still full and inflated, but where it swelled just below the curve of her neck and close to her armpit, she could make out the fine tracery of small wrinkles.

Her tangled mind tried to fix on the filigree lacework where the elasticity seemed to have leeched out of her own skin, but it was difficult to force her mind to make the effort. Even as she looked down, she experienced a powerful craving to chew on chalk or iron rust, and overlying that was the urgent compulsion to hold the baby close to protect it from the cold.

She turned away from the sink where the tap was still dripping like an echoing metronome and passed the mirror on the wall. In that moment, she saw a grey and ridged thing, arms and legs splayed out like a frog, wrapping themselves to clutch on to her skin. Its head was elongated as was its narrow, slat-ribbed back, and the limbs were long and thin and sinuous. It twisted in her arms, sensing her distress. The image in the mirror wavered and blurred again, even as her eyes sparked with tears of anguish and fear, and in that split second it was a baby once more and the overwhelming need to mother the thing came rushing so powerfully that it made her feel she might faint.

Yet in the far depths of her mind she knew who she was and knew it for what it was and she screamed and screamed and screamed in silent terror. She could still make no sound.

Ginny slowly passed the reflection of the pink baby snuggled in against her. Her blouse, now five days unwashed and grey at the collar, was opened right down the front and her breasts protruded, from the gap. They were thick and rubbery, dotted with the patchwork of haematoma bruising, like purple explosions, where it had sucked hard enough to draw a trace of blood through her pores. The breasts themselves were rounded and turgid, twice the pert size they had been only days ago, before the baby had started to change her.

She raised her eyes to her own face and almost reeled back in dull shock. Her blonde hair was streaked with grey close to the roots and the wrinkles on the skin of her body were mirrored red here, in crow's feet on the sides of her eyes, in the fissures spreading upwards from her lips.

Oh Jesus help me I'm growing old.

Heavy bags puffed under her eyes, almost as dark as the bruising on her breasts, and the whites of her eyes were no longer clear and pure. Now they were ringed with a nicotine shade of yellow, as if there were some sluggish poison accumulating in her blood. Less than a week ago, she'd been vainly and justly proud of her high cheekbones, inherited from her mother, which gave her classy hollows that needed no make-up to accentuate. Now they were pits sunk into the sides of her face. They held shadows of their own and her cheekbones stood out in ridges. She was gaunt and emaciated. If anybody who had known the woman who called herself Thelma Quigley had seen

Ginny Marsden at that point they would have thought both women had suffered from the same wasting disease. Ginny saw herself look back, and the dawning realization of the enormity of her disintegration was evident in her own blank stare.

I'm dying.

It was a reality, not merely a notion. She could see it for herself. At the age of twenty-two, she had aged so much – in less than a week – that she looked forty or more. She lay on the bed, very slowly, careful not to disturb its sleep. The squashed-down part of her mind had managed to push open the barrier and was fighting to be free. She tried to calm herself, aware that panic would rouse the thing's senses. Even at that moment her own will was battling the compulsion it forced upon her, but she fought the fear down, making herself be calm.

A thought had formed.

She moved again, pushing very gently at the baby, trying to keep her breathing slow and even, listening to the purr of its own respiration. It sounded just like a tiny baby. Very slowly, despite the grind inside her, she pushed its little hands off her skin, holding her own hand against its back to maintain the pressure contact. It made a little shiver and snuggled against her, letting her turn it slightly. Its legs were now drawn up and crossed over each other. With infinite care, she got the sheet off the bed and began to wrap the baby. She held it close, keeping up the pressure so that it would never know it was being moved. Finally it was cocooned in the sheet, though still held tight against her own body. Its breathing was deep and even.

Outside, a sussuration of ice crystals scraped against the window, reminding her it was still winter. Inside herself she felt as if winter had settled for ever. An icy fear was creeping through her as her mind tried to free itself of the monstrous imprisonment.

Still moving almost imperceptibly, she drew both pillows down from the top of the bed and pressed them firmly against the sheet, piling one atop the other. Only then, when the baby was under the new weight, did she move, drawing herself back out of the bed, moving with glacial slowness. It took an age. At one stage the bed creaked with the motion and the baby made a grunting sound, high and feral. Its head turned, as if its mouth were seeking the nipple again. She put her hand on top of the pillows and pressed down, her own heart speeding up and her mind willing it to slow down. The grunt turned into another snuffle. The head turned back down again.

Ginny Marsden waited a full ten minutes before she eased herself off the bed and, with delicate and deliberate care, stood up. Walking barefoot, ignoring the squeal of protest in the bones of her ankles and the sudden need to cough, she made it to the door.

For the first time in five days, she was more than three yards from the thing that had ensnared her in the mall. From that distance, its influence was fading.

Move now. Go on. Get out. Her own mind, now struggling to break completely free, shrieked urgent and panicked commands. *Go.*

And underneath that, she wanted to turn round and strangle the thing. To batter its head against the solid edge of the basin until its brains burst like the lobes of liver she had gorged. To drown it in the cold water until its unearthly heart stopped beating. The part of her that was completely her own self wanted to destroy it utterly, wreak an enormous revenge on the thing that had fed on her until her skin wrinkled and stolen the life out of her.

Yet, despite its slackening influence, she still had to fight every inch of the way. From the distance of three yards, it was still a baby, though the lines were blurring sickly in a sort of double-exposure effect. The colour was running. She turned round, even as she forced her right foot into her shoe, which she had left by the door, and she could see its head, barely visible against the swaddling of the sheet. It was rippling and pulsing as if the skin itself were melting under the flare of internal heat.

Go. Get gone! her mind squalled desperately. *Run.*

It was now or never. She forced her other foot into the shoe, not waiting, not daring to unlace them. Her heel wriggled hurriedly and bent the back leather edge inwards with the pressure and haste.

Hurry hurry hurry.

The panic was beginning to well up in a dark tide. The thing on the bed was wavering and changing. Its breathing, at first slow and deep, was now beginning to quicken. She sensed its uncanny senses picking up the wrongness of its situation. Any second now it would awaken, and when it woke, it would pull her back, it would make her . . .

She got the shoe on, reached for her coat. The tab caught on the curved hook of the stand, making it wobble. It swung forward then back, clunked against the wall. In the bed the thin, ridged thing, now no longer pink at all, but a mottled, somehow shiny grey, snorted gutturally.

Oh please don't let it . . . don't let it . . .

The coat came free. With her left hand she reached towards the doorhandle. It was cold and smooth under her fingers but the contact sent a jar of pain through her knuckles and elbows. It felt as if her bones were fragmenting and turning to chalk. The handle turned smoothly, without a sound. She pulled, sensed a muscle twist in her shoulder, a small flare of heat. The door refused to open.

Oh God let me out of here.

For a second she was completely bewildered. Her panicked mind could not comprehend the door's reluctance.

The key the bloody key turn it you stupid bitch.

Her hand jerked off the handle. There was a blue plastic tab hanging from the key in the lock. She snapped it quickly in a counter-clockwise twist. The bolt shot back with a solid thump of brass on steel.

The thing growled behind her. Ginny had never heard a stoat in a hole before but that's exactly the kind of sound she would have expected a small, fierce predator to make. Her heart catapulted into her tight throat and pulsed so hard her breathing stopped.

Oh Jesus please . . .

Another sound behind her. The mortise bolt shot back, snapping hard. She reached for the handle and gave it the same twist as before. Behind her something rustled. Instantly every nerve in her body started to shiver. A cold slither dragged across the surface of her mind, not yet focused, just a dull and mindless questing. She pulled the door, trying to make it open quickly, but by now everything was going in slow time as if all her reactions had been frozen to a wintry slowness. It was like wading through glue.

The door creaked loudly, like a branch rending in a high wind, like a plank of wood torquing under pressure. The sound cut into the sudden silence in a jet shriek.

From ten feet behind her, another shriek erupted, though whether it was a true sound Ginny never knew. The rustling noise came again and all the hairs on the back of her head crawled in unison.

It's awake oh it's coming.

She half turned. Inside her head the shriek was going on and on, like a pig in a slaughterhouse. She saw it wriggling in the sheet. Her heart kicked madly. Her mouth opened and she tried to turn away. Despite the shriek inside her head, there was an audible creak and the thing's eyes opened wide, like the aperture of a camera, a sudden blare, a sudden glare. It lanced across the distance and transfixed her.

She was paralysed with fright.

It wriggled frantically, trying to free itself from the swaddling. Ginny stood trembling, coat draped round her, legs braced apart, one hand on the door handle. A shard of blackness showed the door was open six inches, hardly more. Her free hand was a pale bird, fluttering in the air. Her hair, lank and lifeless, was swishing across her shoulder from the motion of turning her head.

The creature growled. Its eyes were wide as saucers, picking up the faint light from outside.

Vampire.

The thought came crystal-clear and cold as ice. The eyes had the red glare of every vampire she'd seen in the cinema, every one she'd ever read about or imagined. But this was no handsome European who would bend to drink the blood of beautiful women. This was a monster, a mindworm who sucked and probed and controlled. In five days it had drained the life out of her and it still wanted more.

It was awake now and it was coming for her. She could see the frantic writhing, feel its dreadful mental blast, its awesome demand for sustenance and mothering. She could also feel the heat of its anger, alien and malignant and utterly, completely ferocious.

She managed to turn her head away. She pushed the door open wider. Down there, down the stairs, she could hear the early-morning stirrings of the hostel, the clatter of pots down in the kitchen. Low early-morning voices. The normalcy of muffled human conversation hit her so powerfully that a sudden desperation welled inside her. She needed them. She needed to get down to the kitchen and warn them of the danger.

The thing snarled inside her head, its inarticulate demands mental claws rending at the substance of her own thoughts. The taste of blood was sour in her mouth.

Downstairs somebody sang a few lines of a song, a warm, woman's voice. It drew her like a magnet. On the bed, the thing tried to hook her like prey, like so much meat on a butcher's slab.

Ginny pushed her way through the door, desperately resisting the compulsion to turn. It was hauling at her. Her hips ground painfully as she took a step. Inside her the liver and the eggs pressed against her abdomen. She wanted to vomit.

Something thumped on the floor and she couldn't help but turn. It all happened so quickly. She was still walking away, aware of the danger, terrified of being caught, needing to get to the other humans and warn them, get to the comfort of their safety. Something thumped on the floor and she turned. It had fallen off the bed. The sheet had half unravelled.

Go, get out of here.

The door swung back and hit the wall.

'You've woken them up with your singing,' a woman's voice came floating up. Another woman laughed infectiously.

'Free bed, board and entertainment, what more could they want?' The second voice chuckled.

'Help,' Ginny tried to respond. Her mouth opened and a small rasp of noise came out that sounded as much animal as the grunting little thing that twisted and humped on the threadbare carpet.

She reached the top of the stairs, forced herself forward, stretching the invisible bonds, feeling them weaken.

'Do you want a cup of tea before we get started?' somebody

asked. The image of a cup of steaming brew flashed in her mind in an astonishingly powerful picture. Tea and sympathy. Tea and comfort and company and protection. They would protect her, surely, her fellow women. They would hold her and mother her.

'Sure. Tea and a cigarette before the day starts. Best way to get the engine running.' Another woman's voice, gruff, rough and ready, full of humour. She laughed again, a smoker's laugh, the laugh of a woman content with her lot. It tugged powerfully at Ginny Marsden who stood poised on the top step, slim and tall, a ghost of a woman, now gaunt and decaying in the shadows. She hovered there, forcing her foot down, working against the pain and the fear and the sudden exhaustion, her hand grasping the cold wood of the banister, gripping it as tightly as she could. She felt herself sway, managed another step, then another, down to the landing. Six tortuous steps in all. Ginny got to the level, turned, sensing the distance weakening the mental compulsion the thing radiated. Knowing she could make it if she tried.

Something clattered upstairs in the room.

Should have shut the door!

The realization hit her like a physical blow. She should have closed the door and locked it from the other side. How could she have forgotten? She could have locked the thing inside the room and it could never have got out. Ginny froze for an instant. She could still go back. She turned, once again feeling as if she was wading in syrup, and looked at the mountain of stairs she had to climb.

Five days ago she would have bounded up there, taken them two at a time, three at a time; skipped up without losing her breath. Now the climb stretched ahead of her, a range of Himalayan proportions. It had taken all of her strength to get down them. Did she have a chance of scaling those heights?

It was six steps. It was a hundred miles. It was only six steps.

She had her mind back again, most of it, the part that wasn't shivering and trembling in abject fear.

It could still get to her. If it freed itself from the wrapping of the sheets it could get her. She had seen it scuttle in the dark of the garden hut, had seen it slither out of reach in the shadows when the cat came in through the flap on the door. She knew it could move quickly, like a spider in the night. Even in her memory, it had that odd double image, a plump and pink baby skin grafted over something so alien it was madness in motion. If it reached the door, it would come clambering along the floor and it would reel her in like an exhausted, dying fish. It would have her again. And if it got her she would die.

Ginny Marsden took the most courageous decision of her entire life.

Down in the kitchen, a woman had started to sing again in a rough but melodic voice. A steam kettle's whistle began to quaver and sing along. The sounds pulled at the very fabric of her being. She turned though, forcing them out of her mind, aware only of the need to close the door on the little monster.

She began to clamber back up the stairs.

CHAPTER SEVENTEEN

'Sure I saw her,' the woman said, holding the picture tilted to catch the light from the faintly flickering fluorescent bar overhead. Her eyebrows, carefully pencilled, arched in twin proud curves, matching her jet-black hair. Her eyes narrowed as she remembered, accentuating the wrinkles around them. She had a kindly, lived-in sort of face.

She turned round to call to the other woman in the steamy space behind the laminated counter where the sausages were sizzling on the flat skillet. 'You remember the girl with the baby, Maisie?'

'The one who sat all morning yesterday, Margaret?'

'Yes. That's her. This is her picture, isn't it?'

The other woman came across, her hair that faded dyed red of an old women who remembers her bright young days. She walked with a waddling gait, her centre of gravity dropped and getting lower all the time.

'Aye, that's the one. Poor soul looked half starved and half frozen. And scared half to death. I thought maybe there was somebody looking for her, or she was hiding from somebody. She never said, though.'

David had gone east, following up some other lead and had left Helen to carry on her own search. It took her two hours to find which bus Ginny Marsden had caught the day before. Two patrolmen thought they had seen a girl with a baby heading for the bus station close to St Enoch's, not far from the Waterside Mall. That had been in the early hours of the morning. Acting on a hunch, working patiently and taking the time to ask questions, she found a bus driver who said he thought he'd seen her sitting in the waiting room of the terminus. She pushed him a little harder, trying to find out which side of the room. It was a long, narrow corridor of a place, with several doors. The position where somebody sat might give a clue as to the direction a person was travelling. The four doors, north south, east and west, in actuality corresponded with the directions the main-route buses would take from the centre of the city. Ginny Marsden had been sitting close to the westbound door, if indeed it had been Ginny Marsden. It was still all surmise, possibility rather than probability.

Another stroke of luck found her the bus crew, now just going off shift. John Skelly, the driver, a beefy man with mutton-chop sideburns, recalled the girl.

'Just about fell upstairs. I thought she was drunk at first, but she was all right. Maybe just stiff with the cold. She gave me a tenner, which I wasn't going to take – you're supposed to give the right money, know what I mean? But what the hell, she was just a young lassie, far as I remember. I've a daughter who's older than her and I wouldn't like to see her out on the streets in the middle of winter, not with a baby. I'd smack her ear if she ever came home with one right enough, but I wouldn't like to see her out in the dark at this time of the year.'

Helen led him back on to the track, thinking for an instant that he'd sidetracked himself the way David Harper was prone to do. She suppressed a smile. She couldn't see David Harper driving a bus.

'Anyway, she went up the back. There were two workmen, regulars, who were already there. They get the bus every morning, but you'll have to get up early if you want to speak to them. I wouldn't bother, for they sleep from here to Kirkland and only wake when I'm turning the bus outside the hospital. So she was up the back. Skinny thing. Looked as if she needed a good feed, big bags under her eyes. I thought she was older at first, but maybe she just had the flu. Oh, and what's more, she could have done with a good wash an' all. You don't often get a girl smelling like that, but she was pretty ripe, I can tell you.'

Helen's ears metaphorically cocked up. 'She smelled?'

'Like a house full of cats. I should know. My auntie, she's a bit wandered, she takes in every stray. The smell up in her place would choke a horse, swear to God. Well, this lassie, she was pretty powerful. I thought maybe it was the baby, maybe she hadn't changed it for a while, for it was rank. Like shite and vomit and cat's piss all mixed in, pardon the lingo. Maybe she had some sort of disease. Maybe it wasn't the flu after all.'

Helen thought that Ginny Marsden, if it really had been her, might have some sort of disease, but not a physical one. Anybody who stole a baby had to be sick in the head.

'No. Tell you what. My uncle Jim, he had emphysema and his leg got gangrene. At the end of the day they had to cut it off at the knee, but it just got worse. The smell of that would have knocked you down for a mandatory eight-count. That's what she smelled like.'

'And where did she get off?' Helen wanted to know.

'Levenford. Just at the junction of River Street and Kirk Street. It was still dark and pretty damned cold. Soon as the door opened, there was snow blowing in. I wouldn't like my girl to be out on her own in that, baby or no baby. It was a damned shame. She just looked like a poor soul. I nearly never bothered taking her money, but if the inspector catches you doing that, then you get your jotters, the sack, the old tin tack and no appeal. They've got hearts of pure stone, so they have.'

Helen Lamont knew inspectors just like that, though not on the buses. She thanked John Skelly, appreciating his honesty and his ineffable cheeriness, and went out of the station. She called David Harper on the mobile, got a busy signal, and decided to head down on her own. She wanted to have something more positive to tell him.

The drive to Levenford – fifteen miles, maybe a little more, west of the city – took nearly half an hour. It was mid afternoon when she turned at Roundriding Road, vaguely aware of having heard the quaint name before, wondering if someone she knew lived here. She drove down towards the centre of the town past the old Burgh Hall that stood bare and weathered in the shadow of the great square red-brick bulk of Castlebank Distillery. A memory tugged at Helen as she went past the squat building. There had been something here, an incident a year or two past. She screwed her eyes up in concentration as she drove past the edge of the building, and saw the looming double hump of the old castle rock down on the mouth of the river.

Levenford. Things had happened here, she recalled. Some crazy killer had stalked the streets in a winter as bitter as this, picking off kids at first. She remembered the stories in the papers at the time, the bulletins on the six-o'clock news. The madman had left a girl hanging from the tall, slender steeple Helen was driving past. She shuddered at the thought of the brazen arrogance, the madness that would lead someone to snatch and kill a young girl and leave her dangling from the weathervane like a trophy.

The distillery building drew her eyes. There had been something there too, had there not? She couldn't remember, but she was glad she was not hunting a madman today. Maybe a crazy girl on a hormonal helter-skelter, but not a killer.

Ginny Marsden was somewhere here, Helen told herself. She had a hunch that she had come here and stopped a while. This old, narrow-streeted town was a place where you could come and find some peace while the chase went rumbling past. Helen parked her car down by the river and walked up an alley of foot-smoothed cobblestones, under the arch of a tunnel-pend that led beneath an old and crumbling building. As she walked underneath, into the darkness away from the weak light of a winter-morning sun, she shivered again, and not with cold. Something had happened here. Helen did not know how she knew, or why. All she got was a tickle that itched at the back of her head, and she wanted to be away from that place. She walked quickly to get to the daylight at the far side out on River Street where the feeling of sudden oppression faded. She told herself not to be a fool. Yet the feeling had been real.

The café next to the bus stop at the end of Kirk Street was quiet when she got there. Margaret and Maisie were grateful for something interesting to happen. They brought Helen a steaming mug of tea, big enough to take almost a pint of strong brew, and a fried-egg sandwich, done just enough to let the yolk burst thick and wet. Both went down just a treat. Helen Lamont knew nothing about Ginny Marsden's recent meal.

'You look as if you could use another one, love,' Margaret said kindly. She pulled a chair and sat down. 'This girl, what's she done?'

'She's gone missing,' Helen said, giving nothing away. 'Her parents are very worried.' She was really amazed that she had actually traced Ginny Marsden's movements so easily. If it hadn't been for the sheer luck of the two patrolmen remembering her, she could still be knocking on doors round the city.

'So they should be worried,' Maisie said. 'There wasn't a pick of meat on the girl's bones. Margaret tried to get her to eat something, but all she would take was a coffee and even then it was hard enough for her to drink that. You'd have thought it was poisoned. She was just a poor soul. Is her boyfriend after her, or did her family throw her out?'

'Nothing like that. I have to find her though.'

'Well, you should try the hostel opposite the Ship Institute,' Margaret chipped in. 'She was asking for someplace to stay and that's the only place I could think of. They take in the homeless there. Big Nina Galt, she helps run the place for the Institute. She's a cousin of mine on my mother's side. Anyway, the girl was looking for a room for the night, maybe longer, I don't know. I told her to go round to see Nina. I think she must have, because we got busy with a crowd of folk off the bus and heading for Creggan. By the time I served them their food and looked back, she and the baby were gone.'

'Did you see the baby?'

'Just a snatch. You know what it's like. You can't resist having a look. She was holding it tight, and I remember thinking the wee one should have a hat at this time of the year. Any time of the year come to that. But she was hugging it in under her coat. I pulled it back to have a look and the girl, kind of, what's the word, jerked back. Like, flinched. I just got a peek at the baby and for a minute I thought it was deformed, honest to God. I felt my coffee and bacon coming right back up again, it was that bad.'

'What do you mean?'

'Och, the old biddy, she needs glasses,' Maisie interjected. 'She wouldn't recognize her sister from across the street.'

'Nothing wrong with my eyes,' Margaret countered. The black eyebrows rose up in tandem arches. 'No, when I looked at the baby, its head looked all wrong. I thought it was a doll at first and that maybe somebody had squashed its head. But it moved and I knew it wasn't a doll. For a minute it was like, like . . .' Margaret searched for the words. 'Like all out of shape, and a funny colour. But it must have been a trick of the light, because I coughed or something and my eyes watered and when I blinked them clear, it was fine, a lovely wee thing. I could have cuddled it to death.'

Helen felt a strange, unexpected shiver run through her. She'd heard those words before.

'It really was a bonny wee thing. I only got a glimpse, but I could see it was lovely. It was looking at me with a big blue eye, blue as the sea. Goodness, that's like a poem, isn't it?' She smiled widely, showing her impressive array of false teeth.

'It made that sound new babies make, kind of shivery, just a wee whimper, and it brought it all back to me what mine were like when they were just born.'

'And that wasn't yesterday,' Maisie interrupted. 'Her eldest's thirty-eight and the way *her* daughter's going, Margaret here's going to be a great-granny any year now.'

'Och, hold your wheesht,' Margaret scolded, but gently. 'Anyway, it smelled just like a new baby, you know that hot-milk smell?'

'Did you notice any other smell?' Helen asked.

'Oh, at first I thought the girl needed a good bath,' Margaret said, wrinkling her nose. 'When I came across to her at first, it was like those tinkers down on the West Mains by the shoreline, dirty beggars. Some of them stink to the high heavens, so they do. Well, at first, I thought she smelled like that, but I must have been wrong. All I could smell was the baby, and you know, I just wanted to pick him up and cuddle him. I really took a notion then. Imagine it, me at my age, thinking about having a baby.'

'It would be a bloody miracle, wouldn't it?' Maisie snorted, and both women burst into laughter.

'And not just for me,' Margaret said. 'I think my Billy's forgotten how it's done.'

He screamed.

She had abandoned him. The realization triggered an uncontrollable fury and panic. He had fed, guzzling on the milk and the thick proteins the mother's changing body had manufactured for him, feeling his new strength swell. Already the skin on his back was tight, shiny with pressure, aching with the need to slough. He was changing again and this was different from those other times. The change was imminent and it was immense. He could sense it with every cell of his body.

He was becoming something *other*. He had not the words or the capacity to understand what.

The past few sleeps had not been easy. He had dreamed again, dreamed of dark and shadowed places, of the long and arduous pain of birth, recalled and echoed in a strange and fearful replay, as if all of his being was resonating with his own long history. He dreamed of hunger and thirst and the overwhelming need now building up inside him, a bewildering, confusing want that felt like another hunger but was something more powerful.

It was the change he could recognize, rushing in on him.

And now she had abandoned him. She had waited until he had slept, stupefied by the feast and the lethargic torpor the changes wrought. She had bound him in the swaddling. He wriggled and fought against the sheets, feeling the fabric rasp against his drying, peeling skin. He kicked and pushed, rolling this way and that. He screamed all the while, sending his mental blast out so loud it rattled the windows and shivered on the floorboards.

He knew she could hear him because the reaction inside her flared in his senses, like a beacon of pulsing light throbbing hard on the forefront of his mind. He located her and demanded that she return. She shivered and her own mind shrieked in awful sympathy with her fear, deliberately defying him as she had resisted him before.

This one was different. The others had been cattle: complacent, contented, bovine. They had taken him and given themselves to him even as he drained them of their substance.

But this one was different. He had chosen too quickly, seizing the opportunity in the midst of his own panicked vulnerability, and he had chosen wrongly. He could not completely dominate her. She would not subjugate herself to him.

She was not a proper *mother*.

Even then he could sense her disintegration. He was leeching her away, sucking her dry, and that too was new. A mother lasted longer than this, so long that time meant nothing at all. He would feed and sleep, feed and sleep and finally when a mother wore dry, he would chose another. This was different, because his needs were different, hotter and more urgent. He

216

could feel the change in his own needs and in the feeding. He was taking not just what she could produce for him, what his own cells, speeding round in her bloodstream, commanded her body to manufacture. His new growth was able to probe into the veins inside her and drain directly, absorbing the elements, the nutrients, the building blocks his rapidly altering state demanded.

Yet she tried to defy him, tried to deny him, and that was new. Now she had bound him in the cocoon of fabric. She had tricked him; marooned him while she escaped.

Awesome anger bubbled up inside him. This had *never* happened before. His mind shrieked in fear and hate and he sensed her falter. He probed instinctively at the fractures within her mind where he could manipulate the responses.

She fought desperately against his touch and he snarled, still frantically wriggling to free himself from the sheet. He worked his head out and rolled to the left, swivelling like a caterpillar weaving its own cocoon. He rolled too far and fell off the edge of the bed. He hit the floor with a solid thump. A sensation akin to pain lanced across his back where the skin was thin and tender. Something tore and the urgency welled up from deep inside him, hot and corrosive as acid.

Down below, beyond the door and down the stairs, he heard the caterwauling of another female, cacophonous in his consciousness. For an instant he debated sending a call in that direction, then he realized, again instinctively, that she was too old to be of any but momentary use. The older ones were harder to control because of their own changes. He screeched again, drilling the mother with the awl of his imperative need. She paused on the steps, almost drew back, then moved further away. He commanded desperately, felt another hesitation, another refusal, a mental protest made in abject fear. She took another step, another. He could feel the vibrations through the floor, seismic ripples picked up by the supersense he possessed. She was getting further away and he knew his influence was waning with the distance. He put out conscious tendrils of thought to the rooms above and below, seeking contact, trying to find another human it could latch on to.

Behind the wall, a hibernating mouse woke up, screeched

and died. The dendrites of its brain sparked and jittered, shattering themselves in the sudden blast of energy. Under the eaves, two roosting starlings fell from their perch and hit the frosted flagstones with muffled thumps. Their eyes leaked out on to the ice. A cat prowling at the kitchen door, looking for scraps, turned tail, yowled a strange sound that was like fingernails scraping down a blackboard, ran out of the narrow alley and under the wheels of the very bus that Ginny Marsden had taken from the city down to Levenford. It made a greasy smear two yards long on the road.

Out in the back yard, a pit bull terrier, the property of Nina Galt's ne'er-do-well brother-in-law Campbell (whose son had once faced something even more preposterous and terrifying than the thing which shrieked after Ginny Marsden, and survived that dreadful contact), suddenly went berserk and attacked the stout door of the old brick outhouse where Campbell Galt kept it out of sight of prying eyes. He had trained it for a major fight set for after the New Year, forcing the wide-jawed, manic beast to bite on an old bath towel and then dangling it from a third-floor window for hours at a time until its facial muscles were so strong and distorted that the dog looked like a grotesque gargoyle. Now those jaws attacked the wooden door, twenty-five yards from the hostel, down an alley which could only be approached from River Street. Nobody noticed until it had gnawed its way halfway through the door, its face a bloodied mess, spiked with wooden skelfs and splinters, its mind completely gone. Campbell Galt killed it with a single, catastrophic blow of a garden spade the following night.

The mother hesitated no more, despite the fearsome command the thing radiated as it writhed on the floor. She was getting beyond his range. He panicked, rolling this way and that, the strange circular mouth rolling back from the almost perfect sphere of tiny, glass-shard teeth. Its mottled face twisted; under the wrinkled lid of a protuberant eye, the skin tore in a series of jagged rips, exposing a purplish underskin that looked as if it were filled with exotic poison. Every gland under his upper limbs opened and pulsed, but he was still entangled. The powerful pheromones that he had used to manipulate the mothers and other humans before his mind had grown strong enough to command, sprayed directly into the fabric, almost dissolving the cotton, but it absorbed them so efficiently that the smell could not escape.

For an instant he was completely powerless. She was escaping, leaving him on his own. If he remained here, he could be discovered. He might be found by another human who could not be influenced – a male. The chemical messengers in his glands could take a mother, make her love him, but they would only drive a male mad with rage. He knew from somewhere in the past that a male could not tolerate him. Instinctively he knew he could be destroyed.

Fresh fear erupted. He was not strong enough yet to survive alone. The change was imminent and disabling. He could not travel on his own. He would be trapped here, trapped without a mother, and in an hour, maybe less, he would have to feed again.

Then the mother stopped. The vibration in the floor faded and died. She had stopped on the landing, no more than thirty feet away.

Everything went silent. He stopped breathing. Very slowly, finally figuring it out, he rolled to the left again. Almost miraculously the sheet began to unravel. His brain, or what passed for a brain, an organ that worked more on instinct than true, coherent thought, recognized the possibility of release. He rolled further until he fetched up against the base of the bed, then, astutely, he wriggled back to where he had started and rolled some more. The pressure of the sheets lessened. He managed to get his shoulders out.

She was still stationary on the stairs. Even as he moved, he could sense her slow turn. Her hesitancy was a vibration on the air, her awful apprehension a tremble resonating across the distance. The mother turned completely. She took one step upwards. The board creaked under her foot, a protest that sounded like a small animal's alarm. Now he had his shoulders free, his arm reached out and clawed on the carpet, dragging it towards him. The carpet's far corner was snagged under the leg of the bed. Its slide across the floorboards stopped. He got his other arm out, clawed his elongated fingers on the rough, matted pile. The motion drew him out of the wrap of the sheet, like a caddis fly emerging from its protective case. His breath whistled as he hauled strongly, and a small grunt that was both satisfaction and exertion mirrored the groan of the stair tread under the mother's weight.

Enormous excitement washed through him. She was coming back. He pulled again and rolled free of the wrapping, tumbling right across the rumpled carpet to the bare floorboards. His skin slithered and scrabbled on the polished surface. His nails got a purchase between two boards and he got himself to all fours. His lower limbs, scrawny and stick-like and oddly jointed, took his weight. She came up the stairs, the exhaustion evident in the heavy drag of her feet on the boards. He could make out her laboured breathing and the rasp of grinding pain in her joints. Still she came.

He moved in a scuttle across the floor to the edge of the bed, half covered by the trailing sheet, small and scrawny and slat-ridged, a grey, blurring thing. She got to the door, an unseen presence beyond the doorpost. A pale and fluttering hand reached in, fumbling in the air, as if the mother were too afraid to look inside herself, which was utterly true. The door had hit against the wall and rebounded slowly. The blue plastic tab dangled from the key in the lock. Her arm reached out for it. He could see her shoulder, then the side of her face. Inside he felt the irresistible pressure building up, the unendurable strain of his glands as they powered and clenched. He held it, held his own thoughts, instinctively waiting for the moment.

She half turned, her eyes catching the scuttling motion on the floor. They flared wide. Her fingers touched the key. Her mouth began to open as she saw him.

He screeched his command and his glands blew, sending an almost visible spray into the air. She froze, eyes so wide they looked as if they would blurt blindly from the sockets.

Then he *moved*.

Helen finished a second cup of tea, a decision she knew she would regret later. Mentally she made a note to find a toilet before she started the drive back up to the city. A group of grey-suited clerks from Castlebank Distillery had come in, all looking like accountants or lawyers. They ordered burgers and sausage rolls, quick food for the office class, and both Margaret and Maisie had reluctantly to give up their gossiping to serve the food. Helen put a few coins under the outsize saucer and made her way out into the cold air. The sky was clear, the glassy blue of a cloudless midwinter, and the haze of river mist was curling round the corners of the alleys which led down past the old bakery on the other side of the road towards the quay. The air was still and cold and the tendrils of river-mist *haar* were like translucent tentacles probing the day. Even in the watery brightness they crept eerily. Helen shivered with more than just cold. She turned, took a step along River Street and shivered again, this time more violently.

'Somebody must have walked on my grave,' she muttered, feeling the shudder still ripple insistently down her back.

It was as eerie as the probing fingers, an odd and inexplicable sensation of wrongness.

She took another step forward, two, then she stopped. It came to her with sudden clarity. She'd felt it before, the feeling of being watched. She was young and certainly attractive enough to be aware of the glances she would draw from scaffolders or road workers, the traditional public oglers. She was aware of it from men in cars, catching their pale faces turn away as she glanced to challenge their stares. She was also aware of it, more strongly, at other times, when she walked into a crowded bar and she would feel eyes peeling her, picking her clean, some hostile, some hungry. It was a kind of sixth sense which was valuable when it alerted the other senses to the possibility of danger.

Now she felt it again, though more strongly, inexplicably so. It was somehow different.

She stopped and turned, drawing her eyes quickly back along the walkway to where Kirk Street connected at right angles with the main road through the town. Two burly men in thick overcoats were walking quickly together, a matching pair of lawyers coming round from the sheriff-court sitting. By the bus stop, a couple of teenagers were hunched, sharing a cigarette, their shaven heads vulnerable and cold. For a second Helen did not recognize them as girls until one turned round and blew a plume of smoke into the air through pouting rosebud lips.

The sense of being observed died abruptly. The inspection, if it had been that, was over. For a brief moment, Helen felt disoriented, as if she had imagined it, but she was left with a strange and uneasy sense of contagion. It was as if something had touched her and left a stain. She shivered again, an invisible vibration, told herself to get a grip. There was no one else around, apart from, further along the street, several stout old ladies weighed down by age and large bags of groceries. She moved on away from the café.

The Ship Institute was on the other side of River Street, up a narrow lane. The Victorian building had been imposing in its day, when the town was rich from shipbuilding and shipping. Now it was a mouldering monument to days gone by. The town built no more ships. These days, it built nothing at all.

The hostel, which once housed sailors home from the windjamming run from Cathay, was opposite the building, sheltered from the prevailing west wind, and therefore better preserved than the institute proper.

Nina Galt took a wary look at Helen's warrant card. 'We're not really supposed to talk about our guests,' she said.

Helen couldn't be bothered going through the rigmarole of worming her way in. 'I don't want to fall out with anybody or have a dispute on the doorstep,' she said flatly. 'I could go and get some paperwork and come back. But that's going to mean an awful lot of trouble for me and naturally, that's going to spoil everybody's day.'

Nina Galt started to speak, but Helen held up her hand: 'Here's the base line. I've got a missing girl whose parents are worried to death, and my boss has asked me to find her. She might be here, or she might not. What I want you to do is have a look at a picture and tell me. On and after that, we'll talk, but in the meantime, just have a look for me, OK? We both want to have a nice day.'

Nina Galt looked Helen in the eye, weighing her up. She'd had a hard life, growing up with a family of boys who were never out of trouble with the law, and then marrying a husband who had spent many a Friday night in the slammer of the police station down by College Way. She had no love of the police, but she was herself a law-abiding person. She did, however, have a loyalty to the people who passed through the hostel, some of them on the run from trouble of one sort or another, some of them not wishing to be found.

'She's really missing?'

'Yes. And she's not in any trouble, not official trouble.'

'Show me the picture.'

Helen took it out from her inside pocket. Nina Galt held it up, drawing her eyebrows into a frown. 'Yes. She came here yesterday. She's got a room upstairs. There's always a couple just before Christmas. We give them a room until social services find them a place.'

'I told you, there's no trouble for her, not from us, nor her parents,' Helen said, though she wasn't telling the entire truth. There could really be trouble for Ginny Marsden. She'd taken the baby. Yet something inside Helen, an intuition, told her that the missing girl was in a different kind of trouble altogether.

'Is she in now?'

'I reckon so. We don't keep much of a check on the clients. We give them bed and board and make sure they're not taking anything illegal. They're free to come and go as they please.'

'Did she give you a name? Show you any identification?'

'Celia,' Nina said after a moment of concentration. 'Celia Barker. It was on her bank card.'

Out at the back of the hostel, a dog was barking furiously, the sounds hardly muffled by the distance or the thickness of the walls. Nina Galt got a master key from a hook underneath the front counter and led the way towards the stairs. Just at the foot of the steps, where the ornate banister curled round in a smooth, polished sweep, she stopped and looked along the narrow corridor behind the stairway where a line of coat hooks, old brass, stood out from the wall at eye level.

'She's moved her pram,' Nina said. 'It was there this morning.'

Helen's heart sank. She wanted to get this over with and get back to what she considered real police work: catching criminals.

'Maybe somebody shifted it,' Nina went on. 'We don't like to have the hallway cluttered up. The fire-safety inspectors don't like it, but we can't expect the girls to haul their prams upstairs. It could be out in the back yard.'

'Let's check the room first,' Helen suggested. Nina shrugged and led the way upstairs. She was about to slide the master key into the hole when she stopped abruptly. An oblong of blue plastic was lying on the floor, partially hidden under the door itself. She stooped, picked it up, drawing the key through the narrow gap as she did so. She straightened and, without hesitation, opened the unlocked door.

'Jesus God,' Nina said, turning back, nose wrinkled in a sudden grimace which sent frown ridges gathering on her forehead. 'Something's gone and died in here.'

Helen moved past her. The smell was thick and stale, and she recognized it from the previous times. It was weaker than before, as if it had faded from the air, but it was still discernible. She felt her eyes sting and her heartbeat cranked up to a faster rate. For an instant the bright outline of the unshaded window wavered in her vision. She shook her head and backed away from the door.

The entire room was visible from the hallway. The blankets were swirled on the bed, the way they had been in Heather McDougall's home, and on Celia Barker's neat little divan. On the floor a sheet was stretched out, crumpled but unravelled. A dried bloodstain, the colour of old rust, was smeared down the middle of it. The carpet was twisted and rumpled.

'What the hell's been going on here?' Nina asked.

Helen stood stock still. Her eyes scanned the room quickly, taking in the open door of the tiny bathroom, and the wall cupboard on the far side. The room was empty.

Something wrong, her instinct told her. A shivery sensation scuttered over the skin of her back, prickling the follicles on the back of her neck.

Nina Galt turned to look at her. The young policewoman's face had gone pale, chalk-white in contrast to the black sheen of her short-cropped hair. Helen Lamont stood, breathing hard, wondering what to do next. The memory of what had happened in Celia Barker's kitchen, when the dead cat had got up and danced and the walls had begun to pulse and breathe and the two-headed monster had come rushing out, twisting and distorted in her vision, all came back in a rush.

She did not want to go into the room. All of a sudden she knew she should call in, get David Harper here. She did not want to do this alone any more. The voice of instinct was so powerful that she could almost hear it clamouring in words. She was not dealing with anything natural. The realization abruptly crystallized within her.

Outside, beyond the window, the dog howled and slavered quite madly, adding to the insanity of the scene. Behind the brick outhouse door, she could hear it throwing itself against the wood which slammed against the uprights. Below, on the ground, two dead birds were being slowly covered up by tiny snow crystals blowing off the roof. In a cavity in the wall, the soft and jellied brain of a mouse was leaking from its southernmost ear.

Helen's nerves felt as if they were all on the outside of her skin. She was aware of Nina Galt looking at her askance, even though the other woman's throat seemed to be involved in its own contraction, trying to choke down a rush of bile. She was conscious of the other woman's presence on one level, but deep in her primitive core she was only aware of a dreadful feeling of supernatural fear.

On the video, she had seen Ginny Marsden stop dead in her tracks as if she'd been garrotted, just when Heather McDougall was writhing in her death throes, and the girl had turned and lifted the infant the woman had brought from the pram. Now, here, the air was still thick with the scent that had sickened Helen in McDougall's house. It was the same smell as at Celia Barker's apartment, the girl whose name Ginny Marsden had adopted.

It was all connected, she understood now. The strangeness of it all twisted once more in her, contaminating her with the unfathomable sensation of threat.

'Close the door,' she said. 'And lock it.' She backed away while Nina Galt swung the door closed, her throat still working against the reaction caused by the cloying, rancid smell. The key went into the lock, turned and clicked. The smell faded almost instantly. Beyond the door, the noise of the madly barking dog was muffled down to a series of distant howls.

'What on earth was that?' the other woman finally said. She could see the policewoman's hands were trembling slightly, as were her own, for no reason. She felt dizzy and nauseous and disorientated. The policewoman looked scared to death. 'What in the name of God is that smell?'

'I don't know,' Helen finally said, 'but I'll find out. Don't let anybody in there yet. I'll have to have it checked out.'

'I'll have to have the place fumigated,' Nina Galt added. 'That would make you sick, so it would.' She pulled back from the door, shoulders working in a swivelling motion as if she itched. She lifted a thumb and dug it in under her own armpit and twisted, pulling the fabric away from herself. Helen recognized the motion. She was adjusting a bra that had suddenly become uncomfortable. She froze, realizing that she herself was doing exactly the same thing.

She looked down at herself while the other woman was turning away to walk to the head of the stairs. Her nipples were throbbing, pulsing with every beat of her heart, and the pressure of the cotton weave was suddenly uncomfortable. The nipples were straining against the thin sweater she wore under the flying jacket, standing proud. She pulled her jacket closed, hiding the tell-tale swellings, but the sensation of pressure continued as she walked down the stairs.

Helen thought the thick, cloying smell would make someone more than just sick. The sensation that somebody had walked over her grave came back to her, strong as the vibration of a bowstring.

It had come at Ginny fast. It had come at her like a spider. She was reaching for the key, while a fear so terrible it felt like it could shatter her into fragments was shuddering inside her, blacking out everything except the urgent need to close the door and lock the baby – *monster it's a fucking monster it's a devil* – inside the room. She had to trap it inside. It was the bravest thing the girl had ever done in her life. It was the first time she had ever had any need to be brave.

She had almost got away. She had stopped on the landing

and then trudged back up the impossibly steep cliff of staircase. She reached the doorway. Inside the room it was panting desperately, like a vicious animal, and making that horrible screeching sound that was so high she couldn't physically hear it, but her brain could somehow pick it up. She fumbled for the door handle, knowing she had to expose part of herself to its gaze.

Ginny thought she could do it, imagined she could get the key, turn it in the lock. She held her breath tight against the demand for air caused by her painfully thumping heart. Her vision wavered, going dark then coming light again.

The key was stuck in the lock, but it was on the other side of the door. She had to reach further while all the time the white sizzle of its distress and anger burned on the bones in the back of her skull. She forced herself forward.

It hissed. It called to her. It demanded. It *commanded*.

She tried to force her fingers round the key, but they were white and numb. Pins and needles danced on the skin of her arms and throbbed in her hands along with the new and grinding pain. It commanded and she felt her head turn, entirely against her will. The sheet was unravelled, unravelling still on the carpet which was pulled into a crumpled roll, caught by the leg of the bed. A small, dark and angular shape moved and she tried not to look.

It shrieked inside her and she gasped with the ferocity of the hurt its sending caused deep in her centre. Ginny tried to turn away, hearing the small metallic tinkle as the tab twisted on its loop. Her fingers got to it, fumbled for the key. It rattled, pulled out a mere fraction.

Her head was jerked round again, hauled by the irresistible force of its demand.

The thing rolled and squirmed beyond the edge of the bed. Her hand pulled at the key. It tumbled out of the lock, slowly twisting in the air in slow motion, whirring softly as it fell. Her senses were cranked up to supernatural perception. Every cell of her body was suddenly and completely aware.

The monster twisted round to face her. Flat red eyes glared in a small face. The round mouth opened and closed in a sucking motion, showing her the lamprey circlet of teeth slivers. Its limbs were scrawny and stick-like, its skin wrinkled and mottled and grey, the way she had seen it in the mirror.

It came at her like a spider. It scuttled across the floor, small and spindly, so fast she could hardly make her eyes follow it. The key hit the floor with a low, metallic thrum and bounced out of sight. Down in the kitchen, a million miles away, the sound of the woman singing was now a monotone drone, drawn out and slowed to incomprehensibility. A steam kettle's whistle sounded like a distant ship's foghorn.

The thing came in a rush. Its outlines fuzzed and blurred as the swellings on its sides pulsed and clenched like small lungs, like poison sacs, sending a fine mist into the air around it. Ginny's mouth instinctively shut like a trap. She tried to move, but found her feet were glued to the floor. Her hand was still reaching for the key that had long gone when the thing on the floor launched itself at her.

The smell hit her at the same time as the monster took her at waist height and climbed up with arachnid speed, its small, wizened hands reaching to grab the sides of her face just under the jawline. The fingers, elongated and warted digits, like the hands of some reptilian lemur, clenched on her skin, almost hard enough to break through into the underlying tissue. The great red saucer-eyes were so close against her that they lost definition, like twin flaring lava pools. The stench enveloped her, infusing her pores and passages with its chemical power while the thing's mental blast seared her mind.

In that instant she was recaptured.

Its outline wavered and blurred in her vision, first grey and rough, then pink and smooth, then back again, as if the camouflage were no longer completely necessary. It fixed its eyes on her, drilling its singularity into hers. Her heart seemed to expand like a balloon under her ribs, swelling with sudden pain. She gasped and its essence went down her throat, swirled into her lungs. Every nerve bucked, every muscle twitched, every joint ground like stone. The compulsion to mother the thing vied with a powerful desire to kill it and be gone. She wanted to run and hide, to kick and scream, to twist free of its grasp and go somewhere to be sick while alongside that she was forced to obey its overriding domination. Over all of it lay an appalling weight of utter despair and loss.

It had her now and she would never be free.

Ginny Marsden backed against the wall, hit it with a thump, slowly slid down to her haunches, her coat stripping off a loose sliver of old flaking wallpaper. The thing in her arms continued to mesmerize her with a brutal mental blaze. A rope of saliva drooled from the corner of her mouth. She moaned slightly, while out beyond the window the mad dog went even crazier, attacking the wooden door with snout, teeth and skull.

After a while, after a long while, she began to stir. The thing loosened its grip a little and the great red eyes, glassy as garnet, slowly closed. It lowered itself, moving like an emaciated and scaly monkey, down over her breasts and began to burrow in once more. After more of a while she felt it clamp on her skin and then she sensed the thin and slick probing between her legs.

But this time she was not aware on any conscious level.

What there was of Ginny Marsden's own self, her own comprehension of being, was trapped in an impervious bubble within her, buried down there in the dark where its screaming, panicked cries could not be heard.

Ginny Marsden, the mother, let it suck on her, let it probe her until, once more, it was sated. The draining sensation deep inside her was like a cold and constant trickle. She ignored that. All she knew was the need to do its bidding and the creeping ache that had invaded her whole body.

After yet more of a while, the baby told her to move. Her eyes could make out its shape. Somewhere within, her thoughts translated the visual image into something resembling a baby, but by this time it did not matter. She belonged to it.

Outside, as she pushed her pram down to River Street, it held her tight. Every now and again, she would bend down, leaning under the hood, a mother does when she is comforting an infant, just letting it know she is there.

The pram's left wheel squeaked its protest as she slowly went down the alley, moving like an old woman.

CHAPTER EIGHTEEN

'I don't know what on earth's going on here,' Helen said into the phone. 'But I've locked the place and I'm not going back in there again until I have back-up. I can call in and get a patrol team but, honestly, I'd rather you were here. We're both in this.'

'All right,' David said, his voice tinny and fragmenting. He was obviously in his car. Bursts of crackling interference split his sentences into senseless islands of words. 'I should be there in . . . an hour.'

'Say again?'

'Wait . . . half an hour . . . through traffic.' She got the message. There was one final burst of electronic heavy breathing and the phone went dead. He was on his way, just passing the centre of town. He'd come down the motorway and across the bridge that spanned the river near Barloan Harbour. She felt a warm glow of more than just relief.

Down in the kitchen, Nina Galt was trying to remember exactly what the girl had said. Helen was on her third cup of tea of the afternoon and the pressure was getting to her, but she was reluctant to move. The toilets were beyond the stairway which led up to the room where Ginny Marsden had spent the night and had now, somehow, been contaminated with the foul, disabling smell.

'She looked more than twenty-two to me,' Nina Galt was saying. 'She must have had a bloody hard life. If I'd looked like that when I was her age I'd have put my head in the oven. I thought she was at least late thirties, maybe even older. I remember thinking she was pushing it to have a kid, know what I mean? There was grey in her hair and it looked like she could use a good shampoo. You could see places where it had fallen out. Has she got Aids or something?'

'She's pretty sick,' Helen conceded. Once they'd come downstairs, Nina Galt seemed to forget the fact that she was a policewoman; any hostility she might have initially harboured melted like spring frost on a south wall. She had seen the look of unaccountable fear on the younger woman's face and some of it had transmitted itself to her. They were now two women sitting in a big kitchen, drinking tea and trying not to be afraid. What she should fear, Nina had no idea, but if Helen Lamont, who for all she was young and slightly built and good-looking, looked tough and capable (had to be, going by the way she had faced Nina down in the front of the hostel), was scared, then there was something to worry about.

'What about the baby?'

'We don't know. She may have kidnapped it.'

'She never did,' Nina said, more of a question than a statement. 'She didn't look like somebody who'd do that. A good breath of wind would have knocked her down.'

Helen had brought in the register from the front counter and had it opened on the table. Ginny Marsden, confirmed from the photograph (though Nina Galt claimed she looked at least fifteen years older), had given her friend's name and shown a bank card as identification. Nina confirmed, yet again, that she didn't have a pram when she arrived, but had brought one back later in the afternoon, leaving it in the space behind the stairs in the hallway.

'And nobody saw her leave?'

Nina shrugged, blowing a dragon's-breath double plume of smoke down her nostrils. 'They come and go. We give them a roof and a kettle and hotplate, a bed and somewhere to put their clothes. It's a charity, a kind of halfway house. The social services take them in after that, some of the time anyway, and sometimes the council might find them a permanent place, if they're really lucky, for this council's been broke for years, run by loonies and gladhanders. As I say, they come and go. It looks pretty much like she's gone.'

She drew in another heavy drag of smoke, held it for a while, her eyes fixed on Helen. She let it go and spoke through the smoke. 'I hope she doesn't come back. Whatever she's got, I don't want to catch it.'

David Harper arrived twenty minutes after the telephone call and Helen knew he must have broken the law to get there so quickly. She felt a glow suffuse her at the thought of his concern.

'Plenty to tell you,' he said. 'How did you find her?'

'Solid police work while you were running around chasing your tail. And I haven't found her. I've only found where she's been. She's gone.'

'Great,' David said, brows drawn down. 'You could have told me on the phone and it would have saved a trip.'

Helen's glow vanished. She bristled. 'Don't come the smart-ass, David. You should have been here and you'd be telling a different story.' She stopped herself, realizing it was his very concern that had spurred that response. 'Sorry. Anyway, she's on foot, with a baby' – she waited for his eyes to register that – 'and a pram. She won't be far, and it doesn't look as if it's in danger, but the girl herself could be. Mrs Galt says she's sick.'

'Call me Nina,' the big, not quite natural blonde insisted, favouring David with a wide and predatory smile. She looked as if she could swallow him. For some reason, it annoyed Helen. Nina went through the story again and then they went back upstairs, Helen trailing cautiously behind David, noting this time how Nina wiggled her broad but shapely backside in an almost comic come-on. The door opened and Nina stood back to let them both inside. Immediately Helen felt her heartbeat speed up.

'Same smell as the McDougall place, and Barker's house,' David noted. 'But a lot fainter.'

'What is it?' Nina wanted to know. 'Should I get the health inspector in and have the place fumigated? Is it some kind of disease?'

'Don't think so,' David told her. 'A good scrub with soap wouldn't do any harm.' He was looking around, noting the rumpled carpet and the swirl of blankets on the mattress, like the nest he'd seen in both McDougall's and Barker's place. Round the back of the hostel, the dog was still barking, though the sounds were more muted. Every now and again, the clatter of its charge against the door and the sound of wood tearing would rattle the ancient sash window in its frame.

'Somebody should put that beast out of its misery,' David said.

Over on the work surface beside the sink, David picked up the polystyrene package which still contained a shallow, diluted pool of blood. It bore the name of the butcher's shop on a stick-on label. Nina told him the shop was less than a hundred yards away. An empty eggbox lay close by, with twin trickles of hardening albumen glued to the wooden surface of the well-used breadboard.

The scent was almost gone, though Helen's nose was still wrinkled in disgust. When he had walked into the room, David had experienced a sudden thumping double beat of his heart and an odd, burning sensation in his temples which spread to his ears. He recognized it as his angry mode, a mood-marker that had been part of him since childhood. His father had always teased him about it, telling him to go cool his ears whenever the younger David had lost his temper in frustration. It was nowhere near as bad as the twist of violent emotions that had shunted through him in the house he'd thought of as Thelma Quigley's, but it was similar enough to make him realize that Helen had been right to call him. There was indeed a very bizarre connection between the rotten – and if he admitted it, strangely exciting – smell and the two women, one dead, one still missing for now. The baby was the other connection.

For an instant, a thought tried to grab his attention, danced away, then came back. He snatched it. Was the smell something to do with the baby Ginny Marsden had scooped from the pram? Was it sick?

Was it dead?

That was something to consider, a possibility, however remote. David made a quick and professional search of the room, realized there was nothing more to be learned, and went out.

The big and typically beefy butcher told them that a girl had bought more than a pound of ox liver and some eggs. He couldn't recall exactly when, but he remembered she looked stooped and cold. 'I remember thinking the liver should do her some good,' he said. 'Plenty of iron and vitamins. Put some meat on the bones. A good steak would have done her some good too.'

Of Ginny Marsden, however, there was no sign. Nobody else had seen the girl with the pram with the one squeaky wheel, except the assistant in the charity shop who had sold it to her, and she couldn't remember what the girl had looked like.

It was only after speaking to the butcher that David's thought came back to him, that the baby might somehow, however improbably, be dead. But when he voiced it, Helen countered the notion. Old Maggie in the café had told her the infant had turned and looked at her with big blue eyes.

'She said it made a noise, and it smelled like a new baby. Smell of milk. They're all like that. Every weekend my mother's house is full of them. They smell of worse than milk, I can tell you.'

'Not your scene?'

'Believe it,' Helen assured him. 'I'm the black sheep of the family 'cause I haven't gone into mass reproduction yet. My sisters give me pitying looks, but it's not me that's stuck with changing nappies and getting up in the middle of the night to pace the floor with teething babies. It doesn't look like fun to me.'

David smiled at the idea of Helen pacing the floor, but at the same time he recalled June's ever more frequent complaints that time was moving on; that her biological clock was ticking off the days.

'Oh, probably some time I might go for it,' Helen said. 'When I meet the right guy. And after I reach chief inspector level. My mother doesn't believe women should have a career. She thinks we should populate the earth, but as far as I'm concerned, the earth is doing very nicely without my help. Anyway, I haven't met the right guy yet.'

She looked up at him and they both smiled.

He had sensed the other one.

Immediately a tingle of strange and fearsome excitement had washed through him. It brought a hollow yearning that was hot and fierce and infinitely powerful.

He was spent from the effort of bringing the mother back under control after the terror of abandonment. The anger bubbled inside of him, anger and fear and the realization of his own vulnerability. That was another new thing that he had learned since the moment the old mother had failed, something that he might have known long ago but had forgotten in the years of complacent feeding. *Fear.*

There had always been a mother, back, back as far as his strange, wordless memory would allow him to look, all their bovine, bland faces merging into one, all their teats melded into one great feeding. When one was finished, another would come to take her place, without fail, without question.

And now there was this one, who had fought against him as he drained her.

Inside her, he could perceive the dissolution, and instinctively he knew she would not last. His hunger quickened at that. He would need more, much more as the change burgeoned. Already, he could feel his limbs lengthen, his muscles strengthen, and there was an even deeper hunger than the one he was used to, now awakening from dormancy within him. It scared him as much as it excited him. It was the first real new thing in his life for as long as his memory could ascertain. He could not remember his beginning.

But he remembered the other one, the new female, with that tingle, unexpected and strange: the stirring of his growing want. The fearsome excitement had ripped inside him in a tide of sudden ferment. It was mixed with the fear and the inexplicable sense of vulnerability.

She was *threat.*

Yet she was more, though he did not have the words or the thoughts to explain what or why.

He had made the mother move after a while, when he had damped down the fires of rebellion, stamping on the sparks until there was little left but some distant, bubbling flares that were far enough away to cause no concern. He had expended himself in that huge burst of energy, draining his glands of everything they had, using up his vital growing sustenance in the singular effort of concentration that harnessed her. He had to rest, but even then, while he made her move, he could not let the link between them subside.

There was danger here now, he sensed. Outside, the animal screeched, its mind crazed by the mental shriek that had almost turned its brain to slush. The mother moved slowly and he could feel the vibration of the grinding bones and the heat of the inflammation in her joints as all of her goodness was leeched out to make his frame strong for the next stage. She had carried him down the stairs, wrapped in the shawl, much as she had wrapped and trapped him in the sheet, but he sensed no danger now. He made her put him in the carrier, in the dark. In another room, another of them, an old, spent one, was singing low. He stretched a curious tendril of thought to touch her and picked up her dry fruitlessness. There was no feeding there.

Outside he closed his eyes against the light, however dim, that managed to get between the storm cover and the hood, turning his head to bury his face against the cloth, all the time holding her with a loop of his own thoughts, a rein of attention and compulsion. The pram rattled and jounced on the flagstones. She walked on in the narrowness of the street where there was no direct sun, just moving slowly.

Then he touched the other one.

His outreach trailed across her and a sudden panic flared inside him. The mother stopped dead in her tracks. Another one, again old and dry, muttered something in passing, annoyed at having been held up. The different one, the one he had touched before, was very near, so close her presence was like an itch on the surface of his skin. His attention wavered out in an expanding circle of apprehension, ready to draw back at the first real hint of danger.

He touched her again and felt her response. Her mind was already open. She had been moving, quite slowly, in the other direction, but now turned, very quickly, swivelling towards him. He stroked the different part of her mind, that rare part in one of these creatures that could perceive. It was weak and unused, but inside it the potential was vast. As soon as he felt it, he withdrew very quickly in great alarm. She too could reach.

She was questing, and the crevasse in her mind was beginning to open, triggered by, responding to, his initial alien invasion. He knew she could feel his touch.

Go go go go NOW.

The mother headed back up the alley. He pulled back, let go, broke the contact with a psychic snap that was almost a pain.

Mentally, for some reason, he was cringing away from her,

confused by the seismic heavings inside his head and his body. He felt the glands puff up, draining his own substance, and he had to concentrate to force them back to quiescence. The tingle, fierce and unexpectedly violent, shuddered under his skin. He experienced a new hunger and a savage gladness that mixed in with the fear of entrapment and the uncertainty of being hunted.

She was hunting him, he could feel that. She did not know what he was. Was unsure of his very existence, on the conscious level, but already she had breathed him in and the chasm inside her own mind, where the coiled power lay hidden, had sensed the strangeness of him.

She did not know it, but they had already met, already touched.

She had savoured him.

He forced the mother to keep walking. The wheel squeaked and the mother's bones ground together. He made her put as much distance as possible between him and the other one. That was all he could do for now: get away, make a retreat. If she was hunting for him, she would find him, maybe, but by that time, he might be prepared; he might be able to do something about it.

For the time being, all he wanted was the quiet and solitude he instinctively knew was needed for the change. Despite that, as the mother took him further from the touch of the other one, the strange, unique excitement shuddered through him.

Barloan Harbour's small railway station looked like the centre-piece of a Victorian Christmas card under the light fall of snow which sent flakes floating silently to earth beneath a sky that was mysteriously clear to the east. Overhead, the moon, low in the early-evening winter sky, was round and bright, ringed with a soft and fuzzy halo – a bomber's moon, they used to say in the old days. It picked out the sluggish waters of the harbour basin, now at half-tide and on the rise. The scattering of snow lined the stone slope down to a few feet above the waterline where a few hardy gulls and oystercatchers bleated hollowly. The moon-light limned the rail tracks which led east to the city, or back west to Levenford where Ginny Marsden had laboriously pushed the pram, still squeaking, up the ramp and on to the first train to pull in, heading eastwards. Something urged her to get off here at the harbour station, in the shadow of the soaring bridge which crossed the broad tidal river in an elegant double curve.

It had been difficult to get the pram off when the automatic doors had opened. A boy, maybe a student, had taken the heavy end, hardly looking at her as he did so, and eased it on to the platform. 'There you are, missus,' he said, courteous and friendly, hefting his full shoulder bag and sauntering away into the gathering dark. Five days ago, he'd have given her the eye, taken in her long and elegant legs, maybe even sat next to her on the train as soon as he spotted her tumble of blonde hair. Now he only saw a woman with a pram, hardly giving her a glance. Ginny Marsden was hardly even aware of that. There were other matters demanding her close attention.

She slowly shoved herself and the pram towards the small, old-fashioned waiting room, which, as luck would have it – if luck has anything to do with this story – was the only one in the whole line, from Kirkland right up to Central High, to have a coal fire, and that was only because the stationmaster, who lived in a small brick house just beyond the edge of the platform, could get as much coal as he wanted from the scuttle boats that stopped to unload at the far end of the harbour.

A couple of schoolkids stopped canoodling when she slowly pushed the door open and trundled the old pram in ahead of her. She hardly noticed them but, disturbed now in their private place, they pursed their lips, exhaling in suffering sighs, and went out to find another nook in which to further their acquaintance. Ginny walked slowly towards the flicker of the fire, spent a few moments effortfully turning the pram so that it was broadside to the heat and then sat down, trying to ignore the dreadful pain in her hips and knees. Her fingers were red from the cold in Levenford's elevated station where the wind had been gentle but insistent and frigid. She had no gloves and she'd had no mind of her own, at that time, to tell her to put her hands in her pockets. They had stayed motionless, clenched tight to the handle of the pram. Now in the warmth of the waiting room, they were red-raw and scadded, each knuckle swollen to twice its normal width. When the blood began to run again into the shrunken veins, the pain in her hands corkscrewed deep under the skin and she was aware of it constantly. She could do nothing about it. She could not, at this time, even weep.

Outside, beyond the dusty window, an occasional flash of bright blue light would jitter and sizzle on the overhead electric line where the hard frost allowed a trickle of power to escape. It was an eerie lightning, a hissing spark that sounded like the wordless hiss of the commands inside her head. Moving with infinite care, she sat at the end of the slatted bench, feeling the heat on the side of her bare leg. Her head ached and her breasts ached and in her womb blood trickled thickly, radiating the constant cramp, but these sensations were almost pleasant in comparison to the awful tides of hurt that juddered into her bones.

She sat there, passing the time in a daze that allowed for hardly any thought. The baby still had her battened down, its manipulation almost absolute.

After a while a train went past, clattering over the cold-widened gaps and making the waiting room shudder. Once past, under the soaring arch of the bridge, it howled like a beast and was gone. The baby jerked in the pram, its attention momentarily grabbed by the noise and vibration. The brief escape from the pressure of its will let Ginny's consciousness bubble up to the surface.

'Please God,' she prayed silently. 'Please God spare me from this.'

Out in the night, the train's clatter diminished and the blue sparkle jittered again on the overhead cables.

I'm dying, Ginny Marsden realized, but there was nothing she could do about that. She was too tired to move, too desperately weak to do anything but bear the pain. In the momentary respite from its attention a tear welled up in her eye, making the already dim shapes in the sparse room waver and dance. It spilled out and trickled down her cheek, a brief, transient warmth on the dry skin of her face. It slid past the corner of her mouth where the surface was fissured and puckered into creases that aged the young girl so violently that the student on the train had taken her for middle-aged.

The single tear trickled to her chin, hung there for a moment, then dropped to the matt of her coat. It was a tear of utter despair. It was all she could do.

The baby's attention turned back to Ginny Marsden.

She felt its probe and her own mind flinched away from the contact, quite fruitlessly. It did not even have to waste its substance by spraying its chemical messengers now. Yet when it demanded to be fed, she would feed it. When it demanded to be held, she would hold it. When it wanted mothering, she would mother it.

Later, another train, this one heading west, went thundering past, not stopping at Barloan Harbour. Ginny stirred and, with enormous effort, stood up. There was no one else in the waiting room, but had there been, he would have heard the awful millstone sound of bone grinding on bone. Ginny paused for breath, unable to let out a cry, even a moan. She went out and along the narrow platform to the white gate that led to the cobbles of the narrow sloping road. She pushed the pram ahead of her up the hill just as a small girl on a big boy's bike came flying down, pigtails flying in the slipstream.

'Watch out, Kirsty,' another girl called, swooping down the hill on a smaller bicycle. 'You nearly hit that woman.' The pigtailed girl wobbled and turned her head to watch the woman push the pram, but the bike's momentum carried her beyond the stooped figure, away from whatever had attracted her notice. Both children, carefree and excited, whizzed past, leaving Ginny Marsden alone on the road.

It took her half an hour to get to the main through road. By the time she reached the small end cottage with the bed-and-breakfast sign in its window, she was limping heavily and the nerves in her left foot were completely numb.

The old woman who answered the door wore glasses as thick as bottle ends, which made her eyes piggy and shrunken. While her vacancy sign was out in the garden, an old-fashioned 'B&B' plaque hanging from two chains on what looked like a hangman's gibbet, she hadn't expected any business so close to Christmas. She had two rooms on the top and one on the bottom and that was the one she offered the gaunt, ill-looking woman who stood at the door.

Mrs Cosgrove, a dumpy little woman with a wizened leg – a legacy from the old polio days before the war – told her the rate and said she always took cash, never trusting those plastic cards. Ginny fumbled, almost absently for her bag, searched it and said she would have to go to the bank the next day. Her voice was hollow and distant, as if she really was sick. The old woman looked her up and down suspiciously. There was a silence as she peered through those magnifying lenses, then, at that moment, the baby whimpered. Mrs Cosgrove looked for a second as if she'd been slapped. She blinked several times and, without hesitation, bustled the woman and the pram inside.

Ginny hardly said a word, merely nodding like an automaton, as the woman, as wide as she was tall, shooed her into a ground-floor room, lit a gas fire, and then brought her a steaming plate of soup and a mound of buttered bread.

She asked if the baby might need a bottle, explaining that she had one of her grandson's still in the house. Ginny shook her head and bent to drink the hot soup.

For some reason, it tasted slimy and alien and almost made her sick, but she forced it down. She wanted something with blood and calcium, something raw and rich. The tastebuds of her tongue seemed to stand out on their own when the strange appetite came upon her, but still, she supped the soup until it was gone.

The woman finally left her alone and, after a while, the baby demanded to be fed.

Ginny Marsden, looking like a woman more than twice her age, now aware of the imminence of her own death, obeyed.

June rang the bell after ten, just as Helen was leaving. The three of them stood awkwardly in the hall, David, wrong-footed again, not sure whether to let Helen out first or invite June in. Finally June made the decision, pushing her way past and throwing Helen a look that should have pinned her to the wall.

'See you in the morning,' Helen said, giving him a wide smile which also conveyed her mirth at his discomfort. Quite archly, very mischievously, she added: 'And don't sleep in, sergeant, we've a busy day ahead of us.' Before the door closed, she winked at him and turned away towards her car.

'What was she doing here?' June wanted to know.

'She was collecting some of the papers we've been working on.'

'Are you screwing her?'

'Jees . . .' David started to say. The question, so bluntly put, had startled him to bewilderment. He'd never heard her use that word before. 'What do you mean?' he finally asked.

'I mean, are you screwing that bitch? Are you giving it to her? Huh? Like what you and me never seem to do these days?'

'Don't be so bloody stupid,' he snorted, all the while sensing a hot and turgid flare of excitement at the now-conscious thought of it. He hadn't actually considered the idea, not deliberately, he told himself, and even then he knew that was not quite true. He had thought of her, even though he'd always tried to keep his working relationship separate.

He had pretended he hadn't understood the other night when Helen had told him he didn't have to do a runner, letting him know by her very posture, that he was welcome to stay, at least a little longer. Maybe he had picked it up wrongly, though he didn't think so. He recalled the unexpected surge of desire that he'd had to clamp down, not as strong as the unnatural sensation in the dead woman's house, but a powerful need within him just the same. They were partners, but now there was something else sparking between them that confused and wrong-footed him. He could have stayed at Helen's, but he hadn't, because he *had* made the effort, even though on the way home he'd swung between lust and loyalty, pinned between the physical drive and his own sense of fair play.

'Then what was she doing here?'

'I already told you.'

'You're a bloody liar. You've been seeing her behind my back, haven't you?'

June pushed past him, along the short, wide hallway where some of his best pictures were lined up in large frames alongside his favourite elemental shots: a skein of geese passing in a chevron across the face of the full moon, a world-famous piece shot by Flora Spiers; one of his own, from early autumn, a woodcock in sharp and perfect focus while the trees it flew between were only blurred shadows. The centrepiece was the one he'd taken as a boy, a close-up shot, so close the edges were distorted, of a dragonfly on a stalk, glittering in the sunlight, while the empty paper skin from which it had emerged hung down, transparent and useless, and as ugly as the larva from which it had transformed. She strode past the photographs and into the front room. He followed.

'Well?'

She had stopped in the middle of the room, winter coat swinging round to catch up with her. She looked neat and capable, a matching beret at a jaunty angle. She was looking down at the scatter of papers and books all over the floor. There were two half-empty coffee-cups on the table.

'I've been seeing her every day. I told you,' he said. 'We were working.'

'For the past week?'

'A few days, you know that.'

'I've left messages all over the place. You've not answered any of them. It's just not good enough.'

'For God's sake, June. I've been up to my eyes. I just haven't had time.'

'Don't you love me any more?' She spat the words out.

That question really caught him on the hop. 'Of course I . . .' he started without thinking. 'Yes, of course.' Even as he said it he realized it was a conditioned reflex. She had needed him to say that, right from the beginning of their relationship, driven by the need to love and be loved. For a while he had thought he meant it and after a while he had stopped thinking about it. Now he realized he should have. He had not been entirely fair, with himself or with her.

She turned to look at him. 'No, you don't. You really don't. We've been going out for nearly two years and in the past six months I've hardly seen anything of you. The last time I did see you, did you stay? No. You gave me some limp-dicked excuse and left.'

'Steady on,' David started to protest. She was so fired up all her sentences were crammed up against each other, and she was using language he heard every day of the week, but never from her. 'That's a bit unfair. You know I'm in the middle of something important.'

'A dead woman in the shopping mall? A missing girl? That's hardly the crime of the century. You must be losing your touch or your reputation. But I don't give a damn about the job. I care about us. What am I supposed to think? Look at me.'

He did. She was standing in the centre of the room, one hand on her hip and the other stretched towards him, a finger jabbing the air. Her nail was long and red and looked as if it could stab him deep enough to draw blood.

'You spend all of your time with her.'

'That's because she's a police officer. She works with me. We work together.'

'It's more than that. I know it. I'm not stupid. Otherwise you'd have stayed with me the other night. But you didn't stay, did you? You haven't stayed over in weeks. You won't move in with me and you won't let me move in with you. All my other friends are engaged or married. They've got children, for heaven's sake. And all the time my clock's ticking. I don't want to wait until I'm forty. I can't wait, don't you understand?'

'So that's what this is all about, is it?' David said, quite needlessly. He'd already known that. 'It's about kids.'

'It's about *us*, David,' she said passionately, her eyes flashing blue. Right at that moment, he felt ashamed of himself and sorry for her. She had drives he could not, would not, comprehend. 'It's about us,' she repeated, her voice high and almost desperate. 'Us and the future. I can't wait any more, watching you run around with her, spending all your time working or taking your stupid pictures. I need more than that. I need a relationship and, yes, I do want children. I want to be part of something, part of a family.'

'I told you I would think about it,' David said, and again he realized he wasn't being fair. 'It's a big step.'

'What are you?' she demanded, eyes glittering again. 'Are you sterile? Or have you turned gay? I'm beginning to think you might have, for your sex drive seems to have died the death. I remember when you couldn't get enough.'

Quite involuntarily, David burst out laughing as irritation

and guilt and exasperation and sudden anger tumbled inside him. 'I can't be gay if I'm screwing Helen Lamont, can I?'

Her jaw dropped and for an instant he enjoyed it. 'Are you telling me . . .?' Her voice trailed away.

'No, of course I'm not. It was you who said I was, and if that's what you want to believe, no matter what I say, then it's up to you.' He stopped, closed his mouth on the anger. He started again. 'Listen, this is out of order. Let's just sit down and calm down and talk this through like intelligent adults.' He put his hands out, reaching to place them on her shoulders. She wriggled away from him.

'No,' she said with a quick shake of her head. 'I need an answer now. We're either together or we're not. I need a commitment and I need it now.'

'What kind of commitment?'

'A real one. Something definite. I don't want to waste my life hanging around for something that might happen, maybe, some time. Like never. I need to know where I am, where I stand. It's easy for you, but it's hellish for me when you're never with me and when you miss dates and don't phone. Yes, I want a commitment that says you'll be where you say you'll be, and that you'll take me out and that we can live together and, yes, have babies. And, honestly, David, the way I'm feeling, if I can't get that commitment, that's it. End of story.'

There it was, hanging there. He wanted to squirm away from it, spend some more time picking it over, thinking it through. He wasn't a weak man, not in any real sense, but he hated hurting her, hated hurting anyone except the occasional villain who had a go at him. Yet he was beginning, however belatedly, to understand that sometimes kindness wore a face of stone.

The silence stretched out for a long, frozen moment while the two of them stood motionless.

'All right,' he said finally. 'You're right. I haven't been fair. But I really don't want to move in. I don't want to have children, not yet. I don't want to get married, not yet, and I don't want to settle down.' He stopped talking, looked at her. 'Not yet.' Her mouth opened, closed, opened again. He held up a hand. 'I don't have the same drives you have. I don't have the same needs either. I really love my work, honestly, even all the crap that goes with it. And I can't take you with me when I go up the hills and take pictures, because that's not your thing. If you want more, then I'm sorry. I can't give you more, not yet. Maybe . . .' he started, looking into her eyes and now seeing the need to say the obvious. 'Maybe not ever. I'm sorry.'

June rocked back as if she'd been slapped. Her mouth goldfished some more and David felt an unaccustomed tear springing in his own eyes as he picked up her distress. It was an awful moment. For an instant the blood drained from her face and he thought she might faint. Instead, she recovered quickly. Her brows drew down into a frown and her mouth pulled itself into an angry twist. Without warning she moved, striding past him, coat flapping again. He half turned, a word trying to blurt out. She stopped, turned, and then, striking like a snake, she balled her hand into a tight fist and hit him square on the nose.

The tear of anguish and remorse died unborn. Real tears of blinding pain sparkled instantly and made his vision waver. 'Jesus fuggig Gryst,' he said.

She stormed past him, through the door, down the hallway. She swiped again and knocked one of pictures from the wall. The Spiers shot of the skein of geese took off, flipped over and landed with a crash of smashing glass. The front door opened, banged hard against the wall.

'Bastard,' she snarled just before the door swung again and slammed shut. The hallway shook with the vibration.

CHAPTER NINETEEN

'You sound like you've gone eight rounds.' Helen's voice was sleepy and soft at the edges as if she were stifling a yawn. 'What time is it anyway?'

'Late. Or early,' David said. 'I had a thought.'

'So you just had another thought, to wake me up and share it with me. Woke up my niece as well.' Helen said, but without rancour. The initial drowsiness was fading as she became more alert and now he could hear the suppressed smile. 'You looked all set for a right hook and a possible knockout tonight. She did not seem to me to be a happy lady.' David thought she didn't realize how close to the mark she was. She would see the bruise in the morning. 'Were you in big trouble?'

'Deep shit,' he admitted. 'It's over now.'

There was a silence on the phone as she considered the permutations and possibilities.

'Over.' Another statement and question.

'We finished. Split. And yes, she did hit me. On the nose. It bled a bit.'

There was another silence that stretched between them. He wondered whether she'd laugh or sympathize. She did neither. 'So you just thought you'd wake me up and cry on my shoulder?'

'No. Not at all.' He didn't really know now why he had called. He'd thought he did when he dialled, but now, in the spotlight of her question, he wasn't so sure. He'd dreamed, slouched in the seat in front of the flickering screen, surrounded by the papers that they'd been going through earlier, and he'd woken with a start when his arm had slipped and banged against the still tender side of his nose. He'd woken and he'd wanted to reach out and make contact.

'I had a weird notion I wanted to bounce off you,' he said. He took her silence and the odd whickering sound that sounded like a stifled laugh as encouragement to go on. 'You'll think I'm crazy. I mean really out of the park. But I think we're looking at this from the wrong point of view.' He paused for just a moment then ploughed ahead. 'I asked Mike Fitzgibbon what sort of woman steals a baby.' He closed his eyes and recalled the tall doctor's response. He could see him frown, hear the measured tones.

'I've dealt with several in my time,' he had said. 'Though it's a fairly rare phenomenon. Many people consider it, but few carry it further. It's a major taboo in our society – in any society. The drive to mother is inherent in most women, despite what the feminists say. It's a programming thing, as much instinct and inherent as learned. More so in fact.'

Mike had taken David back up to his office and called for two cups of coffee. He turned and looked out of the window over the neatly laid out garden where the standard roses were frosted with snow. Two magpies, resplendently iridescent, chattered to each other on the tall wall.

'You get bereaved mothers, women who have lost a child or children. They're the rarest, but occasionally, their sense of loss is so great that they can be motivated to take another woman's child. They are found almost immediately because they go home and normally present the partner with the problem, which is often a great shock. He usually, almost invariably, reports the matter. These are simply traumatized women who are not at all responsible for their actions in the short term. Their depression is often treatable and it rarely develops into full-fledged psychosis.'

Mike held up his hand and counted off his thumb, moving to the next finger. 'Then there's infertile women, or those who believe themselves to be incapable of bearing children and have developed an obsessive compulsion. It is a distortion of the normally powerful mothering instinct. They are the hardest of all to find because, despite their clinical depression, they will have planned the move in advance, like a bank robbery. It is rarely a pram theft though. They tend to take neonates from hospitals, or even go so far as to pose as social workers or district nurses to remove them from homes. Often they build up an elaborate background story and rehearse earnestly, even to the extent of having a name for the child and all the paraphernalia, feeding bottles, cribs, toys, that sort of thing. That's the kind who take longest to trace. So far, in the UK, there has not been a case which has not been resolved. In America, there are several every year, but then there's more murders too.'

Mike ticked off another finger. 'You get sociopaths, psychopaths, who want to damage another woman. Again, this is very rare. Most woman who take a child are doing it from a deep-seated need. There was a case in Boston of a woman taking a neighbour's baby to get revenge over a garden fence argument.'

A fourth finger was marked off. 'You get sexual sadists, equally uncommon, but not unheard of, who want to damage a child. For them a baby's cry hits the wrong programming. For most folk, even for men, the pitch causes anxiety and stress, as a number of tests clearly demonstrate. That's pure evolution. It's how a baby gets into your mental software and presses the buttons. For a psycho-sadist, the sound brings pleasure, and of course, in an infant, it's easily induced. There was a very distressing case in Brisbane back in the eighties. The woman kept the baby fed, but made a blanket out of fibreglass insulation. The baby's back was suppurating with gangrene by the time it was found.'

Mike held up his small finger. 'Lastly, and this is more common than you might expect, even in this country, there's witchcraft. I read a paper on babies being sacrificed in Gambia, Zaire and Haiti. Some of them, it is believed, were stolen, but the majority probably were sold, or even given willingly. There were two suspected cases in Bristol two years ago as far as I remember. That's about it.'

The coffee arrived, two small cups, lukewarm and bitter. Mike grimaced, as if he'd made the same gesture many times.

'So, what about Greta Simon?' David asked. 'Do you think she's telling the truth?'

'With what's left of her brain, it's hard to know. But she could be. The short-term memory is gone, which means that by now, she wouldn't remember your face or your name. She might, one time in a hundred, remember who I am, but I wouldn't put money on it. Certainly, as I told you, there were no signs of her ever having given birth, but signs that she had cared for a baby, and of course, there was nothing to show why a woman of her advanced years was still lactating. That was a mystery.'

'It sounds very like the case I'm working on.'

'I know. But as far as Greta is concerned, she lives in a small series of bubbles in time, if you'll forgive the analogy. She is not in the present. That temporal part of her brain is damaged beyond repair and at her age, there will be no new neural pathways established. Whatever she's lost is gone for good. I can guarantee that. But whenever she is in one particular time zone, as I like to call it, she sees things perfectly clearly. If she tells you she is holding a baby, then she believes that is what is happening, because the memory is forming a perpetual rationality loop. The brain is a wonderful and mysterious organ. It tries to rationalize what it cannot comprehend. It can also recreate, more vividly than any memory, the exact conditions relating to any given period, so long as the recalled input has been strong enough initially.'

David said he didn't quite understand that.

'Basically the cerebral cortex is a time machine. You trigger the response and it puts you back to where you've been. The injury Greta Simon suffered caused lesions and scarring which did considerable damage. She has lost the bulk of her memories. The brain compensates, of course, boosting inherent and surviving memories, giving it some frame of reference. Basically, there are a few parts of her life which are still extant. Each of these parts, at any given time, is real, and because her short-term memory function is gone they are more real than the present. For Greta, the present does not really exist. Her whole life is encapsulated in those surviving areas of memory. At any given moment, she could be back in the sixties, or she could be five years old again, and she can tell you the name of everybody in her school class, where they are sitting and what they wear. It never varies, because she actually believes she *is* there. Most of the time, she's cradling a baby, Tiny Tim. She sees him as vividly as we see each other. Now that itself leads me to believe that at one stage, probably very shortly before the accident, she was indeed responsible for, however temporarily, the care of a child. Greta has no capacity to lie.'

'But not her baby?'

'No. Quite unequivocally not hers.'

Back in his own place, David had poured himself a drink, still shaken by June's anger and the stinging blow to his nose. He let the Jack Daniel's bubble over ice and then sipped it slowly, letting the smooth burn spread in his throat. He tried not to go over what had happened, still feeling guilt, but a certain strange elation as well, which added to the guilt-weight. After a while he pulled together the papers on the floor, collected them into a neater pile, and put them all under the coffee table, realizing that he would get no more work done tonight. Instead, he poured himself another whiskey, popped a can of lager, sat down on the carpet with his back against the couch and thumbed the remote control. The television came to life and offered him a choice of golf, a chess match, or old soap repeats, none of which were worth staying in for. Instead, he checked his list of tapes, possibly the most organized part of his life, and selected the wildlife series he'd been compiling week by week.

The beer was almost ice cold and after the first swallow, he held the can against his nose, letting the chill numb the hot throbbing.

On screen, the famous naturalist was hunkered down observing a troop of baboons spread over a rocky clearing. He turned to the camera, his well-known, almost beatific smile wide and excited. 'And here,' he said, 'the subordinate male protects itself from the Alpha, the leader of the troop.' The camera zoomed in on a bulky primate, tail held high over its rainbow backside, as it snatched a tiny baby from its mother. She screamed in protest and the baby whimpered in fright, but the baboon ignored both. From the edge of the picture, an even more massive male came powering in, its mane hackled and forelegs stiff with aggression. The first baboon began to run the tiny mite's fur upwards against the grain and immediately it shrieked its discomfort.

The dominant animal stopped in its tracks.

'Like us,' the presenter said, 'like chimpanzees and the great apes, baboons have a defined family structure. Instinctively, they react to the sound of a baby's cry, which is pitched at such a level as to cause distress in the adults. As you can see here, the Alpha male has stopped in its advance. It wants to fight the Beta male, driven by its natural response to dominate the troop. But the inferior male is using the baby's shrieks as a shield. The dominant male is anxious and agitated, because the baby's cries for help trigger the adult's protective response, in the same way that an infant's cry automatically attracts attention from a human. Confused by the interference of the baby baboon's cry, the Alpha stops, unable to attack. In this way we see that the baby's genetic programming coincides with that of the adult. It demands attention and the adult is powerless to ignore it.'

Almost miraculously, while the tiny baboon shrieked its glassy cry, while its mother chattered in real distress close by, impotent to snatch her baby out of danger, the huge male stopped, sat still and looked quite comically confused. The rival continued rubbing the infant's fur up the wrong way as it sidled off, far enough to be out of danger. Then, quite casually, he dropped the baby on to the ground. The mother rushed in, snatched it up and held it close, checking for damage. Instantly the baby buried its head against her fur and began to suckle. Its cries stopped immediately.

David watched the programme through, but his mind kept jumping back to the scene with June which clamoured for his attention, demanding to be picked over and analysed, and for some reason, when he thought of her, Greta Simon's strangely sly, lopsided face would intrude in to his thoughts.

I found him, the old woman had said. *I took him and he's mine.*

He'd been thinking about June, how she'd get depressed whenever one of her friends announced a pregnancy while she wasn't even married. He recalled asking Helen, quite clumsily, about the reproductive imperative and how she'd laughed, telling him that her sisters had it in great abundance.

'Because of that, I've got a tight rein on mine,' she'd said. 'I make a terrific aunt – costs me a fortune at Christmas – but the rest of it I can do without.' She'd looked up at him and given him a teasing smile, nudging him with her elbow. 'Unless I find the right man, of course.'

He'd smiled at that recollection, faintly embarrassed despite the third Jack Daniel's, and then again, with no warning, Greta Simon's face floated into his memory.

She fell down and the baby called to me and he needed a mother. The good eye had rolled round to face him, pinning him with its oddly iced sharpness. *I look after him and I feed him. He's so hungry all the time. He could suck you to death, but he needs me.*

The old woman had believed she was suckling a baby. Her hands had moved, the way the baboon mother's hands had moved, a natural hugging motion as she pressed the imaginary child to her thin, shapeless chest. Superimposed on that image, he saw the baby baboon, skinny and flat-faced, its arms stretched and fingers clenched on its mother's fur, nuzzle in against the black teat.

Oh, not so hard, Timmy. You'll empty me right out, Greta Simon had complained, pretended to complain, as the invisible baby suckled.

There was something in those images, an important connection tugging at him. As before, he reached for it, but it danced away. By now he was on his third can and the effects of the liquor and the events of the day began to overtake him. He tried again to make the connection and failed. He considered calling Helen, but dismissed the notion.

On the screen the camera swung round past a crackling flame which ate its way up a trailing vine. It zoomed in to a hollow in a tree where a bird, something small and plain, a lark or a maybe a linnet, sat on its clutch of eggs. The flames of the brush fire made the air waver and dance in heat mirage, but behind it, the bird's eye, black as coal, could be seen sparkling. The camera zoomed even closer, a terrific feat of photography, and even managed to capture the red flames flickering angrily in the eye's reflection.

The red eye glared, sending a strange and unexpected shiver of intuitive recognition inside David, despite the numbing effect of the beer and whiskey.

'As you can see,' the famous naturalist explained in hushed, awed tones, 'this bird continues to sit on the nest. The other animals, the lizards and the snakes, the meercats and the other birds, have fled the approaching flames. In this bird, however, the urge to protect her chicks is too strong. This is genetic programming at its most implacable. The bird wants to flee the flames, but it senses the danger to the nestlings. The need to protect its children is stronger even than its own natural imperative to survive. Again, we can see the command children have over their parents, and this it to the death. The mother bird will sit here as the fire consumes the bush she chose as a safe haven, defying the heat and the fear. All to no avail.'

The flames crackled as the scene began to blur on the screen, the great red eye staring desperately out. The mother bird sat there until the heat and the smoke filled the screen, blotting everything out.

'The natural imperative, the drive to reproduce, to protect its offspring against all dangers, is so powerful that it has overruled every other instinct,' he said. 'In the end, it has killed them all.'

The credits rolled and the dramatic music swelled. David leaned back against the settee and closed his eyes, listening to the soulful notes while the images – June, Helen, Greta Simon, the baby baboon, the dreadful red eye – all came swimming and circling in his memory. By the time the next programme began, he was half asleep.

The tape rolled on. On screen, a mass of moving twigs resolved, as the camera pulled back, into a mound of ants. The voice came on again, whispering atmospherically, explaining the army ant bivouac. As the teeming mass of insects broke up, the camera followed the monstrous, swollen thing that was the queen, hauled hither and yon by the nurses, bloated and helpless.

'She lays eggs constantly,' the naturalist said. 'While the workers, her daughters, are programmed to raise them. They will die to defend the queen's offspring, obeying the queen's own reproductive imperative. She needs to breed. It is her sole function, and it is that drive which powers the whole colony.'

David did not hear those words, not consciously. He was fast asleep. And in his sleep, he dreamed.

'*Bastard.*'

June's face twisted in anger as she spat the word and all of the pictures fell from the walls, spinning away from him, each of them warping and twisting, each of them now a screen in which the subjects moved in their own separate cells of life.

'Bastard.' The word echoed from the walls as she turned to face him, her face white and eyes wide. 'You must be impotent!'

He looked down and thought he might be impotent because

he was naked and nothing was happening where it should and when he looked up again, Helen Lamont was coming towards him, hunched against the cold in her flying jacket. Somewhere in the distance a cuckoo hooted and they were sitting beside a pool where dragonflies swarmed in fighting squadrons, snapping insects out of the air.

'You're one of the good guys,' Helen said and smiled at him while June was storming across the field, her skirt blowing in the breeze. 'I might have one if I find the right man.'

He had turned towards her and she had smiled again and the flames were in her eyes and they were all red.

The cuckoo hooted again, closer in now, and he could see it flutter from bush to bush, seeking the pipits' nest. He turned away from Helen and watched it settle on the nest, furtively pressing down, head swivelling from side to side. The egg came out, soft and membraned, and it wriggled and swelled and then burst open to show the big-eyed bird that jostled the others out of the way, out of the nest, and then shrieked for food.

'Poor little thing,' Helen said and he turned back to her while the baby cuckoo begged for food. 'It needs fed.'

'Of course it does,' he told her, edging forward to plant his lips on hers. 'We all need fed.' The words came out smooth as oil and he marvelled at how cool he was and her tongue came out and he tasted the freshness of it and closed his eyes, lifting a hand to her breast.

He touched the leathery skin and his eyes flicked wide open. Heather McDougall was writhing on the ground, the three moles like risen cancers on her cheek, while he was pressing against her chest, trying to get the heart to start and the smell of her blood and vomit was like a cloud in the air. Helen was screaming at him to do something while June just kept telling him he was a bastard and that he'd destroyed another one and that she wouldn't have his children if he were the last man on earth.

He turned back to the dying woman and Greta Simon leered up at him with that monstrous dent caving in the side of her head and forcing her red eye to look at the other one, madness swimming in her gaze and her laughter cackling out. 'I left my baby lying here,' she screeched. 'And went to gather blueberries. She took it she took it she TOOK IT.'

'I did not,' June hissed. 'I didn't want that baby. I wanted *yours*.'

David spun, confused, and the sun was going down and the dragonflies came whirring in on their helicopter wings, great eyes redly reflecting the setting sun. Helen lay back in the grass beside the water-filled crater. He bent to kiss her again, now strangely excited. She put her hand down between his legs and trailed her fingers up against his thigh. He felt the heat expand on the side of his cheek and she leaned into him once more, pressing against him and he was inside her, slowly surging, back and forth, smelling the heady scent of her body and feeling the shudder and gasp as she pressed against him. She lay back and looked at him with the sun in her eyes and after a while the water rippled and something dark and devilish broke the surface and began to haul its way up the stalk of reed, expanding as it came until it reached eye level and the skin on the back split down the middle and something else came out. He raised his camera to get a picture of the light reflecting on the bulbous, predator's eyes, but it was no dragonfly emerging, it was a small, fragile baby baboon, screeching in fear and alarm and he felt the sudden anger build up inside him.

'Bastard,' June bawled fiercely. 'It's your baby, don't you see?'

He turned, whirling, and saw Helen was gone and spun back to June who was turning slowly away with the red sun in her eyes. Over in the bushes the pipits were feeding a huge bird, the size of a turkey, and the baboon squealed harshly as it sank slowly into the water.

He awoke with a sudden start, heart hammering, thrown out of sleep by the sudden fear of the incomprehensible and by the sudden flare of pain in his nose when his arm knocked against it. The heat on his cheek was almost a pain and a real pain was jabbing in at the muscle of his neck. In the video recorder the tape was screeching to a halt, rewinding itself back to the start.

Groggily he forced himself up on to one elbow, then pushed again until he was sitting. He had slid down to the thick rug, too close to the gas fire. His cheek felt as if it was baked and for an instant he imagined he could smell scorched hairs. The tape

256

squealed shrilly then clicked to a stop. The terrified baboon sound, or what had seemed like a baboon in his dream, died instantly. He moved again and his neck protested in a stab of stiff pain. He groaned and knocked his glass over, spilling a tablespoon of Jack Daniel's on to the carpet. The scent of whiskey overpowered everything else and David came fully awake.

The after-images of his dream danced in his vision, fading slowly. June's face still held the expression he had seen when she'd stormed out. Old Greta Simon's distorted head slowly fuzzed out, leaving Helen Lamont, eyes glazed and mouth open, as she had been in the strange dream. Embarrassment and sudden lust challenged one another and cancelled each other out.

For a few minutes, blinking the sleep away, he tried to recapture the details of the dream, but they faded as quickly as the images had done, leaving him with the slightly disoriented, half-bewildered sense of something not quite achieved, of something half grasped and now lost.

He got up, went to the bathroom to wash his face in cold water, massaging the cramped muscles of his neck with a cool hand, and then came back through to the living room. Somewhere in the ten yards from bathroom to where he'd fallen asleep, the notion he'd been reaching for came in on him with complete, crystalline clarity. The connection.

He sat down by the table and clenched his hands together, resting his chin on the lattice his fingers made, thinking about a concept so monstrous he could hardly believe he was even considering its possibility. He let out a long, slow breath. The dream images had fragmented and vanished, but the core of the symbolism remained with him, mental pieces interlocking, parts forming a monumental whole. He wondered why he had not put them together before, because his interest in the natural world had already provided him with all of the clues. He had known about the drives and the imperatives without having to see them again on a television programme.

Drives. Imperatives. Programming.

Pieces of the jigsaw. Could they all fit? He sat and forced himself to think, drawing on the dream images, sizing them up. The naturalist on television had spoken of the basic instinct that is the engine of the vast and intricate biosphere of the earth, the urge to replicate. The cuckoo of David's dream came back to him, the hairless and blind chick, murdering its foster-siblings by throwing them from the nest while its new parents could do nothing but follow their programming to respond to its cries for food and work themselves to exhaustion to feed their giant ward.

A brood parasite, the cuckoo was. There were worse para-sites, but this one used the parents' drive to protect its off-spring. Like the baby baboon's cry, which drove the adults to feed and protect. Like the bird suicidally remaining on the nest, the genetic programme was clear. The bird had no choice.

And in humans, biologically no further along on the evolution-ary trail, did they have any real choice? He thought of a baby's high-pitched cry and knew that even he would experience the quickening of his pulse and the tightening of his nerves if he heard a child's wail. That response was an evolutionary necessity. It was how the infant controlled the parent.

If, *if* there was a kind of thing that had evolved to use humans, how best to be protected? There was one answer to that.

The concept he'd arrived at was such a stupendous one that he really had to sit down and think it through. The bottle of Jack Daniel's picked up the light and gleamed from the far side of the table. He almost reached for it again, changed his mind, and hauled himself out of the chair, his stiff joints protesting at the sudden motion. He flipped the switch on the kettle and paced the kitchen, still juggling with mental images, until the kettle boiled. He made a pot of coffee, strong and aromatic, downed a cup, had another and by the time he was on his third, he was almost completely awake.

'Say that again?' Helen said, on the other end of the line, her voice quizzical. 'And slowly this time, so I can understand it.'

'I asked Mike Fitzgibbon the wrong question, I think – what sort of woman would steal a baby? What if it were the other way round?'

'You're serious?'

'Sure. Maybe. Christ, I don't know.' He stopped, pulled him-self tight. Took a mental step forward. 'Yes. I'm serious. It sounds crazy, and it is crazy. But we've done the checks and this is not the first time it's happened, and there's no real evidence of any other babies. Not ever. People have seen the prams, maybe even got a glimpse, but there's no name, no real identity.'

'Are you drunk?'

'I've had a drink. But I'm not drunk.' He wasn't sure if that was the actual truth or not, but right at that moment he felt absolutely sober. For a moment of misgiving, he felt that he might have made a complete idiot of himself, but then he realized how it all fitted.

'You think we should look for a baby that steals mothers?'

The silence drew out for longer than before. He hadn't heard a click on the line, but just as he wondered whether they'd been cut off, Helen's voice came back. She spoke quite softly.

'I don't want to talk about this just now. I think you should get some sleep and we'll talk about this in the morning.'

This time she hung up.

She never got back to sleep that night. Now that she was awake, now that he'd put the idea into her head, she couldn't let it go, and the more she thought about it, the more – however preposterous the notion seemed – the more it seemed to fit with the facts of the case.

What if? *What if?*

He'd told her about Greta Simon when they'd arrived back from Levenford where the trail had suddenly gone cold. Greta Simon who had been on the bridge where she'd been hit by the front end of a lorry and lost too much of her forebrain to exist in anything but an institution and a sphere of time somewhere back in the distant past. Who had had a baby which had gone missing, presumed drowned. But nobody knew who the baby was, or, more to the point, *whose*. And it was never found, dead or alive.

Heather McDougall who had vanished on the same day. She turned up dead in the mall, with a baby in a pram, caught on camera in the moment of death. The baby who was caught too, blurred, on the screen and then vanished also.

Ginny Marsden who had gone missing so dramatically while the McDougall woman lay writhing on the ground. Ginny

Marsden who had stopped and snatched the baby, cuddling it tight against her body.

The baby.

The link was there. It was clear, and yet Helen was reluctant to reach for both sides, because that would make her a conduit for the connection between one case, another, a third. If she was a conduit, the electrical connection, a canal linking them all, then she could be contaminated by this thing. Something inside of her mind, a part of her brain which might not quite operate on the truly rational level, the part of her mind that the little parasite had recognized over the distance when she had felt someone walk over her grave, shied away from this.

The fingers trailed down her spine again. Out in the dark, at the far end of the hallway, one of her nieces wailed faintly in dream distress and Helen remembered the same feeling of impending danger that she'd sensed when Nina Galt had opened the door and the bitter smell had come wafting out from the hostel room. The part of her mind that could reach out of the rational and pick up a taste of the other-natural, flexed, still weak, still unready, and gave her a sensation of shadowed and threatening prescience.

There was danger here and it was real.

What sort of baby would steal a mother?

Helen closed her eyes and tried to sleep, but the shiver of prescience wouldn't let her go. *Yet.*

She had sensed something that morning when she'd come out of the café where Margaret and Maisie had told her of the girl with the baby – the unnerving sensation of being watched, the touch of something sliding across her consciousness, leaving her with a feeling of contamination. She had dismissed it then, in the cold light of day, but in the dark of the night, with the dust motes dancing in a strip of moonlight, it came back to her, and she knew why she had been scared in the hostel. She had pushed the idea of being watched away from her, but it had clung. Now she knew her instinct had not been wrong. She had received a warning then, just as she felt the warning now.

And who had been watching unseen? Had it been Ginny Marsden? Had it been someone else? Intuition buzzed inside her head, an angry, insistent insect. Had it been some*thing* else?

Damn David Harper, she thought. He was probably fast asleep by now. He'd sounded thick and mumbling when he'd come on the phone, as if he'd just woken, or as if he'd gone the distance with that bottle of Jack Daniel's. He was most likely snoring like the proverbial pig by now, while she tossed and turned and tried to shake off the images that came dancing into her imagination, images she did not want to consider in the cold shallows of a midwinter's morning.

The baby's blurred, unclear and wavering likeness on the monitor screen stayed with her. It had no face.

CHAPTER TWENTY

There was no sign of Ginny Marsden on Christmas Eve. Both David and Helen had visited her parents again and he was struck by the resemblance in posture and expression between Winnie Marsden and old Catriona McDougall. At least Winnie knew her daughter was still alive.

'But why is she doing this?' she wanted to know. Ginny's boyfriend Tony hung about at the back of the room, looking uncomfortable and out of place. The western division which covered Levenford had assigned two patrols to make inquiries and both David and Helen had spent a cold day collating the information they had. It wasn't until the afternoon before Christmas that word came back that she might have boarded a train again, heading for the city. That would complicate the search.

David drove Helen to her mother's house and found the place filled with sisters and brothers-in-law and a confusing array of children. Almost everybody, it seemed, was wrapping presents, hanging Christmas cards, or crowding into the kitchen to cook or eat. It was a benign bedlam. David was introduced all round and promptly forgot most of the names. Helen told her mother they had to go back to the office just to sort out some paperwork. Mrs Lamont, whose hair was still dark and thick and whose smile showed how well Helen would weather the years, expressed harassed sympathy and told David not to keep her daughter out too late at this time of the year. He promised, not sure whether he had any control at all.

Outside in the early-evening cold he asked her, 'What paperwork?'

'It's a madhouse in there. I need some quiet. Let's go back to yours. My own place will be just the same. Families at Christmas. Who'd have them?'

David had to stop at a corner store for another bottle of Jack Daniel's and added a bottle of gin to the list. He bought two six-packs, selecting cold ones from the fridge, threw in crisps of all flavours and a variety of peanuts.

262

He hung her heavy jacket on the hook beside his dragonfly picture, which had escaped June's wrath. He hadn't had much time to reflect seriously on her dramatic exit, because he'd been busy since the morning, but he'd been surprised when he'd woken that the swelling in his nose had gone down without leaving a tell-tale bruise which would have caused comment at the station. There was hardly a twinge of pain.

He poured a drink for each of them and, without ceremony, Helen pushed some cushions off the sofa, bundled them into a little nest and made herself comfortable on the carpet in front of the fire. Outside, the sky was still clear and the forecast promised a sharp frost. The moon was haloed in crystals of ice. Helen sipped her drink while he talked about the difficulty of finding anybody in the city, especially someone who did not want to be found, until finally she stopped him and asked him about the previous night's phone call.

'Oh, that was just the drink talking,' he said, not meeting her eye. He'd been hoping to avoid this and during the day, because she hadn't mentioned it, he'd thought she might have forgotten. In the heat of the night, the thought had been so positive, so clear. In the cold of the morning, however, it was such a colossal concept that he had to get some distance on it. It had been a mistake, he knew, to dump it on her. 'I'd had a blow to the head.'

'Don't bullshit, David.' The words came out sharply, not angrily. 'There's something happening here that I don't understand. You were trying to tell me something.'

'Look, I was just trying to rationalize all of this,' he admitted. 'I told you I spoke to the old woman, Greta Simon. Her story is just a reprise of the Heather McDougall story. Simon said she lost a baby. It happened on the same day McDougall went missing back in the sixties. We have incontrovertible proof that Ginny Marsden took the baby from the mall, and it was the same one McDougall had wheeled in a few minutes earlier before she threw a thrombo on the floor.'

'Nice turn of phrase,' Helen said. 'Very sympathetic.' David ignored her and went on.

'So I'm just trying to establish connections. We already have links I suppose, but nothing that makes sense. Nothing I'm ready to put in any report to the boss or to Scott Cruden.'

'But you said something about babies stealing mothers.'

'It's true. I did. I'm sorry, but my imagination was running away from me and I apologize for waking you.'

'No, it's more than that,' Helen said. 'I can tell. You're back-tracking right now. I wondered why you never mentioned anything about this today. I kept waiting for you to bring it up. And that's the real reason I dragged you out of my mother's. Well, part of it. Anyway, you'll be pleased to know I lay awake all night after you called because I realize there's something not quite right here. You know more than you're telling. Don't ask me how I know that, for I don't know myself. But call me a liar if you dare.'

'No, ' David conceded. 'I know as much, or as little as you. But as old Sherlock said, whatever's left, however improbable, is the truth. Has to be. So I have to think on even improbable things. There's a similarity all down the line, and I mean going back to the forties when old Greta said *she* had found a baby. Mike Fitzgibbon says she's incapable of lying, so I have to take that as the truth. She had a baby in her care in the forties and then again in the sixties. McDougall had one in the sixties and another one this week. Where did the babies come from? Why were both of these women lactating? Old Hardingwell told me McDougall was carrying something in her blood, major-league molecules, long peptide chains, something that was very like the structure of a virus, so Hardingwell says, and I'm thinking maybe that's another connection. Greta had something in her blood that they couldn't identify, not then. It was probably the same thing. Maybe this baby's some kind of carrier. Maybe it's got a virus, or some kind of bug that alters hormones, for instance. '

'You think they're sick?' Helen asked and when she did she felt a tremor again. *Someone's walked over my grave again.* She remembered the odd moment on the stairs when both she and Nina Galt were adjusting the pressure of their bras.

'I don't know,' David answered her question. 'There's just a strange chain of events. It could be something like rabies.'

The shiver ran through Helen again. Had she herself picked up some contamination? 'What do you mean?'

'Rabies is a very smart virus. It programmes its hosts. First it infects the bloodstream, then gets to the saliva glands. After that it spreads to the central nervous system, drives the host mad, and then makes it bite others. The saliva in the bite carries the virus on again, right down the line. Smart.'

'And you think that's what we're dealing with? Something that could infect us?'

'No. I don't think there's any danger. I'm just thinking aloud. Maybe there's a virus that alters a woman's drive. Maybe. I don't know. But Ginny Marsden stole a baby. So did Heather McDougall, at least so we have to surmise, because she never gave birth and nobody has reported the kid missing. As far as I know she stole one from Greta Simon, way back when I was in shorts. Greta herself says somebody took it, and Phil Cutcheon now believes the baby never died.'

'So what happened to the babies?'

'That's the million-dollar question. We know, or have to assume, that the Marsden girl still has this one, but we don't know where it came from. Nor do we know what happened to the one I believe Heather McDougall might have picked up at Duncryne Bridge. Did it die? Did she give it away to somebody else? And where did *that* one come from, because old Greta never gave birth, and as far as I know, nobody ever reported that baby missing. As you say, it gets pretty weird.'

'So there could be some disease that makes women steal babies?'

David laughed. 'There would have to be one that made mothers fail to report the loss too.'

'So far we're talking of at least five, because McDougall has been seen with kids for the past five years, off and on. Unless it's the same baby,' Helen said, trying to make it sound light, but the shiver stole through her again.

'It would have to be a pretty old baby,' David said, but he gave Helen an odd, almost surprised glance. 'Greta, she had a baby back in the forties, during the war. That would make it close to sixty by now.'

'Older than my mother,' Helen said, wishing the strange feeling of uneasy prescience would leave her.

'Anyway, that was just one of the things I was considering

last night, and I shouldn't have mentioned it. I'd been looking at some of my natural history tapes and I started seeing similarities. Now it sounds a bit crazy. I'll have to think on it some more.' Even as he said it, he knew he was not telling the entire truth. What had started out as a simple sudden death in plain sight had turned into something completely different. David was experiencing the same thrill of forewarning that was making Helen's skin stick out in goosebumps. *Unless it's the same baby*, she had said. That had brought out his own gooseflesh.

Just as he mentioned his tapes, he recalled his dream again, and instantly he felt his ears redden in the way that they did when he was angry, but this time the flush was embarrassment. In a flash of recollection he smelled the scent of her body and felt the shudder and gasp as she forced herself against him. He felt her eyes on him and tried to look away casually.

'It might sound just as crazy, but I think there is something wrong in this whole thing. I don't like it.' Helen said. 'To tell you the truth, it gives me the creeps.' She was turned towards him, looking up, her face raised, almost aggressively. As she moved, his memory superimposed the dream Helen who had turned and trailed soft fingers on the length of his thigh. Another flush of embarrassment, and of something entirely different, crept up from his open collar and he rubbed his fingers on his jawline, as if to check his day's growth.

She said something else which he missed.

'Are you listening?' She was looking right at him and the gleam of the side-light was in her eyes, the way the sun had been.

'I was thinking back,' he said truthfully, wondering if she could see the flush of colour. To cover it, he poured her another drink, while she held the glass up to him, her arm outstretched. The glass trembled slightly, breaking up the light from the fire into diamond sparkles. She raised herself up and sat beside him.

'What do you really think?' she demanded. 'And no bullshit this time.'

'As long as this is between the two of us?'

She nodded, staring earnestly into his eyes. 'Of course it is. I'm one of the good guys too.' She smiled, but there was something else in the smile. He couldn't identify it.

'You know anything about the natural world?'

'I know a brachiosaur from a brontosaurus,' she said. 'Which is more than you do. Yes. I grew up in the country. My uncle's a gamekeeper. His brother's the best poacher you ever saw, and they still drink together. I know where the dipper nests and where the big trout lie in a stream. It's not all dolls and prams with us girls, you know.'

'I was thinking about cuckoos last night.'

'Brood parasites.'

'Exactly. I was putting two and two together and coming up with a lot more than four.'

She pulled back and looked him straight again. 'You think we're dealing with some kind of parasite? Like a vampire?'

'I don't know. Maybe. Possibly. As I said, when everything else is exhausted . . . anyway I think I'd like a day off, and get my head clear of all of this. Too many names and too many babies. Maybe I need a week off.'

'That's a good idea,' Helen said. 'I wish I hadn't brought the subject up. I think we should declare an amnesty from work, at least for now.'

'Suits me,' he said, wondering how crazy she thought he was. He leaned back. This time she took his glass, poured another measure and handed it back to him. She drew her feet up, tucked them underneath her, took a sip of wine.

'So what are we going to do?' she asked.

'Christ alone knows.' He looked at her and she looked back at him, dark eyes still catching the light. That expression was back again and it looked like hunger.

'I don't mean what will we do about work,' she said. 'That can wait. It's Christmas, isn't it?'

He turned to her and without any hesitation she leaned forward and kissed him. He was so taken aback that he did nothing for all of five seconds. She pulled back, eyes scanning his, left to right and back again, her own eyes wounded and moist.

'Do I need some mistletoe?' she asked softly, now uncertain. 'Or have I grown two heads?' He tried to shake his head, opened his mouth just a little. She tried again and this time, more prepared, he responded to the press of her mouth and the heat of her skin. Her tongue slid out very slowly and licked the inside of his lips, a glide of sensuous contact. He met it with his own. She made a very small noise that could have been a whimper or a sigh. There were two simultaneous, almost identical sounds as they reached blindly to put their glasses down on the table and then slowly leaned against the back of the sofa.

Some time later, he took her into his bedroom.

The moonlight sliced its slash on the wall, catching the bright and beady red eye of a fighting black grouse cock framed on the wall, though neither of them saw that.

Some time after that, deeper in the night, he'd lain there, listening to her breathing in the dark, watching the moonlight on the curve of her neck, feeling guilt about June and uncertainty about getting involved with somebody he liked and somebody he worked with and wondered how he'd got himself into this mess. He also recalled the shiver and sigh that he'd seen in the dream and then felt against him in their deep contact, and marvelled at her responses.

Later she woke up and heard him snoring softly and cuddled into him, grateful for his presence on a cold night, delighting in the press of his tough body. She knew, she told herself, that she hadn't exactly planned this, but she was glad it had happened. There were some drives that had a control all of their own. In the dark, she remembered his touch and the sudden ripple that had started deep within her and become a shudder, and she remembered crying out, almost laughing with the force of it. She remembered the urgent demand that overwhelmed her and the spark of warm tears as it began to ebb. She remembered shaking her head when he had looked at her to see if there was anything wrong.

Some time, even later, she roused him with more kisses and told him she had to go home before midnight. When he sleepily asked why, his face a picture of confusion and then drowsy comprehension, she told him.

'It's Christmas. They'll expect me. It's a family thing and I can't break the tradition.'

Ten minutes later, wrapped in his dressing gown and looking

even more slender and defenceless, she dried the short-cropped hair that gave her the pixielike, innocent look which belied her toughness. She came out of the bathroom and gave him a smile that dimmed the light.

'I found the birthmark,' she said, laughing and he went along with it, trying to squash down the feelings of guilt and uneasy elation. June's angry face floated in his memory, scolding and accusing. He made her image fade away and knew that he had turned a corner. Exactly where he was going, he had no idea.

Helen changed back into her jeans and flying jacket while he got his winter jerkin out. She turned to him, easing his collar up to protect his neck, while he did exactly the same thing to her.

'Listen,' she said. 'If you go all guilty on me, I'll feel we did something wrong. But I know we didn't. No pressure at all, but I'd like to do it again. You're one of the good guys. I've known that for a while, since even before you saved me from getting my ribs stove in, and there's hellish few of you around.'

He pulled her close and kissed her again, savouring the taste and the texture, and suddenly he did not want her to leave. June still tried to intrude, but he mentally straight-armed her away. When he and Helen broke apart, almost fighting for breath, he reluctantly walked her down to his car, enjoying the close clutch she had on his arm, then drove through the bitter cold night and waited outside her house until she went inside. It was just less than an hour short of midnight and the moon was riding high. On an impulse, he drove to his parents' house, and slept in the bunk he'd used as a boy.

In the morning, when he woke, for a confused few moments he thought it all might have been a dream.

On the day before Christmas Mrs Cosgrove woke early and prepared breakfast for the woman and her child. They had gone to bed early, the thin woman moving slowly as if she'd walked a thousand miles and had more to go before she reached her destination. The old woman remembered thinking it was a darned shame that anybody, any woman and child, should be away from home at this time of the year, staying in a bed-and-breakfast with strangers.

She looked at the line of cards along her wall, pictures of

angels and glittery Santa Claus figures. At the far end there was a big one from her youngest son in Canada. It was a picture of the Virgin Mary and her child, in a wooden stable. Another young woman, thought old Mrs Cosgrove, a long way from home with her baby. She put the kettle on and decided to give the woman two eggs and another rasher of bacon.

As it happened, the stranger only ate the yolks and never touched the tea. She went out early and came back a while later with money which she handed over without a word. There was enough for a week's lodgings, and that meant the poor dear meant to stay here right over the new year. Mrs Cosgrove wondered if maybe the girl was running away from something, if she was in trouble with the police. She leaned back, taking the weight on her good leg and had a good look at her paying guest. The girl's bones were pressed out against her cheeks, making the hollows under the ridges as dark as caves.

As she told David Harper some days later: 'I thought then that she was really sick. You know, that new thing, the Aids plague. There wasn't a pick of meat on her. Just a rickle of bones. She should never have been out with that baby. I took a peek inside his pram and he looked healthy enough to me. He had big blue eyes and a smile that would break your heart. I could have picked him up and cuddled him. But the mother, she looked as if her days were numbered, poor soul. You know what she looked like? She was like one of them Jews in Germany in the war. The ones in the camps.'

This was some time after what happened in Barloan Harbour came to light.

The mother was finished.

She would not last much longer and already he felt the panic of imminent vulnerability rise up like bile inside him. The old dry woman, who had a familiar scent, one he remembered from days long past, hovered around, desiccated and done, while the mother's milk turned sour and thin. He was hungry now and there was little sustenance left.

He had to find another one quickly. His senses told him that he would be discovered here if he did not move on. The others, the man and the woman – the very thought of her made the new hunger swell under the old one – would follow and the mother was not strong enough to carry him much further.

It was time. He lifted his head from the mother's teat and forced his thought into her. She sagged back, twisting away from the hurt of it. Her eyes screwed themselves into slits. There was a dirty smell of old blood on her breath, partially from the pound of raw minced beef she'd got from the corner shop and also from the three gaping molar sockets where, during the night, the teeth had loosened and come out. He touched her inside and she slowly sat forward and began to wrap him up.

She was almost finished. He had to act.

Ginny Marsden had no strength to resist when it made her rouse.

It made her take it out into the cold again when all she wanted to do was close her eyes and let it all drift away.

Hail Mary, full of grace, please, mother, take this thing away from me. The thoughts linked together in a profound litany. *Holy Mother, please.* She had never been a religious person, not since the piety of early childhood and bedtime prayers, but the words all came back to her now in her extremity. Some time that day she had turned to a mirror and the part of her own mind that was still hers had perceived the witch in the reflection and she had known it was herself. She had been too exhausted to be shocked or frightened. She sensed the end rushing towards her. The witch in the mirror looked like death itself – death warmed up, as her mother used to say a million years ago, and a tear sprung into the eyes of the decrepit, desiccated woman who used to be Ginny Marsden the girl. The glistening tear tumbled over the blood-purple bags under her eye and trailed down the cavernous hollow of her cheek, getting lost in the fissure cracks around her lips.

The approaching end was not rushing fast enough.

Her joints ground like sand in gearwheels, and the rasp of the friction vibrated the deadly abrasion through her faltering frame. Her mouth hurt and her eyes hurt. She began to button her coat over her breasts, noting vaguely that they were not as swollen as they had been. The nipples were red and raw, and beside them, where it had sucked blood through the capillaries and the pores, the skin was beginning to map itself in islands of scabs.

It made her move although everything inside her burned. If she had been able to, she would have got on her knees and prayed, though the pain of that would have made her scream out or pass out, she was sure, before the thing woke her up to urge her on. It stared into her eyes and she stared back, unable to pull away while inside of her head, her mind was shrieking uncontrollably at the knowledge that she was damned.

Devil. It's possessed me.

And when she thought that, the corner of her mind that had a kind of rational capacity suddenly recalled what she'd learned a long time ago, of Christ in his passion in the Garden of Gethsemane, when he was so raddled by the fear of the manner of his death that the blood had come bursting through the pores of his body and he had appealed to his Father to take this chalice away.

Ginny Marsden might have prayed, but the monster reached out with brutal force and made her stand up. Her joints squealed, both in pain and in actuality, rusted door hinges protesting. She shuffled to the door. Somewhere at the front of the house the television was on and old Mrs Cosgrove was talking to someone, possibly on the telephone. It didn't matter. Ginny was made to walk towards the back door, down the narrow little lobby that separated her bedroom from the kitchen. The door opened easily, though the motion of turning the handle sent needles of pain up to her elbow. She went out, almost tripping over the lip of the door edge, and down the broad path where the skeletons of the summer's sweet peas and nasturtiums waited to be cleared away in spring. The air was cold and froze her lungs, but she moved on, turning at the gate, not even looking back.

The thing in her arms pulled at her, making her move, right, left, pain, hurt, right, left, *please God, take this chalice*, agony. She staggered not down the hill – as she had before to get to the little bank and the corner shop – but upwards, along the road, with a brief pause to let her gather her failing strength.

Oh please make it stop.

It made her go on. Here the hedges were frosted in the cold, rimed with ice that blew in from the estuary on the misty sea-*haar*. Down in the distance a monster howled and she did not even realize it was a foghorn blaring from a blinded tanker slowly feeling its way upriver.

Behind her came a hollow clatter and she half turned, regretting the motion instantly as the shock-waves ran up the length of her spine and seemed to explode in her head. For an instant the whole world went black and she felt herself stumble towards the ditch. The light came back on instantly and she managed to keep her feet. Two women on horseback passed by, eyeing her curiously. The horses whickered nervously.

'Watch out for the ice, Kate,' one of them said, 'the ditch has overflowed close to the hedge. They're worried they'll slip.'

The one who spoke passed by. Ginny Marsden looked up just as the woman at the rear, auburn-haired, darker than Ginny had been and robustly healthy, looked down. Her eyes widened, not in shock, but in surprise, the way people do when they see the deformed and the grotesque. Ginny had no strength to react to it. All she felt was the pain and the rasp of bone on bone. The horse skittered nervously, snorting through dilated nostrils and shaking its head, and the woman had to pull tight on the reins. It got over the patch of ice, hooves sounding like mallets, to dance on beyond, still spooked. The woman up ahead called back and the second woman caught up on her. The horse settled down again, slowing to a walk, and moved on with its companion, both sashaying like proud women, backsides swaying from side to side. They quickly passed by, and carried on along the road to where it turned uphill. At the turn, the one who had stared at Ginny turned back to look again.

'Come on, Kate, I have to go and fetch Jeremy from the airport,' her companion said, and the horses moved on. The cold was beginning to sink into Ginny's bones and for a little while, she was grateful for the numbness that spread into her throbbing fingers. She too kept moving, slow and faltering, forced onwards while the thing at her breast kept its eyes closed tight against the weak winter sunlight that came through the gap between the buttons of her coat.

It took her more than an hour to make it to the barn. In that time a jeep almost knocked her into the ditch, just pulling up at the last moment as the woman, the one who had been on the leading horse, realized there was someone walking on the narrow farm road. The headlights, on full despite the hour, seared her eyes, causing her to turn away from a fresh input of hurt. Her breath was coming hard and sore, like an asthmatic's in the midst of a final, catastrophic attack. The pain in her feet had gone completely now, as if the nerves had been eaten away. She heard her shoes slap down on the hard road metal as she approached the gate. In the near distance, horses whinnied, their hollow voices magnified by the slope of the stable roof. Overhead, a flight of honking geese passed across the now deepening sky, and off in the distance, a magpie machine-gunned its aggressive call from a stand of trees.

It impelled her to climb the gate. The metal clanked as she hauled herself over it, not knowing where she was or where it was forcing her to go. In her head, her own befuddled mind was chanting the prayer over and over again, *Holy Mary, Mother of God, pray for us sinners, pray for me. Let this chalice pass.* The prayers went unanswered. She got down on the other side of the gate, slipped on the slick ice and felt her left thigh bone pull right out of the socket. A momentary shriek of anguish ripped in there, but still she was goaded onwards, the mad puppeteer that had control of her volition tugging on her strings. The next twenty yards were easier, because the bone was now outside its own socket. Somehow, she was able to walk, in an odd, stagger-ing, crablike motion, and the immense pain screamed only in the right thigh where the joints still grated. She had no will-power to be thankful for this tiniest of mercies, only enough of herself to repeat the mantra over and over.

She stumbled onwards. Out beyond the whitewashed walls, a dog barked, high and agitated. Closer in, from the roof of an ancient dovecote, a throng of pigeons clapped their panicked way into the air. The sky was getting noticeably darker now. There was a light at the side of the farm's small courtyard which sent the shadows of the hawthorn hedge reaching to-wards her. The light hurt her eyes, but she still shambled towards it. The whinnying was closer now, though the barking had stopped. Out of sight a galvanized bucket was kicked over by a careless foot and she stopped, still muttering madly to herself. Her feet were bleeding where the bones had pushed into decaying flesh, and it was hard for her to keep her balance. At her breast, the thing nuzzled, sucking hard at her skin.

The barn door yawned and she went inside. It was musty here, musty and dusty, with harsh motes of hay dancing on the air in the light that speared in solid beams through the holes in the wall. The bales were piled high, great oblongs of fodder, stacked one upon the other. It made her climb up the giant steps of hay, higher and higher, her heart now pounding with the enormous effort, her feet unable to feel where they were stepping, her dislocated hip making it almost impossible for her to bend her leg properly, but still it drove her, onward and upward, now far above the village of Barloan Harbour. Finally she could go no further. Up at the back the hay bales formed a natural hollow which had actually been carved out by a teenage boy from down in the basin who had found the ideal place, out of the cold and away from prying eyes, to copulate at every opportunity with the red-haired, heavy-set girl who occasionally helped out in the tackroom. The place, this close to Christmas, was empty except for the faint squeak of the rat colony which burrowed far under the hay.

Ginny Marsden hated rats. She would have run a mile, under normal circumstances, had she realized what was making the sound, had she even heard the feral twittering beneath the bales. But these were far from normal circumstances.

Ginny Marsden was dying.

She slumped down in the shadows, gasping for breath, lungs rasping air and hay dust, her sides heaving like an exhausted animal.

Holy Mary, Mother of God, pray for us sinners now and at the hour of our death.

The dark crowded in on her, and in the depth of it, despite the disastrous wasting of her body, she saw her mother's face floating just in front of her, wavering as if seen through a film of liquid. Her mother was calling out to her, anguished at her loss, and Ginny tried desperately to call out to her. The illusion wavered, rippling in the forefront of her mind, and in that moment, Ginny knew that her mother was crying for her. She did not even know that this was Christmas Eve and that all of her presents were wrapped and neatly stacked under the tree.

The thing on her breast snuffled and gobbled. Its mind was loosening its grip on her. She was suddenly aware of that, that it was withdrawing. Tears welled up in her eyes as equally suddenly she was able to think of her warm house and her mother's hugs and the safety she had once, so long ago, taken for granted.

Way in the distance, down in Barloan Harbour, a choir from St Fillan's church sang carols through a public-address system and the faint melody floated uphill, even as far as the farm, even as far as the barn, even as far as Ginny Marsden's dissolving mind. The tears rolled down the hollows of her cheeks while the thing sucked. Inside, she could feel the breakdown of her organs and her body. It had made her come here, overcoming the defeat in her own body, showing the power of its kind of mind over her kind of matter, making her achieve what should have been impossible by the force of its desperation and its unnatural drive.

Monster.

In the distance the choir sang about three kings and a babe in a manger, huddled in a barn. Here, the thing that sometimes looked like a baby and sometimes looked like a beast from a black nightmare lifted its flat head. In the dark, its great eyes flicked open. Ginny Marsden saw them, big as saucers and emitting a strange light of their own, but they were not fixed on her. Lizard-like, spider-like, it clambered off her prostrate and almost paralysed body. It rustled in the hay. Down in the depths, a small thing squeaked and then went silent. She heard a kind of breathless snort and the monster moved away.

She tried to move but could not. The pain in her fingers was draining away, mercifully. The hurt in her spine was still a throbbing shudder, but she knew that too would fade in the end.

About the time David Harper and Helen Lamont found their way into his bed and into each other, something burst inside Ginny Marsden with an actual sound of tearing. She twisted to the side with the force of the rupture. Her bowels pulsed and her whole lower intestine began to protrude from her anus, while her womb, that part of her that should have carried children of her own, turned itself inside out and prolapsed grotesquely down through her vagina into the cold air.

She rolled over and coughed hard. A gout of wet came up her windpipe and through her throat to burst in her mouth and then drip down to the hay. Liquid bubbled inside of her. The dark took on a strange lightness and a succession of faces paraded in front of her: Celia Barker smiling as she waved goodbye and told her to look after the cat and the fish, Mork and Mindy; her mother again, an elegant, oddly young face leaning over a tiny Ginny with a soft sponge in her hand and a smile on her face; the dark-haired woman who had come stumbling into Celia's kitchen; old Maggie and Maisie in the bus-stop café; Mrs Cosgrove and her big breakfast; the woman on the horse. And glaring past them all, the red and ferocious eyes of the monster that had snared her and drained her of everything that she was.

Holy Mother of God, pray. Holy. Pray . . .

Prey.

Something else burst inside Ginny Marsden. Just before everything began to fade, she thought of her father and his big manly hands and his gentle eyes and then she thought of Tony and how she had never let him touch her, saving herself for a special day, saving herself for the first time. Saving herself for motherhood.

She coughed again while, down in the hay, the thing snuffled, moving towards the door of the barn. The choirboys sang and in the distance the beast in the fog moaned far down the firth.

In the Lamont household, there was laughter as sisters and cousins kissed and hugged Christmas in. David Harper kissed his mother and poured a good shot of whiskey for himself and his father, thinking about Helen Lamont and wondering what to do with the present he'd already bought for June.

In the Marsden house, a man and women cried in each other's arms and prayed to God for the safe return of their daughter.

On the other side of the country, in the tiny house where Heather McDougall had been brought up until the day the monster had snared her, Catriona McDougall wished her husband a happy Christmas and pecked him on the cheek, though he should have been in bed a long time ago. Something had made her stay up and she treated herself to a small, thick sherry. She watched her man stare drooling at the fire for a time, then she lay back and, inside her head, a small vessel burst. She died without even knowing it. Old Callum, too far gone to realize that his wife was never going to wake up, died in mid morning when the heat of the fire drained away and the house slowly froze.

Ginny Marsden coughed violently and some other bloodied part of herself gouted out. The darkness expanded in a blare of white light which quickly fizzled down to a point of intense luminescence. All pain fled from her and she let out a rattling sigh which went strangely silent as very quickly the pinpoint of light expanded again and she was swept through it on a wonderful wave of warmth.

CHAPTER TWENTY-ONE

'Now *you* look as if you've gone ten rounds,' David told Helen as they went up the steps at the city station in the sharp cold of morning. He was tired too, but Helen looked as if she had some way to go before she'd be properly awake.

'Christmastime exhaustion,' she said wearily. 'Family, food and fornicating.' Her words made breath billows on the frosted air and her cheeks were rosy with the cold. Her dark eyes sparkled with mischief.

'What, again?' he stopped, turning towards her. She laughed out loud, a natural explosion of mirth.

'No, silly bugger, not *again*.' Her mirth bubbled into the words. 'You were enough, thank you ever so much. Aftermath and afterglow, and I'm suffering from two mornings after in a row. It's good to get back to some semblance of sanity, if there is any sanity in all of this. I need the break.' She straight-armed the fire door, giving it a surprisingly vigorous push (though he should not have been surprised for he'd felt the strength in her supple body), almost slamming it into a young policeman who was adjusting his cap and not paying attention.

'Have a good Christmas then?' she asked.

'I told you on the phone. It was fine. Quiet, friendly. My mother fussed over me and I loved it.' He gave her an apprais-ing look in the empty corridor. 'I could have used some other company though.'

'Me too. "I just called to say" . . .,' she started to sing, then burst into laughter. 'I just called to make sure you weren't floun-dering in guilt and angst. I'm glad I did. My mother's getting suspicious, naturally. She sees every man as a potential rescuer from spinsterhood, so we'll have to be careful.'

He opened the door and held it. She walked past, did a quick visual sweep of the room, saw there was no one there and gave him a very quick kiss, right on the ear, pursing her lips and smacking hard. He pulled back fast as his eardrum almost burst with the sudden vacuum.

'Be gentle for God's sake,' he said. She laughed again and pushed past him. He sat down at his desk and the phone rang almost immediately. He snatched it up while Helen rummaged for change and went down the corridor to the coffee machine.

Phil Cutcheon, the former CID boss from the east side, apologized for calling so early. He exchanged brief seasonal pleasantries and then got straight down to business. The two of them talked for five minutes or more. Helen came back with two coffees, and placed one on the edge of his desk just as Phil was winding up. David said he'd see him in an hour.

Two other detectives came in, both broad and beefy men who just looked like cops in grey suit uniforms. They looked bloodshot and grizzled with festive overload. One belched loudly, apologized to the nearly empty office, wished David and Helen a merry Christmas and asked if they'd both spent the night in the office. David felt his ears begin to colour. Helen said she wished she had.

David had turned from his desk with the hot coffee and opened a filing cabinet when the phone rang again. The big sergeant lifted the receiver in passing, growled a word, listened for a couple of seconds then passed it to David. 'It's your missus,' he said, winking.

Helen watched David over the rim of her plastic cup as he took the call. June's voice had that broken, hiccup quality of someone who's been crying for a while and might start again any moment. She apologized for her outburst and her ultimatum, told him how much she had missed him over Christmas, said she still had his present all wrapped up and how she had suffered a blighted day. He listened, feeling his face colour now beneath Helen's gaze. She narrowed her eyes in mock threat while June babbled on the phone, cramming her words and sentences together. Finally Helen tilted her face, almost challenging, and then, surprisingly, mouthed him a silent kiss – not arrogantly, more in support. At least, so he thought. The other thought that occurred to him was the no-holds-barred status of both love and war.

'I'll have to think,' he said flatly. 'I really will.' He felt suddenly wary of being trapped and he wanted to fight against it. She was having second thoughts, no doubt exacerbated by the fact that she and he had not been together at Christmas, and she wanted to make up. He did not want to hurt her by turning her down flat, but at the same time he recalled the powerful relief he'd felt when she had walked out. 'No. I can't right now . . . No. I'm too busy.'

It made him feel cruel and heartless, but right at that moment he wanted her off the phone. He needed space to think. Already the complications had set in, and he'd had a full day to think about Helen Lamont and himself and, strangely, he did not feel any entrapment there. He'd always considered it a mistake to get involved with colleagues, but that was the voice of reason. He'd woken up on Christmas morning thinking about her and spent most of the day doing the same thing. She'd called to tell him the same story. He did not regret what had happened at all. Finally the phone went down. Helen came across, walking as casually as she was able. The two other men were at their desks, bent over paperwork.

'You're still one of the good guys,' she said in a whisper. 'I just want you to know that. Even if you do go back to her.' She looked him right in the eye, and that quick look conveyed a number of messages. One of them was that she didn't give herself to everybody, that she had put her trust in him. Her voice was almost inaudible, even though she was right up against him. One of the other men looked up, noticed the closeness, grinned and looked away. 'But I'd really prefer it if you didn't. That's the truth.'

The phone rang. The first man picked it up, listened, then called over to Helen. 'Transferring to you,' he said. 'Some chick asking for you. Says you left a message on her machine. Lost her cat and her wallet.'

Helen picked up the receiver and spoke for the first time to Celia Barker.

In the corner of the barn, in the dark gloom of that cold Christmas Eve, he had been dimly aware of the mother's racking cough, but his attention was focused forwards. She groaned, and for a moment it sounded like the wind through the eaves, but on this gloaming winter afternoon, there was no wind.

Somewhere outside the barn, a dog barked, the high-pitched, narking aggression of a small terrier. Beyond it, a cockerel bawled its hoarse territorial cry. Close by, a horse whinnied and jostled a stable door.

He was alone now and all of his instincts were wound up tight, all of his needs and hungers. He was afraid too, caught almost in the open while the mother was disintegrating. The sense of danger and vulnerability swelled inside him like a cancer. The skin on his back was peeling away, cracking into fissures while underneath the tender new skin protruded. He scratched at his back, twisting his oddly jointed limb round to hook a nail there to ease the dreadful itch.

Behind him the used-up mother was finishing. He could sense her glow diminish in his mind. Already he had released his grip on her. It had taken effort to bring her up this far, forcing her every step of the way, over the gate and up into the hay, while everything in her was shutting down, the muscles and the nerves. He had drained her even as she staggered upwards, stealing the last of her, emptying the store for his coming change.

It was not quite dark, not yet, but it would be soon. He would move then, when it was safe enough. Over in the corner, something squeaked. He considered it, sitting as still as stone, but let the creature live, reaching out the merest tickle of thought to encompass its glow. He might need all of his energy for the next stage. He crouched there near the door, eyes closed, just sensing. The big beasts were nervous, somehow aware of his presence and not liking it at all. They skittered and banged on the stalls. He ignored them. They would taste bad, his own senses told him, but if necessary, if he had to, he would change one of them if he could. He did not know if that was possible, but intuition told him the creatures were big and warm and female.

The moon finally rose in the sky, dim at first in the fading of the day, but gathering brightness. The silver light did not hurt his eyes the way the day did, the way the street lights burned. The moonlight was a cold balm on his dry and itching skin. He edged closer to the barn door, letting his eyes open slowly to take in the new night. With equal care he moved out of the barn, a small, thin thing, scuttling on all fours, back arched and blunt face held low. The cold was intense here and automatically he speeded up, getting close to the stable wall. He rounded it, almost rat-like, keeping very close to the masonry. Here, the smell of horses was powerful, but there were other smells too, the dry scent of birds' feathers, the bitter reek of cats and the flat odour of dogs. Over and above that, the real smell came, thin and far off. Enticing and intoxicating.

The smell of a mother.

He had sensed her before, as he instinctively led the old one up the hill towards the new.

He scuttled round the whitewashed corner of the stables, skirting the rain barrel, into the farm's small courtyard. Here, the angle of the roof cut off the moonlight, throwing this part into inky blackness. He sat there, sending thought tendrils to probe ahead. He touched a trundling black beetle under a slate and it died with a click of its jaws, legs folding up under the carapace. Over in the dovecote the pigeons panicked again, taking to the air in a clatter of alarm. He saw them as warm, fluttering dots of light in his outreach.

He took two crab-steps, then emerged into the courtyard proper. Two of his glands pulsed, audibly hissing as they expelled their payload into the air. He waited while it drifted away from him, revelling in his own scent. He paused for a few tense seconds.

Bedlam erupted.

On the far side, the wire door of a small brick chicken coop punched outwards as every bird went into a frenzy of hysteria. Feathers tumbled out into the cold air, wide snowflakes slowly swinging towards the ground. A tall cockerel came barging out from an outhouse doorway, crest erect, chest feathers bristling with instant outraged aggression. It stood on its toes and started to crow, harsh and brittle.

From the shadows nearby, a black cat came rocketing out, screaming in absolute fury. It clamped its jaws on the bird's head. Bone crunched and the cock's brains dribbled out of its skull. Instantly its wings thrashed in its death convulsion. The cat did not even stop. It crossed the courtyard, a black streak, heading straight for the corner.

He turned to it and touched hard with a pulse of thought. The cat went veering off and ran straight for the chicken coop, hitting the door with such a crash that it shook on its hinges. Its claws snagged the wire and it hung there, screeching like a demon while inside the coop the already mad chickens pecked ferociously at each other and whirled in crazed circles.

The two terriers, half asleep in their basket just inside the storm door where coats and boots were stored, jolted instantly awake and came bolting out, ears erect, sniffing at the air, growling in the back of their throats. He hardly needed to touch them at all, such was their sensitivity to the powerful scent. One flopped to the ground, then got up again, snarling, saliva already beginning to foam in its mouth.

Inside the byre, just through the wall from where he crouched, seven Jersey cows, sheltered from the harsh winter, simultaneously began to leak milk in identical streams from each udder and, inside their vast wombs, seven unformed calves died. Beyond that, two fillies began to stamp their feet in the stables and then, as one, began to lash out at the door with their heavy hooves, sending shards of wood whirling into the air. One of them, the lead horse on the way uphill, kicked so hard that a bone in its foot broke and burst through the skin. It bled until morning.

The second terrier jumped on the first, clasping it round the chubby waist and started bucking uncontrollably. The first one, still drooling saliva, howled in protest as its brother mounted it and penetrated in two savage thrusts. It turned, fighting the weight, and snapped hard, taking hair and flesh in its jaws, rending both. Its teeth clamped on the carotid artery, bit through and blood fountained. Its brother, a white cairn terrier, kept on thrusting even as its lifeblood drained away. It was unable to stop. After a short while, both dogs toppled over, the first one still twitching but dead, the second covered in blood and gasping for breath, bleeding from its ruptured anus.

Over at the coop the cat still hung on the wire, screeching like a banshee.

A flock of starlings, as ever susceptible to the emanations of the alien mind, were first startled by the howling of the cattle as their udders expressed their milk, then the touch scraped over them. They took to the air in a whirr of wings, trying to find an escape. As one they wheeled and as one they crashed into the far wall of the byre and dropped with soft little plops to the ground.

The moon rose over the roof of the outhouse as he moved forward towards the door, all of his senses now sharp as fangs and his glands pumped up so hard he could feel the skin over them rip and tear.

Inside of him the hunger and the need was vast.

'I always thought he was a bit cracked, the old fool,' Phil Cutcheon said. 'Now it could be me that's been the fool all along.'

Between them sat a folder which bulged with papers. It was tied with an old-fashioned piece of ribbon, like a lawyer's brief.

'I dismissed old McBean way back in the sixties, but it might just turn out he was a better policeman than anybody ever gave him credit for. Way back then, before the Duncryne killing and the thing that happened to Greta Simon, old Ron had a theory. It became an obsession with him. He approached me in confidence much later, maybe the year after Heather McDougall went missing. I thought it was just a fixation with him, and it probably was, but he was certainly a methodical old beggar. This is his obsession box. I got it from his grandson, who was on the force. He left to start his own security firm.'

'And what is it?' David asked. The office was still half empty at this time on Boxing Day. All he could offer the retired policeman was a bitter coffee from the machine, but Phil smiled and told him it took him back to the good old days. 'Coffee and ulcers. Sore feet and rain always dripping down the back of the neck. Good old days? I must be dreaming.' He took a big swig of coffee and smacked his lips, relishing the nostalgia, then opened the file. 'It was when you came to see me that I remembered this. I hadn't thought about it for a long time, and if I'd done my job properly, I would have made the connection.'

'But what is it?' David repeated. Helen had gone round to Celia Barker's house, alone again, though she was hardly in any danger now the girl was home. He would have preferred to have gone with her but something in Phil Cutcheon's tone had made him stay.

'It's a list of connections, just like yours, only much older. I have to be honest, I probably rejected them because I was busy with a murder and because I didn't have the balls even to consider the possibilities. Old Ron McBean came to me with a crazy story and I told him to shove it. I didn't want anybody to think I was insane.'

'What are the connections?'

Phil leaned forward and drew out an old-fashioned police notebook. 'You told me about Greta Simon and the McDougall woman and now this young girl from your neck of the woods. You've got a connection between Greta and Heather and now you've found a link between Heather and your girl.'

'Ginny. Virginia for long.'

'Yes. Her. Now, this little lot takes your links and makes a daisy chain of the whole lot. You might be able to make some sense out of it, for what I think doesn't make sense. Either there's something getting passed on like a disease, or there's something really strange happening that I don't want to think about.' He sat back and his brows gathered down, making his seamed and benign face look very grave. 'Ron McBean stumbled on to something that he couldn't let go. His grandson tells me it became a real obsession with him, long after he left the force. He died about ten years ago.'

He tapped the file, flicked open the flap and drew out a few sheets of paper. The top page was white except for a yellow border at the very top where it had been exposed to sunlight at some time. The writing was thick and blocky, a big man's writing, slow and careful. Phil turned it so David could read it. He drew his finger down to the third paragraph, drawing David's eyes with it.

There is no doubt in my mind now, none whatsoever, that the chain will continue. It confounds all reason and the Good Lord alone knows the whys and wherefores of it all. I remember speaking to the divinity professor at Heriot Watt University who told me there was no historic proof that Herod sent out soldiers to slaughter the innocents. He told me that was from a more ancient Hebrew myth. He told me there have been many occasions in history when baby boys were hunted and slaughtered without mercy. There are books in the library which confirm this. There is a necropolis in Ghassul, in the Holy Land, by the Dead Sea, where hundreds of infants have been uncovered, all of them with wooden stakes through their heads. In the mountains near Lake Titicaca, they have uncovered the dried remains of many baby boys, all of them murdered. The professor told me of this madness happening again and again all down through the years. Perhaps the hunt for a newborn baby was not a search for the King of Kings at all. They could have been looking for the devil incarnate.

The Simon woman does not have all of her faculties back yet and the doctors say she never will again. Dr Tvedt tells me it is a miracle that she is alive at all, though in all honesty I am hardly minded to consider miracles. The opposite in fact. I only wish the records went back further, but they do not. All I know is that it appeared on record some time in the past century. It will appear again, but where and when, who knows. All I can say, with absolute clarity and conviction, is that it will emerge again and anything that can do that, time and time again, is not natural.

Nobody is prepared to accept any of this research, and I can hardly blame any of them, even seasoned officers. They do not believe in the unnatural, but as God-fearing men, there is no shame in it. I have tried and failed, but I will continue to try. It will be seen again, with some other poor woman. All I am able to do is check the library for news of a sudden death and the disappearance of a child and I will know it is still alive. It may not be for many years and I don't know how many I have yet allotted. God willing, and I pray every night that He is, I hope I am alive and I hope I can hunt it down.

'A shade dramatic,' David said. 'And pedantic.'

'He was a bit old-fashioned, and a bit serious too,' Phil agreed. 'He was an Elder of the Church, but not a Holy Willie. There was never any harm in him, so people, including me, turned a blind eye. I kept it turned, most of the time, but I did go along to see Greta Simon every now and again and I was never sure why. I never told you that. I thought you should see her for yourself. Anyway, now I don't have a pension to lose. Old McBean's grandson says we can have this. He's not interested. Thinks the old man was a bit wandered.'

'Sounds as if he was,' David said guardedly.

'Aye, there's that possibility. But he was just following leads, and he was never even a detective, just a small-town sergeant and a God-fearing man. Not sophisticated like you and me.' David recognized the irony in Phil's voice. 'But like you, he thought he was on to something and he dug away. Like you. You turned up at my door because you're just doing your job, checking out the possibilities. Most folk would have got an ID on the dead woman and left it at that, but you stuck with it. You think there's something odd going on here and when you mentioned this baby and the women involved, it gave me something to really consider. I wasn't going to turn a blind eye like I did all those years ago.'

David started to speak but Phil held up a hand.

'At the end of the day, there might be nothing in it, nothing at all, and I would rather like to believe that this is the case. But if you put what you know and what Ron McBean turned up, put them all together, then I have to tell you I have my doubts. You're on to something, and I don't mind telling you that it makes my skin crawl.'

Something was wrong.

Kate Park heard the racket from the back of the house and for a moment she thought it was something on the television. The baby whimpered softly in its cot and she pulled back the coverlet. The child's eyes were crinkled up tight and she was making little blind sucking motions, even though she was fed and fast asleep. Kate's cousin Jill, who had baby-sat while she and Anne Collins had gone for a canter down on the bottom fallow, had got a lift home in Anne's jeep, and while Kate herself had felt a pang of guilt about getting a baby-sitter less than a month after the birth, the easy ride had felt good, even if her muscles were unused to the exercise and the saddle stretched the tender skin where she'd been stitched. The hot shower had soothed the stiffness of the muscles. Her hair was still damp, ringletted in dark auburn curls. She was tucking the cover back when the racket started up out at the front of the farmhouse.

Instantly she knew something was wrong. The skin between her shoulderblades puckered, drawing over her spine in a creeping contraction. She moved out of the bedroom, closing the door slowly, aware of the tremble in her hand and unable to explain it. She shivered, pulled her dressing gown close.

Out beyond the front door the dogs were howling. Or one of the dogs was howling, or coughing. Two of the cockerels were squawking as if they were in a fight to the death. Behind her, in the baby's room, little Lucy whimpered again.

Something wrong.

The slam of the horses' hooves against the stable doors came like hammerblows, muffled only by the thick walls. The cattle were lowing, their cries, high and pained, echoing out through the ventilation slits of the metal-roofed byre.

She stood in the hallway, undecided. The dogs were not howling, they were snarling as if they were tearing each other's throats out. There were other sounds. The caterwauling of the cat, the frenzied clucking of the chickens.

What was happening out there?

Something wrong something wrong something wrong. The message came from deep inside her, as clearly as a voice in her head. There was somebody out there. Kate wondered what to do. Jack's guns were in the front-room cabinet. His cartridge belt was still hanging in the hallway stand, illegally of course for they should have been secured, but this was a working farm. She stood undecided, her heart tripping joltingly, breath held in. She lifted a hand to her brow to push back her short curls.

A faint noise came from just inside the porch. Her eyes flicked to the door. The dogs normally sat there in the corner of the porch, out of the wind. The sound came again, a soft scrape of noise that was suddenly and incongruously loud, reaching her over the madhouse cacophony out in the yard and beyond.

Something made a faint whining sound, almost like a kitten, but unnervingly, terrifyingly alien. Her blood turned to ice. She backed off. The letterbox rattled; the knocker rapped several times in quick succession against the plate. A faint squeal, the familiar sound the postman made when he delivered the mail, creaked out from the slot where Jack had always promised to oil the hinge and spring.

A hand and an arm came through. For an instant it looked grey and slender and somehow tattered. Her heart stopped, kicked, stopped again. Her vision swam.

A baby's hand was scrabbling through the slit.

Oh my . . . oh my . . .

Her mouth worked but no sound came out. She thought she would pass out and that thought seemed to shunt her heart back into life again, hammering against her ribs, suddenly as loud and as violent as the horses' hooves on the stable doors.

The baby's hand reached out into the hallway, the small pink fingers splayed. A baby whimpered, soft as a lamb and as insistent, and she knew it was not Lucy. Behind her Lucy cried out, a shivery, pitiful little cry. In that instant, Kate Park felt her soul wrenched one way and another. Yet her mind was suddenly frozen in abject terror. She was here alone with her baby in a farmhouse, a mile above the town. The animals were going crazy out in the yard. A baby's hand was reaching through the letterbox of her front door.

Poison, she thought. Jack had warned her about the sheep-dip organo-phosphates that had caused a series of hill farmers no end of mental and physical problems. Had some of it spilled, sprayed from Upper Loan Farm and drifted down on the wind?

Yet she knew it was not poison. She was here alone with her baby and another baby, a mite hardly bigger than her own, was clambering on her door, reaching its hand inside, grasping mutely at the air, trying to get in at her, trying to come in.

It was the most terrifying sight. It was a scene from a mother's worst nightmare, made more hellish because her own motherly instincts were so strong.

It was impossible. It was completely impossible, she tried to tell herself, but her eyes were watching the creepy waving motion as the small baby fingers grasped emptiness.

'Go,' she heard her voice blurt. 'Go away. Get away.' She backed up the hallway. The hand stopped moving. It stayed there, still and outstretched, completely and utterly incomprehensible, completely and utterly terrifying.

Lucy squealed and Kate's heart kicked again as her mother-self recognized her baby's fear and alarm. Lucy had somehow sensed the threat. Kate felt her knees give way just a fraction. She was a strong and robust woman, a farmer's wife who could confidently do a man's work on any day of the week, yet the sight of the baby's hand had simply robbed her of strength.

Without warning, the hand withdrew. The letterbox lip slapped shut with a rattle of metal. A weight dropped to the tiles outside. Something scuttled. Kate leaned against the wall, willing her heart to slow down. She did not know what to do, what to think. The apparition had been so unnatural, so *alien*, that her entire reasoning process was struggling to cope. In the room, Lucy was howling frantically and Kate wanted to turn towards her, but she was scared to take her eyes off the door, in case that impossible little hand came groping for her again.

Think, damn you, think.

She tried. There was something she should consider. She knew that, but her mind, fizzing and sparking under the horror, wouldn't let her think rationally. She turned, bumping her substantial breast on the corner of the wall, ignoring the dull thud of pain.

There was something else. Some other danger. She heard the scuttle, imagined she heard the scrape of dog's nails on the flagstones round the side of the house where she kept the kitchen garden. Imagined she heard the scurry of some small but heavy thing crunching over the smooth stones bordering the path. Imagined she heard the creak of the – *Oh no it can get in through the* – cat flap.

The sound came from the back of the house. The cat flap opened, then snicked closed with a whump of compression. Something skittered on the red tiles just inside the door. An insane fear shuddered up the whole length of her spine. Lucy screamed. The sound of movement came down the back hall. She whirled to face whatever it was, every nerve glassy with tension, the hairs on her neck crawling with a life of their own.

Something dark came around the corner of the back hall. Its limbs pistoned, hit against the wall as the momentum carried it to the side, then surged down the narrow hallway. Kate Park saw it black and tattered, then grey and thin, altering, blurring as it moved towards her, turning into the pink form of a baby, still moving with spidery swiftness, its round face held up, eyes fixed on her. She gasped, tried to turn. Her heel caught the carpet and she fell backwards, slamming against the door which whipped open to crack against the wall.

Kate tried to scream, unable to get her balance while the

monstrous little baby scuttled towards her, the lines of its face wavering as if melted under heat. It was a baby, and it was a monster, a double-image monster which shrivelled out of the pink as if bursting out of a skin, to become a red-eyed, staring thing with a flat grey face and a circular, pouting mouth which opened and closed like a sphincter, showing a ring of glassy needle teeth.

It moved like an awful insect.

She went clattering to the floor, feet scrabbling for purchase. Lucy was screeching, infected with the horror and the panic, her blank baby mind sensing some kind of threat. Kate rolled, got a hand up to fend the thing off, to slam it against the wall.

It came scrambling up her body, faster than she would have believed, a nightmare in motion, its nails digging into the towelling of the robe, snatching at the rough dry fabric, digging into her skin. Its eyes opened, flat blank and fathomless red depths with the dry texture of polished stone. It looked right into her eyes, bored its glare deep inside her.

Lucy, she tried to say. Oh Lucy it's got me.

It clung there. Some dark and foul touch scraped across her mind, poked and probed, snagged like black and poisonous thorns. The thing flexed, arched its back. The swellings down its side seemed to expand and then deflate. For an instant a watery, unpleasant hiss seared the air. Then the scent hit her.

She opened her mouth in a soundless scream. The eyes began to close, rippling down from red. The scent invaded her pores. The room spun crazily and the baby on her chest looked into her eyes with its own which were turning from red to black and then to blue, and now closing very slowly. It held her tight, fingers digging into her skin while the scent, at once bitter and rancid and somehow sweet as honeydew, flowed into her. Instantly her breasts ached. Her nipples swelled to painful tautness. A shudder of some desperate need swelled deep inside her and an awful warmth spread down in her tender womb.

Behind her Lucy screamed in fear, but Kate never heard the sound of her own child. The baby on her chest looked in her eyes and stole her away.

'I knew we should have checked,' Helen said. David had waited until she came back, unsure of what to tell her. He had read the papers Phil Cutcheon had dropped on his desk and what they contained had set up a powerful oscillation of thought. They had brought back the conversation he'd had with Helen the day after he'd phoned her in a blur of alcohol and confusion.

What kind of baby would steal a mother?

He had not been the first to consider that possibility, however impossible. It was all in the laboriously written pages in the file, compiled by the careful hand of an old policeman who had got a glimpse of the unusual and had followed its trail. The dead hand of old Ron McBean led him down through the years.

Was it real? Was it true? David had asked himself the question over and over again, always coming up with the same answer. It was a history, a strange and continuing history, of lives touched, lives affected, and by the looks of it, lives distorted and destroyed. Where McBean had broken off, David Harper had started, linking the past to the present. There was now no doubt in his mind that this was real and that something dreadful was repeating itself over and over and over.

'I knew we should have checked,' Helen repeated when he looked up from the papers. 'Celia Barker confirms that Ginny Marsden was supposed to look after her pets. She had a key to the place. She's just back from holiday, lucky little bitch, and she finds out her bank card's missing. Ginny Marsden has her PIN number.' Helen was flushed, most likely with sudden heat inside the office, but she looked elated. 'We should have checked to find out where she was staying and contacted her direct.'

'But she wouldn't have known the bank card had gone missing.'

'Or about the dead cat. You'd think she'd stumbled across the bullet-ridden bodies of her parents the way she's going on. I told her the cat probably starved because nobody fed it. She found it in the bin.'

'That's where I put it,' David said. 'The flies were at it. Its eyes were gone, poor thing.' Even as he said that, he realized there was something wrong there, something he'd missed. He tried to reach for it, but his mind was full of other matters to consider. It wasn't that important.

'Anyway, all we have to do now is get to the bank tomorrow. They'll tell us what branch the Marsden girl's been dipping and we'll find her.'

'Assuming that she's used the card,' David said. He was itching to show Helen the old McBean file.

She turned on him, telling him not to be such a pessimist, her dark eyes flaring just a little but more theatrically than in anger. 'So what did you tell her?'

'Who?'

'The girl who wants to kiss and make up and come back.'

'I told her no,' he said, not quite truthfully, wishing he had, now determined to make it the truth. The smile Helen gave him made the small lie worth while. All was fair in this war, and it was that smile that finally made his mind up completely. It conveyed a feeling so powerful and so welcome that he wondered at the strength of it, and the instant effect it had on him. He only wondered why he hadn't felt its power before.

They both went back, at his request, to David's place when they finally cleared their desks. One of the other detectives said something, leaning across to his colleague who sniggered. Helen stopped at the door, turned back and bent over the desk, putting her face right up against his. 'I can hear the slither of your grubby little mind,' she whispered, quite softly, almost seductively. 'You should go back to vice squad where you can get free rides any day of the week. It's better than playing pocket pool with yourself and letting your imagination run riot.'

'But I . . .' the other man started to say.

'But nothing,' Helen said, very slowly. 'I hear any rumours and I'll be back, big boy. Got me?'

The man, who tipped the scales at twice what Helen weighed, nodded. She had a reputation for taking no prisoners.

'What was that all about?' David asked. His mind had been on other things and he hadn't noticed the exchange of looks and the laugh.

'Nothing I can't handle,' she said. 'Girl talk.'

CHAPTER TWENTY-TWO

Jack Park came trundling up the road in his Range Rover, feeling the car bounce and sway as he took the corner, avoiding the ice patch picked out by the beams where the ditch had spilled over from the field drain. He'd had a long drive up from Leyburn in Yorkshire, pushing the limits, desperate to get home for Christmas Eve. He'd checked out a couple of yearlings that might make an addition to his stable. Already he was planning for an end to recession and brighter times ahead when people had more money to spend. He was ready to open his paddocks as a riding school and get rid of the cattle altogether. At the height Middle Loan Farm stood, high on the hill overlooking the estuary, with a commanding view up- and downriver and with the orange lights of the sweeping bridge a magnificent string of jewels in the winter mist, the farming was a marginal business. Weekend riders and summer trekkers would be money-spinners when the time was right. It had been Kate's idea, one he'd initially looked at with some reluctance, farming being well grained into his tough hide. His family had farmed Middle Loan since the middle of the last century.

He eased the car round the last bend and on to the narrow straight that led up to the farm, noting with no surprise the mounds of horse droppings, pleased at the evidence that Kate had got back in the saddle again so soon after her legs were in the stirrups. He smiled at his own joke and looked forward to a good malt whisky, and after that, a great grilled steak festooned with mushrooms and tomatoes. More than that, he was glad to have made it home despite the delays on the motorways. He wanted to help wrap little Lucy's Christmas presents for the morrow. He'd phoned from the pit stop down the motorway and Kate had held the baby close, letting her snuffle into the receiver and instantly Jack had felt that warm, urgent twist in his belly.

That was something completely new. He was in love. For the first time in his life, he was completely, irrevocably, absolutely in love. It was different from his love for Kate, vast orders of magnitude stronger, though what he felt for his wife was a powerful emotion in itself. He loved Kate truly and deeply. They were friends and lovers and partners. He had hungered for her since the first time they'd met at a young farmers' barn dance. Her auburn hair had been longer then, glinting chestnut under the lights, and she'd been a pound or two lighter, no featherweight but her sturdy curves had been well within his own ideal, and her thick red hair which faded to a fair matt beside her ears had hinted at a hirsute secrecy which he had discovered and revelled in. He had lusted after her and he had liked her, and now he loved her, he imagined, as much as any man loved a woman.

But when he saw Lucy the hammerblow had hit him so hard he was still, a month later, reeling from it. It hit him in his heart and in his soul. He had seen her head push out from between Kate's quivering, straining thighs and seen the ugly little twisted face and then they'd handed the slippery bundle to him and to her and he had almost died of it.

Parental love kicked him down, lifted him up, made him fly. It had been the most momentous occasion of his entire life. Up in the high field, bringing the Highland cattle down to the low pasture, he would savour the moment over and over again. Coming up the motorway, he would relive it time and again so that the distance passed without him being able to recall any of the road. Lucy had transformed from a lump to a squirming thing and then to a complete human person as soon as he held her in his big, strong hands. He'd been a man who was comfortable but vague about the idea of impending parenthood. Then Lucy had arrived and he was a father and what he had considered before as sunshine paled to twilight beside the radiance she put in his heart.

He gunned the engine, feeling the back fishtail on the black ice now forming on the road, and got to the gate. The light was on at the corner of the byre, the warm and welcoming glow reflecting off the whitewashed corner to illuminate the side of the barn and the smooth cobbles of the entrance to the courtyard. He got out of the car, arching his back to take the stiffness of the road out of his muscles, glad he was driving a high-topped four-by-four and not some low-slung saloon which would leave him creaking for weeks. He walked to the gate imagining he could feel the heat of the halogen lights on the back of his neck, and as he pulled back the bolt, something flickered above him.

Startled, he turned. The flock of pigeons, racers and fantails, the doves white as snow in the beams, went fluttering with a whistle of wings, wheeling all together across the road, circling the dovecote.

Jack pulled the bolt against the spring and swung the gate forward, once again reminding himself that one day he'd get a remote control to open the gate and save him the stop-start every time he arrived home. The pigeons wheeled round again, flying in tight formation. They looked panicked and he wondered if a stoat had got into the dovecote. A stoat or a ferret, or one of those wild mink from the old farm on Langside, any of them could do a lot of damage in a henhouse or a pigeon loft. The birds hardly ever flew at night and when they did, they sought a place to roost as quickly as possible. Something must have spooked them to keep them on the wing. He thought he'd get the gun out and check out the roost after he'd something to eat.

He drove the car through, got back out again, closed the gate. For a third time the birds circled, trying to keep within the circle of light the lamp afforded, certainly unwilling to settle. Ahead, one of the horses was whinnying. It kicked the door and he thought maybe it was a fox, though the horses rarely bothered about vermin. The car door closed again and the heat inside, after the cold of the night, was suddenly quite oppressive. A bead of sweat trickled down the back of his neck, making the skin pucker. He was halfway along the track, along the home straight as he and Kate called it, when he realized it was not a hot sweat at all.

The hairs on his forearms rippled.

Something wrong?

He shook his head. He was just tired. On the way up, apart from thoughts of his beautiful daughter, he'd decided the price was right for two fillies. He'd phone later and make the deal. All work and no play made Jack a tired boy. That's what he told himself as he slowed down at the end of the drive where the close-cropped hawthorn hedge glistened with frost. The lights bounced off the whitewash of the wall, making the mist sparkle. With the ease of long practice he swung the wheel, feeling another little slip as the tyres spun on the cobbles, then he was past the gaping door of the barn.

He eased the car into the yard, hauled hard to the left and drove straight into the garage.

Something wrong?

A twist of odd sensation gripped the muscles of his belly and gave a squeeze. He was out of the car, still in the dark of the garage. For some reason, his senses seemed abnormally acute. He stopped for a moment, put his hands on the roof, leaning. His breath made pale clouds in the dark and he tried to slow it down.

Why was he breathing fast?

'Must be coming down with something,' Jack muttered. He hoped not. Not now when they were getting ready to celebrate their first Christmas as a threesome. He'd told both his and Kate's parents that they would see them all the day after Christmas at the earliest. The big day, he swore, was going to be spent at home, all of it. The tree, the presents, the dinner, it was to be their special time and he wasn't going to drag his baby daughter round from one side of the country to another on a cold winter day to visit grandparents.

'Maybe it's the flu,' he wondered aloud. He really hoped not. He didn't want the baby catching something. If she got sick he'd shit himself, he knew that. He'd be unable to move for the fear of it. The hairs on his forearms were all marching together, standing proud like proper little soldiers. The skin puckered and tensed and he thought that was very odd indeed. 'Maybe it's just the cold.' The cold. A cold. Maybe even just the tiring journey. He pushed himself away from the car.

Something wrong?

He walked out of the dark, into the yard and stopped. The moon was high and dented, a slumped face in the velvet sky. Over beyond the byre, the birds were still flying. What was different? He knew what was different, his instinct and his years on the farm told him. Something was out of place.

There was noise where there should be silence. There was

silence where there should be noise. It was inside out and back to front.

Out behind the cowshed, where the sturdy stables gave on to the paddock where the old dovecote stood, the horses were whining and snorting. Inside the byre, the cows were all howling. They were not lowing, the way they would in the spring as they headed along to the pasture, or the way they would when it was time for the afternoon milking. They were howling the way cattle did when their calf is straining to get out, head turned back the wrong way, stuck in the passage. The hoarse, high grunts made the building shiver.

'What the hell . . .?' he began to say. Where was Kate? Had she gone for the vet? Were they sick?

Something wrong.

The chickens were silent. There was always, even in the dark, a squawk as the pecking order was maintained. He turned and walked past the coop. A black shape came scooting from the side of the shed, startling him off balance. The cat, the best ratter they'd had in years, went screeching past him, ran towards the door of the tackroom, missed and hit the wall with such a thud that it somersaulted backwards, landed on its back, got to its feet still screeching and then shot right out of the yard.

Where were the dogs? They always yapped him a frenzied welcome. Always.

'What the fuck is going on here?' he demanded to know, speaking aloud.

He almost went straight to the house, but something held him back. He could not explain it, but suddenly he felt a shudder of real apprehension. Instead, he crossed to the byre, got his weight against the door and slid it open on its rollers.

The cows were crying, each one in its stall, crying in the darkness. He reached a hand and hit the light. The fluorescent bars flicked on one after another, drenching the place in their pale glare. He walked into the centre, breathing in that familiar scent of hot milk and warm cattle. He turned round by the stalls and his jaw dropped so far his chin hit his chest.

He was standing in a pool of milk. Six of the seven cattle were tensed, legs spread, sides convulsing while all of their milk poured steadily in pulsing spurts from their grotesquely swollen udders. One of them managed to turn round, like the others a gentle Jersey the colour of old honey. Its great black eye rolled, showing white all round, pinning him with the desperation of its pain.

'Jesus God,' Jack said finally.

The six cattle were standing and each of them was covered in blood. Behind them all, in the drainage gully, their part-formed calves, calves that would have been born in the late spring, lay in greasy heaps of placenta and blood. They had all aborted, every one of them.

A chill stole right inside Jack Park. Were they sick? Had they caught a disease?

He saw his milk profits and his calf profits gone for the year. The sick feeling of apprehension lurched inside him and he staggered backwards with the force of it, feeling his own gorge rise at the grotesque sight of all those slimy packages that would have been calves. The seventh Jersey, his best milker and mother of three others standing in the stalls, was lying on the ground, her head at a strange angle. She must have slipped and the collar had choked her, retaining all the blood in her head so that her face was swollen and black and her tongue lolled grotesquely. Her legs were splayed and from just under her tail, her calf's hind legs protruded like a growth.

Jack moved back. His good-to-be-home feeling had evaporated instantly.

'What the fuck? What the bloody fuck?' he demanded to know, almost incoherent. He bulled his way out of the barn, leaving the cattle to bellow their pain. He crossed the yard at a trot and almost stumbled over the terriers, still locked in a dead embrace.

Poison, he thought. Had there been a leak of something? Had there been a chemical emission from the big incinerator over the hill towards Drumadder? His heart was beating so hard it made him dizzy. Nausea and vertigo came on in waves. The front porch loomed and the fear gripped him with a cold and merciless hand.

'No,' he said aloud, a panicked blurt of sound.

This was all madness. His dogs were dead. His cattle were dying. What was happening? The pigeons flew round again in their sweep and he wanted to shoot them down, make them stop. He wanted the cattle to stop their wailing, the horse to quit kicking. He wanted the pressure inside his head to slacken because suddenly he was afraid to open his own front door.

Had somebody done this? Had somebody killed his dogs and poisoned his cattle? The irrational thought did not seem irrational to him, not at that moment. His wife and child, his wife and his baby girl, they were inside the house – *were they?* – waiting for him to come home to them.

'Oh please,' he whimpered, his voice breaking, gaining two octaves in height, making him feel like a helpless boy again. He moved towards the door, then stopped. Maybe there was somebody here. Maybe strangers had come and were inside there now.

Anger suddenly flared up under the dread, twisting him this way and that. He tried to think. They would expect him to come in the front. They could be waiting for him. *They*. He turned and, moving as quickly as his quivering muscles would let him, went to the path at the side of the house up beside the vegetable garden, unwittingly following the trail of something else.

The mother's breath came harsh and shallow, panting for air. She was fighting him, even in her shallow slumber, the way the other one had fought him, but he had been prepared and he had battened her down, using the last of his resources to subdue her. Now she lay slumped in the darkness, dazed and numb, her body shaking all over, vibrating with a delicious frequency that set up a sympathetic resonance within himself.

His glands had squeezed him almost dry, filling her with his essence. Her massive teats were filling now: he could feel the swell of them and smell the nourishment surge inside. He had clamped his sucker mouth on one of them, letting his tiny teeth dig just enough into the surface of the skin so that the trickle of blood and new milk mingled. Strength began to flow back into him in a hot stream.

After a while he was aware of the rumble of the engine as the car trundled along the road he'd been carried along when the day was fading.

Immediately, all of his senses went on the alert.

Ginny Marsden had coughed the last of her blood on to the hay and she died only an hour before little Lucy Park's life was stolen.

The baby's mother had been powerless, bound in mental webs and chemical manacles that prevented her from moving. She remained slumped against the wall with the image of the thing's eyes burned into her brain. The whole world had taken on a red tinge, turning the light of the room into a strange purple. She was gasping for breath, trying to clear her lungs of the acrid miasma that had sprayed out from it. Behind her the baby whimpered and the thing, the other baby, turned its head, quite unnaturally, almost completely around on its narrow shoulders, like an owl responding hungrily to a squeak in the dark. She needed to mother it, was compelled to feed it, yet at the same time she wanted to kill it. She had tried to reach and clasp it by the throat, but her hands were only capable of stroking its smooth, unblemished skin and pull it even closer to her own body. She could not make them grasp and strangle.

Behind her Lucy cried again, and the thing moved quickly. 'You can't walk,' she tried to reason, mouthing the words while dribbling saliva on to her bare chest. 'Just a baby.'

It clambered off her and moved to the little wicker Moses basket Jack had brought back from a trip down south. She heard the scrabble as it climbed up and she tried to scream a warning. The baby was climbing up to her child.

Not a baby, she tried to think, but the thought couldn't break through the membrane that encapsulated her own mind.

Out of sight, she heard a sucking, wet sound and her heart slumped, giving a slow double beat that was shock and loss and dreadful despair. She tried to move once more, but her limbs were incapable of anything more than a slow-motion, direction-less flop. Lucy cried out, thin and fearful, and then the sound faded out. Kate's mouth stretched wide in a silent scream and all that came out from between her quivering lips was thick and ropy saliva.

The baby, her own baby, gurgled again, a sound that was liquid and high. The cot rattled violently but she could not turn to stop it, could not turn to protect her own. After a while, the sound stopped and her baby was silent and the other one came crawling back to her, climbing up between her breasts again. She felt the terrible touch inside her head and the need to mother this thing came rushing back into her. Down in the depths of her belly, blood trickled. The baby's eyes bored into hers and forced her once again and she drew her arms around it, let it suckle, and after a while the appalling pain in her heart was crushed by the touch in her mind and she fell into a numbed daze.

It was some time later when she awoke, fuzzy and drugged, rising up from a black pool of sleep where terrible things happened in nightmare visions of death and destruction. She slowly got to her knees, clasping her baby tight, pressing its tiny frame against her. There was somebody outside and he was coming for the baby. She knew that without doubt.

She quickly moved to the front room, robe flapping. Someone was outside. She heard the engine, over and above the howling of the cattle. Someone was coming and the baby was in danger. She could feel its demands for protection: *mother me, mother me, mother me* . . . a mantra of wordless demand. She could do nothing except obey.

It was dark in the room where she sat in the corner, prepared now.

And all the time, her very soul was riven by the unspeakable knowledge that her own baby, her Lucy, was gone.

His guns were in the cabinet in the front of the house. There was a spare key in the roll-top desk in the same room, but it was still at the front of the house. He was sure nobody could break into the gun-case where the two twelve-bores stood side by side, but whoever was in the farmhouse could still be armed. He had convinced himself that the threat was human.

His heart was beating somewhere in his throat, making it difficult to breathe quietly. Fear and anger were battling it out, each a powerful force, but utter desperation overshadowed them both. His hands were shaking as he grabbed the spade from the side of the greenhouse and hefted it in two hands. It had been well used in the summer and autumn and the moonlight reflected off the abraded blade.

'Let them be all right,' he whispered under his breath in a hoarse prayer. 'Let them be all right. Please.' He appealed to any god, any force. What he was saying was, *Let them be alive.* Cold dread twisted inside him, and he could feel the loop of sudden nausea force upwards. He swallowed it back, telling himself he had to be clear, he had to be strong.

There was light inside the house, but no sound at all. He made his feet move silently on the flagstones, avoiding the small decorative chips that would crunch underfoot, and got to the back door. Very carefully, he turned the handle. The door opened a crack.

Something here.

The perturbing smell reached him and for an instant he thought again about poison or some sort of pollution. His heart leapt at the notion. Maybe they were safe. Maybe . . .

He opened the door further, pushing it quickly to prevent a squeal. He got inside, slunk along the narrow little corridor to the corner where it turned beside the baby's bedroom. Here the smell was thick and clogging and he felt his heart speed up with sudden vigour. Without warning, the desperation evaporated and the anger suddenly soared to ascendancy, making his temples pound. His vision wavered as the adrenaline punched into his bloodstream. He moved quickly, carried on the surge of rage, holding the spade right out in front of him, ready to decapitate the first bastard he saw. In his mind he saw an ugly head topple from shoulders to land with a thud and the image gave him a savage sensation of gleeful anticipation.

'Fuckin' bastards,' he growled, unaware that he spoke aloud. He barged, not quietly, into Lucy's room. It was empty. The little Moses basket was askew on its stand, and he knew instantly that Kate had grabbed the baby to protect it. She must have. He turned, about to storm out, then halted, garrotted by some new information. He spun back to lean over the cradle. A dark stain smudged the tight basket weave. A smudge of deep red.

His thudding heart hammered against his ribs with such violence it was like a minor explosion. A waxen doll lay on a red-stained pillow, a small and inhuman thing with plastic, stiff fingers, and half-closed dark eyes which glinted in the overhead light. A darker smudge indented under its chin, like a bruise. Twin trickles showed where tears had trailed from its glassy eyes.

The bolt of nausea made it into his throat, hard and bitter lumps hitting his palate only to be swallowed down in a little acrid stream. He turned away, stumbling, his brain in a state of complete rejection. He saw a doll, he told himself. It was just a doll that Kate must have bought for the baby.

The stiff little fingers reached up into the air. He could see them in his mind's eye and he knew they had to be plastic because they were still and unmoving, not like his baby girl's soft and gentle, perfectly formed hands. He made himself walk out of the door, trying to call his wife's name, but unable to get his mouth to form the words. The muscles in his belly were heaving and twitching and all across his back they were moving in conflict with each other as if the nerves had been disconnected and rewired wrongly. A singing noise filled his ears in a juicy, high-pitched monotone.

He staggered into the kitchen. On the stove a kettle was billowing steam. A pile of washing lay on the table. On the work surface by the sink, two substantial steaks were lying on a flat plate, each in a dark pool of blood.

'Must have been the steak,' he said. 'Must have been. Sure.' He giggled and the sound had a taste of madness in it. 'Should have washed her bloody hands first.' He laughed again, high and manic. 'Bloody good pun.'

Inside him, his inner voice was trying to make him go back into the baby's room, telling him to look again. His subconscious had taken in the shape in the cot and recognized it for what it was. Jack Park's conscious mind would not let him accept it.

He shouted his wife's name now. 'Kate, I'm home.' He still held the spade up like an axe as he walked into the front room.

His hand reached for the light, but even before he touched it, he saw her in the corner, slumped or crouched against the wall. Her robe was wide open and she held a small monkey in her arms. He blinked once, twice. The smell here was dreadful, nauseating. It stung his eyes and he felt the surge of emotions shudder through him again. He hit the switch and the thing on Kate's chest – both of the breasts were bared, rounded and full – its wizened form blurred. For a second it was grey and emaciated, ridged and flat-faced, and then its outlines ran and expanded. It was Lucy. He shook his head, trying clear his vision. The baby screamed and changed again, wavering into some ridged and blotched little gargoyle. The scream sounded like grinding glass. It scraped inside his head like fingernails down a blackboard. Sudden pain twisted in both ears.

'What the fu–?' The red eyes flicked open and glared at him.

A fucking alien Jesus it's a –

He didn't even think. He reacted, taking two steps forward, raising the spade at the same time. He would smash it off her. The thing twisted. It was Lucy again, small and fragile, bleating in fear. He was about to smash his daughter's head with the garden spade.

The picture of the doll in the cot, the doll with his child's face, suddenly leapt into the forefront of his mind. Utter horror swamped him. His brain almost stopped functioning under the overwhelming visual and mental and chemical assault. He managed one more step forward.

Thunder erupted from the corner and smashed him backwards into the wall. He spun, hit his knuckles against the cupboard door and saw a crimson slash appear on the paint.

'Wha . . .?'

Thunder roared again and slammed him in the side. His hip hit the wall and a strangely numb but somehow fizzling pain expanded in his arms and his side. The spade spun away and landed next to the desk, clanging like a cracked bell.

'Kate, it's . . .' he started to say when he saw his hands, torn and ragged where the shot had blasted them, trying to comprehend the immensity of the damage. He tried to make his legs move, failed, and toppled to the floor. His feet did a jittery little dance and then were still. Huge pain bloomed in his side and in his back and he knew the heavy goose shot had done more than ruin his hands.

A cool realization soared above the pain. *She must be mad*, he thought. *She's bloody well killed me.*

He lay on the carpet, feeling his very essence ooze away so quickly that the room darkened almost instantly. Over in the corner, he heard Kate moan and for some reason the sound was the distillation of all fear, even though she had used his own gun on him.

A picture of the doll in the cot came back to him and he saw his daughter lying face up, his brain now able to comprehend a greater enormity than the fact of his own death. 'Lucy, darling . . .' he managed to blurt before his lungs emptied in a frothy gush. He fell forward and died. The last thing he saw as his vision faded to black was the grey and ragged thing that squatted over his wife's trembling body, one great red eye fixed on him while it sucked at her flesh. In the last moment of his life, Jack Park thought he saw the face of the devil.

Much later, long after the bottom of the kettle had melted on the stove, while her baby's body was stiffening with rigor mortis, while Ginny Marsden's disintegrating corpse was turning rigid with the bitter cold out in the barn and while her husband's mutilated, slumped shape had dripped its last through the devastating wound in his side, Kate Park got to her feet and went through to the baby's room, cradling the thing close to herself.

Over there in the little Moses basket, there was something she should know, something she had to see, but she had no wherewithal to make herself cross the short distance. Her mind was not her own. She bent to the clothes chest and wrapped her new baby up in the wonderful christening shawl her mother had passed down, a link from a generation gone, her grandmother's, to a new one just begun. She wrapped it tight against the cold while its huge blue-lagoon eyes held her attention and her mind.

While she wrapped the new baby, in the core of her being she was screaming madly, as Ginny Marsden had done. Her breasts were full again and there was a tingling in her veins as her temperature rose, her body fighting a futile war with the new chemicals, the long and complex molecules now driving through her bloodstream. The twist in her belly proclaimed the start of her period after ten months of freedom from cramp. Without pause, she stripped off her robe, not noticing the new bruises on the ballooning skin or the scratch marks where small thin fingers had clenched her tight. She dressed herself like an automaton, knowing she would have to move soon, while ignorant of where, or when, or why.

CHAPTER TWENTY-THREE

Kate Park picked the baby up and went through to the living room where the log fire was just beginning to burn itself out. The baby turned its face into her and felt its change come rushing on.

Half a mile further north-east, on the brow of the hill at Upper Loan Farm, the old shepherd looked out of his window, wondering if Jackie Park had got the fox he was hunting a while ago. The two shots had not been repeated.

Down in Barloan Harbour, old Mrs Cosgrove wondered about the woman who had come limping with the baby in the old pram. She had gone out in the afternoon, after paying for several nights' board, and had not returned. It would be a couple of days, in this weather, before the old woman would venture round the back of her house to empty the trash. Until then she would be unaware of the old pram angled against the wall. She blinked behind her big glasses, eyes watering, and she whipped a huge handkerchief out to blow her nose vigorously. She always got a cold at this time of the year. Despite that, she was sure she could smell something. She wondered if maybe a bird had got in one of the vents under the eaves and had died. Oddly, she felt a wrench of cramp deep down between her hips, a pain she had not felt for a long time, and her old and sagging breasts tingled strangely. She wondered if her cold was turning into something worse.

All of this happened on the day before Christmas, while the choir from St Fillan's went round the doors of Barloan Harbour, singing of peace on earth to men of goodwill and about a new infant, born in a manger, who would save mankind from its sins.

Two days later, on the night of Boxing Day, David Harper and Helen Lamont were discovering each other all over again.

It had been a long day and a long night. He had brought the papers home with him after reporting their progress to Scott Cruden, who was quite reasonable about the delay. He told

David he could borrow another two patrols for some house-to-house inquiries the next day, once the shift patterns got back to normal. David wondered if that would do any good, because if Ginny Marsden was back in the city, she would be hard to find. He wondered whether he should ask the public relations folk to put out an appeal in the press, maybe get a picture flashed on the tea-time news. It was still early days yet, he decided. He'd let Helen make an inquiry at Celia Barker's bank. It was a long shot, but she'd done a fine job so far and he knew she had an instinct for this. They had picked up a pizza, both of them agreeing on a seafood topping (and he was pleased to find they had something else in common) and gone back to his place.

June had left two messages on the answering machine and Helen felt herself bristle as he played them back. Both messages began with an apology and the first asked him to call her. The second almost demanded that he return her call. He didn't, but while he reheated the food, she rang again. The pizza was warm by the time he got off the phone.

'Doesn't she give up?' Helen wanted to know.

He gave her an apologetic look and shrugged wearily. 'It's not easy for her. It's been a while for both of us.'

'But she claimed you and I were having an affair, and she half wrecked this place. Plus it was she who told you it was over and you were never to darken her doorstep again.'

'And I've told her it's over,' David said. 'I don't like hurting her, that's all, because she'd not a bad person. We just came to the end of a relationship and that's the best thing. Convincing her of that is something else. It'll take time. She's just lonely because it's Christmas, and she thinks she made a mistake.'

'You bet she did,' Helen retorted, fire in her eyes. 'But that's over now.'

He smiled awkwardly and busied himself with the plates. He knew June and realized there would be more telephone calls, more messages on the machine. She was stubborn, and when she was fixed on something, she wasn't easily side-stepped. 'She'll be fine in a while,' he said, though he knew a while might be a while longer.

They ate the pizza and had a beer apiece while he changed

the subject and drew out the old and detailed report a long-dead policeman had compiled.

Greta Simon had disappeared in the middle of May 1941. She had been a scullery maid in Overburn House, the dower house to the mansion in the valley behind Lochend where the Coleraine family had held their clan seat for centuries. At this time the dower house was owned by an English ironfounder who was rolling out tank treads and armoured panels for the war machine and would later be elevated to the House of Lords.

She had been a skinny, plain girl in her late twenties, with thin hair and large teeth. There had been a rumour that she had indulged in a passionate affair with a married man from Levenford, where she'd initially been raised, the only daughter of a widow who had died five years before. The unnamed man (known from her letters as Mars – she called herself Hesper, after the morning star, a fine play on words, linking the god of war with the goddess of love), the unknown lover, some folk believed, had been killed on the beach at Dunkirk. Greta Simon had gone missing from the dower house in 1941 and people believed she had killed herself. She had failed to turn up for work on the seventeenth day of May. The next time anybody heard of her in any official capacity was in 1967. Nobody knew how she had evaded official notice. There was no indication of how she had made a living. Her tiny apartment held only the bare essentials and a strange collection of toys and baby clothes, all of them hand-made. Her landlord said she had paid the rent in coins. A neighbour said there were always coins in the pram and she even recalled that she herself, the neighbour, had put money in for the baby several times, luck money, an old Scots tradition. That was a puzzle to her, Sergeant Ron McBean noted in his stolid hand. The tradition only calls for one donation of silver. The woman could not remember why she had been moved to be so generous. She could not recall what the baby had looked like. It had just seemed the right thing to do.

Ron McBean had noted the strange, rancid smell in Greta Simon's house. He had smelled it before.

It had been routine work, more than two decades prior to

this, when McBean had been a young constable in Lochend and he had stumbled on the mystery. If he had not, five years later, taken a transfer for promotion to a town on the other side of the country, he would never have made the connection between Greta Simon and Harriet Dailly.

The connections were laid out in a chart, on sheets of yellowed legal-pad paper which had been stuck together with glue. The glue itself was old and hard and looked like a fine amber. The rest of the report was written out in McBean's clear, laborious hand. He had been a good, methodical policeman. What he had discovered he could hardly believe himself, and he had been unable to get anyone else to believe there was more than coincidence involved.

Phil Cutcheon had been too busy with the murder inquiry to be concerned with myth and fable as he had called it then; but now, more than fifty years after Greta Simon walked away from her job (to her death, some thought at the time, suicide from a broken heart), Phil Cutcheon had changed his mind.

Harriet Dailly had been a woman of sixty-two when she jumped off the Pulpit Rock, an outcrop of slate which overlooked Loch Corran, famed in song and for the mythical creature said to swim under its dark surface, and for its own connection to the low roads of the underworld. She could possibly have been saved, because the teenage son of the ironfounder who ruled the dower house was fishing for salmon nearby, in a boat rowed by his own bailiff. Unfortunately Harriet landed on a half-submerged tree-trunk and caved her skull in. She had died instantly.

There would have been no real interest, had it not been for the baby Harriet had been seen carrying in her old shawl on the path up to the rock. A few girls from the dower house, Greta Simon included, had been given the afternoon off to pick elderflowers for the season's wine. The bushes near the Pulpit were a traditional source. Two of the girls had seen Harriet jump. It was May 17, 1941. An immediate search for the baby turned up no sign at all. There was speculation that dogs or foxes might have taken it. Or perhaps that Harriet had killed the infant herself and then committed suicide. That part of the loch was searched by a team of Navy divers in cumbersome suits, but the water dropped straight down from the edge more than two hundred feet to blackness and nothing was found.

Nobody knew where she had come from, not immediately. Constable Ron McBean was charged with finding her nearest and dearest. A perfunctory post-mortem showed that the woman had a degenerative condition, a loss of bone tissue at her joints which would have made movement almost impossible and, at the very least, excruciating. Quite unbelievably, according to the young doctor who would soon be carrying out triage on the awful wounds of war, she was still producing milk and showed signs of menstruation. She had been chronically anaemic and her liver was grossly enlarged.

It was not until a quarter of a century later that Ron McBean would read a similar report, by sheer luck or coincidence, in a similar town separated by the narrow width of the country, and he would start adding up the coincidences.

McBean almost by accident found a clue in Harriet Dailly's shabby little house, down an alley at the west end of Lochend, a crumbling little shack tacked on to the end of an even older dye-house. It had a bed and a sink and the gutted remains of two rabbits: liver, kidneys and brains all gone, the rest substantially chewed. The place stank, possibly of the lye from the old dyeworks, or possibly from rot. There was a hardboard chest full of baby clothes and the bed was piled high with hand-crafted toys. McBean found a pile of bones in an old wooden barrel in an outhouse. Some of them had been chewed. There were rabbits, pigeons and a couple of cats. Nobody remembered the old woman having a dog. Everybody had seen the tightly swaddled baby and had believed it was a grandchild. They had taken her for an old tinker woman who kept to herself. People passing by gave her money for the baby.

The young policeman, whose career would take a four-year vacation during which time he would see more murder and mayhem in North Africa and then in France than he would experience in the rest of his life, discovered a photograph of a young couple, alike enough to be brother and sister, and an old letter to 'Dear Harry', signed 'Yr Lving Bro, Chas'. The address on the envelope was faint, but legible. The letter told Harry that Chas would be coming home on leave in less than two weeks and he was looking forward to a break from all the square-bashing. It was dated 1918.

It was a fifty-mile train ride to Lanark where Ron McBean found the Reverend Charles Dailly, a short, portly man with the ruddy cheeks of a committed drinker and the smile of a jester. When he saw the picture of himself and his sister, instant tears sparkled in both eyes and he had to dab them with his spotted handkerchief, blowing his nose vigorously, much as old Mrs Cosgrove would do more than half a century later. By sheer coincidence, if anything relating to this could be, the old woman who did bed-and-breakfast in her cottage in Barloan Harbour had been one of those girls who had seen Harriet Dailly jump from the Pulpit Rock. She and Greta Simon had both been singing that old Gaelic song about the fairies who stole babies from their mothers.

'I haven't seen Harriet since the year the Great War ended,' Charles Dailly said when he composed himself. 'Dead, you say? How, where?'

The minister explained that his sister had grown up in his house, the old manse in Lanark where his father had been the incumbent before him. 'Harry and John, that was her husband's name, you know, they had been hoping to have a family, but she couldn't have babies. Something wrong with her innards, you know. But she helped foster the youngsters from the orphanage, and she told me she would adopt as soon as Johnny came marching home. She had taken responsibility, she told me, for the child of a woman who had been admitted to the sanatorium down in Carstairs, a poor soul who had gone mad. That was on the same day she got the telegram that John had bought it in France. He was killed just before the end of it all, poor fellow. I never saw Harriet again after that. I went round to her house and she was gone. Someone said they had seen her at the train station, and somebody thought she might have been carrying a baby, but from that day to this, there's never been a word, not a whisper. We reported her missing, of course, but that was under her married name of Burton. It was a long time ago, but we never thought she'd go back to her own name.'

The red-faced minister gathered himself together. 'In fact I

314

had always had the notion that she'd killed herself all those years ago, from the grief of it all. She and Johnny were made for each other. He was a handsome devil, and quite a catch. His father had the strawberry farms down the valley, and they made a fortune out of preserves.'

Ron McBean had not told the minister, feeling it was neither his business nor necessary information, that his sister had jumped into the loch. He did not elaborate, but left the bereaved brother with the idea that she had fallen accidentally. There was no harm in that.

When he mentioned the possibility that the old woman had been carrying a baby, Charles Dailly said that was quite in character.

'Loved them. She would have had a dozen if the Lord had blessed her. She was always looking after other folk's children and it was a real shame that she was cursed to be barren.'

'What happened to the baby she fostered?' McBean asked. It was only curiosity, as his older self would later write. Obviously the child was now a man of twenty-three, unless he too had died in this new war.

'Well, nobody knows. Who could know? She just disappeared. I didn't know if she even adopted it. It was all very confused at the time.'

Who could know? It was just a loose end, but McBean was a painstaking young policeman who would always do a job to the best of his ability. He turned down a sherry while the minister wrote down the address of the sanatorium at Carstairs. 'It would be June 7, 1918. That's when the telegram came. I remember because it was Harriet's birthday. My mother had baked her a big cake. We gave it to the orphanage.'

The place in Carstairs had been a madhouse at one time, and now it just seemed like a madhouse, in the May of 1941. The three main wings had been given over to the wounded, the men of the Scottish battalions who had been blasted and broken on the shoreline in the dreadful retreat. Some of the men, young boys hardly out of their teens, with dreadful injuries and missing limbs, were sunning themselves on the grass or on benches, all of them smoking, and the ones that could see staring into the distance with that long-range stare of men who still looked into the fires of hell and felt the heat.

Ron McBean recorded in his personal notes how the dreadful damage, both physical and mental, made the place look like an image of another hell. He would also later record in his personal papers, after his own war experiences, how familiar that look became.

Matron Ducatt, a squat, grim-faced woman with a transforming smile, took him to the records office. She had been a nursing sister back at the end of the Great War and remembered Harriet Burton. She had gone to school with her cousin. She could not remember any adoption, though Harriet had taken several children into her care, easing the burden of mothers whose husbands had gone to war. McBean gave the date and the elderly nurse checked the records of admissions.

'Oh, I remember that day,' she said when she looked up the entry. 'It was awful, and I shall never forget it as long as I live. That was the day we brought Mrs Parsonage in. She had killed her husband with a coal scuttle. She said he'd tried to kill her baby. She was quite demented of course and she was sent away to Dalmoak when they made it a state mental hospital. We had the charge of her until then, and no matter what treatment we gave her, she stayed in a straitjacket for most of the time.'

'What happened to her?' Ron McBean wanted to know.

'Well, she killed her husband all right, but she never had a baby, not one of her own. She had adopted the child, some time before, after its guardian died, some relative of hers, an old washerwoman from down in Dumfries. The baby was thought to be her granddaughter's who'd had it out of wedlock. Mrs Parsonage's husband, he was a planter in India and he was never home from one year's end to another. It's all coming back now. Anyway, he came home and he never took to the baby at all. Even the minister said he asked him to come down to the house to make his wife give up the baby. He said it was possessed. Whatever the case was, she hit him with a coal scuttle and killed him and she was completely deranged when she came here. They found her in the garden of her house, all covered in blood, and with hardly a stitch on. She was trying to feed the baby herself, poor soul, at her age.'

'And what happened to the baby?'

The matron looked at the old file, flicking several pages over before turning back to him. 'Mrs Burton, Harriet Dailly as was, she was on the parish board at this time and she took the child to their care, for adoption. I imagine she did. Didn't she?'

The parish records showed no such admission. It was getting dark by the time Ron McBean discovered this, apologizing to the old church clerk who'd got a box of redundant ledgers and records down from the loft where they'd lain untouched for many years. On the way home, he pondered over what he had gleaned, but at that time, he had nothing at all to make him suspicious. But McBean was methodical and he was conscientious. He may also have had a trace of the fey Highland touch, being the seventh child of his family. Over the years, his notes revealed, he had thought about the strange case, wondering what had happened to the baby that a demented, bloodstained woman had tried to suckle in the garden of her substantial home.

As time passed, through correspondence mainly, he built up a kind of picture which made no sense at all. He had, after speaking with Charles Dailly, discharged some of his duties, but *if* Dailly's sister had adopted a child, now obviously a young man, he had a further duty to try to trace him. Yet the parish orphanage records showed no such adoption, and though she had been seen with the child, both by witnesses and by her brother, there was no subsequent record of the baby after she had run away.

That left him with a series of mysteries which nagged at him down through the years. Who was the baby that Harriet Dailly had cared for when she had died? Who was the first baby adopted by mad Mrs Parsonage and then taken by Harriet? What had happened to them both?

There was a possibility, he had to consider now, that Harriet Dailly, crazy old lady that she seemed to have been, had killed both children.

Over the next two years after Harriet Dailly's death back in the war years, McBean discovered, with the help of a local undertaker who was an unofficial historian down in Lanark, that Mrs Parsonage had become a sort of recluse during the year before her breakdown, since she had taken the baby into her home. The unregistered adoption had come after the suicide of that distant cousin, the impoverished washerwoman widow from Dumfries, some forty miles south, whose death had caused some notoriety, as she had leapt naked from a stone bridge which spanned a narrow, rocky gorge. When recovered, her whole body was found to be covered in bleeding lacerations and bruises which a doctor described as very similar to the sucking circlets caused by lampreys on salmon from the nearby River Nith. McBean automatically noted the similarity in the odd circular lesions uncovered in the autopsy on Harriet Dailly.

It was to be almost fifty years after that strange suicide, following the accident at Duncryne Bridge which took away most of Greta Simon's brain, that Sergeant McBean was moved to dig further. The records by this time were sparse, but what had started as a routine inquiry gathered a mass and momentum of its own for McBean as he counted up the coincidences.

The cousin in Dumfries, an Emily Melrose, youngest daughter of a hatmaker who had succumbed to the madness of mercury poisoning, had left her home in Lanark to work as a seamstress, though she had ended up in the parish workhouse in 1890. She had disappeared from there, vanished from sight in fact, on the day after a fire in which an elderly woman and her baby grandchild had died. No trace of the infant was ever found in the ashes of the poorhouse.

Ron McBean's personal investigation became an obsession. He listed, in his papers, his growing consternation and concern:

In all this time, I have never been able to identify any one of the children alleged to have been involved. I can draw a number of conclusions, but coincidence is not one I can honestly infer, not any more.

'Do you believe in coincidence?' Helen asked David as she finished reading the old policeman's account.

'Sure I do. But I'm with McBean. He was a cop's cop. And nobody believed him, the same way nobody would believe us if we came up with the same idea. They'd lock us up, wouldn't they? Phil Cutcheon says he's on the point of belief, though he hasn't a pension to lose. What I don't believe in any more is that there is any coincidence in all of this.'

'Me neither,' Helen said. 'The woman who died in the fire, Agnes Lassiter, she had a baby with her, but after the fire, nobody could find out whose it was. Then Emily Melrose, who was in her fifties, and was looking after a child, and she was long past her sell-by date. She took a dive and killed herself, just like Harriet Dailly.'

'They're all connected, in time and in space,' David said. 'Lassiter, Melrose, Parsonage and Harriet Dailly. Like a chain, down the years. They die or they disappear or they go mad. McBean did not discover until very late on, a quarter of a century later, the connection between Dailly and Greta Simon, but it was there. Nobody sees the obvious when it cannot be explained in rational terms.'

'And how would you explain it?' Helen asked.

'I'll show you something in a minute that you're going to think is very crazy, crazier than the idea I had before. But let me get the sequence right. Greta was there when Harriet jumped and she disappeared the same day. There was no sign of the baby, though there were dozens of people who knew the old woman had one. Twenty-five years later, Greta gets hit by a truck and her baby disappears, presumed dead. On the very same day, Heather McDougall does a runner, turning up nearly thirty years down the line, and once again, she has a baby which very strangely disappears, taken by a woman who, as far as we know, is acting well out of character.'

He turned to Helen, counting on his fingers, much as Mike Fitzgibbon had done. 'Look at the conditions in Harriet's house. Exactly the same as Greta's place. Kids' clothes, toys; hardly anything else. Same with Heather. McBean mentions the smell in the house in Lochend. Probably the same as the stench that's been getting up our noses since this whole thing started. I don't think it's poison. And I don't think it's a disease.'

'So what do you really think?'

'I think it's what McBean believed.' David reached down into the side of the box and found the slim envelope that had been jammed down the lining. He took out the thin sheets of paper. The top one had the yellow band at the edge where sunlight had dulled its whiteness. He read beyond the first page of this separate letter which was undated and unaddressed. He drew Helen's attention to the part near the end, the few paragraphs Phil Cutcheon had showed him that morning.

. . . All I know is that it appeared on record some time in the past century. It will appear again, but where and when, who knows. All I can say, with absolute clarity and conviction, is that it will emerge again and anything that can do that, time and time again, is not natural . . .

When I was a boy, my mother used to sing a song, the same one that Greta Simon and her friend were singing back in 1941 while picking elderflowers. You could say my mother was an old, uneducated Highland woman whose first language was the Gaelic, and who clung to the old ways. 'Hovan Rovan' was the song, about the fairies who would steal a mother's baby and leave another of theirs in its place. The infant was a goblin, a thing they called the Tachara. The mother felt the pain and loss of her child, but the goblin had the power to make the mother love it and nurture it and raise it as her own, and the woman was damned for ever and her own child was gone. An old wives' tale from the Highlands, but somehow, it strikes a chord now.

My mother would have said that the Tachara had stolen these mothers. She would have said that somewhere in the past, a real baby had been spirited away and this goblin put in its place. They called the thing a changeling. It is possible they were right. I pray they are wrong.

As Helen read, her eyes widened. Finally, very slowly, she put the sheets of paper down on the table and turned to him. 'That's just what you said. "What kind of baby would steal a mother?"'

'He thinks it's been going on a long time,' David said. 'I know it's hard to believe, but I'm very close to going along with the old guy on this.'

He put the file back in the box and put it away, not wanting to read the dead man's words again. Helen was about to say something else, but he motioned her to silence with his hand while he reached for a videocassette. 'I spent a couple of hours compiling this lot. I just want you to look at them and tell me what you think.' He jabbed the starter and the screen flickered to life. The bird in the burning bush glared wide-eyed and desperate over the rim of the nest, while the naturalist explained the unbreakable conditioning that made it sit on the eggs until it was consumed by flames.

The screen blurred, danced then focused again as the scene switched to another shot of a baby cuckoo in the next, blindly ejecting its rival foster brothers from the pipits' nest, arching its back to roll the eggs up and over the rim. A commentator described the hollow in the naked little bird's back, an evolutionary design which allowed the bird to carry an egg and eject its rivals forever. 'The cuckoo,' the narrator said, 'is a successful brood parasite. It is driven by instinct, because it obviously cannot learn this behaviour from its parents. Within an hour of hatching, helpless and completely blind, it gets rid of all competition by killing its rivals. It is an efficient little murderer, and now it will reap the benefits. The pipits will feed it, unaware that they have adopted a killer, and it has adopted them.'

Another flicker, pause, another scene.

A Pepsis wasp battled with a tarantula spider, forcing the curving fangs away from its thorax while it manoeuvred its abdomen right underneath the poison needles to plunge its sting into the arachnid. 'This is a pendulum battle, win all or lose all,' the voice-over informed. 'The wasp risks death, driven by her procreative imperative. If she wins, then her genes will carry on to the next generation.' On screen the insect paralysed the spider and dragged it into an underground chamber where she laid an egg on the former foe. 'Alive, but motionless, the spider is now a food store for the emerging grub. It will be eaten from within.'

Helen shivered. 'I hate spiders,' she volunteered. The screen flicked.

A baby looked directly into its mother's eyes. 'Humans, like animals are programmed by their own genes,' the well-known anthropologist intoned, 'programmed to recognize a human face. That is why we see faces in patterns and in rock formations, in the craters of the moon. We first recognize our mother, both by smell and eyesight and, later, by voice. It is a two-way process. The human infant, like the young chimpanzee, like the

321

nestling bird, is dependent on the mother for food, shelter and protection. The mother is made, genetically programmed, to respond to its demands. A human baby's cry is pitched at a level which causes her distress and impels her to rush to its defence or its aid. The smell of a baby, human or mammal, imprints upon the mother, increasing the flow of hormones from the pituitary and other glands, reinforcing the mothering instinct. If this system had never existed, then higher mammals, primates, the human race, would never have existed. You could say that the most powerful force on the planet, the controlling influence, is the power a baby exerts on its mother.'

David switched the machine off. 'There's plenty more, but that should do for now.'

Helen gave another exaggerated shudder. 'That,' she said, 'is the creepiest thing I have ever seen in my life.'

'Ah, but does it really apply?' They looked at each other, both wondering. Both on the cusp of belief in the impossible.

Some time in the night, he woke with a start, drenched in sweat and shaking in the aftermath of a surreal dream in which an unseen baby whimpered and cried while he searched for it in the dark of a derelict house, following its high echoing cry through the nooks and crannies and cobwebbed hollows, all the time knowing that it was trying to lure him into danger and that if he set eyes upon it, it would ensnare him.

Helen held him tight in her arms until the aftershock of the dream faded.

CHAPTER TWENTY-FOUR

'Oh, she looked a lot older than this wee lassie,' Mrs Cosgrove
said, looking at Helen through the thick lenses which made her
eyes seem huge and staring. She stoked the coal fire in the front
room of her little cottage in Barloan Harbour. Both the old
woman and Helen Lamont were ignorant of the fact that Mrs
Cosgrove had already crossed the long and sinuous trail of this
affair many years before, as a friend of Greta Simon. 'And she
didn't look well, the poor soul,' she quavered. 'If it had been
back in the war, I would have said she was sick with consump-
tion. There wasn't so much as a pick of meat on her bones.'

The description mirrored Nina Galt's observations and
Helen wondered just what was it that Ginny Marsden had that
could transform her from the healthy and fit girl on the video
into the seemingly emaciated, much older woman that people
perceived. Since the first time she had entered Heather McDougall's house she had experienced that strange and disturbing
sense of foreboding. Now that feeling was getting stronger all
the time. Whatever Ginny Marsden had, she did not want to
contract it.

And David, adding his own weight to the old policeman's
years of obsession, had almost convinced her of the sinister
connection. He had told her, in the early hours of the morning,
that the baby was probably some kind of mutant, though what
kind of mutant he couldn't even speculate.

They had fallen into each other's arms again, both of them
tired and yet strangely excited by the new, menacing overlay to
their investigation, and in the night she had whimpered as she
clutched at him, desperate for his strength, matching him
motion by motion, thrust for thrust, carried on an irresistible
wave of her own drive and her own need.

Some time in the cold hours of the morning she too had
woken from a dream, in which a wasp had stung her and laid a
grub in the pit of her belly that it was eating her from within.
She had jerked awake, trembling with fear, disoriented in the

unfamiliar room, with a burning, acid pain twisting under her breastbone. It slowly died away and she lay back, listening to the sound of David's breathing, pressing herself close to him for warmth and protection against the images in the dark. The fear diminished, but it did not go away.

It was with her still, faint yet insistent, the next morning, a prescience that she could not shake. She had experienced tickles of forewarning before; this was something deeper. She did not know how or why she knew that, but a part of her she did not even comprehend recognized the approach of danger. The odd, exposed feeling remained with her when she got the call back from the bank. Celia Barker had contacted them first thing, authorizing them to give CID any information they needed. From the description she had of Ginny Marsden's condition, Helen had not expected her to make a withdrawal from a hole-in-the-wall auto-teller, but when she had thought back to the image of Heather McDougall on video, dying, maybe even clinically dead, yet still crawling towards her baby, she had wondered. Even as that thought struck her she knew that she had crossed a threshold. She had stepped from the world of the rational to a dimension where the inconceivable could actually be considered possible.

She wondered if Ginny Marsden were lactating now to feed her baby.

'She's in Barloan Harbour,' she said excitedly, turning round as she put the receiver down. 'She made a withdrawal three days ago.'

'I know it,' David said. 'It's just a village. I used to fish on the canal and take pictures of kingfishers when I was a kid. It's not a big place, so if she's there we'll find her.'

'And it's between Levenford and here,' Helen said. 'It's on the same train line as Lochend, where Greta Simon came from. Ginny must have got the train, but she got off after a few stops instead of coming back into the city.'

'When was the withdrawal?' David wanted to know. His face fell when she told him it was Christmas Eve. The girl had had plenty of time to move on, but they wouldn't know until they had checked it out. They got to the village in less than half an hour and by the time they turned at the bridge over the canal and down to the small station, clouds were beginning to gather, billowing up the estuary, promising dank and dismal rain or a heavy fall of snow. The harbour here, where the waterway that meandered through the city emptied itself into the wide river, was old and weathered and at this time of the year there were few signs of life apart from a pair of mallard ducks in the broken reeds. Further along the waterway, the same canal that looped through the parkland close to June's apartment, was lined with old and gaudily painted narrowboats. They all looked deserted and empty and one or two were slumped on their sides in thick patches of weed. David took a minute to reclaim childhood memories of birdwatching here where the fresh water met the tidal brack, attracting waders in their thousands, marsh harriers and herons. He remembered this place in sunshine and summer warmth. Now it was cold and bitter and somehow empty.

The railway angled past the canal harbour and under the arches there was a little restaurant where he'd once taken June. It was closed now, possibly for the winter, maybe for ever. There was little passing trade in a place like this. Most of the village was to the north of the canal, and further away from the flat where the old locks held back the water; the land rose up to the Langmuir Hills, whose heath- and bracken-covered slopes were powdered with snow. This had been a good place to come as a child back then, armed with a fishing rod and a camera and no complications.

In less than an hour after they arrived, he and Helen had got their first clue. A thin, birdlike woman with hungry, gossip's eyes in the corner shop recognized the girl in the photograph from her coat and told them she had bought a pound of minced beef and had gone up the Loanhead Road. 'It's a dead end,' she said. 'She'll be in one of the houses there. They take in lodgers, most of them.'

In five minutes, old Mrs Cosgrove was making tea. 'And her pram's out the back,' she said. 'I couldn't believe she would have left it, but she must have just taken the baby and gone.'

There was a faint, familiar smell in the old woman's house, hardly traceable, but enough of a taint to make them both recognize it. Ginny Marsden had been here. The baby had been here.

The old lady told them she hadn't smelled anything, but she said there had been a bloodstain on the sheets and she'd had to wash them in bleach. 'I don't think the poor girl was all there,' she said, tapping her temple. 'Maybe she's one of those unfortunates they're putting out of hospital and back into the community. It's a terrible shame. Maybe she's gone back to somewhere she knows?'

They left the cottage knowing they had picked up Ginny Marsden's trail, hoping they could find it again. 'Where now?' Helen asked. David shrugged. The trail, first hot, could go cold. The pram left few clues, for it had been outside since Boxing Day and had only been discovered that morning. Even the blanket was hoared with frost. They went towards the car and David was just about to put the key in the lock when a white patrol car came labouring up the road. David held his hand up, motioning it to stop.

The policeman, a young man, who looked too thin for his shirt collar which gaped over a prominent Adam's apple, seemed irritated at the delay until David showed him his warrant card.

He hadn't seen the girl in the picture, but he'd been in bed with a cold since Christmas Eve. This was his first day out since and he maintained his belief that he should have stayed under the blankets. David thanked him and was about to move away when, for no particular reason, he asked the local cop where he was going.

'Up to Middle Loan Farm,' he said. 'Got a call to check out the Parks' place. They're not answering the phone. Their in-laws have been trying to get them for a couple of days. Lucky buggers have probably flown out to Barbados and away from this bloody winter.'

He drove on up the road and they got in their car. David started the engine, thinking.

'Do you think we should . . . ?' they both asked at exactly the same moment. Another coincidence. A cold and clammy sensation caressed Helen's mind. Without another word, David put his foot down and followed the patrol car.

The policeman had stopped at the gate on Jack Park's home

straight when they caught up with him. 'This is the worst thing about working out in the sticks,' he said. 'You spend more time opening and closing these things than anything else. That and rounding up the livestock when people forget to close them.' His name, he told them, was Jimmy Mulgrew. He'd been in Barloan Harbour for three miserable months of winter. Out of the warmth of the car, he looked as if the wind blowing up the estuary would knock him down. His nose was scarlet with the cold and raw from rubbing with tissues.

'Jackie Park and his wife Kate.' He dropped his voice. 'She's a looker. Big girl, but classy.' David gave him a man's look which said he got the drift. 'Had a kid a few weeks ago and they were staying home for Santa Claus and then going to visit her parents yesterday. They're not answering the phone. He does a lot of travelling, so maybe he's stuck somewhere. There was a hell of a fall of snow over the borders in the past couple of days. The sergeant asked me to have a look, just for the record.'

'We thought we'd give you a hand,' David told him, and that was fair enough with the local man. He was a city boy, ill at ease with the big shambling cattle on farms, not quite ready to believe they weren't about to kick maybe and gore him.

'Don't see smoke from the chimney,' Helen said. The cold and troubling shiver that had gone through her had left her with a quiver of inexplicable apprehension.

Something wrong.

Even she did not know how many times that mental warning had flared in other people's minds. All she knew was that, quite unaccountably, this didn't feel right.

Something wrong. David Harper could sense the wrongness, though he did not know why. An instinct had made him follow the patrol car, an instinct that had no foundation in reason, yet . . . *yet* . . .

It was Christmastime. Up here, they'd have log fires and there would be smoke. Over by the whitewashed edge of an outhouse he could see the stack of wood piled on the lee side out of the wind. There would be smoke on a day like this.

Something wrong.

David was no city boy. He'd spent his childhood up the hills, helping on farms, taking his wildlife shots. Something was not

327

right here. He knew it, not just in the strange and threatening sense of foreboding, but in his rational mind too.

The farm was silent. Dead silent.

Down in the woods a pheasant coughed, tin on stone, jarring the air. Up on the moor a hawk bleated, high and plaintive, a strange counterpoint between hunter and prey. In the farmyard, no animal made a sound. The hairs on David's arms went walkabout again. Jimmy Mulgrew heard nothing and did not realize that was extraordinary.

There were no cattle lowing, no dogs barking. Almost any approach to a farm will get a response from the guardian dogs. Even more peculiar, there was not a sound of poultry. Chickens did not have the sense to stay silent. A cockerel did not have the ability to stop proclaiming its territory. Yet there were no sounds of either. As Mulgrew closed the gate with a rattling clang, David looked over the cropped hedge. A pigeon loft, one of the old-fashioned stone dovecotes that might have braved the storms of centuries, stood squat in the middle of the field beyond. Beside it, scattered around its stone bulk, light shapes fluttered in the gathering wind.

David held up a hand to shield his eyes from the watery glare reflecting from the snowclouds but he already knew what the shapes were. A flock of dead pigeons lay on the short grass, their hapless wings fluttered by the impending storm. The sensation of cold expectation swelled. He waited until Mulgrew got back into the patrol car before following on.

'Something's not right,' Helen said, 'But I don't know what it is.'

'You got the second sight?' he asked, trying to make it light. 'As the cavalry say, it's too quiet. It *is* too quiet. There's no sound at all, and that's unnatural.'

They drew round the corner in to the gap between byre and barn, and found themselves in the small courtyard. Helen turned in her seat and pointed to the gaping door of the garage. A Range Rover stood next to a small Volkswagen. Two cars. The four-wheel drive's door was wide open.

'Wonder how many they've got,' Helen said. Both of them knew this just didn't look right.

*

He heard their approach.

It was a faint vibration at first then a rumble in the air. He stretched his perceptions and an instant panic flared when he felt something familiar.

They were both coming now.

He forced himself to be still, listening, now fully alert after the miasma of the shedding. He had pushed and squeezed, expanding and contracting until the split had widened down his back and then he had laboriously freed himself from the dry sheath. A breeze had carried the discarded, papery skin away across the field as soon as the mother had opened the door. It had flipped over, that translucent, fragile image of his former self, shrivelling in the cold as the wind scraped it over the far thornbush hedge. He had taken a while to rest, but now he was fully awake. The mother moaned. The gate clanged, the same sound he had heard before, when he had taken the mother.

With a wrench he had forced the mother to absolute stillness. He could feel the thud of her heart magnified in the hollow of her ribs and he could perceive its liquid rush in the veins of her breasts. The skin there was dry and scabbed where he had fed hungrily, draining this one even more rapidly than he had drained the last.

Up here it was dark and for the moment he was safe, but they were coming. *She* was coming, and the peculiar hunger, the different hunger, tried to swamp his wariness. Tyres rumbled on the cobbles, making the building shiver. The smell of dead chickens filtered up, an oily smell on the dusty air. He sat perfectly still, his great eyes closed, sensing outwards.

Helen felt the touch again, registered the sensation she had experienced before and for a bewildering moment her vision swam.

'All right?' David asked. He too felt his nerves tensed up. Jimmy Mulgrew was whistling. If he had seen the two cars in the garage, he made no mention. Helen nodded in silent response, clamping her jaw to keep her teeth from chattering. Her skin felt as if it were trying to shrink on her. For some reason, a flare of discomfort pulsed in her breasts and her nipples

329

scraped against her bra. Instantly she recalled the sensation in the hostel.

David came round beside her. 'It doesn't sound right, not even a starling or a sparrow.'

'You're right. There's no sound at all,' she agreed. 'That's weird.'

Over by the chicken coop a small whirl of air spun a handful of white feathers in a will-o'-the-wisp circle. By the farmhouse proper, beside the angle of the porch, a white heap lay on the cobblestones. At first it looked like a dead sheep. All three walked forward. For all of ten seconds they stood and looked down at the dead dogs and the now black pool of congealed blood. It was clear that one had bitten the other. They were frozen in their bizarre embrace.

'What the fuck . . . ?' Jimmy asked. He looked at Helen and apologized with his eyes. She hadn't even heard him. Her heart was revving up now, pounding harder and faster. For a reason she could understand, but not put into words, she wanted to be out of there, driving fast down the hill from the farm, looking in her mirror to make sure nothing was racing after her.

The alien touch slid on the surface of her thoughts and a shudder of nausea ran through her.

David went quickly to the front door, eyes flicking from window to window for the merest hint of movement. Suddenly he felt dreadfully exposed. Anyone could be watching them and he didn't even have a baton with him, though he could see Jimmy Mulgrew carried his night-stick. It was still on the loop of his belt and in a flash of uncharacteristic contempt, David thought the village constable must be a congenital idiot.

They got to the door, David taking natural command of the situation, pushing the younger man to the side, away from possible danger. Anything could come through the door: an axe, a bullet. He stood away from the direct front and tried the handle. It turned without any resistance. The door opened.

The smell of blood came billowing out, cold and familiar, carrying with it the smell of death. His heart blagged against his ribs. The knowledge of complete vulnerability was right up there at the forefront. Adrenaline socked into his bloodstream in the instant preparation for fight or flight, made his leg muscles tremble. His throat tried to swallow the excess of saliva. Behind him he could hear Helen's harsh breathing, accentuated now in his heightened senses. Jimmy Mulgrew started to say something and David jabbed him with the edge of his hand.

Very slowly, very silently, his whole body now hypernaturally aware, he edged inside, motioning them to stay back. If someone came round the corner of the hall, pointing a shotgun at him, he could throw himself to the floor. *Maybe* he could. Silence and speed were his best weapons in this situation, he knew. A very reasonable part of his mind told him to get the hell out of here right now. Another part told him that people here could be in danger if they were not already dead. He got to the end, closing his mind to the sickly smell of death in the air. At the end of the corridor, he turned, flattening himself against the wall. A door lay wide open.

David eased over the threshold and saw the dark splash on the wall. He held his breath but succeeded only in making his heart pound a deafening pulse in his ears. He exhaled slowly, drew his eyes down and looked into the eyeless sockets of Jack Park.

Kate Park awoke cold and shivering, her skin almost blue with the cold. There was no sensation in her toes and her mouth tasted of blood. She wondered if she had bitten her tongue. She came clawing up from the pits of hell where her dreams replayed the catapulting body of her husband over and over again. She saw him slam against the wall, saw the spade spin away, tumbling in slow motion while Jack twisted in an ungainly pirouette, his hands disappearing in fragments. *Kate it's . . . Kate it's . . . Kate it's . . .* His voice echoed in its own mantra, the words repeated over and over and over in her head as if an endless loop were running in her brain, impossible to switch off. She had come awake on that black surge of unendurable horror, still seeing him, hearing his voice overlaid by the dreadful sucking sounds the baby had made.

Monster.

The core of her own self recognized it and repeated Ginny Marsden's mental shriek. It had been at the cot, at the crib. It had sucked there and she had done nothing because the baby, the baby *devil*, had captured her.

It had fed on her and it had fed on them all. In the fog of shock and mental paralysis, she had seen its red, glassy eyes blink once, and then it had turned from her and crawled across the room, its image wavering and blurring, and it had sucked at the still twitching body that had been Jack Park, the husband who had tried to save her, who had put the baby inside her. It had slobbered and sucked and then it had come back to her, the mental bonds tight and unyielding. Over by the wall, Jack's mouth was open and his eyes were mere shadows. The dark hollows stared accusingly at her and she knew she was damned for ever.

Now she was here in the cold musty confines of the back barn where they had stored the hay before the new barn was built. It smelled of mice, though not one sound could be heard. It smelled of bird-shit and old hay and the dried-out carcasses of long-dead rats. She had moved once only to get a drink of water from the trough at the corner of the wall, sucking up the icy liquid with her face almost submerged while the baby, a greater weight now, clung tight to her, dangling like a long, thin monkey.

It had changed in the night. She had heard it grunt and strain; for a little while the mental connections had sparked and fused and she was almost herself again. Without warning she came tumbling out of its control, back into the real world. For a ghastly, unbearable moment, everything came flooding back to her, all of it, every movement, every noise. The sounds of the dogs and the horses and the cattle and her own husband slamming in a thudded crunch against the wall. She heard again the gobbling sound from the cot and knew that everything in her life was gone.

It was dark in the old loft. A few stray rays of moonlight came through the holes where a some slates had come loose, solid silver rods in the dusty air. The thing was close *not a baby it's a fucking devil* a twisting shadow, roiling on the floor close to the angle of the roof where the cobwebbed beams sloped down to the flat. Kate did not know that she was only repeating Ginny Marsden's desperate protest. She did not know that the emaciated, skeletal thing that had been Ginny Marsden was lying stiff and frozen less than twenty yards away, feasted on by a horde of rats, the only creatures which had survived the proximity of the thing.

The beast grunted, though the sound wasn't quite a grunt, more a flaccid gulping noise. It was like nothing she had ever heard. She knew, right then, that this was something like nothing else on earth. This was something that should never have existed in this world.

She turned, almost able to hear the protest in her joints. It was squirming there, concentrating on its escape. Its mental pulses swelled, flickering randomly on the surface of her own mind, unfocused little jolts of energy. She could hear ripping sounds, but the motion was oily black, shadow upon shadow.

Yet she was free. Everything in her life was gone and Kate Park had no intention of running now. There was nothing for her to gain. All she could think was that the thing had to be destroyed. She rolled on the rough boards, towards the hatch. She reached the edge of the rickety stair and did not hesitate. Down she went, on hands and backside, like a disjointed crab. She got halfway down when she heard it howl its silent, cerebral shriek above her.

Down at the bottom she turned. It came scuttling like a spider, still making the hollow sound and sending commanding pulses at her. From its hind legs trailed a whispery translucence that for a moment looked like crumpled old polythene sheet. She lurched towards the wall. An old pitchfork, one that hadn't been used since before Jack had been a boy, was stuck into the soft and rotted wood of the walls. She grabbed it without hesitation. The beast came at her, its red eyes glaring poisonously. She hefted the shaft, raising the curved tines. It jinked to the side as she leaned into the thrust, pinioned the trailing flutter which merely ripped away with the sound of dry leaves.

The ghostly thing whipped round, a pale image of the monster floating upwards. It snagged her attention for a fraction of a second. The black and rippling thing scuttled under the prongs and snatched at her coat. She gasped, turned to face it, trying to get the pitchfork down on to it. She lunged hard again. It blared its command into her and a huge pain exploded in her head. In that instant her eyes went blind and her whole body convulsed, as if an enormous electrical charge had gone right through her. The fork's spike slammed down on to her foot, stabbed through the flesh, bored between the bones of her toes and continued through the sole of her shoe into the soft earth of the barn floor.

The little monster scrambled up her coat and snatched her mind just as the hurt of the stabbing reached her brain. It probed; Kate's muscles contracted again, sufficient to pull the pitchfork from her foot. A distant scrape of pain accompanied the motion. The implement dropped to the dry muck where her blood was now mingling with the shit of long-dead cattle. It held her there, her whole body vibrating with the power of its seizing, unable to move a limb. After a while, it made her walk to the door, keeping to the side of the building, and made her drink until her belly was hugely distended. She could not refuse.

When she had opened the door, the ghostly white thing had tumbled away, drawn out in the draught of air. It had looked like a ghost. It had looked like her worst nightmare.

Much later, in the dark of night, she crouched in the cold, waiting for the next thing to happen. At her breast, the baby mewled, now heavier than before, now grown more. Pains creaked out in her joints and every beat of her heart gave her an odd, wrenching discomfort. Her gums bled and her back ached and the pounding between her temples made it hard to see in the dim light.

She could do nothing but watch and wait while the baby drained her and would not let her die. Day and night passed. All she took was water. It fed like a glutton.

When the sounds came, sounds of the approaching cars, she did not hear them. She sat still as stone until the baby roused her and made her move.

CHAPTER TWENTY-FIVE

'We should take a look,' Helen had protested and David had reluctantly agreed, against his better judgement.

Both of them were subliminally and consciously aware of the imminence of danger, yet each of them was now driven to put an end to this, to find Ginny Marsden and the mysterious baby. The young policeman was whey-faced and every now and again his stomach muscles would spasm and he'd double over, dry-retching. He had not been sick yet. Helen had felt the bolt and roil of nausea and swallowed it back. The dead man's awful injuries had not been the worst, though they had been devastating. The shotgun wounds were black and still liquid, while the blood on the walls was black and dry, soaked into the paper. Other things, dotted like flies still stuck there, shrivelling as they too dried. The dead man had not been the worst of it, though his frozen grimace, lips stretched back from bloodstained teeth, had been a sickening sight. So too had been his empty, bloodied eye sockets blindly staring at the ceiling.

The baby's thin and waxen little body had been the worst. David had tried to push her back from it, sparing her the horror, but she had squirmed past him and now she wished she hadn't. The other policeman had not seen the baby. If he had, he would have been a stretcher case by now. She was shaking in fear and in anger and in a sudden pathological loathing for the thing that had done this.

Not human. The words repeated themselves in her mind. *Thing.* She tried to shuck that thought away, but it came back insistently. What sort of woman steals a baby? What sort of baby steals a mother? And what sort of devil could do this to a helpless infant? She had backed away from the cot where a thin trail of congealed blood hung down in an elongated drip, like old black toffee. The baby's little mouth had been open in a perfect circle, its tiny tongue, soft and delicate as a rabbit's, protruding over the toothless gums. Splashes of black sank where the eyes had been. The little chin was angled to the left and below it was a hole in the flesh that reminded her of something. It was not until she got outside that she remembered what it had been. She had once seen the body of a tramp who had died of exposure in an old warehouse. He had not been found for some time, not by humans. The rats had discovered him and had gnawed their way under his rib-cage to eat him from within. The body had twitched in a ghastly, possessed way and the rats had come scurrying out of their fleshy tunnel, glutted and fat. The baby did not twitch or tremble. The tunnel in her little neck showed ragged and abraded ends of tendons and blood vessels. It looked as if something had drilled its way through her skin and flesh. The small arms and legs were thin and wasted, as if all the goodness had been sucked out of her, and though Helen did not know it, that is exactly what the pathologist would discover.

Outside in the yard, where the snow had begun to fall, swirled round by the wind boiling up from the estuary, she had leaned against David while he used Jimmy Mulgrew's radio to call in. He had kept it very brief. She held on to him more for the warmth of another human being than for anything else. He put the radio back in its socket in the front of the patrol car and then moved towards their own car.

It was then that Helen had once again sensed something. Later on she would say it was just like the scrape of awareness that had made her flesh creep down in Levenford as she was leaving the old women in the café: footsteps on her grave. Something touched her and she stopped dead.

'What is it?' David asked. His face was pale and pinched, showing he was not immune to what they had found in the farmhouse.

'I don't know,' she said. 'I got a feeling.'

'What kind of feeling?'

'We should look here.'

'We should wait for reinforcements,' David said. 'I think we should get out of this yard, just in case.'

'There could be something here,' she said. 'The guns are inside, and the used one is on the floor. Whoever did this has cut and run.'

The contact touched her again, a feather stroke on the edge of her thoughts, slightly greasy, ominous as a distant thundercloud. She sensed it and something deep within her responded. 'I want to look around,' she said, suddenly afraid, but needing to move. 'It can't do any harm.'

He had looked at her, weighing it up. She was probably right, he finally conceded. This had not happened today, or yesterday. The damage was a couple of days old and the killer had gone. Yet the other part of him, the part that had read Ron McBean's account and had dreamed of parasites, told him to get the hell out of there. Down the years, there had been a trail of death and madness, suicide, and lost, abandoned lives, and they were all linked. Ginny Marsden had come here with her creepy little baby and they had followed her trail and they had found a tiny infant with a gaping hole in its neck and not a drop of blood left in its body. He lifted up a hand to call her back, but she was angling away towards the corner of the garage. Behind him, Jimmy Mulgrew gurgled like a drain and finally heaved his substantial lunch on to a pile of potato sacks.

David shrugged. She was probably right. The inner voice nudged and tweaked at him, but he ignored it. They were the police, his rational voice said, stolid and definite. This is a murder.

Helen was across by the wall. The touch came again, gentle as fog. She thought she heard the squeak of tiny bats, whispery as insect legs on dry sand. It drew her onward and she did not even know she was being pulled.

Go back, the logical segment of her brain, the one corresponding to David's rational part, urged powerfully. Get out of here *NOW*, pleaded the subconscious core that sensed a deep and alien danger in the shadows. Yet beneath that, something darker egged her on. Her nipples tingled. At first she had been unaware of it as she crossed the yard, feet muffled by the thickening snow. It came as a pressure in her breasts and then a warmth that spread to the tips and suffused them with a fierce, prickling heat. Down in her belly, another warm sensation spread, edged down between her legs, pulsed twice, unexpected and powerful. For an instant her vision swam and she thought she was slipping on ice. She reached a hand out to the wall, found its cold surface, steadied herself. The brief flare was gone, leaving her with only an itch and a sudden sense of need that she could not identify.

Go back! Get out of here!

It came loud, like a physical blow, just as she shoved the faded red door. It creaked open in a shudder. She was in before she knew it. The bat-squeak sub-audible sound in her ears swelled stronger. It felt like a resonance in the bones of her skull. The fillings in her teeth sang in sympathy, sending a ripple down her jawbone. Behind her she heard the clatter of the byre door as it swung along on its rollers, but it sounded far away. She was here and she was now and her whole world was suddenly shrunk right down to this singularity.

Above her, a slow, flopping sound rolled down from on high. The air was cool and dry, filled with dust and another, more familiar smell. She walked inside, across the dry straw-covered floor, between two stalls festooned with ancient harnesses and bridles. Very slowly, and with hardly a sound this time, the door swung shut. The darkness here was not absolute.

Another smell. She breathed in and the flush fluttered over her skin in a hot tide. She turned, feeling the touch stronger now, feeling it close. Deep within her, in her mind and her body, urgent messages were pulsing, jumping from axon to dendrite, from cell wall to cell. They shunted through her nerves. For an instant, everything else was forgotten and a tide of hungry need rolled over her.

Up there, the sound came rumbling, as if heard through several layers of canvas, while the whispery call went on and on and on, insistently tugging at her. She was halfway up the short flight of wooden steps when a shape launched itself from the doorway ahead. It came rushing at her.

The singing in her ears soared to a glassy, brittle pitch, and pain drilled into her skull, but over them, the appalling need swamped everything. It took hold of her and drove her on. She wanted it. It wanted her. She had to have it, protect it, *mother it*.

The shape came lumbering down, pale in the gloaming light, the edges of a coat flapping, while legs, moving slow, as if through glue, thudded with muffled crumps on the treads. She saw a dark triangle of hair and realized this was a woman. She tried to raise her head. There was something clutched tight in the other woman's arms.

The baby.

Uncontrollable ripples of emotion pulsed into her, pulsed out from her. She felt the baby's touch and heard its cry and smelled its smell and for an instant she was utterly ensnared. She reached to take it. It reached towards her. She heard its hunger.

Yes. *Yes*. Come now. Sizzling messages jangled between them and the darkness started to close in on her.

He saw her.

In that moment of recognition, his new hunger yawned, huge and empty, confusing his senses and for an instant stripping his instinct away.

The scent of blood was even now still in the air, the mother's blood with his own essence in it, rich and powerful. She had come for him on the cusp of the change, when he was freeing himself from the fraying shackles of the old skin, and she had almost succeeded – more nearly than the last one. The anger had flared and he had almost put his head against her neck and sucked her dry, but he still needed her. Instead he put the hurt in her, pushing the pain deep inside, and stopped her; then he had pulled the pain out and covered it with a different pressure, making her love him again. She had nursed him in the dark, and he had fed. He had fed ravenously, glutting himself even as she felt her own strength diminish. Another change was already boiling inside him, making his blood sizzle and his muscles tremble. It was coming so swiftly, hard on the heels of the last one, that its speed confused him and he only knew he had to feed fast now. The growth inside him was phenomenal. There were changes within changes, new senses, new needs, waxing with every feeding. He could not resist them any more than he could turn away from the instinct to feed. His instinct was all: he had no conscious thought, though a kind of intelligence burned behind the thick lids that protected his eyes from the day.

He fed and slumbered, holding the mother tight, until the sensation of threat, his ever-alert sentry, woke him. Unconsciously he had reached out and touched, feeling them approach, and he recognized their glow, the way a dog sniffs a familiar scent. He woke the mother brutally. She coughed harshly, for her lungs were filling up with fluid. He made her sit very still, and they both heard the trundling vibration of the cars as they came round into the courtyard. Still he waited, despite the urgent instinct to to fly.

His new hunger confused his instinct and made him wait.

After a while, noises came outside. People talked, unintelligible grunts and creaks to him, and he recognized her sounds again. He sent a tendril down towards her and slid it over the top of her thoughts.

She sensed him and recoiled. A delicious heat spread inside him, and the new thing between his legs swelled, urgent and thrusting.

He waited a while. The mother breathed steadily, her eyes closed and mouth open, horror tumbling inside her mind. Outside, beyond the walls, danger walked. He stayed stock-still, all his senses stretched to their ultimate, picking up sounds and vibrations and the heat of the moving shapes. In the dark, surrounded by the old hay, clutched in the mother's arms, he was safe for the moment.

Out there, the noises faded for a while, leaving a silence broken only by the rising moan of the wind, until a cry came, low and inarticulate. Some more noises, a clang of metal. His nerves twitched. Something was about to happen. The imminence of danger pressed at him. He closed his eyes and reached out just as the door opened below.

The mother jerked, hauled out of her torpor. 'Wha . . .?' she blurted. He punched a command at her and her mouth clamped shut. The door rattled, the old loose hinges protesting. A shape came inside, sensed rather than seen through the gaps of the floorboards of the hayloft. He reached again and touched the other female. An explosion of emotions erupted within him. The mother jerked back, hitting her shoulder against the heavy oak beam. The thud boomed hollowly.

Some reflex made him move. He shoved at the mother and her eyes opened wide, her mouth wider. She got to her feet and moved slowly to the top of the steps.

*

When Kate Park became aware, she was already moving. Her body was a mass of pain and her foot was shrieking loudest of all. The bones of her toes had been dislocated and distorted as the tine of the pitchfork ripped between them. The puncture holes, top and bottom, were now ragged and black. Gangrene was setting in there on top of the infection from the rats droppings. Her joints sung a protest song as they ground together. Her breasts, now thin and dangling, felt as if they had been torn in a clawed vice. She was moving down the stairs from the dark of a hayloft. A blink of darkness flooded her vision, as if an internal switch had been cut, then her sight came back and with it came her conscious self.

Her mind was her own; it had swung its dreadful concentration from her. She stumbled down the stairs, not even limping, though the agony was so immense it felt as if she was riding an impossible surf of hurt. It carried her along, carried her down.

A pale face floated in the gloom.

She saw the woman, saw her eyes widen, all in slow motion. She was slim and dark-haired and she was reaching towards the baby as if her life depended on the contact.

In that instant of recognition, Kate Park became a martyr.

In that moment of time, all three of them were bonded. The other woman's hunger, her primitive need to protect the baby, came sizzling between them. The baby was calling out to her, a feral, mindless demand. The girl was reaching for it, snared by the thing.

The image of her baby's pallid face lying in the cot came suddenly back to her and Kate Park's mind almost broke with the pain of it. She saw her dead husband twitching his last while his blood ran across the floor. She saw the thing sucking down there at his face. 'No,' she grunted, though the sound was hardly even audible. She perceived the young woman's need, knew it would have her, would capture her mind and soul, and in that instant she reacted.

Helen Lamont reached to touch the thing that was still huddled between Kate Park's breasts, overwhelmed by mother-love and by the strange, hot urgency in the pit of her belly that was something entirely different. Kate Park slammed her to the

341

floor. There was no hesitation. The woman swung out a sturdy arm and hit her square on the side of the face. The slap sounded like leather on wood. Helen went spinning away. She hit an upright with a dull thud and fell to the floor.

The beast howled in fury.

Kate's momentum carried her across the storeroom, past the stalls and out the back door. The thing in her arms was screeching madly, its mind still casting round to grab the other woman. But for a few seconds, a few vital seconds, Kate Park's mind was her own, and in that brief, somehow eternal space of time, she refused to let the monster take another human.

She pushed the door hard. It swung back, hit the wall and she was out in the snow. Cold bit at her skin. The thing cowered from the sudden lack of warmth. Its mind was singing in anger and thwarted hunger. She ran along, loose shoes clacking on the hard-packed ground, coat flapping in her wake, right down the line of the hedge, taking advantage of its frustration and confusion, putting distance between her and the farm, knowing she was doomed anyway, but doomed to hell if she stayed to let it take another woman.

Down at the bottom end of the field, where the old fence gave on to woodland, it stopped her headlong rush with a savage twist of demand, but she was too far away now. It pulsed at her and an augur of pain drilled into the back of Kate Park's head. The last thing she knew before she lost control of her own mind was the appalling satisfaction that she had fought it and, on one level, she had won.

Helen Lamont dropped like a sack. The darkness spun and fragmented into crazy whirling Christmas lights. The sound was shrieking in her ears and the smell filled her pores and then everything broke up into shards. She rolled, gagged, got to one knee, fell again and then she burst into tears of loss and anger and pain and relief.

She had almost seen it. As soon as it was gone she realized that it had almost had her. Horror surged inside her at how close it had been. Everything was blurred. She remembered walking away from the car and nothing else after that except the humming sound of music in her ears and an urgent sense of want. She had turned and something had . . .

She reached for the memory, not wishing to see what it might show her, shuddering all the while, trying to overcome the racking sobs that shook her. She turned, got to a crouch, tried to stand.

The image wavered in her memory, trying to get through. Something had come at her, big and white. A woman? Yes. And in her arms she had held something that had reached out to her and demanded her love. Yet even as she had reached back she had sensed the wrongness that jittered under the urgent compulsion.

Alien.

She had almost been there. It had almost had her. She had not been able to help herself at all. The false imperative was now ebbing away fast and on its heels came the fear. It had been an alien thing. It had reached into her soul, and for a moment she had not been herself at all, just a thing to be commanded by the filthy mental touch of something that should never have existed.

Parasite, she thought, breath now hitching violently. It was a parasite and it had wanted to feed on her.

The woman had slapped her, hit her. Had it been Ginny Marsden? Had she inadvertently saved Helen from it? Or had she done it deliberately?

The door opened and David came running in. He took one look at her, hauled her to her feet. 'What happened? Did you see him?'

Helen coughed, felt a bubble swell out of one nostril. She wiped it away unselfconsciously, pointed at the door. 'There,' she said. 'She got away.'

'She? Was it Marsden?'

'I don't know. She hit me.'

'Did she have the baby?' David wanted to know. Helen could not even respond for a moment. She felt a warm itch of blood trickle from a scrape on her temple. David was across at the back door, pushing it open. Here in the lee of the wind, the snow had not gathered. There was a space of about two yards clear behind the building that was bare of snow. He looked up and down, but there was no sign of movement. There were no footprints on the hard mud. Finally he came back to her.

'You sure you saw something?' he asked.

'Yes. I saw something and it hit me. Oh God. It was a woman and she was carrying a bundle. I think it was a baby. It almost had me, for God's sake.'

'How do you mean?'

'It reached inside me and told me to become its mother.' She turned to David, blinking the tears back. 'It felt like leprosy, David. It felt like it had been waiting just for me. And I couldn't do a thing about it.' She held on to the lapels of his coat until a fresh and violent shudder of sobbing passed. He knew he should be out there looking for the woman, yet all he could do was stand and hold on to her.

Kate Park made it to the bottom of the hill hobbling in little spastic jerks, her body bent against the pain of disintegration. Her eyes were wide and blinkless, despite the whipping snow. She was heading for shelter, driven on by the force of its will. She reached the fence and skirted along the treeline, now out of the direct wind. Ahead, the land rose and she forced her way up, every breath a purgatory of rasping pain, but she could not pause or flag. Her mind was no longer her own.

She stumbled on as the light was beginning to fade in the sky and the clouds rolled overhead. At the crest of the low slope, a black cloud erupted from the field that had been ploughed the week before: a flock of rooks took to the air, startled by her sudden lurching presence. There were forty or more, wide and glossy, cawing angrily. They wheeled, took off for the trees, then turned towards her. She reached the corner where a stile gave on to a woodland path which would lead to the far side of Barloan Harbour, close to the soaring bridge over the estuary. As she levered herself to the top of the steps, the rooks came winging in, beaks wide. They swooped down, beating at her with their wings, black beaks pecking at her head. At her breast, the baby thing hissed and spat, sensing their own perception of something alien, but unable to turn his head and open his eyes to the daylight.

If Kate's mind had been her own, she would have known the crows were mobbing her, driving her off as they would a stoat or an owl caught out in the daytime, vulnerable in the open. They sensed the predator and the parasite and instinctively drove it away. She stumbled over the stile, landed heavily and twisted her ankle. There was no stopping. The crows followed them a short distance into the tangle of the woods and then pulled off, still cawing deafeningly. She moved on, down towards the old railway, lugging the weight she was forced to carry.

It had all been his fault, David knew that. The sirens howled like banshees and the ice-blue lights pulsed like electrical sparks on the home straight. Jimmy Mulgrew was shivering and not from the cold. His eyes rolled every now and again and he would grab something to stop him from falling. He had been sick so often and so violently he believed the next spasm would turn him completely inside out.

David sat with Helen, merely holding her hand. She too was shivering like an aspen leaf. He could feel it vibrate into him. Her eyes were wide and dark and she was looking into the distance as if she had gone blind. Two red grooves angled from her ear to the point of her jaw and the side of her face was swollen alarmingly. It reminded David of Greta Simon's slumped leer and he winced at the comparison.

Helen had not been badly hurt, not physically. But the look on her face told it all. She looked as if she was in the middle of a nightmare she could not escape from.

He should have pulled out.

She wouldn't have been hurt if he'd just got them out of there and waited for the cavalry. Yet both of them had been compelled to stay, compelled to look. Christ, they could have been killed, he thought, all of them. He put his arm around her, pulling her close. David and Helen were sitting on an upturned trough, out of the gathering blizzard which had started only a few minutes ago and was now already covering the dead, fluttering bodies of the pigeons.

Exactly what had happened here? He couldn't begin to imagine, he tried to tell himself, but his imagination was all fired up and doing nicely on its own. She shivered beside him, breathing hard, as if she'd run a long way and had some distance yet to travel.

Down on the lane the gate opened, slammed hard against its post with the sound of a heavy bell and the police cars came rolling on, wheels crunching on the gravel that would be hidden when the wind came round to let the snow lie on the track. A big sergeant, grizzle-haired and jug-eared, wide as an outhouse and towering over them all, came striding forward, followed by four other men in uniform and a pair of ambulance men in medics' greens. Another car let out two pairs of plain-clothes men and David recognized one of them as a chief inspector from the western division. He bulled his way forward.

'Well, young David,' he said, recognizing him by sight, or simply from what he'd heard. 'What in the name of God's going on?'

'Two dead,' David said, 'In there.' He pointed towards the farmhouse. 'Plus some dead animals.'

'Signs of violence?' the detective asked. His name, David remembered, was Bert Millar.

David nodded. Helen shivered. 'One of them's gunshot. Shotgun. Haven't a clue about the baby.' She shivered against him again at the sound of the word.

'Jesus. A baby?' The detective turned to one of his men. 'Tell the office we need a full forensic, if it's not on its way. And dogs.' He swung back to David. 'This a today job?'

David shook his head this time. 'Couple of days, I think. The blood's dried and clotted, no sign of mould yet.'

The older man looked at Helen. 'Does she live here?'

'No, she's with me. DC Lamont. Waterside section. City division.' It was almost like a code. Short, rattled sentences, the machine-gunning of professionals.

'What's up with her?'

'Slipped on the ice, sir,' Helen spoke up. She had gone very still. 'Hit against the wall.' David said nothing. He had only seen a shape, a kind of movement along by the far hedge leading towards the trees. He'd considered pursuit, but Helen had been on the ground, hands to her face, obviously in pain. She'd seen it, and she wasn't ready to tell another soul. Not yet.

'There might have been somebody in the barn. I couldn't be certain,' he said, knowing he had a duty to tell them at least that. The senior man nodded, jerked his head to one of the others who strode towards the gaping door.

'I'd get that seen to,' Bert Millar said. He beckoned to the big sergeant who came clumping forward, his collar up against the gathering wind. 'David's going to show us. There's a man shot in there.'

'Is it Jack Park?' Millar wanted to know, but David hadn't a clue, and the young policeman had been no help at all. He had been unable to speak from the violence of his vomiting and he now looked as if his mouth had forgotten how.

They all walked in towards the courtyard as the snow fell in a silent shroud, giving the day an eerie, slow-motion effect. The flashing lights added a winking Christmas-card image as the snow began to pile quickly on the roofs and chimneys and the curve of the nearby barn; yet inside, they both knew, was like a scene from hell. He was reluctant to go back inside again. They passed the door that led to the old hayloft. It was still swinging on its hinge. He felt Helen cringe as they walked by.

CHAPTER TWENTY-SIX

The wind howled along with the sirens, singing in the wires that stretched from pole to pole along Jack Park's home-straight track, catching under the eaves of the barn and rattling at the slates of the farmhouse roof, whipping off a spindrift of snow and leaving miniature cornices along the ridging. The dogs howled in sympathy, snapping and snarling at each other from the backs of the vans.

'Useless bastards,' the Chief Inspector rasped, drawing hard on his thin cheroot and blowing smoke down his nose, trying to burn away the stench. Even though it was midwinter, the mess Jack Park had left of himself on the walls was still putrid. The first wagon with his remains wrapped now in plastic was on its way, lights whirling as it jounced along the track. Inside the farm, men were measuring, dusting, sampling.

'So who the hell is that?' he demanded, jerking his thumb towards the barn.

'It's the girl we've been looking for,' David told him. 'At least as far as I can tell. The coat matches, plus the shoe and the ring on her finger.'

Little else matched. The girl's emaciated body had been found sprawled on the tight-packed bales, and if Helen Lamont had been the first to see it she would have recognized the ghastly twitching in the belly. Sergeant Holleran, who discovered the corpse, didn't; he swore without repetition for almost a minute as he beat with frantic flails of his night-stick at the rats which emerged in panic from the hole in the chest cavity. He missed them all in the attempt.

The big, grizzled policeman had swung the flashlight beam round and seen her face, mouth wide open and thick with congealed blood. There was a gap in the teeth where several were missing and for an instant he thought he'd found an old skeleton. He leaned forward and saw the crumpled, drying eyes and realized that what he'd taken for bone was actually tightly-drawn skin over an emaciated skull. The girl's hair, rat-tailed and filthy, was spread out to one side, its golden waves now a bedraggled grey. After his quite instinctive and frenzied attack on the scurrying rodents, he had taken a good look at the corpse. The woman was lying in an old coat, a skirt and a blouse which was rucked up and unbuttoned far enough to show a wizened, wrinkled breast. He assumed he was looking at the corpse of some old woman who had crawled in here to die.

He clambered down the bales and crossed to the door where he shouted to one of his men to fetch the boss. Some time after that, David took a look at the body and in that first glance, his impression was the same as that of the jug-eared sergeant. This looked like an old crone.

But she was wearing the same coat that Ginny Marsden had worn. One of the shoes was off, leaving a bare foot with toes that had been nibbled by the hungry rats. The other was a fashionable winter walking shoe with a gold chain on the side. It was the same kind of footwear the missing girl had been wearing as she strode into the shopping mall. He remembered what other people had said. She'd grown older. In ten days, since John Barclay's camera had picked up her lithe walk in the mall, she'd turned into a hag. Now she was a corpse.

'So she's not from around here?'

David shook his head, eyes fixed on the girl. He shivered, but not from the cold. Whatever it was that could cause such a drastic metamorphosis in so short a time, it was frightening. He remembered Hardingwell's description of the long-chain molecular cells in the dead woman's blood. Could it have been this? Had she been carrying a dreadful wasting disease that she'd passed on to the girl?

Was the baby the vector?

David shook his head again. He'd seen Helen's face in the barn. The blood had drained out of it and she had been shivering in shock. She had seen the baby, and that had almost driven her crazy.

What were they now hunting? All he had were questions. He had to find the answers.

Helen came towards them, sipping hot coffee from a polystyrene cup. The senior man beckoned them both aside, to the far end of the barn. 'Right. I think I should know what the fuck's going on here. I want to know what you two are doing on my patch, and how the hell you turn up here at this slaughterhouse.'

David told him, speaking quickly. He left out much of it, sticking to the bare bones of the story and omitting all of the history. They had been on the trail of a girl who had gone missing, and they believed she had stolen a baby. They had traced her to Barloan Harbour, to the bed and breakfast run by old Mrs Cosgrove. They had followed the constable up the hill on a hunch.

'Some hunch,' Bert Millar said, swinging his eyes between them. 'And if this is her, where in the name of Christ is the baby? Huh?'

David looked at Helen, she looked back. The Chief Inspector looked at both of them. 'There's something you're not telling me,' he said. 'I don't want to be a pain in the arse, but I've just walked into a madhouse here. I've got three bodies, two of them mutilated, and a farm full of dead beasts including two wee Scottie terriers who look as if they've screwed each other to death. Santa Claus did *not* stop here at Christmas with peace and goodwill to all men.' He paused and smiled without any trace of humour. 'Now, you might think my head zips up at the back, but I've been running murder hunts since you were on the potty. I can spot a lie a mile away and I'm spotting one now. So what you two are going to do is come with me, sit down, and tell me everything I want to know. From start to finish. Because what you've said so far doesn't add up to a spoonful of shit. You know it and I know it.'

'It's difficult – ' David started to say, but Helen forestalled him.

'We can tell you,' she said quietly. 'But you won't believe it.'

'Well, girl,' Bert Millar said. 'We're just going to have to see.'

It was another twenty minutes and two cups of coffee from the dispenser in the mobile unit before David finished talking. He took the senior officer through the story from day one, from the death of the woman they'd assumed to be Thelma Quigley and the later discovery of the video shots showing Ginny Marsden, who had by this time become the subject of Helen's search. He spoke of the puzzling pathology in the autopsy and the inexplicable and confusing series of coincidences.

At the end of it, the Chief Inspector drained his cup and lifted his head. 'And you believe this? It's some kind of mutant?'

'It's getting hard not to,' David finally conceded. 'We've been on her tail for ten days. Heather McDougall had a baby and nobody knows where it came from. Ginny Marsden took her baby and now she's dead. Nobody has ever really clapped eyes on this baby.'

'Just the one?'

'Who knows? There could be several,' David said, still instinctively prevaricating. No matter what he believed, he was aware of how it would appear. 'If there's just one, then it's some kind of mutant, and it's damned dangerous.'

'I think it is, Chief,' Helen interjected. 'We wanted to find her first, to make sure. But I can't think of any other explanation. She's been here, and now the baby – whatever it is – it's gone.' The only thing she'd omitted was the confrontation in the hayloft, and that was only because she refused even to let her mind approach that. Every time her memory veered in that direction, a wave of panic began to swell inside her, threatening to engulf her completely and reduce her to a quivering, weeping child.

'She's certainly been here,' David backed her up. He knew Helen had seen another woman with a baby, some *thing* in her arms, but he sensed, quite rightly, that she was not willing to share that information with anyone else. 'And earlier on, I thought I heard something over by that loft. There was nothing there by the time I got the door open,' – he felt Helen tense against him, knowing he was lying – 'but I'm sure there was. There was movement down by the hedge along the edge of the field. I couldn't make it out, for it was snowing by then, and I thought it was best not to give chase on my own.'

'So who could it have been?'

'I think it could be another woman, maybe even the farmer's wife. There's no sign of the baby, is there? Nobody's found the Park woman yet.'

Bert Millar thought about it. He had a long face and beetling black eyebrows which every now and again drew down so that his eyes were hidden. He looked as if he'd stood out on a lot of crime scenes in a lot of cold winters. 'You say Phil Cutcheon goes along with this?'

'He gave me the old man's files,' David said. 'He says he thinks there's something wrong. I *know* there's something wrong. I don't know the answer, but I think we came close to it.'

'I worked for Phil,' the DCI finally said. 'He was a straight arrow. Still is, I suppose, and he was never given to flights of fancy. But all this gives me a problem. I don't believe in aliens and mutants and I don't even waste my time watching them on television. That's just to state my position so you know the kind of reports I submit. As far as I'm concerned you've got a missing baby. I've got a father and a child killed by some maniac and I've got the corpse of your runaway girl. I'm going to assume this baby of yours has been abducted yet again, because there's no trace of it and there's no trace of whoever left this place in a shambles. Now, until I know better, I'm going on the assumption that there's been some leak, some contamination into the water supply. Perhaps some old chemicals lying around have killed the livestock, made them abort, caused some aberrant behaviour. That's my official line and that is how this inquiry is going to proceed.'

He dropped his voice. 'But you two crazies had better keep on working on your own thing. You're looking for a missing child and at the same time helping me with my investigation, because the two are linked. I'll speak to Donal Bulloch and get him to spare you for the duration. He'll go along with that. Now believe me, we never had this conversation. I never heard a word about sixty-year-old babies, not a whisper about aliens and monsters. OK?' He stood up. 'When you heard something, out at the back of the hayloft, which direction would you have said it went?'

'Down towards the trees,' David said. 'Why?'

'That's where the dogs went berserk. The handlers couldn't get them past the hedge. They sounded as if they were scared shitless.' His brows drew down again, hiding his eyes from them. 'I think you two should think about where this baby might have gone, and who it might have gone with. You're right when you say we haven't found the farmer's wife. If she's killed her own child and run off with another, there's more of a chance that this really is down to some toxic leak. I'd honestly prefer to believe that.'

He turned to Helen. 'Do you think she did this? Or was it the siege of Sunnybrooke Farm? I really want to know, and God save me, I'm beginning to think you two might be able to help me.'

He heard the dog in the distance. He knew the frenzied sound from back in his past, so long ago that it was lost in the haze of all memories. The animals were too far away to pose a threat. The snow was thicker now and he burrowed under the mother's coat, in against her flopping breasts, feeling the beat of her heart. It stuttered and staggered along with her and he knew she was flagging. He goaded her onwards. They had reached the old railway, the one which used to carry the grain to the Littlebank Distillery further beyond Bowling Harbour. The spur line had not been used for years, though in times past he had travelled it, huddled against another mother. He had no way of recognizing it or recalling that mother. It was too, too far in the past and all their scents and flavours merged.

Most of the sleepers were gone, leaving the hard-pack grit which was overgrown and matted with moss to form a pathway, used by small boys on bikes as a shortcut behind the village in the summer. Now it was quiet, all sounds muffled by the falling snow. They had been moving for half an hour through brambles and rose thickets. Her legs were a mass of scratches and her twisted ankle kept giving way, but there was nothing for it. He had to get to other people and shelter before she emptied and stopped.

Almost as soon as he had broken through the ragged confines of the old skin, feeling the new surface shiny and slick and rippling with the strength of growing muscle, he had felt the start of yet another change. It was happening so quickly he had hardly time to act. Now he had to be away, away from the howling beasts and the others who had followed him.

He recalled the shock that had come out from the female, the sudden burst of awareness when he had touched her. He had felt the *rightness* of her, the ripeness of her, and the new hunger had raged within him. His glands had puffed up and the new-grown part of him had swelled in readiness. The heat of contact had made all of his muscles vibrate in monstrous anticipation.

And then he had missed her.

It had been so close he could have taken her right there and then. He could have snatched her and dropped this one to the ground with a twitch of his mind, yet unbelievably, he had been thwarted. His anger swelled but he doused it instantly. She would come again and he would be prepared.

They had come too far for him to be able to sense her now. But she had followed him down the days. From one den to another, from one hiding place to the next. She had followed him and he knew she was important.

Darkness was falling in earnest now. His own eyes were closed, but he could sense it through the mother's dulled reactions. She pushed through a barrage of broom stems, scraping her ankle on a gnarled root, ignoring this little pain among so much of it. Ahead, over the iron bridge which spanned the canal, barely visible in the deepening shadows, was the old station. A dim and distant part of Kate Park recognized it. She had played here as a girl, climbing the trees with her brothers and trying to catch fish in the small stream which ran parallel to the high track and emptied itself into Barloan Canal. That had been a lifetime ago.

It had been her baby's brief and incandescent lifetime ago. It had been Jack's lifetime, ended as he spun twitching to the floor. Now she was groping her way along this track with the beast that had made her kill him, with the beast that had clambered on to the baby's crib. While this small, helpless part of herself knew it for what it was, its control was such that she clutched its weight against her and felt the smooth skin of a newborn baby. The compulsion was so powerful that she kept going, despite the rot of her flesh and the disintegration of her bones as it took all the succulence from her body and used it for itself.

She reached the old ticket office, almost an exact duplicate of the still-used room down in the village where Ginny Marsden had sat by the cooling fire, resting before her next move. Here it was cold and damp; tall trees kept out most of the wind but let the snow billow round the trunks and build up on the west-facing sides. As soon as she arrived, a family of magpies which had been sheltering under the canopy took off into the gloom with loud, racketing cries of alarm. Out beyond the track, a stoat sat up on its hind legs and sniffed at the air, sensing something more mindlessly hungry than its own self. Very quickly and silently, it turned and disappeared into a hole between the roots of a thick beech tree.

The station door was closed, but the lock had long since fallen out of the rotted wood and Kate Park's weight pushed it open. Inside, the air stank of old fires and piss. An ancient mattress, helixed with rusted springs, jutted out from the corner near the fireplace. It smelled of worse, though Kate was unaware of it. She squeezed inside, out of the turbulent wind. Beyond the ticket office, through a wide-open door, was another small room with a bench. The windows here were still intact. Kate stumbled to the seat and lowered herself, eyes wide in the deepening darkness. She cuddled the thing against her and it dropped its mouth on to her, taking another feed. She felt herself drain into it, every pulsing suck taking more of her, but she was helpless to resist.

After a while her eyes closed and she gave herself to the unremitting waves of pain, holding on to them because that was the only part of her that was truly her own.

As the night deepened she sat still, one foot bloated with infection and the other twisted to the side where the muscle had been wrenched. The layer of fat that had given her the substantial round sleekness had gone, sucked out of her and burned by the creature's flaring metabolism. It left her angular and sharp, her cheekbones beginning to stand out the way Ginny Marsden's had done. In three days, it had robbed her not only of her baby and her husband, but of her very substance.

And still she could do nothing. It held her tight and drained her dry.

By a miracle, she survived the night, the deeply buried part of her re-reeling those deaths on a constant loop.

In the morning, when the sun came up, she awoke from a kind of torpor, slowly aware of the sound of howling dogs. It too was awake and aware. It heard the dogs and knew that the danger was coming. It reached for her and made her move.

Kate Park tottered to her feet.

The autopsies of Jack Park and his daughter Lucy were carried out simultaneously with the post-mortem on the body in the barn. Professor Hartley was called down from St Enoch's and Simpson Hardingwell arrived within the hour. By this time, the whole of Barloan Harbour had been blocked off and Bert Millar's squads were methodically making door-to-door inquiries.

Hartley got a positive identification on Ginny Marsden less than an hour after she'd been carried out of the barn, her limbs jutting like stiffened sticks. The identification needed dental records which were already on hand. Helen Lamont had got them on the third day of her search for the missing girl, just in case they were needed. She hadn't told the girl's parents that, to spare their feelings. Now they would hear the worst. John Marsden would face the nightmare of identifying his ruined daughter's corpse.

Had it not been for the X-rays of her upper molars, even this first identification would have been difficult, because Hartley discovered the girl had lost eight teeth in her last few days. The gaps in the gums were frayed and swollen with infection. His notes said that the woman appeared to be middle-aged and extremely emaciated. Apart from the gaping wound in her belly where the rats had gnawed a tunnel into her liver, he found she had been suffering from acute calcium and collagen deficiency in her skeletal structure. Her skin was wrinkled and her hair thinning, much of it turned grey. He remembered the woman who had died in the mall and reflected on the similarity in their pathology.

In his notes he wrote:

> The inflammation in the joints, caused by the abrasion and pitting of the calceous surfaces due to bone degeneration, would have caused acute pain. It is unlikely that this person was able to

walk, at least for any distance. Similar deterioration can be seen in the ligaments and joints of hands and feet and seems to have been spreading to her skull and pelvis where a marked thinning of the skeletal structure is apparent.

Hartley noted the bite-marks all over the body's upper torso and the scarring of the skin on and around the breasts and nipples. There was evidence of lactation, although each breast was now wrinkled and empty. Ginny Marsden's blood was devoid of iron, magnesium, zinc and a host of vitamins. Her white-cell count was huge while the number of red cells was vastly below normal. She was seriously anaemic. The muscle of her heart was thin and the aorta had already become porous, leaking her dilute blood slowly into her chest cavity. The mucosal membrane of her trachea and throat had been stripped clean. Some of the bloody lining had already been found on the hay of the barn. Simpson Hardingwell, the microbiologist, confirmed the presence of large polypeptide molecules and clusters of unfamiliar cells which later proved to contain unidentifiable chains of genetic DNA cells. Hartley concluded that Ginny Marsden had died from blood loss and oxygen starvation possibly caused by an unknown viral infection.

Simpson Hardingwell took samples of the cell material for later study. Despite being kept frozen in liquid nitrogen, the clusters of cells fragmented, spilling their genetic sugar-chains into a soup of amino acids as soon as the samples were unfrozen. Subsequent attempts to identify the cells proved fruitless.

The autopsy on Jack Park was easier. He died from shock and haemorrhaging caused by the two gunshot wounds, first to his hands and arms and then to his side which took away one kidney, some of his liver and half a lung.

The baby, little Lucy Park, only a few weeks old, had died from blood loss. The cause of that was more difficult to determine. The pathologist found a small and roughly circular gash in her neck where the flesh had been cut away. The striations on the skin and muscle showed a scouring pattern unlike an animal bite. In fact it was unlike anything in the experience of the young pathologist who was working in the room next to Hartley. He wondered if there might be some kind of farm implement which could have drilled such a hole. Tests on the few centilitres of blood left in the tiny body showed a type of anti-coagulant similar in chemical structure to the kind produced by leeches to prevent clotting. He could give no opinion as to how the substance was introduced into the body, other than in a kind of bite. He was unable to offer an opinion as to what kind of creature would bite in such a fashion or be the vector of the blood-thinning compound.

While the autopsies were being carried out in the basement of Lochend Hospital, Bert Millar had set up his incident caravan down in the centre of Barloan Harbour, close to the railway station, and his teams were out knocking on doors. Jack and Helen had been seconded, with the agreement of Donal Bulloch. The dog teams had tried again up at the farm but the animals were unable to function properly. They were confused and agitated, and none of them, it seemed, could be persuaded to go down to the woods at the bottom of the slope.

Two teams of searchers combed the thick belt of trees until darkness fell and found nothing on the stretch between Middle Loan Farm and the railway line. The Chief Inspector posted guards on the upper perimeter on the assumption that anybody leaving the town, east or west, by road or rail, would be picked up. The road blocks stayed on until the following afternoon.

Nothing turned up, except a poacher called Snib McFee, who was ambushed by two big policemen as he came scuttling quickly down through the trees beside the canal just before sunrise. The unfortunate Snib was running at full tilt along the path and had not expected a welcoming party, as was clear from the look on his face as soon as the hand clamped upon his shoulder. The flashlight beam caught his look of utter terror. His hand went to his chest, and if the light had been better, his face would have been seen to go a sickly bluish colour as he gasped for breath. The sack with four hen peasants, all of them winter-plump, fell to the ground with a thump and Snib almost did the same. 'Holy mother of . . .' he gasped, hauling for breath. 'I'm having a fuckin' heart attack.'

The burly policeman didn't even hear the protest. All he knew was that a maniac killer was on the loose and he was taking no chances, heart attack or not. He swung his boot and caught Snib in the crotch with such force that the small man was lifted three inches above the path. He doubled over and fell to the ground with both hands between his legs. He was suddenly, violently sick.

The policeman grabbed him by the collar, dragged his hands away and cuffed them. 'Check the bag,' he rasped, hardly daring to take his eyes off the gasping man. 'If there's a body in it I'm going to cave this bastard's head in.'

The pheasants rolled out heavily, their necks twisted at odd angles.

It was to be more than an hour before Snib McFee finally got someone to listen to him and by that time his testicles had swollen to such an extent that he thought they might burst. Sergeant Holleran wanted to lock him up, being the local cop and bearing the considered opinion that poaching was just one degree beneath treason in the eyes of the law. He and Jack Park had gone fishing together up in the tarns on the hillside in the summer months. He'd sat out on many a night trying to catch the McFee boys, a large family who plagued the landowners within a radius of twenty miles.

A valuable hour was wasted before anybody listened to what the little poacher had to say.

Snib had been after the pheasants at Wester Farrow estate where shooting parties gathered every autumn and winter for some of the best woodland pheasants and high-moor grouse. The land was fenced and well patrolled, but the quick and the brave could get in, snare a couple of pheasants as they roosted in the branches of a thicket, and be out again long before anybody noticed. It was simple enough. The pheasants never flew at night, and a noose of wire on the end of a pole would bring them down without a sound as they slept. The birds would buy drinking money for any long weekend.

He'd heard the barking of the dogs in the distance, a couple of miles west at Middle Loan, but he paid them no heed. Big Jack Park was probably out for the foxes; maybe he'd even persuaded the gamekeeper at Wester Farrow to come along for the fun. Snib preferred to hunt what he could eat or sell.

In and out. He'd been quick and he'd been quiet. Just a flash from his Maglite and another bird would come down. Four was enough for a night. He slipped through the pines, following the edges of the forest and the high fence until he came to the break he and his brother had cut weeks before, hidden by a clump of rhododendrons. Through that and into the beech forest with only a mile or so to home. Down on the level, he followed the straight of the disused railway line, his feet now silent on the thick snow that had managed to get through the trees. The wind was strong, rattling the bare twigs high over-head, but on the track he was protected from the worst of it. The pheasants were still warm against his back.

He reached the old station, cupping a cigarette in his hand, and followed the slope up to the abandoned platform. Here it was more exposed and he went round the side of the old ticket office and stood in the lee for a moment, drawing hard on the smoke and looking forward to the sharp burn of a dram of whiskey when he got home. He finished his smoke, hefted the sack again and turned round the corner into the wind, passing the shuttered window which rattled softly in the bluster. He was just beyond the window when he heard the noise.

He froze, one foot still suspended in the air, the way he would while poaching if he suspected the keeper was close. One wrong foot in the forest could crack a twig and draw attention. Snib froze, but at the same time all the hairs on the back of his neck suddenly crawled and the skin down his back puckered in a cold twist.

The noise was just a groan, hardly audible above the whine of the wind through the branches, but it had stopped Snib in his tracks. Very slowly, he put his foot down on to the overlay of soft snow on the platform, making not a sound. His heart had speeded up, quite inexplicably, and something inside him wanted him be off and away along the track. Snib was a crea-ture at home with the night: Perhaps that gave him an added alertness to danger. Whatever it was, he was aware of a chill ripple of alarm.

Despite that, when the soft whimper came again, he could not prevent his feet from taking him back two steps to the window. He leaned towards the dusty glass. Inside, it was black as tar. He caught a flicker of his own reflection looming out at him and started back in alarm. The feeling of sudden menace inflated.

The sound came for a third time, a little louder, and he could not resist peering back again. He drew out the little torch and twisted it until the beam shone, then raised it to the class. What he expected, he could not have said. Maybe a fox, bleeding from a gin-trap bite, possibly even a roe deer trapped inside. He swung the thin beam round, following its pallid disc on the far wall, a small moon arcing across a flat blank sky. It passed a dark shape, moved on. He snapped it back.

The noise came again, that eerie, low moan, and this time the ripple down his back was a physical shudder of apprehension. The torch beam steadied on the shapeless huddle.

The woman's face stared at him. The light reflected back from bloodshot eyes, making them look eerily pink and somehow blind. Her mouth was open, slack and imbecilic. For a moment he thought she was dead until she moved and a moan escaped her. Despite his fear, Snib almost called out to her, for, poacher though he might be, he was not a bad fellow and would never leave anyone, human or animal, lying hurt.

Then he saw something move just under her chin. He lowered the beam and saw she was holding a bundle of cloth up against herself. It was a baby, Snib realized, and he let out a long breath. Just a baby. He wondered what the hell a woman was doing out in the abandoned spur-line station in the dead of a winter's morning. The light caught her eyes as he raised the torch again and in that moment they stared right at him and the look they conveyed was one of absolute and utter loss. Instantly the sensation of menace fell on him again. He lowered the light once more and saw the baby's head squirm round as if it was trying to free itself from the shawl. The cloth fell away.

A wrinkled forehead puckered and a thick lid opened. A large, flat, red eye stared into his and he felt a dreadful jolt of baneful contact through the glass. Snib's heart somersaulted into his throat. He jerked away and the flashlight flicked out. The pane of glass went black.

Snib took one step backwards, breathing hard. His foot slipped on the snow and he went down on one knee. Just as quickly he was back up again. Inside the ticket office he could hear a muffled thumping sound and then a pattering scrape. It sounded like a dog's nails on a hard floor. He reached out a hand to steady himself, turning once again towards the window.

A nightmare pressed up on the other side of the glass. Two great red eyes bored into his. He saw a wrinkled demon face and a round, puckered little mouth with thin, warted lips that pulled back over a circle of glassy shards. In that instant he believed he was looking at a devil from hell. 'Mammy,' he yelped, unaware that he had made a sound, or that, at the age of thirty, he had reverted to the language of his childhood.

On the other side of the thin glass, the little beast glared at him. A thin grey hand came up and scratched at the pane and the lips wavered back from the circlet of teeth. Inside that circle the light flashed on another set of spines. For a second he thought he must be going mad. Then, behind the glaring nightmare face, he heard a woman's hollow cry, a sound so pitiful and desperate that even on the crest of his fear it touched a chord within him and he knew he had heard the cry of the damned.

The thing turned, showing him a flat profile and a receding jaw topped by that alien, rounded mouth. As soon as its attention had swept away from him, he could move again. Without a thought and without a sound, Snib was off and running. He slipped on the snow on the far side of the old platform, rolled, and got to his feet, trying to keep the scream inside of him. He scurried along the track as fast as his feet could take him. If he'd been thinking at all, he'd have dropped the sack, but his fear of a gargoyle-faced devil coming after him through the dark of the trees was so great that the thought never crossed his mind. He went haring along the track until he reached the turn, threw himself to the left, and raced downhill, narrowly missing all of the tree-trunks on the slope. His breath panted, loud as the old steam trains that had once run on the line, and his heart was kicking like a horse inside his ribs. There was no sound behind him, but he dared not stop to look. All he wanted to do was get home and lock the door and get up to his bed and pull the blankets over his head and wait until light.

Then a hand came reaching out of the shadows to clamp upon his shoulder and Snib truly thought he was going to die on the spot. When the foot came up and smashed into his groin, the pain was so great that he hoped he would die.

CHAPTER TWENTY-SEVEN

She was lurching along the track, unable to stop while the baby's mind jittered inside of her own, forcing her on. Her body was a pulse of pain. Behind them men were coming through the trees. The sound of their voices was muffled, but getting louder all the time.

Help me, please help me . . . someone help me. . . The mantra sang out in the deep and barricaded part of herself that was her own, but she could not make the words come out. All she wanted to do now was die, but the thing at her breast tugged her on, its own panic conveying itself to her in sharp drilling spasms of energy. Off to the right, a clump of snow fell off a spruce tree with a quiet flop of sound and she felt it jerk in alarm. In her ears the chittering sound waxed, a fuzzy little crackle that made her ears feel as if they were bleeding. It vibrated in the bones of her jaw and made her teeth chatter together.

Go go go. GO!

No words, but a mental goading, whip and sharp spurs, that could not be denied. She had to run and hide. She had to get the baby away from here. That was the only thing on the surface of her mind. It was crying, whimpering its terror at her. She could do nothing but respond.

The dogs were coming: two of them, howling behind, somewhere in the distance. They sounded like wolves in the early dawn. Over to the east the sky was pinking, slashed in layers of colours under the snow cloud, tinged with the rising sun and with the orange of the street lamps on the main route to the city. On the right, the wide black ribbon of the bridge spanning the estuary was lined with a coruscation of lights. Under any other circumstances it would have been a winter scene to admire. She did not even see it. Her whole attention had been focused on the need to get the baby to safety.

She ran, while rivers of white-hot pain surged in her feet and in her hips. Blood trickled from her mouth and the ragged wound in her sole. The baby cried constantly, huddled against her. The dogs howled and snarled. Somewhere in the distance a siren wailed. Down in the estuary the foghorn bawled hollow in the lessening wind. Snow flurries still blew in, but fewer than there had been before. Kate Park's feet left deep holes in the virgin snow but they made hardly a sound.

She stumbled on.

Behind her, the dog handlers were urging their animals onward, with some difficulty. When they had arrived at the old station, the dogs, at first fired with their normal energy, had taken one sniff inside the ticket office and then they'd gone into fits of frenzied barking. Both of them, powerful Alsatians, had cringed back, haunches low, tails tucked tight. Their eyes had been rolling wildly and they looked absolutely terrified. The handlers dragged them back, wondering what was wrong with them. Already the first team had been forced to pull back up at the farm when the other two dogs had started snapping and snarling at each other, and one of them had tried to mount the other, thrusting away with powerful jerks of its rump while foaming saliva flicked from its gaping jaws.

This time, just after dawn, the dogs looked plain scared. One of the other policemen went inside the office and came out holding his nose. 'Smells like a slaughterhouse dump,' he said.

There were footprints in the snow on the far side of the old building, leading down across the flat where the track had once been and angling into the trees. The footprints stopped only a few yards into the spruce trees where the snow couldn't reach. The handlers pulled the dogs away from the station. The animals howled excitedly, almost like a gathering of wolves, but the trained men could hear the panic in their yelping. 'Something wrong here, sarge,' one of the men said. 'They don't want to go on.'

'They'll go on with my toe up their backsides,' Sergeant Holleran warned him. 'I don't care if they've got broken legs. Get them out and get them sniffing.' The dog men dragged their charges on to the disused track. The beasts sniffed and yelped in obvious distress, but had taken their training better than the previous two at the farm. After a few moments' hesitation they got their heads down, started to snuffle for scent and then began to follow a trail. Every now one of them would back off, yipping in consternation. Slowly and hesitantly, however, they made progress through the damp forest.

He had perceived the pursuit and made her move. In his strange acoustics, he heard the dogs' yelping like the cracking of ice, but he still recognized it as a threat. Alarm jangled through him as she gathered him up and hobbled out into the cold, clutching him against her failing heat. He shared her mind once, twice, for inside she was shrieking, like the other one had, like no other mothers had before. They had all accepted him, they had loved him. But now he was changing, and while he could still control the mothers, he had to push them hard.

He twisted violently and she lurched out and into the trees. Her breath was ragged and her heart was beating too fast. He could sense the weakness there. She would not last. She stumbled on, barging through the thickets of birch and bramble, alder and hazel.

He needed a place to hide. The threat came from behind them in the howl of the beasts and the hoarse rumbling vibrations that were the shouts of pursuing men. If they caught him they would destroy him. That instinctive knowledge burned brightly, not in words but in a complete concept on the forefront of his mind. A sudden dread washed over him. He had never been hunted like this, not in his memory. He had always driven the mothers on whenever he sensed any danger. Now he was out in the cold, exposed and desperately vulnerable, and they were after him.

In his panic he reached out a long way, casting ahead and behind, to identify the points of greatest peril and spaces where the danger was less.

He brushed the other one's mind and recognized her.

Hope flared. A chance. Hunger swelled with it despite his panic. She was coming. She would follow him. If he could find a place, she would come to him, dragged along the invisible lines that bound them. He needed her now.

The mother stumbled on, broke free of the bushes and was down on the track again. Here, for a long straight distance, the rail-route was a broad avenue of pristine snow. She went along it, breath crackling like ground glass, heart thudding so hard he could hear it through the shawl and the coat.

The dogs howled. Men shouted. They were getting closer. Ahead of them, the old iron bridge over the canal loomed, grey and stark. She stumbled towards it, now reeling from side to side, powered only by the force of his will.

'It's ahead of us,' Helen Lamont panted. She and David had been pushing their way through the bushes. Both of them had listened to what Snib McPhee had said and they were the only ones who took his description literally. Helen's mind wandered back in the direction of the barn and then shied away from the recollection. She had seen something but her eyes had swung away, denying what she might have glimpsed in the shadows. It had been a flash, nothing more, and it could have been anything at all, except for the fact that her subconscious mind had snatched the image and burned it deep into her brain.

Monster.

She knew it had been and it had almost had her. It had wanted her and, God help her, in that instant, she had wanted it.

Monster.

'It's a fuckin' monster,' Snib McPhee had said, unashamedly massaging his balls where, according to the two policemen, he had taken a bit of a knock when he'd fallen on the slippery snow against a tree-stump. Snib knew there was little point in protesting about brutality, and anyway his mind was on other things. 'Swear to Christ,' he swore to Christ. 'I saw it with my own eyes. It's a fuckin' monster.' The small man crossed himself several times in quick succession, driving out devils, then slid his hand back down on to his throbbing crotch. 'I saw a woman. She was just sitting there with her eyes open and I thought she was dead, for Christ's sake, and then she moved. I heard her first. Crying like, sort of moaning. Or maybe like a grunt. I thought it was a dog or something, stuck behind the door, but I got a look at her in the torchlight and she saw me. She tried to talk, I think, but I never heard anything and then this baby she was holding, it turned round, and it wasn't a baby at all.'

'What was it?' Bert Millar wanted to know.

'I told you. It was a fuckin' monster. My torch went out and next thing it's up at the window. It had eyes like nothing I ever saw in my life and a mouthful of teeth. A big circle of them, all pointing in towards each other. You put a finger in there and it's never coming out. I'll tell you what it's like. It's like them lampreys you get on salmon. You know those things that eat their way inside?'

David recalled the words of dead Ron McBean in his report. The Melrose woman, way back before the turn of the century, had leapt off a bridge and killed herself.

When recovered, her whole body was covered in bleeding lacerations and bruises which a doctor described as very similar to the sucking circlets caused by lampreys on salmon from the nearby River Nith.

McBean had noted the similarity in the odd circular lesions uncovered in the autopsy on Harriet Dailly. Another coincidence. Whatever this thing was, if McBean was right, it was older than fifty, older than a century. How long had it been around stealing mothers? And what sort of creature looked like a sucking lamprey that fed on living salmon?

'You'd know all about salmon, Snib,' Sergeant Holleran had volunteered, but the CID boss held up his hand for silence.

'What do you think?' he asked David. 'Is he taking the piss or what?'

'No,' Helen said. 'It's probably the farmer's wife. She'll have the baby.'

'Killed her own and then run off with another?'

'I couldn't say, sir,' Helen said, falling back into police-speak. 'But the woman is missing and I can't think of anybody else who'd be out alone with a baby on a night like this. And it also wouldn't be the first time, if we're right.'

Millar drew them outside. 'At least we've got a direction. We'll take his word for it, but as far as the rest are concerned, it's a woman and a baby.'

Half an hour later, Helen stopped, panting for breath. 'It's ahead of us,' she said. They were almost at the edge of the trees now. She had been pushing through the bushes, well to the left of the other policemen, maybe ten feet from David, when she felt its touch, the cold slither of hunger and need. It sent a shiver right into her, because she recognized her own response.

'Which way?' David asked. He saw the look on her face and believed her. In the weak winter light of the morning, her face was pinched and pale, and her dark eyes were like black stones in snow. The wind ruffled her hair and made her seem slender and vulnerable.

'There,' she said, pointing ahead, further to the left. She turned and he followed, up a tree-covered rise and down the slope. The dogs were behind them now. They reached a stand of thin, rotting willowherb, ploughed through and found themselves on the straight.

A trail of footprints, deep and unclear, angled away from them towards the bridge in the distance. From where they stood, they could see the shambling progress, as if both feet had been dragging, throwing up spill-piles of snow into hummocks. The tracks wove left to right, from one side of the line to the other.

David turned and bawled, attracting the attention of the dog teams who came bursting out on to the line some fifty yards behind. He pointed to the tracks and then turned to follow them. The dogs barked frantically, high, fretful yipping sounds that made them sound plaintive and timid, but the handlers urged them on. David and Helen ran ahead, and all the time, Helen could feel the oily, sinful touch of the thing they had pursued now for eleven days.

Kate Park lurched off the steep embankment about three hundred yards past the bridge. Behind her the dogs howled and scrabbled. Footsteps thudded on the far side of the bridge and men's voices carried on the cold air.

Go go go go GET GONE . . .

There was desperation in its urging and she obeyed it. She slipped, fell, arched her racked body to protect her burden, and got to her feet again. Burning, crushing sensations ground from bone to bone down the length of her back. Her heart was a lump of fire in the centre of her chest and the pain in her legs and hips had soared to such a crescendo that the nerves there had simply given out. A dreadful numbness oozed up her limbs, making it even more difficult to carry on. Yet she reeled down the slope, snagged by thorns and bramble runners, down to the low wall of the railway embankment. An angle-iron fence sat atop the wall, its spikes corroded and paint-peeled. She started to climb when one of the upright spars clanged outwards, making a gap. A bolt had rusted. She slipped through, pushing the baby ahead, then drawing herself between the spars until she was on the wall itself, maybe ten feet above a narrow street.

The metal clanged back into place just as the dogs came pounding over the edge of the embankment, whining as they came. The handlers urged them on towards the shape on the other side of the fence, half hidden by the upright spars. The baby squirmed until it could see over her shoulder and risked opening its eyes, despite the ferocious burn even in the half-light of the early winter's morning. Its attention was partly snagged by the other female who was behind with the dogs, but it had no time to waste. It concentrated on the beasts and stabbed into their minds.

The dogs went berserk.

They were halfway down the steep slope when their yelps turned into savage growls. The lead dog turned round, bolted between its handler's legs, knocking him off balance. It pulled the leash from his hand and went streaking for its partner, jaws agape. The second dog reared up, met it halfway, fangs exposed in a ferocious snarl. The two animals collided, growling like tigers. Their teeth closed on each other's necks. Blood and fur flew. The two men tried to separate them, but the dogs seemed to have gone mad. Their eyes were rolling wildly and their strangled grunts soared higher and higher as they savaged one another. One of the men got his night-stick between one dog's jaws, levered hard and succeeded only in snapping two teeth. The dogs ignored them.

Helen and David came running fast over the rise and down the slope. They took in the snarling animals and then saw the shape at the far side of the fence.

Helen felt the touch of the thing, not aimed directly at her, because it was focused on the dog threat, but it still sent a spasm of horror *and feral hunger too, she knew* right through her.

'There,' David said, pointing. A pale face could be seen on

370

the other side of the fence. Someone was sitting on the wall. 'Stop,' he yelled, but the face disappeared from view. The dogs screamed. Blood bubbled from their nostrils, from their throats. One of the policemen was shouting at the top of his lungs. David started towards the wall and Helen followed, her whole mind cringing from the leprous touch.

It turned its mind away from the mother to the dogs. She felt the buzz of mental energy as it threw its command at them. It was like the searing heat of lightning in the air. Her own mind had lurched away from that mental blast, and she was herself again.

Kate Park blinked, coughed, and a trickle of pink foam spun away from her. She felt a scream build up in her shredding lungs, a primal blast from the depths of her fragmented soul, and she clamped it to silence. All of her was in pain: her mind, her heart, and her body. The image of Jack's twitching body came back again, overlaid by the sound of sucking from the baby's crib. She was out of one nightmare and into another. She turned her eyes to the thing and saw its flat, mindless eyes. It was bigger now, more angular, almost insectile. Her hate welled up and in that moment she knew what she had to do.

Behind her, the dogs tore at each other, men were bawling. The beast was concentrating on the animals, trying to combat that threat. It would come back to her, or it might turn on the others.

She was done and she knew it. There was nothing to live for and the pain was too much.

It was turning to the others. She turned too, unable to prevent herself. Through the bars of the fence she saw the young man coming towards her, his mouth open, one hand raised as if reaching to grab her across the distance between them. Beside him was the girl she had seen below the hayloft. She recognized her instantly, although their previous encounter had only been a brief scrape. Her open mind touched the girl's in a flash of empathy. She knew in that instant it had wanted her, and she knew why. The girl's mind touched hers in return, sending a shudder of sorrow and pity and fear.

Kate Park turned away. Down below the flagstones of the

pavement came hard up against the wall of the embankment. The thing's attention was just beginning to swivel to the men when she launched herself into the air. She clutched her burden tight, turning as they toppled, ensuring that they would both land together head first on the hard concrete.

Kill you! her mind snarled. Oblivion rushed at her.

David Harper saw the twisting lurch and bawled at the top of his voice, jumping past the slavering animals. Helen screeched an incoherent warning. The woman disappeared from the other side of the fence.

Kate was falling, but a long runner of bramblethorn snagged her foot as she tumbled, spinning her in mid air. The world spun. The thing in her arms shrieked, stronger now since its change and the spurt of growth, and a pure, distilled pain shuddered into her head, completely shattering the cochlea in her inner ear. Above the embankment, the mind-blast lashed outwards and a policeman's retinas detached themselves and he went instantly blind. In the trees overhead, the flock of crows that had mobbed Kate on her run down by the hedge dropped like fluttering weights to the ground, quivering but not dead, all of them hissing like snakes. Fifty yards away a cat howled, ran across the road, and was flattened under the wheels of a car. Beyond the bridge, a small child in a high-chair vomited and fell face first into a plate of cereal.

Kate Park landed on her hip and her pelvis shattered into fragments. The appalling jolt smashed her teeth together so hard that they bit right through the tip of her tongue. A new lava-burst of pain slammed her breath away as she bounced, dazed, but amazingly still conscious. Unbearable despair overshadowed the inconceivable pain in her damaged body. She had tried to kill them both and she had failed.

'Are you all right, dear?' A voice came from nowhere, thin and wavering. Her head turned as she lay, not voluntarily, but simply with its own weight. An old and weathered face was looming down at her.

'Go,' she tried to say.

'What's that, love? Are you hurt?' The old woman peered down, her head tightly wrapped in a thick scarf knotted under her chin. 'You took a nasty fall there. Did you slip on the ice?'

'Please,' Kate tried to tell her, but the word only came out in a wheeze. Her vision was looping in and out of focus and she felt her consciousness begin to slip away. In her arms, the shape stirred, and it was only then that she realized it was still wrapped in the shawl.

'Oh dear,' the old woman said. 'The poor wee thing. Is the baby hurt?'

She tried to scream, to tell the woman to get away. Beside her, she saw with unexpected clarity a shopping bag on wheels, and got a whiff of freshly baked morning rolls, the first normal scent she had been aware of since the thing had come scuttling in through the cat flap and stolen her mind. Its thoughts were now focused outwards. It knew she was useless. It pushed and kicked against her like a trapped stoat, panicked now and desperate. The old woman with the trolley was leaning closer, using her solid walking stick to brace her weight.

'Can you get up?' she asked.

The thing swivelled, managed to get its head and shoulders out of the confines of the shawl. The old woman blinked, then wrinkled her nose.

Take me take me take me HELP ME!

The wordless command blared out. Kate Park recognized it. Her whole body was making the twitching motions Jack had made as he death-danced to the floor, but even then, in her extremity, she tried to move to crush the life out of it. Much of her weight had wasted away, but there was enough there, surely, to suffocate the monster. She rolled and just then the old woman bent and lifted it, grunting with the effort.

'Oh, who's a lovely baby then?' she crooned, sing-song.

'No,' Kate tried to say but all that came out was a bubble of red. She fell forward and hit the pavement with a solid thud. Her shoulder splintered where the weakened bone took the impact but she still tried to grab the thing from the woman. Already it had fixed its eyes on her. The trolley rolled away on its own and tumbled off the kerb on to the road. A half-dozen rolls spilled out and wheeled around in decreasing circles under the span of the old railway bridge.

'Give me,' Kate grunted, but the words were all bloodied and incoherent. She snatched at the old woman's coat, ignoring the white rivets of pain caused by every motion. Her numb fingers grabbed the fabric and she hauled hard. The little lady was jerked forward, almost off balance. She turned to look down at the crawling, desperate woman on the ground.

The baby held her tight. Its glands pulsed, sending a hiss of chemicals in a visible cloud around them both. An immediate rush of emotion swept through the old woman. Her vision swam for an instant, defying her wire-framed glasses, then it cleared. She looked down and saw some dreadful woman trying to steal her baby. In that hellish moment, she felt her ancient breasts swell and another sensation ripple between her angular, shapeless hips. Sensations she had not experienced for near on fifty years flooded her and she had to protect her baby. The woman on the ground was trying to take it from her. She wanted to kill it.

The old woman dragged herself back with a thin cry. Without hesitation, she raised her walking stick and brought it down with all her weight, her strength now augmented by the baby's powerful demand. The end of the stick came down in an arc and caught Kate Park on the side of the face and her head whipped back in a violent jerk. Without hesitation the club was back in the air and coming down again. It cracked against her jaw and something in there broke like a twig.

'You can't have it,' the old woman squawked. Her stick hit again, right on the bridge of Kate's nose, and this time it was enough to slam her to the ground. The world spun in wavering ellipses and then blacked out. The pain drained away.

The old woman did not pause. She turned and tottered away, off the pavement and past the overturned trolley. Her foot crushed one of the morning rolls under the bridge, but she saw nothing. Her whole being was overwhelmed by the need to get away, to find a place to look after the baby. The bundle in her arms, a heavy, dragging weight, clung tight to her coat and she smothered it in her thin arms.

Move move move move. She heard the commands as her own thoughts and she scurried under the bridge, turned at the corner beyond it, hastening in small, old-lady steps. Behind her, dogs were snarling and men were shouting and she had to get away.

The thing shuddered with a savage, mindless glee. He would escape. He would find shelter and find another mother. He knew this one was empty, despite the twitches deep inside as her body tried to respond, as the old machinery tried to re-awaken. It was dry and barren. There was no feeding here.

They turned the corner and the sounds of pursuit faded away. Here the road was narrow, flanked on one side by the blank wall of the railway where boys came to practise climbing in the summer. The line then turned to allow space for a terrace of sandstone houses. On the other side were a couple of old buildings: the bakery and a newsagent's. They were almost at the far edge of Barloan Harbour. Beyond the cluster of buildings the canal snaked away up from the harbour itself. A strip of grass, covered now in snow and planted with cherry trees in regimented lines, gave on to the bridle path. A mist crept up from the still water where the outlines of the houseboats and converted barges loomed like ghosts.

The old woman scurried along, heading past the shops. In the distance, ahead of her, a bell jangled and a child came scooting down the slope on a bicycle. A couple came out of the newsagent's and started walking towards the bridge.

Up on the embankment, a tragicomedy of confusion was unreeling. One of the policemen was crying real tears as he tried to open the jaws that were clamped and still chewing away at his own dog's neck. He did not care that his own animal's teeth were embedded in the flesh of its attacker. They were partners, he and the dog. He had trained it almost since it was a puppy and it was dying in front of his eyes. He jammed his night-stick in between the teeth and twisted savagely. The other policeman, a close friend, took exception to this and kicked him on the backside so hard his colleague fell over on to the writhing pair of animals. The dogs were howling no longer. They grunted weakly, unable, it seemed, to open their jaws and let go, locked in a deadly embrace. All around them, stunned crows were flapping in little circles, banging into trees and men alike, now cawing raucously in confusion and fright. Another policeman grabbed the first and dragged him back, while a fourth was holding on to the trunk of a tree and bawling for help. 'I'm blind, for pity's sake. I can't fuckin' *see*!'

David and Helen were over at the fence on the wall. David was trying to climb the spiked spars which had been designed to prevent just such an occurrence. Down below, through the close-set spars, he could see some movement, but it was hidden by the ridge of the wall.

'She must have got through,' Helen said shrewdly. She scampered along the side of the fence, trailing her hands on the spars. One of them swung at her touch. 'Over here,' she said. David gave up on his fifth attempt to clamber the fence and came quickly towards her. She pulled the metal back, leaving just enough of a gap for him to squeeze through. Ignoring the men and the dogs behind them, they got on to the wall and looked down.

A woman was lying spread-eagled on the ground, her pale face staring straight up to the sky. A couple of snowflakes landed on her forehead. David assumed she was dead. Down under the arch of a bridge, an old woman was walking, head down. David ignored her.

'Where is it?' Helen said. 'I can't see it.' Both of them peered down. There was no sign of the baby.

'It can't have got away, can it?' Without hesitation he turned and began to lower himself down. There was little purchase for his feet on the damp surface and he slipped downwards, only catching himself at the last moment. Green smears of moss painted the elbows of his coat. Helen turned and started to lower herself on to her belly at first and then down the wall. For a moment the pair of them hung like mountaineers and then both dropped together, fortunately landing lightly. David turned, slipped on the snow and went down on one knee which hit the ground with a sickening thud.

He limped across to the prostrate woman. Her eyes were still open and a trickle of blood was dribbling out of her left ear. Her face was twisted out of shape, and there was a jarring grotesqueness about her posture. She looked as if she had crumpled in on herself. David got a flashing image of vampires after sunrise, then dismissed it. This was an injured woman. Even at a first glance, he could see that she was dreadfully hurt.

Helen scrambled across and knelt beside the woman, ignoring the damp snow under her knees. She took a hold of the woman's face, holding it as gently as she could. Kate Park blinked once, twice, and she took a deep, shuddering breath as she swam up to consciousness. Her eyes rolled, focused and met Helen's. 'Saw you,' she said, and though the damage to her jaw and the bloody wound on her tongue fuzzed the words, Helen understood. 'Couldn't let it take you.'

'I know,' Helen said. 'We'll get help. Just lie still.'

'Find it,' said Kate Park. 'It's got away.' The pain was razoring and twisting through her and not one part of her body was free of it. She had welcomed the dark, welcomed the cessation of hurt, but she forced herself to keep her eyes open. She had to do it because the thing had taken everything from her and she had to destroy it. The pain was a price she was willing to pay.

'Where did it go?'

'Old woman,' she said, gasping for a breath that seemed to take for ever to come. 'She hit me. It got her.'

'Jesus,' David said. He hadn't been thinking. He had seen the old woman turn the corner just beyond the bridge. It hadn't even struck him as incongruous that the woman just walked by after another woman had come flying over the wall and landed on the concrete. He turned to look up the embankment. The dogs were still wheezing but the crows were beginning to get their flight capability back, lumbering unsteadily into the air. One policeman was coming through the gap in the fence. 'Get on to Mr Millar,' David told him. 'Tell him where we are. Get an ambulance here pronto.' The man nodded. David turned back. 'You look after her,' he told Helen.

On the ground Kate Park moaned. She shook her head and a stream of blood blurted from between her lips. 'No,' she said, guttural and almost incoherent, but powerful enough to make sure they understood. 'Find it. Find it and kill it.' She lowered her dreadfully injured head to the ground and the red blood trickled down on to the white snow in a searing contrast. Her body shivered as if in a death spasm, but her eyes were still gleaming bright.

'Go,' she told them.

CHAPTER TWENTY-EIGHT

Old Mrs Williams saw the bike approach in the distance, just a blur in the morning mist. She tottered along the road, moving as quickly as she could, faster than she had moved in years. The urgency drove her on. Her heart was speeding up, clamouring now in twists of effort, each beat loud in her ears with the sound of the sea on a stormy shore.

All she knew was the compulsion to protect the baby. Her stick dropped from her gnarled hands and she got both arms around the burden, hugged it tight, and bent her head forward. A burning sensation ignited under her breastbone. Her breath plumed out, fast, irregular pants and gasps. She hurried on, ignoring the creak of ancient muscles and the painful twist in old tendons that had not been used for so long. All of her was hot and then cold, ripples of alternating temperature bands flowing down from head to foot. A sweat broke out and dripped from her pores, and in her ears she could hear the distressed triple thud of her pulse.

After another five paces she gasped for breath, hauling for air, now almost doubled over. She took another two paces, reached a hand to steady herself against the wall. Her whole body was trembling with the enormous effort. The sky darkened, lightened, darkened again. For an instant her vision failed her, then slowly came back. The only sound she could hear was the wet and gurgling pulse in her head.

She tried to walk on, to get to shelter, to see the baby safe.

Inside her chest something broke with a terrible snap. Instantly she spun to the left, against the wall, thrown by the force of it. Her heart kicked once, very hard, a hammer-blow against her ribs, and then vibrated like a tuning fork. Pain twisted through her and a blinding light burst all around her, fading away to tiny sparkles of luminescence that jittered in front of her head. All sensation faded and the old woman toppled to the ground, her heart burst from the enormous effort of running with the child.

*

Utter desperation flared inside him. It had happened too fast for his primitive reasoning to cope with and now he was in acute danger. The mother had betrayed him for a second time. As they had tumbled from the wall, he had tried to get back into her head, to make her stop, but she had spun in the air, and they had landed with a colossal thump which for an instant had shocked his senses numb.

Move move move! This command had blared; they were coming for him. But the mother would not move. He dug at her, felt the broken places and the hideous pain and he knew that she could not, no matter how much he pushed. He reached further, touched the other one, far overhead. The heat of want hit him, even then, but he had no time. She was too far away and there were others with her, others who would kill him. He sensed the hate of the dogs and the little sparking pulses of anger and fright from the crows and he knew that if the pursuers saw him they would hate him even more and they would destroy him.

Frantic with fear, he turned, squirming in the confines of the shawl. And he touched another mind. Instinctively, and without hesitation, he had hooked it. He felt the connection, locked, and a huge relief washed through him. A new one was coming, she would take him away. He sensed her barren emptiness, but that was no concern. Flight was the only thing he needed. He would find the protection later, somewhere to feed. She was reaching for him and the mother had spasmed, and tried to crush him ... and then he was free, swooped up from the mother's grasp into the air. He had pushed hard and the old one had reacted to protect him from harm. He felt the violence of her blows, acts beyond her strength, which started to drain her immediately. The mother fell back to the ground and he pushed again, knowing he had to be away from here.

The new mother held him in weak arms and he sensed the ruination of her body and he knew he had to find another, find one fast. This one could not last long.

And then, to his utter dismay, she started to falter. Something inside her broke.

He screeched aloud, a thin, whistling, metallic sound that

was lost in the mist coming off the canal. In desperation he dug his mind into her, reaching for something to command, but when he touched the damaged part he knew she was finished. The blood was pooling in her abdomen, pouring out from her ruptured heart, even as she began to slump.

His mind bawled in desperation while behind him, he knew the killers were coming.

Little Kirsty Cameron came down the road on her brother's bike which was too big for her, and if he knew she'd taken it out in the snow, she'd be in trouble, but he had been in bed with a cold since Christmas Eve and that's why she was out on this winter's morning, heading down to the baker's shop for bread while her mother attended to Kirsty's younger sisters. The girl had been one of the youngsters haring down the hill on the day Ginny Marsden had ponderously ascended the road up to old Mrs Cosgrove's house. On that day, something had snagged her attention and she had turned her head, almost falling off the bike in the process. On this day, at ten years old, she was just big enough to reach the pedals as the bike trundled down the gentle slope, crunching the snow beneath its treads. She reached the flat, brown pigtails swinging, eyes down, trying to avoid the piles of slush, tongue sticking out of the corner of her mouth in a grimace of concentration. Ahead of her, through the thin veil of falling snow, she saw someone walking quickly, huddled close to the wall. She braked, slowed, careful lest she hit a pedestrian. It was only when she got to within twenty-five yards that she recognized old Mrs Williams.

Immediately she slowed further. The old lady didn't have her trolley or her stick. She was carrying something in her arms and walking in jerky, speedy steps. Kirsty stopped. She was a bright girl. Old Mrs Williams was never without her trolley and her stick, and she always walked at a snail's pace, each step a strain on her ancient heart. Just as Kirsty stopped, the old woman's head arched upwards to face the sky. She uttered a groan and spun sideways. Without hesitation the girl laid the bike on the ground and ran to help.

The old lady hit against the wall. A terrible, little moan came blurting out of her slack mouth and she crashed backwards like a falling log. Her head hit the concrete with a sickening crack. She did not even twitch.

'Are you all right?' Kirsty asked, suddenly scared. She did not know what to think, or what to do, and she was frightened in case the old woman was dead. She did not want to look into a dead person's eyes.

She got to within three paces of the body and stopped. The old woman was lying with her head to the side. Her scarf had pulled back from her freckled head where the scalp showed through the scant hair. A few snowflakes landed on her face, as they had landed on Kate Park's, and quickly melted. The woman's mouth was slackly open and her top row of false teeth had slipped out, giving her a graceless, somehow imbecilic appearance.

On her chest, something moved.

Mother me . . .

A voice whispered inside her head, not quite in words, but in a context she understood. 'What?' the girl asked. She leaned forward, nerves making her hands shake. She thought she should call an ambulance, or at least get across to the baker's shop and tell someone. Mrs Williams stared at the sky through one open eye. The other was closed in a ghastly, humourless wink. Kirsty knew she was dead, but didn't want to believe it. 'Are you all right?' she asked again.

Mother me! Mother me!

The pulse came stronger. The bundle was moving and for an instant Kirsty thought it was a small dog wrapped up. Maybe Mrs Williams's great-grandson was staying for the holidays and had brought his pet spaniel. She bent down, suddenly curious, drawn to the thing. She pulled back the coverlet.

A face stretched out from the cloth and she jerked back in terror. Lizard eyes blinked, then closed. Her heart thrummed in shock. Her mouth opened, then the thing reached and took her. Her vision crackled and everything wavered. Just as abruptly, the world came back into focus again and she saw the baby.

No, no, no, she told herself. It's not a baby – it's *something else . . .*

Despite her denial and the swelling fear, the girl lifted the thing, grunting with the effort of hoisting its weight. It poked into her head and Kirsty tried to scream but found her mouth would not work. It was a baby and it was a freak, both at the same time. It held her in mental manacles, stabbing and digging, trying to insinuate itself, but she fought against it, her mind swinging between sudden need and dreadful loathing.

No No No . . .

Its glands exploded weakly, denuded of their potency by the effort of taking the old one. The scent surrounded them but the wind blew it away. Little Kirsty squawked. Twin pains flared under the skin on the front of her chest and a different, more agonizing tearing sensation hooked in her belly. She swung away, still holding the thing, part of her trying to clutch it tight, the other attempting to throw it away. It pulsed again, giving its last.

Little breasts budded and started to swell on her narrow, child-like ribs. Flesh gathered, immature glands suddenly dilated, sent hormones flooding her system. Pain twisted on her skin as it ballooned, forced out by the preposterous growth. Down between her skinny hips, her ovaries began to enlarge, draining oestrogen and progesterone into a system that was not yet ready for them. Instant puberty came crashing in on the little girl. A dreadful flush of heat sizzled inside her. She cried out in real pain and real fright.

Somebody called from down the street. The little girl staggered and crashed against the railway wall. On her chest the thing glared at her and tried to make her move. Kirsty stumbled forwards, unable to cope with the sudden flood of chemicals in her veins. Her heart was fluttering like a bird's. The thing was prodding at her head, but she was too young for it. She was not yet a woman and, for that reason alone, it could not completely dominate her.

The girl staggered on, trying to free her mind from it, while inside her the catastrophic physical reactions were beginning to tear her apart. Without warning she was very violently sick.

David and Helen came hammering round the corner under the bridge. Behind them, on the main road that went through the centre of Barloan Harbour, they could hear the wail of sirens.

Over by the wall, hardly more than a hundred yards away, a woman was lying flat out. They reached her in seconds.

'What the hell . . .?' David started to ask. The old woman was clearly dead. Her hands were both arched up from the body, fingers hooked at the air. Helen remembered the dead cat in Celia Barker's house before it had got up and danced.

'Where is it?' she blurted, getting to her feet. At that moment, the old woman did not matter. She was out of this and there was nothing they could do for her.

'There!' David bawled. He was already moving across the road to the patch of grass along the side of the canal. Just beyond them loomed the vast arch of the road bridge. On the grass, moving in a crouching run, a little girl was ploughing through the snow. Just beyond the old woman's body, a boy's bike lay on its side on the pavement, its back wheel still spinning slowly.

'Jesus,' Helen spat. 'It's got her. She's only a kid.'

The small frame was making heavy going, clutching a bulky white cloth which fluttered with the motion. David was halfway across the road, feet splashing in the slush. Helen started to follow just as two patrol cars came roaring round the corner. The leading driver only saw a shape on the road, but stamped on the brakes. He missed Helen by inches. Her heart leapt into her throat as the wind of the car whooshed past her. The car spun round, pirouetting on the slick surface. Its offside tyres hit the pavement beside the woman's body and burst simultaneously with thunderous cracks. The car mounted the kerb, completely flattened the bike and crumped itself against the wall. The second car fared better. It managed to stop three inches from the first. Its driver got out, hands shaking. By this time Helen and David were running along the edge of the canal. The three police officers, two of them women, followed on after checking the fourth, who was lucky to have got off with a bruised nose and a staved little finger. He had however, pissed his pants and he did not want to walk anywhere. Two of the other men who had been with them as they trailed Kate Park through the trees came running out from under the railway bridge.

The little girl was screaming in a high-pitched, pitiful way, but still she continued to stumble along on the grass. Every time she tried to throw the thing away from her an intense pain knifed into her head. Her little nipples were points of fire and she could not comprehend what was happening to her. Even if she had been older, she might not have understood either, but little Kirsty was sure it would kill her the way it had killed old Mrs Williams. She ran on, unable even to slow down, heading through the thick mist on the canalside.

David reached her first and tried to get a hand to her collar. She swerved and he almost fell headlong. Helen had kept up with him, an enormous black apprehension beginning to build up in her: the anticipation of catching the thing and a fear of getting close to it. With her newfound sense she had felt the pulse of its mind when it had reached out after Kate Park had jumped and again as it grabbed the old woman. There had been a third flare, hot like the updraught from a brush fire, and she knew that was when it took the girl. Each time she had sensed it had sparked the loathing and the other want deep within her.

Behind her footsteps clattered on the road then became muffled thumps as the rest of the pursuit reached the snowy grass. David reached; missed. The girl dived through an ornate clump of azaleas like a small animal. David's passage was thwarted. He and Helen went to the left. The others went round the side closest to the canal.

The girl shrieked and every one of the pursuers heard the appalling fear in her cry. A policewoman held her hand up to stop the child.

Everything happened at once. The child spun and tumbled as the policewoman grabbed for her, and the officer's momentum carried her forward flat on her face. One of the uniformed men came barging through the bushes, cursing hoarsely. Kirsty Cameron got to her feet, moving fast despite her burden. Helen got a glimpse of greyish-pink, just the curve of a head under the cover of the shawl. A slither of thought touched her and she rocked back under the force of it.

'Don't get close,' David yelled, suddenly aware of the reach of the thing. He had felt the sear of energy radiate outwards and had not known what it was. But this close he could feel the mind-burn like a singe on the edge of his consciousness and the power of it both amazed and appalled him. In that instant he realized how this thing snared the mothers. The policewoman either ignored him or did not hear his warning. She reached again and the girl ran on to the ice on the surface of the canal. David grabbed at her, almost caught her, and then they both plunged through the thin covering and down into the freezing water. The thing in her arms tumbled away on to the ice. It spun on the surface. A small, thin arm reached out and something screeched with the sound of cracking glass.

The girl went right under. Her scream was cut off instantly. David was right behind her and the shards of ice slashed at him as he went through. Instant cold froze him to the marrow. He gulped, took in a throatful of slimy water, coughed. The water was black down there. His feet were down in the mud and he couldn't free them. Panic flared at the thought of being trapped under the ice. He'd never get out. That thought galvanized him: he spun quickly and his feet came free. In front of him a pale shape floated. He reached for it, inadvertently sticking his little finger up the girl's nose. She bucked, he caught her, and lifted her above him. Her head broke the surface and she hauled in a desperate gasp of air.

Helen saw the thing spin away on the ice, travelling five yards to settle close to the bank where a stand of reeds stood up from the surface. Without a thought she went after it. It screeched glassily and a note of singing pain lanced between her temples. She leapt off the bank and crashed through the reeds, up to her thighs in mud and decaying stalks. She got a hand to the shawl and dragged it towards her, pulling herself back as she did so. She lifted the bundle, feeling its weight, the powerful squirming of the thing inside. She turned it round in her hands.

A red eye opened and speared her.

'Oh my God,' she managed to blurt.

And then it took her. A force reached right inside her and she was lost. Her mouth opened, stayed that way. Suddenly strong, *move move move* it demanded. A pulse of pure energy flooded her mind and she recognized the alien scrape of mindless hunger, yet she was powerless to fight it. The sky went black. The thing closed its eye and locked itself into her. Helen stumbled back under the force of its command. One of the men reached for her and she batted his hand away, pushing herself out from the bank into deeper water. It came up to her waist.

'What the hell . . .' the man snorted, but Helen did not hear him. Behind the man, a policewoman burst into sudden, braying hysterics as she picked up some of the pulses blasted out from its panicked mind. In the water, Helen reached for a floating branch and held it up.

David got the girl to the bank and shoved her up on to the firm ground. He hauled himself out, gulping for air, gasping with effort. The other policeman knelt down beside the girl who was spluttering hysterically. David staggered breathlessly to his feet, heard a commotion in the water and saw Helen wade out backwards. In her arms a grey thing was squirming away from the light.

'What in the name of fuck is that?' the policeman shouted. David could hear the bewildered loathing in his voice. The shape of the thing rippled and wavered, its lines undefined. It could have been anything.

But there was a mad look in Helen's eyes. His heart flipped over and a sudden despair shook him. She brandished the thick piece of wood, warding the others off. Her eyes were wide and flashing and her teeth were clenched and she looked like an animal, like a ferocious panther protecting her cubs. In that awful instant, he knew it had her. Whatever it did, however it achieved it, it had reached out and taken her.

What kind of baby steals a mother?

Now he knew. This ugly, wavering thing had stolen a new mother.

He did not hesitate for a second. That sudden desperation drive him on. He ran along the bank, past the floundering policeman, and leapt right in again, pushing through the thin layer of ice beside the reed-bed. She saw him coming and swung the heavy branch in a vicious swipe, catching him hard on the ribs. Pain exploded as something inside cracked, but not as much as it would have done had his whole body not been already numbed by the freezing canal water. His momentum carried him onwards. He landed with a terrific crack and a huge splash. His full weight hit Helen and drove her under.

She had seen him coming and only saw threat. The other man was pulling away out of range of her stick when she had seen the shadow in the corner of her eye and she had snarled, knowing this was an attack.

He had leapt and she had struck him and then his weight had cannoned into her and she had screamed. Water went down her throat and an appalling anger erupted inside her. She reached for him, trying to scratch at his face and his eyes, to protect her burden.

The water blinded her. She held the baby tight against herself and clawed at the attacker's face, hissing like a cat.

David reared back and slapped her so hard her head whipped sideways. With his other hand he grabbed at the thing she clutched. It was screaming, a strange, high and alien quiver of sound, as if the very air was being torn apart. Helen's nails ripped on his eyelid and raked down his cheek. Blood poured into his eye, blinding him on one side.

The thing shrilled again, a mental blast of energy that felt like nails on glass, yet sounded as if it was scraping right in the very centre of his brain.

Anger exploded. Bright-hot feral rage erupted inside him, completely uncontrollable. The thing's mind-blast had touched that male part of him and catapulted him into absolute savage frenzy. All he wanted to do was destroy this thing. The automatic response to the parasite was to kill it, break it and tear it and rend it. He reached to drag it from her.

Helen screamed too, the sound of a pig in a slaughterhouse. She lunged at him, all her teeth showing. David tried to hit the shape in her arms. She pulled back and he went flying into the water. Some of it went down his throat and he came up spluttering.

One of the policemen ventured a foot into the reeds, appalled by the sudden and incomprehensible violence. Just then, the screaming policewoman launched herself at him, both hands hooked into claws. 'Holy Mother –' he managed before her weight slammed into him and threw him into a dense thicket of scrub willow. The woman came tumbling after him, trying to rend his eyes out, driven by the thing's foul appeal for protection.

On the bank, Kirsty Cameron's body arched backwards with such violence the ligaments actually creaked like old wood, and every muscle in her body shivered as if a powerful electric shock had surged through her.

In the water, David got to his feet and lunged again for Helen and the thing in her arms. She saw him coming and screamed wordlessly at him, desperately trying to reach the bank and be away. He dived full length, got a hand to her jacket, pulled her back violently. She slipped, fell; he reached and jerked at the thing as hard as he could, and it came tumbling out of her arms.

Helen screamed again and then the dreadful contact of its touch snapped. She went spinning backwards, along the side of the bank, out of the reeds and into deep water. A hand hauled her back up again and she gulped, coughing slimy liquid which ran down from each nostril. The baby sent out its shivery demand again and she tried desperately to respond, but David shoved her away. She was shrieking at the top of her voice, in between coughing splutters. Another hand reached down, strong and steady, and lifted her straight out of the water. David went spinning away out of view with the small thing in his hands.

He was dragged down in the water. The mother was screaming for him as she was pulled away but there was nothing he could do. The man had hit him, almost hard enough to break his neck, and a dreadful realization had burst on him. He had been caught and there was no mother and the one he wanted was gone.

Under the water, his glassy eyes opened and he tried to squirm away. It was no use, he was caught in the fronds of cloth and he could not move. His glands opened wide and they filled with water, drenching him in cold. He pushed at the man's mind but could get no response. He could sense loathing and, beneath it, an awful anger. Beneath that there was a sea of fear that mirrored his own. It was the primitive and mindless fear of the alien.

Down they went down into the dark of the mud. He pushed and squirmed, but the weight kept him down.

*

It had tried to take her and it had almost won. David knew that as he pushed down under the ice. The creature in his arms was twisting and turning, all arms and legs and bones, a scrawny yet powerful thing. He could feel its shape through the cloth and knew it had no right to exist. It was a spidery, reptilian gargoyle of a thing. It was a parasite.

The sizzling anger still suffused him, a mindless lust to kill. It was such a primitive need that it bypassed all his other conditioning. It was simply a basic drive.

The thing pulsed sharp shards of thought at him, searing the back of his eyes, sending corkscrews of hurt into his bones. But he could not help himself, he had to kill it. The pain was somewhere inside him, but the anger flooded the hurt and smothered it.

Take me take me take me. The creature's command blasted out. He felt the glassy blades of mental energy stabbing inside his skull, like some dreadful infection. He shuddered, drawing away from it. It sensed retreat and pulsed harder. The awesome anger surged up inside him; he shook his head, unable to control himself. At that moment he was locked with the creature. Nothing else existed except he and it and the need to destroy it. He forced himself downwards, right under the surface at the far end of the reed-bed where the water swooped to its canal depth. It was freezing cold, but he did not even feel it. For the past eleven days he had followed its trail of feeding, its trail of destruction, and he knew that this was beyond any natural law, or any law of man. This was beyond any nature he had ever heard of. It had almost taken Helen Lamont and that would have been enough for David if any form of rational thought could break through the ramparts of his monumental rage.

He went down to the bottom of the canal and pushed the thing right into the mud, kicking his feet hard to force it further down, shoving with all the strength of his body. He kept it there, under the silt, until it stopped moving.

The mind-scream went on and on, but it was weakening all the time. David stayed, up to his shoulders in mud down in the dark, until the shivering stopped and the mental pulses died away and whatever life was in this thing guttered and failed.

Just before the cold came and took him, a wonderful surge of triumph swept through him at the knowledge that he had beaten this thing. His last sensation was one of dim regret that he would not see Helen again, for in his fading consciousness he realized that, indeed, she was the one for him.

He knew that she had been worth dying for.

CHAPTER TWENTY-NINE

David's dreams were beset by visions. In the deep dark the images came looming up close and he saw again the baby cuckoo hunched within the nest. Behind the translucent lids he could make out the red of the eyeball twisting and turning, trying to see. It struggled with the egg, getting underneath it, bracing its legs against the sides, and the egg cracked open and a thin, warted thing came uncoiling to get its sucker mouth on to the bird. Even in the dream he knew this was wrong and he tried to turn away from it, but the creature held him as it held the fledgling and he saw it was no longer a cuckoo, but a child in a cot and the warted thing was hunched over it, its circular mouth straining to suck at its helpless eyes.

He reeled back in disgust and horror, knowing he had seen this before, and he fell into the water, sinking down and down into the thick mud. Under his feet something stirred and he knew it was a sucker-fish, a lamprey with its great flat mouth and its circle of teeth, and he tried to swim away, but it twisted and changed and he saw it was no fish. The black bulk of a dragonfly larva scuttled up, its hinged jaw snapping at him, armoured with deadly spines. He climbed in desperate fear for his life and it chased after him while above the crows were falling from the trees, cawing madly. He risked a look back and saw it stop.

It arched outwards and the skin of its back split down the middle. Two red eyes came poking through, forcing the torn edges of the skin apart. Out of the shell, metamorphosing in the dying light of day, Helen Lamont clambered, but her eyes were now wide and red and her skin was sagging and her breasts were huge. Dark clotted blood dripped between her legs. 'It got me,' she mouthed at him. 'It gave me the sickness and now it's inside me.'

He reeled back, lost his grip and fell away while she looked down on him and he knew he had failed. A heavy weight of loss and regret came rolling over him and he fell and fell and fell and . . .

He woke.

His hollow cry of panic and despair echoed round the room. Bright lights stabbed his eyes and he flinched from the glare. Pain drilled into his side and thudded in the back of his head and he felt reality slip away from him again.

A cool, soft hand slid over his forehead. 'You've come back to us then?' He risked opening his eyes again and the light was less painful. A pretty nurse was smiling at him in welcome and for a moment he was completely bewildered. He almost asked where he was, then realized he must be in a hospital. He drew in a breath, felt it rasp in his throat and he coughed reflexively. Immediately he regretted that. His throat burned like acid.

'Drink,' he managed to rasp.

'Yes, you'll be a bit sore for the while,' she said in a lilting Dublin accent. She sounded like an angel from heaven to David Harper. 'There was a lot of dirt in your lungs and you've had enough antibiotics to stop a horse.'

'How long?' he tried, and it came out a whisper.

'Only a day and a half,' she told him. 'Doctor thinks the cold water saved you. It slows the metabolism, you see.' She took his temperature, gentle with the thermometer. 'You've two broken ribs and a nasty cut on your arm.'

He didn't remember the cut. The nurse checked the thermometer, failed to react and he knew he would live to fight another day. His head was pounding in deep dull thuds in time to the beat of his heart and every breath brought a stab of discomfort. He managed to convey his pain to the nurse and she gave him a tablet. Swallowing was an ordeal, but finally it got past the rawness of his throat. A few minutes later it started to work.

Two hours after that, he woke up again, not realizing he had slept. The nurse brought him a drink, eased him up on the pillow, told him he had visitors and opened the door. He expected Helen Lamont, but, disappointingly, it was his boss, Donal Bulloch, along with Bert Millar from the western division. Their bulk and height cut out a lot of the light, which was a blessing. His head still ached.

The two senior men sat down and looked him over. 'You'll

live then,' the Chief Superintendent half asked. 'Bad time of the year to be swimming.'

'Is she all right?' he asked.

'Which one of the many?' Bulloch asked. 'I suppose you mean DC Lamont. She'll live as well. A bit of hysterics and a bit of a chill, nothing much. She's tough. The farmer's wife, she's still alive, but for how long, nobody knows. Another tough one. She's beat all the odds so far.'

'Did you find it?'

Both men looked at each other, then back at him. 'When you say "it", what are we talking about?' The Chief asked.

'The thing. The baby.'

'We've had two teams of divers down the whole stretch,' Bert Millar said, 'and the place has been dragged. We got four dead dogs and two large pike and an expensive artificial leg that hasn't been explained. Nothing else.' He leaned closer to the bed. 'Did you get a look at this baby?'

David shook his head. 'Just a glimpse. It was no baby. I couldn't say what the hell it was.'

'That's our problem,' Donal Bulloch interjected. 'There's a lot of media interest in this. I've spoken to Phil Cutcheon, after Mr Millar here briefed me on what you told him. Now I have to tell you that I have no interest in any of old Cutcheon's theories, not officially and not personally. We're all policemen here and we all want to stay policemen and enjoy our pensions. Wild speculation does nobody any good. Officially, for the record, we were acting on information on a missing girl and happened to be in the vicinity when a child fell into the canal and was rescued by a passing policeman. All true. We might even find a medal for the gallant lad. As far as the Park killings are concerned, we are looking for a shotgun raider, and we will go on looking for one. As far as you are concerned, you were never at Middle Loan Farm and there was never any baby there.' He leaned over and looked David straight in the eye. 'You'll understand what I'm saying?'

David nodded. He was tired and his head and ribs ached. He caught the drift. Donal Bulloch and Bert Millar had talked it over and they had done a deal. That was fair enough with him. It was dead and that's all that mattered. It was down there, below the mud, and there it would rot. His boss had obviously spoken to everyone concerned and all of their stories would be matching by now. Bulloch did not want to see what was down there. He was a policeman. He upheld the law. He saw no devils except in the hearts of men. He was lucky.

'Suits me,' he said, working up a smile. 'That's exactly how I remember it.'

Bulloch nodded and left the room. Millar stayed for a moment. 'I spoke to Phil Cutcheon. Whatever the hell's going on, you've got balls. You and the girl did a good job. You want to work for me any time, you just ask.' He stood up, put on his straight look which drew his brow down so that his eyes were almost hidden. 'But no more ghosts and ghoulies, OK? That's enough for one career. Remember what your chief says. You know it makes sense.'

It was the following morning when Helen finally came in, bearing a huge basket of fruit. She leaned over and kissed him hard, accidentally pressing down on his cracked rib and then jerking back when he groaned in dismay. The nurse looked in, smiled, went back out again.

'Is it dead?' she asked as soon as they were alone.

'Last thing I felt it was at least a yard under the mud. Must be pretty deep if the divers haven't found it, though I don't know how hard they were told to look. It stopped struggling before I did, and I was down there for a long time.'

'I know that. Everybody stood around and that stupid constable just sat on her backside crying. The poor little girl was in better shape than her.' Helen told him that it had been Jimmy Mulgrew, the young policeman who'd been so sick up at the farm, who had dived into the canal fully clothed and had finally, after two unsuccessful attempts, found David's foot and dragged him up to the surface. 'He got you out and got most of the crap out of your lungs too, so you owe him,' she said. 'And I owe you too. I can't remember anything of what happened after we got to the canal. It's all a blank.'

'You broke my ribs, you silly cow,' he said. She sat back, taken by surprise, but then he laughed, though the laughter cost him plenty. 'But I'll heal.'

Kate Park was alive. She was in intensive care in St Enoch's

394

Hospital where a succession of specialists queued up for the chance to examine her. She was alive, but barely, in the depths of a coma. Her hold on life was so tenuous it hardly existed. It was a miracle that she had any at all. According to the X-rays and the cat-scans, the damage to her system was phenomenal. Apart from the multiple fractures of her hips and chin, the deterioration in her skeletal structure and musculature showed she had lost almost thirty per cent of her bone calcium and all of her body fats. Dr Hardingwell and senior bacteriologists and virologists speculated on a new super-organism that could cause such catastrophic damage. Kate Park's body contained more samples of the large proto-genetic compounds that had been discovered in Heather McDougall and Ginny Marsden. It was studied at length by many eminent men, but no two of them drew the same conclusion. Some said it resembled a kind of virus. Others claimed it was a protein complex that could trigger responses on the cellular level. Most agreed that its components were amino acids, the very basic building blocks of life, but that was where agreement ended. It remained and still remains a mystery.

Teams of people worked round the clock trying to keep Kate Park alive and to rebuild the lost elements of her wizened body. Occasionally she would twitch, as if coming awake, but then she would go still. Nobody knew what monsters scuttled in her dreams. Her husband and her baby girl were buried in the same grave in the family plot in the churchyard at Barloan Harbour; most of the town turned out for the funeral on a cold winter's morning. The priest at St Fillan's prayed for the repose of their immortal souls. For Kate Park's soul, as yet, there was no repose.

Little Kirsty Cameron spent a week in hospital and was then transferred to a psychiatric ward where she underwent intensive therapy for a hysterical fugue state. The girl's little breasts were black with bruises and medical examination showed severe damage to the subcutaneous tissue caused by sudden violent expansion and stretching. Blood tests showed that she had gone into a rare, instant puberty. Her ovaries were fully developed and were now producing vast quantities of adult female hormones. She was also almost catatonic, responding to no stimuli, or hardly any. Only when she heard a baby cry would she react, going into such fits of hysteria that she had to be subdued with thorazine. She would remain in the psychiatric ward for some time.

David Harper got out of hospital in three more days, during which time Helen visited him every day, and, awkwardly for them both, so did June, fussing at his bedsheets and plying him with outspoken concern at his treatment and fruit for his speedy recovery. Eventually both of them accepted her attentions, though she was brusquely and sullenly hostile towards Helen. He drew the line when she turned up on his doorstep, and she stormed off in an angry flood of tears. It was to be a further four weeks before he was allowed back to active duty. Donal Bulloch welcomed him back to the squad, shaking his hand gravely and thanking him for his efforts in tracing the dead woman.

Between them, David and Helen completed the report that an old policeman had started before they were born, but they never showed it to anyone else.

They closed the chapter.

CHAPTER THIRTY

'Did you hear something?' Jasmine Cook raised her head up from the pages on the table. 'I thought I heard a noise.'

'It's probably a coot, or a mallard duck,' Flora Spiers told her. 'Spring is about to be sprung on us, and a young waterfowl's fancy turns to whatever it is waterbirds do at this time of the year.' She was chubby and had thick, short, grey hair and shrewd, jolly eyes. She was beyond the door in the galley, over by the stove, stirring a mixture of Chinese vegetables in an old, blackened wok. In the low, narrow room Jasmine could smell the aroma of garlic and soy sauce and crisping beansprouts.

Jasmine scratched out two words she had written and replaced them with ones she considered more apposite, reached the end of her paragraph and then sat back, pushing her glasses up on top of her head. At the age of fifty, she had well-cut dark hair which was still natural and framed a youthful face. She was slimmer than Flora, and when she smiled, her teeth were perfect and even. She collected the pages, which were scattered over the low table, shuffled them together and put them into her case. 'That's the last chapter but one,' she announced with a satisfied smile, raising herself from the seat to stack the case on a shelf before coming through the narrow passage.

'Well done you,' Flora said. She turned round and kissed Jasmine on the lips. 'It's been a long time.'

'But worth it. The final chapter's a real climax. The perfect end.' She put her arm around Flora's shoulders and hugged her, letting her hips slide close. 'And thanks for the support. If it hadn't been for you, I'd still be floundering.' She leaned to the side and rubbed her head against Flora's, feeling the rustle of greying hair against her own, then hugged her again.

'I think spring is springing,' Flora said. 'The magpies are out in force on the willow. I got a shot of them this morning when the mist was thick. The sun was coming through the branches and everything was fuzzy and monochromed, except for the velvet of their wings and tails. I got another shot of two whooper swans taking off towards us, coming right along the canal. If my exposure was right, it'll make a magnificent illustration.'

'Your exposure is always right,' Jasmine said, almost bawdily. She slid her hand down Flora's back, feeling the warmth come through the blouse. Flora moved back, just a fraction, to press herself against the touch, almost like a satisfied cat.

The noise came again. A small whimper of sound.

'Did you hear that?' Jasmine asked.

'Hear what?' Flora said. Despite the close contact, she was still gently stirring the vegetables on the heat. The oil sizzled.

'I heard a noise.'

'The canal's full of noise, if you listen. There's ducks and moorhens and all the finches in the bushes. If you sit quietly enough you can hear the voles in the reeds.'

'No,' Jasmine stopped her. 'I thought I heard someone crying.'

'That's your imagination. That's what makes you the writer.' Flora gave a little laugh. 'I wish I had that talent. I can only work with what I see.' With her free hand she drew her fingers very gently down Jasmine's cheek. The touch was smooth as silk and for an instant she felt the wonderful surge of desire and a deep swell of love. 'Which reminds me,' she said, forcing her mind down from such springtime heights. 'If it's still calm tomorrow, we'll have another morning mist, and I can take your picture for the book jacket. We can get something really atmospheric, something with impact that people will remember.'

'And a fog to hide the lines,' Jasmine said.

'You don't need that, love. Not ever.'

Jasmine smiled. 'I wish we had more time here,' she said. 'It's so peaceful and private. It's like being in a world of our own, just you and me, and the mist to keep the rest of it at bay. I don't want to go back.'

Flora was about to respond when the thin little cry came again. 'There,' Jasmine said. 'I told you I heard something.' She pulled away slowly, turning to listen. The sound shivered again.

'Is it a rabbit in a snare?' she asked. Flora frowned and listened too.

398

Very weak, very faint, the whimper broke the silence of their held-in breathing. Jasmine felt it resonate inside her head and a strange, sense of loss went through her. 'It sounds like a child,' she said, pulling further away, moving towards the galley doorway. Flora's hand followed the motion, trailing down between her shoulders, almost in an attempt to hold her back. The touch altered the cringing feeling that was somehow squeezing on Jasmine's skin.

'Don't go out,' Flora started to say, but then the cry came stronger. It ended in a small, choking sob. Flora could not help but take a step forward. In her ears there was a ringing sound, very high, almost sizzling, the way it was when her sinus pressure was bad in the winter. The pressure spread along her temples. Jasmine was moving through the narrow hatchway.

The door slid open and a cool swirl of damp evening air came tumbling down into the warmth of the narrowboat. Far off, on the estuary, oystercatchers cried to each other, like lost souls, drowned spirits on the watery mudflats. An owl moaned in the stand of chestnut trees on the north side of the canal.

A child sobbed. It was a wordless cry, but eloquent of need and helplessness. Flora felt her heart kick and then quicken. Jasmine felt a terrible pang of melancholy, and over that, she experienced a fierce twist of inexplicable hunger.

She stepped up on to the deck, feeling the mist catch in the back of her throat. It twirled in pallid tendrils here, not freezing, but still cold in early spring air. It curled around the deckhouse and oozed inside, a questing miasma that seemed to have volition and direction.

Flora shivered. 'Can you see anything?' she asked, still aware of the fuzzy pressure in her temples. Jasmine had stopped, head cocked to the side. There was no wind. Further down the stretch of the canal, on the flat and shimmerless water, the moonlight reflected a perfect sphere that limned the trailing willows. In beside a bank of tumbling ivy, a vole squeaked and then took to the water, sending out concentric circles of jewelelled light which faded out slowly as they reached the far side and merged with the floating weed. This part of the canal was wider, a place where two barges could pass each other with still enough space for a third to be moored. A stand of reeds edged out into the water, tall and greening now after the winter slump. Something rustled in the depths, though there was no wind. It could have been a duck heading for shelter, or a wild mink hunting.

The soft whimper shivered the reeds. Jasmine's head swung round. Flora saw her breath billow a hazy plume. 'Who's there?' Jasmine asked. The moonlight caught her hair and turned its shine to a glint of blue steel.

A small shape came slowly out from the reeds. At first, before it had moved, Flora could have sworn there had been nothing there. She had looked when she'd heard the rustling sound, looked with her trained eyes that could spot an adder sunbathing on autumn leaves or a lacewing on a green stem. The moonlight had reflected from the black water between the new-grown stalks and there had been no shape here.

But now there was a small child.

His face was in shadow, but she got a glimpse, maybe just an impression, of a haunted look, like the melancholy face in the moon. He was thin and pallid, as insubstantial as the mist. He moved, holding a thin, starved arm out to them, a waif in supplication. He took a step forward, yet when he moved there was no sound of his passage through the bed of reeds.

'He's making no sound,' Flora said distractedly. 'Isn't that strange?'

'Oh, Flora, it's a child,' Jasmine said, cutting across her thoughts. 'The poor thing.' She stepped out along the planking to where the edge of the hull rubbed gently alongside the edge of the canal, pressing against the old tyre buffer. Flora followed, suddenly almost supernaturally aware of the night and the blare of the moon. It was as if every sense had been powered up to new levels of perception. She could feel the water-mist scrape against the skin of her neck and cheek. Way down on the estuary, far beyond where the canal emptied out into the tidal basin, she heard the mewling of dunlin and the piping of redshank. Somewhere in the willows, an early cranefly rustled its wings and then fell silent. Flora got to the edge of the barge as Jasmine stepped off and down to the turf that lined the bank. She was turned away, walking quickly towards the stand of water reeds.

The small boy was ankle-deep in water. The moonlight limned the gaunt outlines of his frame, giving him a silver-blue aura which seemed more substantial than the rest of him. His arms were held out towards her, his body bent. He took one silent step, the kind of step a heron might take, putting his foot back into the water so delicately, so deliberately, that there was hardly a ripple.

Help me, please.

Jasmine heard no sound, but whatever she did hear, her own brain translated it into a language she could understand. Every cell of her body responded.

Help me help me help me.

Behind her, Flora too felt the irresistible tug. The child stood with the scart water up above his ankles, naked and slender, with great moonshadow eyes and delicate limbs. His whole posture begged for help. It sang out from him. He whimpered, and in both women the most basic instincts of all switched themselves on and waxed strong.

'Poor little tyke,' Flora heard Jasmine say. *Poor little tyke.* The words had been on her own lips. Jasmine was bending. The little figure reached for her.

In that bare instant, Flora felt a shudder of fear. It rippled through her in an inexplicable rush of dire threat. She opened her mouth, suddenly wanting to urge Jasmine away from the child. The boy's slender arms seemed to lengthen. The moonlight wavered on the skin as if his surface was twisting and melting. The little round head inclined.

Jasmine put one foot in the water, crushing the reed stems and splashing down. On the other bank, maybe a hundred yards from the barge, a duck took off in a whirr and crackle of alarm. Down in the water, unseen by anyone, a whole swarm of tadpoles, so numerous they turned the water black in the light of day, stiffened, convulsed and sank to the bottom to form a sludge of slime. A large pike cruising in the dark of the willow roots suddenly rocketed out from its shelter and went rippling down the waterway two feet below the surface, moving at such panicked speed it sent up a powerful bow-wave and did not stop until it reached the lock a quarter of a mile distant.

Don't touch it, stay away! Flora almost blurted the words but they stayed unsaid in her mouth. The little head turned towards her and dark eyes looked at hers. She tried to look away, tried to step off the barge and on to the bank. The eyes locked into her. Something stroked inside her mind and the alarm deflated as quickly as it had swelled.

'Oh, Flora, he must be frozen stiff,' Jasmine crooned. She lifted the child into her arms, the way a mother will do when her child has fallen. She spun round to take it away from danger, from cold, from the night, smothered the boy in her arms and then turned towards Flora. 'He's shivering,' she said. 'I can feel it going right through me.'

'What's he doing here?' Flora started to ask, but Jasmine cut across her again.

'Quick, get the kettle on. He'll need a warm drink. He's like ice.' Jasmine opened her baggy cardigan, jamming the infant against the swell of her breast and then wrapped the cardigan closed. She could feel the damp cold ooze from him into her. It was as if he were sucking the heat out of her. In a few short steps she was back on deck. Flora had done as she was told and was already stooping to get down into the cabin. Jasmine followed quickly, shivering now with the cold of the contact. The small frame wriggled against her, seeking comfort. Her heart swelled with the sudden need to protect the little boy.

'How did he get here?' Flora was asking. 'Should we call an ambulance?'

The boy whimpered. He looked about three, or maybe four. The dim oil lamp threw more shadows than it cast proper light, but even so he twisted away from its glow.

'It's hurting his eyes,' Jasmine told her. 'Turn it down. We can use the light from the galley.' Again Flora obeyed. 'He just needs to get warm. He's obviously lost.' Jasmine brought her other hand up to clench the shivering little frame against her. There was a little fruity hum inside her head, almost like the sound of a fly trapped in a bottle. It touched here, it stroked there. She felt nothing except the growing need to protect the child.

'What's that smell?' Flora asked.

'What smell?'

Flora sniffed. She closed her eyes and sniffed again, then very slowly, she shook her head. 'I thought I smelled something, but it's gone now.' She raised her own hand and used the back of her wrist to rub away an itch of tenderness just under the skin of her breast, mirroring almost exactly the same motion in Jasmine. She turned and went into the kitchen, put on the kettle, then came back. Jasmine was sitting back on the corner seat, clutching the little fellow tightly. The child was lost in her shadows. In the dim light, Flora could see the contented smile slowly spread on her face.

'Come sit with us,' she told Flora. 'We can heat him up together.'

Flora slowly crossed the narrow room from the galley door and squeezed in at the corner. There was a smell here, the scent of a small child. She recognized it now. As the little boy warmed up, she could smell warm milk and washed skin. It reminded her of her own sunny childhood when her mother would soap her in the bath. She drifted off in the wave of reminiscences, overtaken by a sense of gathering fulfilment.

Some time later, when the moon was high, they went to bed, not daring to allow much distance between them, or between themselves and the child. They had discussed nothing at all since they had come back on board with the poor little tyke. In the narrow bed on the narrowboat they huddled close for the warmth that they needed, pressing their naked skin together, while between them, smothered and protected in hot mounds of flesh, the boy was safe from all harm.

In the night, they dreamed hot visions of touching and probing and slick wet contact.

Helen Lamont woke up in the night, gasping for breath. Her eyes were wide and staring into the dark of the room and a cold sweat sheened her skin. *Oh God*. Her chest heaved and the back of her throat was dry and the intense feeling of overwhelming catastrophe rocked her whole body.

She had been dreaming and then the dream had broken and she had snapped instantly awake, all her nerves taut and bristling. A shaft of moonlight speared between the curtains, making her damp skin gleam blue. The fear rippled within her, a nameless thing, a shadowed, stalking beast in the night. In the depths of her sleep, something had reached outwards with a foul touch of rot. The wary sentry inside her own mind, the fey ability to sense danger, had felt its approach and had slammed her from sleep.

Sudden, unbidden tears glistened and spilled, making her vision waver. She reached in the dark for comfort and safety and protection. Somewhere inside herself she realized that there was none to be had.

He had come to awareness slowly. It was almost as if he had never existed before the moment in time when sensation came back to him. For a moment all his receptors went into sensory overload. He awoke with a start, though in fact this wakening had been a long time coming, a slow rise from a great depth that had taken for ever, but when it had come, it arrived with such a violence that he was wrenched out of his dead slumber.

Panic blazed and his first instinct was to scrabble back to the dark and stay there until all danger had passed.

Yet he could not deny this now. He was different. From what, he did not know, but the change was complete and absolute. He stilled, feeling the depth of the cold inside him, yet knowing it was warmer than before. Down here in the soft cold, small things wriggled against his outer skin, tiny things clambered on many legs. He reached out with that part of himself that mind-snuffled, touched one, tasted, spat. It died. He needed richer fare than this.

His limbs twitched and a grind of pain burned in them. They had not moved in a while, and they too were different now.

He stilled again, gathering strength, exhausted with the effort of thought and emotion. He crouched there in the cold, gasping like a half-born hatchling.

This was just another beginning. He could sense it. In the silence of his rest he gathered himself. Down his back there was pain, a pressure pain, and all of his bones ached, but it was a good pain, the hurt of growth. He felt as if much of him was new again, but there were still parts from before. He tried again, twisted his thoughts in one direction, cast back.

Inside his mind, a scene flicked. *The dogs were after him, slaver-*

ing in fear, howling in anger. He felt the powerful flip of the throw and saw them attack each other while blood spattered the dead leaves.

Another flick. *She was coming for him through the fading light of the day, turning towards him, and he had felt the urgent need for her. The other one hit hard and pushed her away and the anger had blurted so hot it was like a light stabbing in his eyes.*

Flick. *They had been behind him. He could sense the pursuit in the skin of his back, in the bones of his spine. He had almost had her. Then there had been pain, bright and burning and then cold.*

He had gone down in the cold, into the dark depths where the light was out of his eyes. Hands were on him, ripping and squeezing. He had tried to push his mind into the man's thoughts, but he could not force his way through. Something inside him had broken but that did not matter now because the desperate chase and the danger had brought on the next metamorphosis. It had come on him so suddenly that he had not even recognized it. All he sensed was the enfolding cold and the collapsing darkness and he was down there in the clammy black. Feeling began to ebb away from him. After a while, the weight eased and he knew the man was pulling up and away. Here in the wet dark he burrowed deeper, down where the water pressure was heavy and the mud was thick. He kept moving, ever slower, twisting and squirming until he reached a crevice. He got inside and waited while the sediment settled around him and all went quiet.

The dark grew through him. Up there, far away in the day, the sparks of other minds began to fade. *She* was still there, he could sense, but all was muffled and after a while, they all went away. Some time later, there was more noise, the close proximity of another mind, but it was as if seen through thick insulating layers. His mind was freezing down, his skin was thickening against the cold and the change was on him. This time it was an immense change. He crouched under the ledge of stone, swaddled in the winter-mud where other small lives had burrowed away from the bite of winter. His skin hardened and the cold too faded away as if it did not exist. His breathing had stopped, but now his skin took in what it needed, even as it hardened like insect chitin. After a while, even this stopped. Around him, the larvae of the smaller predators curled asleep in their pupal cases, waiting for the warmth that would transform them. Unconsciously, he mimicked them. His thoughts slowed, flickered, slowed further and then died, all except the singularity that was his continuing self.

He was, on almost every level, unaware of the profound changes going on within the shell of thickened skin. Yet very deep inside his own existence, he accepted the power of it and waited. The dark time went on for ever and ever, seemingly without end.

And then he had awoken.

Awareness slammed him out of the miasma with sudden violence and he was himself again, and yet he was *different* now. He explored his newness, the different configuration, and he knew, in his wordless, instinctual way, that he had attained a new level of being.

The hunger came.

And it was a different hunger. It yawned deep inside him, a searing wild emptiness that needed to be filled. As soon as the hunger gnawed in his belly, his higher awareness told him he was still changing. He needed to feed to become what he would yet be.

He flexed and felt something rip down between his thin shoulders. His limbs were still crossed over each other, still, as far as he could perceive, flexible and unhardened. He flexed again, bunching unused muscle, gathering strength and the harsh rending came more strongly. Something gave, the sound of a membrane bursting, like living hide ripping. This skin was different, for it had protected him from the cold. He pushed, felt the scrape of the casing on his back, pulsed again, and felt more give. This went on, pulse and give, then rest. Pulse and give, then rest. Cold water was oozing in between the shell and his own flesh and that eased the passage. His new skin shrank from it, allowing water pressure to help his own effort. He pushed hard and the shell split up the back of his head with a ricketing vibration that felt as if he was being wrenched in two.

And suddenly he was free again. His limbs found their way out to the open. He arched again, turned in a slow, muddied somersault (and if David Harper had seen it, he would have recognized the dark, demonic similarity to the dragonfly larva arching out of its chrysalis) and drew himself right out. It was still dark here, still cold, but he was less vulnerable than before. He crouched tight, ignoring the press of thick mud, until he had his strength back and then started to move. The tide was within him and he knew the time was right. His senses picked up the darkness above and the light of the moon. It drew him towards it. Very slowly, very purposefully, he burrowed upwards from the deep ledge. After a while he came to a dense place where old roots and dead reeds matted the bed of the canal and he had to claw his way through them. Here it was still dark because his movements had sent up clouds of sediment, but he crawled on, feeling the tug of the other gravity, got past the muddied water and out into the clear.

Above him, high up there, the thin circlet of silver light danced in a watery sky. He slowed again, waited unbreathing, then very deliberately clambered up the slanted bank until his head broke the surface. Water expelled from his blunt nostrils and he snuffled air for the first time in a long while, like a scenting animal.

It was night, but it was no longer cold. He got into the shelter of the reeds. He cast out a thought, now with almost casual ease. That power had increased in the long sleep; he could sense its strength. Some distance away, he touched the warmth of another creature and he slowly made his way towards it. Behind him, the lights of the bridge dazzled him and he kept his eyes averted. Some distance away, where a road paralleled the canal for a span, lights flashed past, making his eyes sear with hurt. After a while, he was past a higher bank that cut off the glare and then the canal took a turn that hid the bridge from him. He was in a shaded part where willows overhung the deep water. Ahead of him, closer now, were the warmths he needed and he quickly and silently eased his way forward.

He emerged, silent as death, from the patch of reeds, and trailed out a cold quest of sense. He touched the one and then the other and pulled them towards him. A hunger like a yawning chasm opened up inside him.

Jasmine Cook woke up in the night and shivered. The boy was

staring into her eyes and her heart did a little heavy flip. She reached to pull him close. His skin was damp and he made the little whimpering sound that touched the deeps inside her and made her want to hug him against any threat of danger. She rocked him, humming wordlessly in the dark. The boy flattened himself against her to gain her heat.

'Poor little thing,' Jasmine crooned. 'But you're all right now. All right now, little tyke. You've got someone to look after you now.'

In the dark, Flora snorted and Jasmine smelled a warm scent on the air, a cloying thick odour that was at once familiar and strange. When she had awoken, the boy had been on the other side of the bed, close to Flora. There was no envy at all in Jasmine. They were together, friends and lovers. They had talked many a time of having a child, though time had passed them by and the imperative that had swamped both of them, each at different times, different ages, had faded. Now it was back. They had a child to protect and nurture.

It just fitted, a gift from God.

'Little Moses,' she said, smiling contentedly in the silvery dark. 'Out of the water, in a basket of reeds. You'll be our little prince, and you won't ever have to be cold again.'

She held the child while the thick smell wafted round. Flora snorted again, but Jasmine was already falling into a deep slumber. Once again she dreamed, but this time she dreamed that she was pinned down by a weight that prevented her from moving. Her legs were spread out and the weight on her was bucking very slowly. She felt cold penetration and a burst of pain. Inside her, something ripped and she tried to scream, tried to wake, but she was trapped in the dark and the dream went on and on through the night.

In the morning, she came out of the troubled slumber. Still pressing the child against her, protecting it, unaware that she even made the motherly motion. Beside her, Flora was lying on her back. Both of her eyes were open and her mouth gaped in a black yawn. Her hair was rumpled and sticking up in little corkscrews.

Under Flora's mouth, another black hole gaped. A dark trickle, thick as a mooring rope, dripped down from her bottom lip, while under her chin, an even darker, shiny hand's width covered the skin. It had soaked into the bedclothes.

Jasmine pulled back. A hand clutched her heart and squeezed it to sudden stillness. The dim shadows of the room spun and blurred. The hand let go and her heart bucked once, twice. A pulse throbbed in her temple and a scream started to expand somewhere in the pit of her belly. 'Flo –' she started to say, but the word got caught in the desert at the back of her throat and ground to a halt.

Under the blanket, the small boy stirred. Jasmine tried to reach for him, to turn him away from this. Her mind was still making the colossal effort to take in the horror on the bed beside her. Flora had grunted in the night. She had made the little gurgling sound and the blood smell had rolled up from the bed. 'Oh,' Jasmine moaned. 'Oh no . . . ' That was as much as she could manage. The wet of Flora's blood was on her. She had been lying in it and the brown-red clots were smeared on her own skin. A dreadful juggernaut fear was winding up.

She pushed the boy, getting her own body between him and the gaping thing on the bed that had been the woman she had loved and was now a dripping, ripped abomination. Her motion made Flora's mouth jiggle wider. A slew of viscid dark dribbled. Flora's eyes did not waver. They were fixed on the ceiling. A thin, translucent sheen, like peeling skin, or perhaps like the cocooning web of some monstrous grub, covered the naked surface of Flora's skin. Under it, Jasmine could see the flaccid, collapsed breasts. Her body was caved in as if she had been drained by some unearthly suction.

Under the sheet, the boy turned, using her body to clamber upwards. She tried to hold him down, overpowered by the need to protect him from the dreadful danger that had befallen Flora. She drew her eyes away from Flora's body as the boy came up and his eyes opened. She saw a glassy sheen of red that held her own eyes.

He was bigger now. His belly was grossly distended and swung obscenely as he moved, glutted with his latest feeding. His frame had extended, grown in the night.

And then he was on her. She could do nothing at all but fall back against the headboard. Without using any physical power, he forced her head back and nuzzled. Down between her legs, she felt the cold penetration and a shock of realization rippled through her.

It held her with its eyes and its mind while it fed from her. Her limbs spasmed and deep in her mind she screeched and writhed and tried to pull away, the way Ginny Marsden had done, the way Kate Park had done. But it held her and inside her depths its cold spread in a deadly baneful creep, while on her neck a small popping sound told her the blood was beginning to flow.

After a while Jasmine's vision began to waver and fade. The thing that lay astraddle her, forcing her arms wide and her legs wider, sucked noisily on her neck while that other part of it found sustenance deep inside.

CHAPTER THIRTY-ONE

'That's the fourth time this week,' Helen said as David rewound the tape on the answering machine. 'I never thought she was God's gift to intellectuals, but I thought at least she'd have got the message by now.' The tape clicked to a halt. Helen's eyes held a mixture of pity, contempt, and a flash of anger too. 'You'll have to tell her.'

'I did tell her,' David said. 'I can't seem to get through to her at all. She's got herself convinced that everything's going to be sweetness and light again.'

'She's got a problem, David. She really needs help if she can't get it into her head that it's over between you.'

'And I could surely do with the break.'

'Me too. She'll have to understand that it's you and me from here on. It may not be easy, but it's a tough old world. To the victor, the spoils.' She gave him a look that measured him up and down, managed a half-smile.

'Even if the spoils are spoiled and don't amount to much?'

She ruffled his hair with a fast hand. 'Tell her. After what we've been through, we're sticking together. You won't get rid of me easily.'

'Or at all,' David said, 'That's a promise.'

June's ever more demanding messages were becoming more than an irritation. She'd sent him a mass of flowers while he was in hospital and then arrived in person, elbowing brusquely and with obvious hostility past Helen. David had been mildly embarrassed then, but now he was becoming concerned – not for himself, though he wished she would take no for an answer in the hope that they could all get back to some semblance of normality, if anything ever could be normal since the frantic conclusion in the freezing water of the canal. David had dreamed of the thing for nights after that – still did, though he never told Helen. He didn't know that she was keeping the same secret from him. The thing preyed on their minds all through the rest of the winter.

Neither would June let him go. He'd had the Christmas present, an expensive Gucci watch which he'd almost been tempted to send back, except that that would only have been an insult. He still felt pangs of guilt that he hadn't been able to give June what she wanted. She'd sent him Valentine cards. She'd sent him letters. She called him at the office and she left messages on the tape at home. She contrived to bump into him in the street and every time he met her she had that desperate, hopeful, needful look on her face that made him feel at once ashamed and repulsed.

'She's one creepy lady,' Helen finally said. 'She can't control her emotions, and if she thinks she's going to have your kids, then she's got another think coming. You'd better watch or you'll end up in a fatal attraction scenario. You don't keep a rabbit she might be tempted to cook?'

'I'll tell her,' David said. 'I will. Honestly.'

'Good man,' Helen told him, favouring him with a quick smile. 'If anybody's going to have your kids, I want first crack at it.'

He spun round so fast he felt a harsh crick in his neck.

'Kidding,' she said. 'At least for a year or so. I want to make chief inspector before you do.'

'No chance.'

'Maybe, but I'm serious about the other thing. I'm sorry for June, but it's us against the world now. I'm not a grasping person and I don't plan to be a weight around your neck, but I don't believe I'm going to let you go, not after what we've been through.'

David eased towards her and drew her close. He remembered his regret down in the mud before everything had faded. She had been worth dying for. 'Thank heavens for small mercies,' he said, and she leaned into his warmth.

Helen had transferred to the western division to work with Bert Millar not long after David had come back to duty. It had been a good move for her, and the right move for both of them. Working in the same office and living together would have done neither career any good and would have put too much pressure on them off duty. David was rewarded with what he wanted, a transfer to the murder squad. The drugs wars were heating up in the east and south of the city and the subsequent rash of street killings kept him busy as winter turned to spring.

Apart from June's pestering, life almost got back to normal. Then, in early spring, two bodies were found on a narrowboat in the canal.

It may have been coincidence (though both of them had long since stopped accepting coincidence so lightly) that David and Helen found themselves, that spring morning, on the banks of the canal. The sun was already high and the morning mist was burning off in the heat of the day.

When she had arrived here, the memory of the frantic battle for mind and body had come rushing back to her, and she shivered silently, getting the same feeling she'd had in Levenford when she'd imagined that someone had walked over her grave. *Something was wrong.* A sense of threat scraped on her mind and she tried to tell herself it was only the association with this place and the memories it brought. The water here was deep and turbid, and in the early hours, the air was still except for the occasional twist of wind coming off the estuary where the wading birds piped and whined. The ice was gone, and there was a sense of life under the still waters of the canal. A dragonfly whirred by, metallic green on helicopter wings, and Helen recalled David's photograph where he'd caught the insect emerging from the ugly skin of the larva. She shivered again, wishing she were elsewhere. This place gave her the creeps, she told herself, and always would.

At night, in the dark, she could still see the thing glaring at her, while it stole her soul away. In the daytime, the image often came unbidden. She blinked the memory away. A group of people were coming along the track and that distracted her enough. She turned, drawing her eyes away from the dark water, and saw the murder team arrive. Helen gave David a small, not quite surreptitious wave when he got to the side of the canal with two young men and a tall, bulky man she knew was a chief inspector on the squad. David had told her he was very hard, but also very good. The narrowboat had been barricaded with police yellow tape. But for the numbers of police in uniform and the curious crowd of onlookers, nothing seemed out of the ordinary. The surface of the canal was almost glassily placid, except for that part just beside the barge where the added weight of the police made it dip slowly and send out a barely perceptible ripple. An early kingfisher flashed past, an emerald glitter close to the surface heralding the summer to come. David recognized it immediately, almost automatically noting it for future reference. He could come back here in the late spring and get some shots of the bird on fast film.

Bert Millar came striding up the path, ducking under the tape, shook the senior man's hand, then turned to David and did the same, favouring him with a nod of familiarity. 'Two women,' he said. 'Dr Robinson estimates they've been here for more than a month. We've got one of the McPhee boys banged up as we speak. He's talking his head off. Crying his head off more like. That's one light-fingered wee bugger who wishes he'd never broken into a boat.'

'Bad?'

'Nothing much left of them. You'll have a problem getting anything here. And another problem.' Bert Millar stopped and drew them towards the narrowboat and away from other ears. 'I had a look at them. No matter what Robinson comes up with as the cause, I'll give you any odds you name that it's the same as that Park baby up in Middle Loan Farm.'

A cold touch trailed down David's skin. The Chief Inspector raised his eyebrows. 'David here knows what I mean,' Bert Millar said. 'He was there.'

'I heard,' the murder-hunt leader said. 'You'd better come with me then.'

Helen watched as both of them stepped on to the barge. A light breeze riffled through the green reeds at the edge of the canal, making them rasp together in a conspiratorial whisper. The still water shimmered in the eddy of wind, bearing the scent of early hawthorn flourish and willow pollen. Overlaid on that, there was another, much fainter scent, barely discernible on the air.

Helen breathed for an instant. The fine hairs on her arms were standing out against the cotton of her blouse. She sniffed, twice, caught the hint of it again. An itch crawled across the skin of her breasts.

'No,' she breathed. Beside her, one of the other policeman

turned, thinking she had spoken to him. The eddy passed by and took the trace of scent away. Helen shook her head, wondering. Her eyes scanned the slow water. If there had been a movement there, if some rounded head had poked out from the weeds, and if a glassy red eye had fixed upon her, she might just have run along the towpath and run and run until she had dropped. The dark corner of her mind that could reach forward and sense the danger in the future touched against something and she recoiled from it. David was at the edge of the barge, walking towards the cabin. The prescience suddenly swelled inside her, a black tide of foreboding. She wanted to call out to him, to tell him to stop and turn and get of that damned boat, but she knew she could not.

'I know her,' David said, once he got his breath back. Despite the open door of the hatchway in the cabin, the air was thick with that musty scent of old death. Bert Millar's men had searched the boat and despite the obvious difficulty the forensics boys would have in getting an identity on the two women, there had been enough personal effects to be fairly sure. 'She's one of the best wildlife photographers in the country,' he said. 'A world expert.'

Flora Spiers's battered old camera bag was stacked on a ledge at the foot of the bed. On the wall, a world-famous shot of a wedge of geese crossing the face of the full moon dominated the other photographs, the same picture David had on his own wall. David had long admired the woman's technique and style. If he hadn't become a policeman, he would probably have tried to make a career of his hobby. 'I never knew she lived here.'

'According to the harbour keeper, they spent weeks here at a time. They're both from London,' the other policeman said.

On the bed, two mounds which bore little resemblance to human beings lay parallel to each other. Any blood had long since dried and much of the flesh that had been left had been taken care of by the flies, even at this time of the year. The inside of the cabin was festooned with cobwebs as the spider population exploded to cope with the glut.

Jasmine Cook's head was canted to the left and her jaw was open so wide it made her appear to be screaming silently and eternally. A spider scuttled across one sunken eye socket. Her perfect teeth showed brilliant white against the grey of the taut flesh. On the side of her neck, where the flesh had shrivelled and dried, a gaping hole showed ragged edges. The mattress was matted with a hoary white fungus that rippled in the stir of air when any of the men moved. It looked like a dreadful infection, but David had seen it before. It was feeding on the dried blood. Jasmine's legs were spread apart in a dreadful invitation that made the obscenity somehow blasphemous. At the junction, the white fur had grown up the trail of blood to meet the dark triangle. On either side, both hips pushed like budding horns through drum-tight skin. The body looked hollow.

Flora was on her side, neck twisted back so that her blind sockets gazed up at the ceiling. Thin, empty and leathery breasts hung down on either side of her arched chest. David could count every rib which poked up through the surface. Both hands were curled into claws, longer now that the flesh had withered and shrunk. Her nails seemed like black talons ready to hook and gouge. The hole in her throat was even more ragged, as if whatever had killed her had used considerable force. As if it had been very desperate.

'It's back,' David said aloud. He remembered Helen waking in the night, her body shivering like a tuning fork, unable to say what had scared her. She couldn't express, not in words, what was happening. But she had known.

'What's that?' Bert Millar asked, turning back towards him. David only shook his head. The smell here was now quite cloying, rasping on the soft membranes in his nose and throat. He had tried to kill it, the thing that had sometimes looked like a baby and sometimes wavered into something else entirely, and he had failed. He had put it down under the mud and it had not died.

His mind flicked back to the cot up at Kate Park's farm. He had crept into the bedroom, his nerves jumping, every one of them expecting attack. He had looked over the rim of the crib and seen the strange circular wound in the baby's neck. He was looking at the same wound now, only this time, the ragged gape was bigger.

Both women had been raped too. He could see that from the

trail of fungus up the trickle of blood. At least they'd been penetrated, damaged inside.

What in the name of God had it done? Mentally he rephrased the question. This had not been done in the name of any god.

His eyes scanned the cabin, looking for any trace of the thing, but he saw nothing and smelled nothing except the powdery odour of flesh that was bloodless and dry and the bitter, somehow alien scent of the hoar-fungus. The thing he'd shoved down into the mud was back. Of that he was suddenly and completely certain. It had somehow stayed alive after he'd been dragged unconscious from the bottom of the canal. The frogmen had searched and the stretch of waterway had been dragged with weighted hooks and nothing had been found except for a couple of pike, a false leg and some drowned dogs. They had missed it. It had got away, and now it had come back to kill again.

The wizened corpses on the bed might tell the forensic team a few tales. David knew, because he'd seen it before, that they would find veins collapsed from lack of blood. They would find torn ligaments and muscles, and burst blood vessels. He knew that as a fact. The experts in minutiae would come up with reams of documents to show what had caused the deaths of these two women.

But they would not show the killer. David knew it had a shape and a face, something that rippled and changed and hurt the eyes. It was a face from nightmare.

Some time later, Helen saw him come out from the cabin and step down on to the bank. Even at the distance separating them, she could see the blank, hollow look on his face and she knew something was badly wrong.

He was moving. With uncanny and utter silence he followed the line of the hedgerow, ferociously hungry again. He had come out of the stand of spruce trees, a dark and shadowed place bounded by a high fence. He had left the last skin there, an opaque but translucent remnant caught on the sharp branches, a pale image of himself. After all the changes, after all the mothers, he had finally *become*.

The feeding frenzy as he drained the two mothers in his

penultimate transformation had glutted him. His belly had distended like an insect's abdomen and as soon as he had fed he had felt the numbing drowsiness overtake him, but he had shaken it off because he knew he could not wait here. He had to find somewhere dark and isolated for the next development that already was beginning to work inexorably on him and within him. Driven by instinct he silently followed the strand of willow that bracketed the canal until he found a coppice of thick rhododendrons and brambles. He stalked through them, a bloated shape on thin, stick-like legs, moving with predatory quiet. In the sky a cloud moved slowly and let the light of the moon shine down through the thick branches, limning his body with its silver, making his skin gleam like exotic metal. Things scuttled and rustled down in the undergrowth, but he ignored them. Early bats whispered their subsonic chatter, chasing the few insects flying at this time of the year. They avoided him as instinctively as he headed for the centre of the coppice, through the impenetrable mounds of bramble and hawthorn. Over in a gnarled oak, a tawny owl opened an eye and saw his shape moving. It opened the other, let out a hoot of alarm and took off on silent wings. He felt its fright radiate in the air, but ignored it, his concentration fixed on his own need.

In the centre, he found a hollow under an elm that had toppled over an ancient stone hut that must have existed before the trees themselves had taken root. He forced his way inside. A family of rats bolted out into the night, shrieking their terror. He found a corner filled with leaves and bracken and swirled them around him until he was covered, the way a weasel nests in the heat of the day. The sleep was rushing on him and in the sleep he knew there would be change again and he sensed that this would be the last. The moonlight sent a shard of silver down through a hole in the dry stones and that was the last thing he saw. The pressure in his belly pulsed and his eyes closed and he sensed his organs already begin to disintegrate.

It seemed no time at all. It seemed for ever.

He woke again, so suddenly it was like a birth. He woke trapped in a hard case. He flexed and the case split with the sound of snapping branches. He opened an eye. His limbs creaked into motion and he uncurled his body. He opened the other eye, snuffled the air. He smelled the roots and the insects. He scented birds in the air, but they meant nothing to him at all. He snuffled and got a far-off scent, so faint it was no more than one or two atoms, and a hunger wrenched inside him.

He was grown now. The last change was over, and the new hunger was a hot pain deep inside him. He could no more deny this than he could have refused to feed before, when he had needed the mothers.

Now his needs were different.

He stretched his limbs and got to a crouch, squeezed himself with some difficulty through the narrow entrance hole, which was much smaller to him now. He was strong and powered by the fierce new imperative. His nerves sparked and behind his eyes a pulse throbbed. Whatever passed for blood in his veins was now pumping fast within him, vital and urgent. Overhead a cloud was pushed across the sky, just enough to let the moon shine through. It was full again, leprous-pale in the black of the sky. It swelled the tide within him and drove him on and on.

This emerging had not exhausted him, because his blood was singing with the energy the final mothers had provided. All of his senses were keyed to fever pitch and he moved silently and fast, a thin, gaunt thing of shadows and edges. Here and there, little points of lights would flicker on his consciousness, lives flaring briefly. He could extinguish them if he only looked, but he had no time. The new urgency spurred him on. Every now and again he stopped, sniffed the air, turning his small, domed head this way and that, before moving on.

The clouds swung closed and the world went dark. It was morning, but black as pitch here. He had followed the line of the canal, using its hedges and trees and reeds as cover as he moved east, ever east, following that wordless demand. His whole being was tuned to that and could not deviate. Here and there, on the locks, there would be lights, but he was able to cope with them now, even if the glare seared his skin. The orange glow of the road lights would have melted his eyes if he stared into them, but now he had a nictitating membrane, a secondary pair of lids that came flicking down to dim the glow. It allowed him to see as he moved.

The canal wended slow and sluggish towards the city, a snake of water that had been redeveloped for the new millennium, an inland waterway that bisected the north side before it crossed over to Blane on the east coast. It may have been coincidence that all of the towns that had featured in his long and alien life, through all of the changes, had been connected by river, lake and waterway. It *may* have been coincidence.

The morning air was still and damp. Once or twice, he heard the incomprehensible sounds of human voices, low and muttered from inside an outhouse close to the canal, loud and fretful from a house some distance away. He heard the clump of a policeman's feet and had to fight the instinct to strike. He heard the patter of a vixen as it crossed a pipe spanning the canal. He did not know that she had smelled him when it reached the far side and had instantly aborted, in dreadful agony, the seven cubs she would have borne the following week. They writhed weakly on the grass until the cold stopped them.

He drew nearer where he had to be. The drive inside him was now a singing screech of physical demand. He was complete now and this was his hour.

He only had one purpose.

June Lavery had come by taxi, bearing David's birthday cake. She had called him at the office and discovered he wouldn't be home until later. She had arrived at ten and it was now close to midnight. It was dark, but not too cold, though there was a hint of rain in the air. She wondered if she should get a taxi and go back home again, but she wanted to see him on his own.

She had made a big mistake, she knew, and if she could only get the chance to make him see, everything would be back to normal again. When she had walked out, it had been in the heat of the moment. She had rushed him, and that had been the wrong thing to do. She knew that, deep in his heart, he loved her and she knew, with the same certainty, that they would be together again. He would come round. They would get married as she had always planned. They would start a family and he would see she had been right all along. It would just take time, and she had time. She was still young.

There was no question of her trying to find another man. She had been crazy about David since the day they had first gone out together, and she still was, no matter what arguments they had had. That was all in the past. She could make him see that, no matter what silly mistake he had made with that other bitch. There was no one else for her.

She waited on the corner, knowing he would arrive any moment. He would drive round the side, to the off-street car park in the shadow of the trees that led on to the waterway park. She hummed to herself, as she strolled round the corner where the Virginia creeper was just bursting into a leafy tumble on the wall.

The air stirred. Something moved. She heard a high-pitched buzzing in her ears. She turned.

'Who's there?' She was not alarmed. There would be no danger next to David's house. Maybe, she thought, he had come from round the back. She took a step forward down the path, out of the light. A shade moved and she stopped, saw it was only the shadow of the juniper tree ruffled by a gentle breeze. Something moved again in the deeper shadow at the side of the house. She stopped once more and a figure came looming out. At first all she saw was a black silhouette, about the height of a man.

'David?'

It came towards her and as it did, she heard the fruity little hum get louder. The air thickened and a powerful, sickly scent enveloped her.

'What –?' she began. For an instant her vision wavered. She blinked, turning to the side.

The shadow came forward, very quickly. It took hold of her shoulders. It turned her round to face it and two eyes flicked open with audible fleshy clicks. They glared into hers and she felt the power of its will force its way into her brain. Her mouth flew wide open. A scream formed in her throat but died there unblurted. The world went red and then it went dark.

Helen Lamont was on her way home after a long, footslogging day. She had walked along most of the western end of the canal, as far as Barloan Harbour, asking questions of the few boatmen who were on the water at this time of the year.

Every step on the bridle path reminded her of the chase after the girl and the gargoyle thing clutched in her arms, every swirl in the water when a pike came rising to snatch a minnow would cause her to start and turn, eyes wide, alert to the potential threat. Since she had breathed in the faint, cold trace of its passing, she had realized that this was not over. She could not share her fear with anyone else, here with her new team-mates. She told herself she should be thankful that this was not the high summertime when the waterway would be teeming with weekend navigators and the basin filled with yachtsmen and power-boaters. Yet it would have been better if there were more people on the stretch of canal. In the distance the arch of the bridge showed movement as cars and trucks passed over the wide span, but here there were few people. She felt vulnerable and exposed. At night she would have felt in dreadful danger.

She also told herself that she was wasting time. She had seen the photographs of the two women on the barge. She had read the report and she knew they were looking for no murderer. They were looking for something which killed and fed. Bert Millar knew it too, but he was obliged to put normal procedures into operation.

She and David had talked it over and they both knew the little beast was back again. If she hadn't seen the evidence, she would have known anyway. Her prescient sense itched and nagged, telling her to beware. The thing would no doubt kill and feed again. They would have to wait until it did, and then they would have to kill it dead. They would make sure this time.

Helen steered the car round by the trees to the little car park behind the house. The wind was picking up, rustling the branches that overhung the quadrangle. The light was off in the house, all the windows dark hollows on the wall. She knew David might not be home for some time. She was only on the periphery of the inquiry, but David was there, unable to say what he thought, what he knew. The night before he had woken, lacquered with sweat, gasping for breath, just as she had done. In his dream, he later told her, sides heaving in the aftermath, he had been fighting with it again, down there in the mud.

'It's been a month,' Helen said, trying to convince herself and failing. 'And nothing's happened.'

'It was at least three months before that, and it still came back.'

'You're sure?' Stupid question. She was sure herself. There was no mistaking it. She had sensed its existence.

Now she eased herself out of the car, pulled her bag after her and slung it over her shoulder. She turned, stuck the key in the lock, and crossed the little yard under the trees, walking towards the house.

Then she froze.

Every cell of her body lurched. She stood rigid, still as a statue, completely motionless, mouth agape, while inside, her heart fluttered like a trapped and desperate bird.

Something had touched her.

It had reached out. *It* had stretched to touch her. She felt its caress, its damp dank slither, and she recognized it from before, but now it was different. The foul tendrils slid over the surface of her mind and she recoiled in utter disgust. Right on the heels of the uncontrollable repugnance came the fear, so powerful that it almost spilt her to the ground.

'Oh God,' she managed to blurt out.

Oh God, it's here!

Her legs had simultaneously frozen solid and turned to jelly. She tried to back away, and her feet refused at first to move. The breeze carried the smell towards her, not faint now, but a harsh reek, a foul taint, and her vision wavered. Her heart stopped fluttering and kicked madly, painfully in her chest.

Something moved in the shadows, deeper black on black, and for some reason, the fright unlocked her. She turned, grabbing her bag as she did so. She snatched the mobile phone and was keying the number as she moved. The bag spun away and landed against the garden fence.

Behind her a snuffling sound seemed so close she could feel cold breath on her neck. She scuttered across the yard, head down, and got to the car. She tried to open it, couldn't get the key in the lock. Feet scrabbled behind her and she realized she'd never make it in time.

The scabrous touch reached into her and she reeled in horror from the appalling sense of filth in the alien contact. She turned from the car, unable to make herself look back, knowing that if the thing fastened its eyes on her it would sear her brain. She jinked to the side, trying not to whimper, trying to concentrate despite the eruption of fear. She got to the far side, where the privet hedge bordered the thicket. She was running under the overhanging trees. The telephone beeped at her as her thumb keyed the numbers, pressing so hard that her nail bent back in a rip of pain which she never even felt. In her mind she could see the gaping wounds on the dried and shrivelled bodies of Jasmine Cook and Flora Spiers side by side on the narrowboat. She saw the white fungus growing up the scab of dried blood between their legs and the fear bucked madly inside her. She ran under the light, breath suddenly tight and constricted as if her lungs could not haul enough air to fuel her escape.

It scuttled behind her. She could hear the scrape of *nails? claws?* feet on the road, a deadly, predatory sound of pursuit.

'Emergency, which service do you require?' The operator's voice came loud and clear, with none of the tinny interference she would normally expect. The woman could have been standing next to her. The sound of another human voice was somehow miraculous.

'Help,' Helen managed to blurt. 'Please.'

All her training, all of her toughness had gone, evaporated in the flick of an eye when she had smelled the sweet-rancid scent and seen the shadow move. It had changed her into a primitive, fleeing organism, running in abject terror for her life.

'Which service please?' the woman asked again. 'Hello?'

Helen's feet pounded the road. Her eyes swung ahead, beyond the house to the left. She was in a cul-de-sac. The road dead-ended at a picket fence. Her heart almost stopped. The touch slithered on the surface of her mind, trying to force its way inside. She felt the feral hunger, sensed the sizzling heat of its need. Mindless panic exploded.

'Please,' she whimpered again. Her fingers were clenched so tight on the plastic case that the thin shell creaked. Even as she spoke she was swerving to the right, cutting across the road, pulling out of the dead end. It had gained silently on her as she turned, she sensed with quivering nerves, but she put on a mad spurt of speed, getting to the far corner under the spread of chestnut-tree branches which overhung the pavement.

'Hello? Can you give me a number? Hello.' The phone was still pressed to her ear and the woman's voice, the wonderful, natural human voice was speaking directly to her, an illusion of contact, of succour, while the diseased touch of the shadow chasing her tried to clamp her down and burn her thoughts.

'Get away,' Helen screamed. 'Get away from me. Oh Jes–' Her foot caught the edge of the kerb, twisting her ankle violently and throwing her off balance. A crack of pain bolted up to her knee as she fought to compensate, still clenching the telephone. Her shoulder hit against the upright of a trellis fence with a crash and the thin partition vibrated with the impact. The force of it threw her round, wheeling for balance. Behind her the shadow snorted. She could feel its eyes on her, sense long arms and hooked talons reaching for her, and she spun through the gap in the fence.

'Police,' she shrieked, almost incoherent. 'It's hunting me it's going to get me it's – ' Her voice cut off.

'Hello, please, where are you?' The operator sounded suddenly very concerned indeed.

Helen had crashed through the gap which gave on to the little woodland bordering the waterway park. As soon as she was off the pavement, she realized she had made the wrong move. The cul-de-sac would have been better. There were houses there and lights. She could have run to one of them and demanded sanctuary. She could have done, but she had not thought. The primitive fear had swamped her and all she had known was the need to run, to cover distance, escape from this nightmare. Her other shoulder slammed into a birch sapling and spun her again. She almost fell, but still she held on to the telephone. Her feet crackled over twigs and through burgeoning brambles.

Behind her, the beast-nails scraped on the road metal again, then went silent for an instant before it reached the grass under the trees. A twig snapped loudly, the sound of breaking bones, and the immensity of her mistake sunk in to her. She should have kept on the street and not come into the trees. Even then she knew to have done so she would have had to turn and face the thing and that would have destroyed her. Yet here, in the dark, it had the advantage. It was a night thing, she now understood. It was a devil. She ran, blundering through the dark of the copse, the phone held up against her ear, one hand outstretched to push through the undergrowth while all the time she could hear the steady, fleet pursuit of the thing that snuffled ferociously behind her.

The beast reached out to her and she felt its hunger yawn. Hot and febrile thoughts scurried and scratched over her own. It was getting closer, she could feel that, and she could hear its progress, quieter than her own, swift and deadly, a rustle here, a scrape there, and all the time the fast and feral snort of its breathing. She got down to the pathway between the trees, reaching the flat ground, forcing her legs to move, though they threatened to stop working and simply spill her to the earth. Helen knew she had to put some speed on to get away from it.

All the while, through the thicket and the bramblethorns the operator's voice was scratching out from the receiver, but Helen had no breath to spare now, no time to waste. Her breathing came in ragged, desperate gasps. The moon stuttered its light through the trees, a pallid strobe that marked her frantic passage. Off at the edge of the forest, something small panicked and screeched. Close by, to her left, a shadow flickered in her peripheral vision.

The touch squeezed at her and a bolt of shattering pain slammed into her head.

'Oh,' she gasped. Nausea looped. The pain flared, burned, faded a little. Sparks danced in her eyes. The moving shadow veered towards her, hurtling in from the side. It hit against her, surprisingly light, grabbed hold of her neck. She felt a sharp abrasion, like sandpaper. It hauled, letting its weight slow her.

She spun and hit at it, cracking the telephone against the side of its body. The blow jarred her right up to her shoulder. It was like hitting rough tree bark. Its skin was hard and leathery. It grunted, its grip on her momentarily broken. It twisted, a mere blur in the dark. The eyes glared briefly but she was turning away and missed the force of them. The shape came at her again, reached in a flick of motion. She batted it away again, feeling the scrape of the skin, like sharkskin, and she knew this thing did not belong to, should never have existed in, this world. It grunted, leapt to the side, came bulleting in once more. A hand, a claw, whatever it was snatched for her, crabbed her shoulder. She hit out at it, but it gripped her hard enough to drive fingers or nails almost through her skin. A grip like a thin, hard bird claw snagged her ankle, tripping her forward and her feet slipped on wet leaves from the winter's decay.

A cry escaped her. The beast snuffled, questing at her, the sound of an animal in the shadows, the sound of a hunting predator. The image of Jasmine Cook's gaping bloodied neck came back to her again and she bucked in terror, trying to shuck it away.

She screeched again, stumbling to the side, trying to gain her balance, failing, tumbling. She hit the ground with a wordless grunt as the air whooshed out of her. Her head slammed against the soft loam and sparks whirled and spangled in the darkness. She hit out again, a desperate flap of her hand which accomplished nothing. She tried to kick out and connected with air. The thing had downed her and leapt back quickly, spidery fast. It came rushing back and she got an image of a slender, disjointed shape that was all edges and angles, like a black mantis. Its arms shot forward with incredible speed. Fingers clamped themselves to the side of her head. Two hands gripped her ankles.

She was screaming now, screaming high and clear, an ululating blast of pure fear. The thing's eyes opened and its glare burned into her soul. The eyes were huge and glassy, polished stone slabs that had no iris, no pupils, just a red surface that caught the moonlight and looked as if poisonous blood vessels pulsed just under the surface. Its need shunted into her, a dreadful obscene hunger.

She screamed and the operator pleaded tinnily, a whisper of noise now from her outstretched hand.

The smell came and invaded her. She saw the baby in the cot and the horrible apparition that Ginny Marsden had become. She saw the scuttering thing at the side of the canal, pulling on her emotions and dragging her with it. She saw Kate Park's wizened, raddled body.

More than that, she saw herself in all of this, a prisoner of the thing.

The smell pulsed again and infused her head and in that instant she realized that this thing did not want to feed.

'No,' she bleated. 'Oh God no . . .'

The eyes blared into her, connecting her with a consciousness that was old and evil and deadly and so appallingly different from any other that her mind twisted desperately in a futile bid to break that awesome link. The probe touched in a deadly sharing and the hollow of other sense in her mind opened up and *she saw* . . .

She saw Kate Park. Her face was angled up, as if seen from below, eyes wide and staring at something in the distance, a dribble of saliva running down her chin. Her cheeks were hollow and she looked as if she was damned for ever.

She saw Ginny Marsden, hurrying through the dark, her face a pale oval. A grinding vibration creaked upwards and Helen felt it inside herself, as if she were two people at once. She felt Ginny Marsden's pain of disintegration and dissolution, and the desperate, mute prayers for help.

Ginny's doomed expression faded and Helen saw Heather McDougall, young and fresh, with the three moles in a constellation pattern on her cheek, gazing down, mindlessly obsessed. In her own breast she felt the sucking of its lips and the drain from within.

The images came in rapid-fire succession while the thing stole her mind.

Greta Simon crooning a lilting lullaby . . . Harriet Dailly in her little shack . . . another face with cheerful, healthy cheeks . . . a thin woman with mad eyes . . . They came flickering like an old film: faces, postures, sensations, all riffling on the front of her consciousness.

She saw hawk-nosed men in armour drag babies from their mothers' arms in a night of fire and screaming and impale them on stakes and she knew she watched the hunt for vampires.

She saw different, darker men rampage through a dusty city dragging newborns into the dark while the narrow streets ran with blood and madness was loose in the night.

She saw men in skins cast out a woman and her child into the dark away from the fire, back in a distant, awful past.

Her mind catapulted back from then and Helen Lamont saw something in the future and the force of it was so dreadful it almost killed her. The awful realization slammed her into the present and she squirmed against the poison of its scan and the pestilent scent of its body. All she could hear was the whistle of its breath and the crack and rustle of the leaves and twigs under her writhing body.

It had her by the wrists. Prehensile feet on the end of skinny shanks grasped just above her feet, clamped so tightly she felt the bones grind together. It flexed powerfully, irresistibly, and stretched her wide. It sniffed its strange and terrifying scenting breath, a mindless sound that was completely alien. She felt the pain in her joints and muscles and knew she could not compete with its supernatural strength. Helen tried to free her hands, her ankles but it was futile. Panic soared.

'David,' she screamed. 'Help me. Please. Oh. *Help me!*' Her desperate cry reverberated from the trunks of the trees and vanished in the depths of the thicket.

She was now hysterically aware from the picture that had flashed into her mind that the hunger was truly different from before. It did not want to feed. It had no need now. Its wants were deeper still. It spread-eagled her further, making her muscles and tendons stretch beyond their capacity. Something tore in her pelvis, then another thing, a dreadful thing that was rigid and sharp and hard, jabbed in at her. She felt a rip of fabric, felt a rip of skin, felt a burning pain that at first was outside of her and then *oh then* was shrieking and rending inside of her, in the very depth of her being.

The nightmare bucked on her spread body and its cold was through her, the alien cold of pure badness. In the heat of her pain she felt the unnatural cold spear inside as it thrust viciously again and again and again.

She soared on the crest of unbelievable pain.

Helen's scream went on and on and on.

CHAPTER THIRTY-TWO

The screams echoed round the room, desperate and shrill and conveying so powerful a fear that everybody visibly flinched. The sound cut off abruptly and they could hear the crashing sound of twigs being broken, of bracken crackling underfoot. There was a thump and an animal grunt which could have been human, could have been the sound a desperate woman might make when she fell heavily to the ground. A cracking sound of branches breaking. Another thud, like a sharp blow.

A snuffling noise, like a dog in the dark, like a pig rooting in the undergrowth followed. It was a somehow unnatural whistle of panted breathing. Something, or someone gulped. A thudding sound came loud and clear, another hard blow landed against a rough surface.

'No,' Helen's panic bleated. 'Oh God no . . .'

'Jesus, turn it off.' David bent and put his head in his hands. His shoulders were twitching as if he was holding tight to prevent himself exploding into violence

'David,' Helen screamed and he jerked back as if garrotted. 'Help me. Please. Oh. *Help me!*' Her rending cry reverberated, staccato, as it bounced from one tree-trunk to another, fading all the time before dying completely. They heard her try to say something, heard the words choke in her throat. Something else snuffled once more like a hungry beast scenting prey. There was a harsh cry of pain that ululated high and soared to a peak, a pure and crystalline shriek of utter agony. It climbed to an unbelievable height, sounding more animal now than human. It continued for a stretched-out minute and then it was cut off.

They could hear frantic breathing and more grunting and a noise that could have been anything at all. After a while the sound stopped altogether. There was a hard crack, presumably when the handset fell, and then a silence that was like a physical weight. Somebody reached to turn the recording off. David felt the violent shudder inside, a combination of anger and rage and impotent distress. At that moment every eye in the room was on him, all of them aware of his agony, all unable to reach and touch him. It was something he had to hear.

'That tells us nothing,' Donal Bulloch said. 'Nothing of any great help.' He looked at David and managed to convey his sympathy and understanding in the same glance.

'Except that she was hunted down and raped.'

'Oh, it tells us that all right,' Bulloch said. 'Dr Robinson tells us the same thing, more or less. The tape only lets us know when it happened. If her attacker had spoken, we might have got a voice-print. If there had been any background noise, we could have got a pattern, maybe even got a computer analysis. But there was nothing at all. He never said a word. The dogs found nothing at all. There's no shoe-prints, scraps of clothing, nothing under her nails. Some blood.'

David winced, tried not to show it. Everybody in the room saw it.

It's hunting me it's going to get me it's . . . Her voice continued in his mind. She had begged for help and no one had known where she was. *Get away. Get away from me. Oh Jes–* Her desperate plea drilled into his head. He wanted to be sick. He could feel the waves of nausea build up and subside again, like squeezes of pressure. His head was pounding in a dull, ceaseless ache.

'Bruising and lacerations,' Bulloch continued. 'No sign of semen at all. There's a possibility there were two of them, because she's been held in a tight grip, hands and feet. More than a possibility. There probably were two, or more. Perhaps they were disturbed before they finished.'

David kept hearing the dreadful screams. They overlaid everything else. Every time Bulloch paused, David could hear the demented shrieks. Worse, he could hear the snuffling sound as Helen's legs were forced apart and something sharp and spiked had been rammed inside her so hard it had ruptured the neck of her uterus and punctured her bowel.

'I know it's a tall order, but I'm sure you'll agree that we have to get a description,' The Chief told David, keeping his voice even. 'She hasn't spoken to anybody at all, and we have to get some response if we're going to find them. It's possible you might get some reaction.'

David looked at him blankly, trying to get his mind to switch off the interminable screaming. He cursed himself for being late, he condemned himself for not picking up the signs quickly enough. He had arrived home, tired from a long day, looking forward to a good whiskey and the chance to get the chill out of his bones. He parked the car, began to walk round the side of the house and then stopped. For some reason, he turned. Had there been a smell on the air? He sniffed. There was a scent of spring growth, perhaps a hint of perfume from daffodils and primulas in the next-door garden. Maybe something else, faint and almost gone.

The hairs on his arms were crawling again. He could feel them brush the fabric of his shirt-sleeves. A trickle of sweat ran down the sides of his ribs. It felt cold. His heart speeded up and a flush of odd, anxious emotion, like a quick anger, twisted inside him. He turned, sniffing the air again, recognizing this odour yet scenting something different within it.

He was not alarmed, not yet, but the anxious sensation, and an odd new feeling of foreboding made him walk back through the gate. All of his senses, flagging and dragging only a moment before, were now wound up to sharp alertness. He scanned the little yard, saw Helen's car parked in the corner. There were no lights on in the house.

He paused for a moment, then turned quickly and ran up to the front door. It was locked, and that would be usual if Helen had arrived home first. His heart gave a double beat. The key rattled on the outside of the lock and he cursed at the delay. Finally it clicked and the bolt slid back. He pushed the door open and got inside. It was cold. The heating had not been switched on. He called her name and the foreboding swelled blackly within him. She was not there.

David did not hesitate. He went straight back outside, forgetting to close the door behind him. He ran to her car, found it locked. A breeze shivered the topmost branches of the trees in a whisper of sound. He turned, and the street lamp on the corner glinted on something on the ground. He bent, found the car keys only feet away from the door.

His heart stopped.

Two yards away, Helen's bag was lying close to the hedge. It was wide open and the contents had spilled out.

A premonition shivered through him. Without hesitation he reached for his own handset and called the office. In ten minutes four patrols were in the little yard, lights flashing on the walls of the surrounding houses.

The tracker dogs were howling in the trees. One of the searchers found the telephone. It was another six hours before they found Helen Lamont, bloody and bruised, huddling at the side of a disused boatshed close to the waterway. She had been unable to speak.

The memory of her bruised and torn body hung with him, hooked into his heart, the way the terrible screams on the operator's tape lanced through him. He told Bulloch, in a slow, mumbling voice, that he would do what he could. He got up from the room and left them, feeling their eyes on him, not caring at all.

Helen was huddled on the bed. The clean white sheets showed up the scratches on her face and the bruises under her eyes. Her hair was jet-black against the pillow. Her eyes were open, staring at the wall. David sat down at the side of the bed.

'We've managed to repair the damage,' Dr Robinson had told him. David wanted to kill. Helen's dark eyes were unfocused, hollow smudges, bereft of their life and fire. Her breathing was slow and measured, but every now and again, her chest would hitch as if she was about to burst into tears.

The tears did not come. She said nothing.

He held her listless hand, finding it difficult to comprehend the turmoil inside himself. She did not respond to his touch or to his presence and that too upset him. Her hands, badly scratched and abraded, stayed flaccid, not returning his grip the way they had before. She had always been a tactile woman, eager to hold and caress. Her hand was cool and the skin dry. Her eyes did not so much as flicker.

He spoke to her, low, leaning close so his words were private, just for the two of them. Her pupils remained fixed on some point far beyond the wall. He told her he loved her, promised her that everything would be fine, that they would be happy together. She did not react.

Helen made no sound at all, except that when David was about to leave, she began to hum, very faintly, almost inaudibly. A trickle of saliva drooled down from her slack lips and he thought she had groaned. He turned round, leaned close again, willing her to respond.

She was humming tunelessly. He did not recognize the notes. For an instant, though, her eyes flickered. She blinked slowly and she looked at him. For that instant he thought she was trying to make some sort of contact and he took her hand again. Then the expression changed. The eyes slid away. A muscle twitched on her cheek, drawing her mouth into a small smile. For another instant, for a brief flash of time, David thought he had seen that look on someone else.

It was only when he was leaving the hospital that he recalled the last time he had seen that almost sly expression. It had been on the face of mad old Greta Simon, in Blane Hospital, when she had begun to hum the old Gaelic tune.

Helen sat in a world of strange and numbing sensations. She was Helen Lamont, a part of her understood, but she was more than that. It had looked into her eyes and it had connected with her depths and in that sharing she had touched them all, all of the past ones.

Her mind had fragmented and at once she had been among them, sharing with them all, down through the years, feeling their powerful need, needing their powerful presence. They were one. They had all had one purpose. But now that purpose was different.

Helen had reached into her new memory and had plucked out songs that she would sing to herself, in words that she now understood, from far, far back. She hummed these softly while others clucked and fussed around her, seen as if through gauze curtains, heard as if through fog, part of a different world now. She had been broken and shattered, then all the scattered parts had coalesced once more and she was alive again.

He had come to speak to her, murmuring words that she could not understand, trying to touch an emotion that she could no longer possess, because there was only one emotion. He had touched her hand and she had felt her skin crawl. He did not realize that she could not bear to be touched any more.

None of them realized anything at all.

She blinked slowly, turning away from the light, and tuned in to herself, listening to the slow beat of her own heart and the rhythm of her own cycle.

June's parents both came round to David's house the evening after he had been to the hospital and surprised him when they asked after their daughter. They had been astonished to learn that she and David had split up, for she had not mentioned the parting at all. In fact she had continued as if nothing had changed. They had wanted to know if she was staying with him, for they hadn't heard from her for a few days. David was irritated by their presence, because it reminded him of a dead relationship while his own relationship had been shattered by Helen's rape. He held himself in check, because they were a nice couple and he'd always liked them. The three of them went round to June's flat, found the place cold and empty, with two days' milk outside the door and two days' mail behind it. He took them down to the station and helped them fill out a missing-person report.

Within himself, however, he harboured dark and irrational suspicions. Had June taken revenge? Had she somehow set Helen up in the hope that she could win David back? A miserable, smouldering anger started to twist inside him again and he could not quench it.

The rapists were never found. Neither was June Lavery.

David spent a couple of hours with Dr Mike Fitzgibbon, the psychiatrist who had taken him down to see Greta Simon what seemed like years ago. David was hoping to get some answers.

'She wants to forget what happened,' Mike told him. 'It's the brain's way of coping with an overload of trauma. It is not catatonia, more a withdrawal. I'm sure she will pull out of it, with help and therapy and counselling. Your division's got some good rape-crisis people.'

Mike also explained David's own feelings of panic and anger, of complete helplessness. 'It's another side effect of your own drive. You feel the need to protect your mate, and you consider that you have failed in that. If there was a visible threat, another human, you would fight him, but you cannot see it, only imagine it. Your brain is doing the fighting for you because you feel the overwhelming need to protect what is yours.

'You asked me some time ago what sort of woman steals a baby and I explained about the mothering need. It is a primitive, built-in instinct. Men sometimes have a corresponding drive which generally manifests itself after the birth of a child. All of these drives are linked to the great fundamental, which is more powerful and basic than the day-to-day survival instinct. Our whole lives, our very existence, revolves around the compulsion to reproduce. Everything is secondary to that, yet everything is linked to it. The reproductive urge is the most powerful force on the planet. Yours has been threatened, in a very literal sense. Humans suffer stress because of that. Helen is suffering enormous stress and so are you. The problem with humans is that we can think. We are not mindless animals. If we were, it might be easier.'

David still wanted to lash out. He needed a target to hit. Something to kill.

Helen Lamont came out of her fugue state after two days, but while she seemed more aware of her surroundings, she remained silent and unresponsive. She walked stiffly and painfully, her eyes huge in her pale face, still focused on the far distance. A battle-weary soldier would have recognized that hopeless look into infinity. She looked more slight, more vulnerable than ever. A woman colleague of Mike Fitzgibbon, along with two rape specialists, tried to coax the story out of her, but Helen, when she spoke at all, managed to convey to them, haltingly, mumblingly, that she remembered nothing at all. After another day, despite David's panicked protests, she signed herself out of the hospital. Failing to dissuade her, he told her he would take her back to his place, which in recent times had become their place. She shook her head dumbly. Helen refused to go to her mother's house either, or her sister's, where he knew she would get love and care. She went back to her own apartment, sitting silent in the car as he drove her there, ignoring everything on the way, eyes fixed ahead of her. She let herself in with her key, easing the door closed on his hurt expression.

At the beginning of May, two small boys found something in a dense coppice four miles along the waterway parkland. They were not sure what it was, but they said it had skeleton hands and it might be a body.

David was merely going through the motions, unable to cope with what had happened to Helen. She still could not return to work and she still refused to communicate with him or, it seemed, anyone else. Her mother had called, hoping for some help in getting through to her daughter, but he was as powerless as she was. Helen had simply withdrawn into a cocoon of solitude. On the two occasions when she let him into her flat he picked up a sense of anxiety, and more, a sense of dumb hostility towards him which he found as painful as a physical blow. Her eyes were lustreless and she cocked her head to the side, absently listening to some imagined sound. He got the impression that she only wanted him to leave. He begged her to get medical help, but she told him in a listless voice that she neither wanted it or needed it. She only wanted to be alone.

'What about us?' he asked clumsily. She looked at him as if she did not quite understand. He got no reply to his question. In the breaks of conversation, breaks that stretched out into dismal, uncomfortable minutes, she would hum to herself as if her mind was roaming elsewhere. Her hair was getting longer, but it was losing its shine. She was developing lines at the side of her mouth. The bags were still heavy dark curves under her eyes. Occasionally she would smile to herself, as if harbouring a secret. David wondered if she had simply gone insane. He felt impotent and angry and bewildered all at the same time, and added to that was the guilt he felt for harbouring such a selfish attitude.

He tried to throw himself into his work and when the call came in that a body had been found in the woods on the parkland, he welcomed the chance to get on a case.

'Over there,' the local policeman said when he arrived on the cycle track that shadowed the waterway. 'Don't know what the hell it is.' Two small boys, both red-haired and freckled, obviously brothers, were sitting in a police car, looking scared yet puffed up with importance at the same time. David spoke to them first then went into the coppice, pushing his way through the bramble runners and dog-rose stems which clawed and tugged at his coat. Finally he reached the shape in the centre of the thicket.

It looked at first like the decomposed body of a man.

There was no wind here in the coppice, but the day was warm and the smell was overpowering. No direction was upwind. A horde of black buzzing flies crawled over the body. A long, thin hand reached out to grasp a sapling. The other one was stretched overhead, hooked on to a branch. The skin was purple and fluid, as if it had been burned or melted. Bones, long and slender, strangely gracile and oddly jointed, showed through in places.

'What in the name of Christ is that?' a uniformed sergeant who had followed him through the undergrowth wanted to know. David heard the man's harsh gagging as he tried to cope with the smell of rot.

He stepped closer and saw that whatever it was, it was not a man. It was more like a spider monkey, in a way, with those elongated arms and grasping fingers. The lower limbs were almost identical, slender and jointed, almost insectile. For a moment, the image of a mantis came to him. The feet were prehensile, each of them holding on to an upright stem. It hung there, head down on its narrow, ridged chest, an obscene Christ from a Dali nightmare. Flies crawled all over its flat face. David risked getting closer, shooed them away and they buzzed up in an angry cloud. Two wide sockets, each big as a fist, gaped in a flat face.

There was no mouth at all.

David took a step back, suddenly nauseated, not so much by the smell, but by the dead thing's hideous appearance. It defied the senses. It was an obscenity, an *offence* against the natural order of things.

Yet to David, this crime against nature was somehow familiar. But for the lack of mouth, it was just a larger, more elongated version of the thing that he had shoved down into the mud of the canal. Such a thing could never exist, not in this world, but it was there, decomposing in the shadow of the copse, suspended from the branches, a slender, slatted horror with purpling, viscous skin which dripped on to the brambles below it. Its proportions were all wrong, yet it looked somehow predatory. He could imagine it stalking, like a mantis, like all other mindless creatures.

Between its legs curved a spike which looked like bone. It pointed outwards and upwards, a vicious stabbing thing. Donal Bulloch's words came back to him. 'Something sharp and spiked has damaged the walls of her uterus and punctured her bowel,' Bulloch had said after the tape had stopped playing and the silence had echoed with screams.

As soon as he recalled that, the image of the mantis faded. The deadly insects killed only to eat, even to the extent of snatching a potential suitor and tearing it to shreds. This thing without a mouth was different. As he stared at it, his encyclopaedic knowledge of the natural world dredged up for him a picture of a male octopus, in a scene captured underwater by the camera of the now dead Flora Spiers. It had copulated with the female and, after the successful fertilization, its role in life done, it had ceased to live. It had completed its purpose and it simply disintegrated and died.

He remembered another picture, taken by himself when he was only ten years old, of spent mayfly bodies on the still water of a river pool. They had metamorphosed from larvae to emerge as adults for their final flight, the incandescence of the breeding dance on the summer air. They had fed all their lives and now the feeding was over. They had emerged with only one drive, to find a mate. To breed. They had no need of mouths, not any more.

'Oh sweet Jesus,' David muttered. He stumbled backwards, his mouth open, eyes fixed on the dripping shape.

The clawed hands gripped the branches in a death lock. The feet were hooked round the slender saplings. David now recognized the bruising on Helen's wrists and ankles.

And in death it showed its living purpose, the stabbing spike between its scrawny limbs curved up like a horn. It was only then that he realized the cause of the dreadful rending wounds inside of her. He stood back, groaning, eyes suddenly blinded by the violent, uncontrollable pounding of his heart.

Helen Lamont disappeared that day from her flat. She was never seen again.

CHAPTER THIRTY-THREE

Down in Barloan Harbour, old Mrs Cosgrove, peering through her thick lenses, had not recognized her when she came knocking on the door, keeping her face to the shadows. It was no surprise that the old woman who offered rooms for bed and breakfast did not know her. She had changed.

The nights had been filled with strange dreams and the days with strange hungers. Her ears buzzed and crackled and her sense of smell was changing too. She needed hot meat, flesh and blood. Sweet tastes nauseated her and made her retch violently. She had pains deep in her belly, wrenching, swelling pains, but they did not distress her.

She sat in the dark now, most of the time, keeping away from the light, huddled in the swirl of blankets.

It had been right to move, to get away. There was danger in staying where she was known, danger not just to herself. Instinct had driven her on, tugging her wordlessly to a safe place, somewhere she could hide and wait.

The time was almost on her. The pressure in her belly was intense. The skin was stretched until she felt it might rip asunder. Inside she could feel the small movements and the hot pains and the glow spread through her. It had not taken long and the waiting would soon be over.

In the night, something stirred and she awoke with a ripple of alarm, but she saw it was the other one turning in her sleep, the one she had known from that distant time before. Her name was May, she recalled. Something like May. The name of a month. The name mattered not at all now. No name did. Her sister, her brood sister, was stirring awake. The moonlight streamed through the narrow window, fuzzed by the condensation on the glass from the heat of their bodies and the warmth of their breath.

A third one was already awake and her eyes were gleaming in the light. The fourth and fifth were starting to move. She did not know their names. They had no names. She had almost forgotten her own. Identity, too, meant nothing now, yet they all recognized her and the difference inside her.

She moved too, careful of the weight in her depths, careful of her precious burden.

She hunkered down, ignoring the small and distant pain as her knee pressed on the bent frame of Mrs Cosgrove's glasses. Eyes glittered impassively in the dark. Without a pause, she joined the others in the moonlight and they shifted slowly, giving her preference, as was her natural right. She bent and used her teeth to strip the plump, rich flesh from a cold, spread-eagled thigh. She gulped it down without chewing and the blood trickled down her chin and over the swelling curve of her breasts. The others watched her as she fed, naked in the dark. Over the smell of the meat, she could sense their own imminent birthings. They would produce only males.

She was different. The vessel that had been Helen Lamont nurtured a special burden. No man would ever resist her offspring. It would live for ever.

A drop of milk leaked out to merge with the blood and the birth pains began to pulse deep inside.